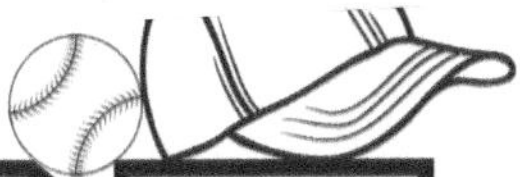

KNOT HER

Catch

an **MVP: MOST VALUABLE PACK**

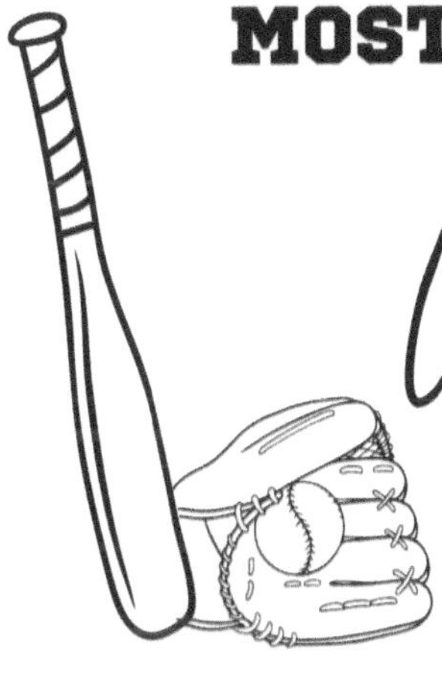

Published by Blue Eyed Books.

Knot Her Catch

MVP: Most Valuable Pack, book 5

ISBN: 979-8-9914464-7-1

ebook ISBN: 979-8-9914464-8-8

Cover Art: Staci Hart at Quirky Bird

*to the ones who find endless kindness for others
but nothing for themselves:*

listen closely, the love is there

WHAT IS
an omegaverse?

An **Omegaverse** is an alternate universe wherein humans have evolved a biological hierarchy based on three individual designations: **alphas, betas, and omegas**. In an Omegaverse, every person falls into one of those three categories (or "designations") by the time they reach adulthood. Their **designation** then determines certain elements of their physiology, psychology, and physical appearance. The humans in this Omegaverse are not shifters.

Alphas are large, strong, dominant, possessive, and territorial. While civilized, they often struggle with the urge to use force or exert their dominance over others; particularly fellow alphas. Optimized anatomy makes them physically superior in many ways, including reproduction.

Male alphas have a "knot" at the base of their penises. This **knot**, much like the penis itself, becomes engorged when they are aroused and expands to its full size upon completion, "locking" an alpha into his partner. Female alphas have a "lock" inside their vaginas that perform a similar locking maneuver on their partners.

Alphas are biologically compelled to find compatible partners based on individual scents. They also tend to form **packs** with others. Omegas often become the center of packs because they are the only designation capable of creating **bonds** between others. There is rarely more than one omega in a pack. Once a pack bonds with an omega, all of their scents alter subtly. This shift helps protect bonded omegas from unwanted advances.

Betas remain the most similar to everyday humans. They do not have intense scents or the same biological compulsions that alphas and omegas share. Many beta-beta relationships resemble traditional monogamous partnerships. Because they cannot bond among themselves, they often choose to marry instead.

Omegas are smaller and softer in stature, naturally submissive, wary of violence, fearful, emotional, empathetic, and magnetically attractive. Omegas' bodies are built to endure the demands of an entire pack of partners, emotionally and physically.

Omega biology draws alphas in. When omegas are aroused, their bodies send nearby alphas a signal by **perfuming**. Omega perfume is a concentrated hit of their specific scent, intended to lure an alpha to their aid.

Alphas and omegas each have distinctive scents. Their bodies produce these scents at all times, but they are particularly strong when the individual is sexually aroused or emotionally distressed. Alphas and omegas can have very intense, all-consuming physical and emotional reactions to each other's scents. While uncommon, the phenomenon is called **scent-sensitivity**.

Scent-sensitive alphas and omegas are referred to as **mates**. By some twist of fate or biology, they are near-irresistible to one another. Separating from their scent-sensitive mates would cause an omega extreme pain and distress.

Omegas experience **heat cycles**. These "heats" are spurred by the biological imperative to mate/bond with an alpha (or group of alphas) who will provide for and protect them. When an omega goes into heat, he/she will experience intense physical pain unless they are knotted by their alphas regularly. Heats send omegas into a state of limited lucidity that is known as a **heat haze**. This haze makes them extremely vulnerable and unstable.

Omegas can take **suppressants** to lower their hormone levels.

Suppressants help make the pain of heats tolerable for omegas who do not have alphas. Unfortunately, over time, suppressants become less effective.

Unbonded alphas who encounter an unbonded omega can experience **rut**. Rut is a condition wherein an alpha loses his/her mental faculties and gives in to the biological imperative to knot/lock an omega. Rut is often dangerous for omegas.

Omegas **nest** in order to feel secure. An omega's nest should be a soft, round place that feels low to the ground and dark. Omegas take great pride in building their nests to their individual tastes and their alphas' approval. It is their alphas' duty to provide this space and the resources to outfit it.

Courting is the process by which alphas can press their suits with an omega of their choosing. It is generally a task undertaken by the entire pack in pursuit of their one chosen omega.

Alphas and omegas are not required to be scent-sensitive/mates in order to bond; however, bonding with one who is not your mate means forgoing the future possibility of building a pack with a scent-sensitive match. **Packs and omegas can be scent-matched without being scent-sensitive/mates.**

foul ball

(content warnings)

I'm so glad you're here!

Knot Her Catch is the fifth installment in the *MVP: Most Valuable Pack* series. If you haven't read the other books, please don't worry, this is intended to be read as a *complete standalone*!

This is a why-choose Omegaverse romance. It includes lots of knots, tons of spice, and absolutely no choosing!

If you don't like rowdy alphas, swoony mates, and group sex scenes (including packmates lending each other a hand), this may not be the HEA for you <3

Content Warnings: age gap, alcohol dependence, fake engagement, bullying (not among main characters), lack-of family support, medical gaslighting/suggested weight loss, scars, public spectacles, body shame/body shaming (not among main characters), injury/recovery, car accident (off-page, in the past), free use kink, exhibitionism, voyeurism, sexual domination, hand necklaces, "Daddy" kink, double penetration (DP and DVP), oral/anal sex, pierced genitals.

remember the packs?

Don't worry: Knot Her Catch is a stand-alone!
These are just the names of the packs from the first four MVP
books to help with character cameos in this one!

ASH PACK

OMEGA: Meg

PACK LEADER: Ronan Ash

PACK ALPHAS: Declan Howard

Dr. Archer Monroe

Theo Matthews

PIERSON PACK

OMEGA: Remi Skyes

PACK LEADER: Smith Pierson

PACK ALPHAS: Damon Mathers

Cassian King

remember the packs?

THORNE PACK

OMEGA: Serena Swanson

PACK LEADER: Tristan Thorne

PACK ALPHAS: Spencer Thorne

Avery Thorne

Jonah Thorne

BECKETT PACK

OMEGA: Emma Matthews

PACK LEADER: Knox Beckett

PACK ALPHAS: Grammar Sinclair

Zane Madani

Micah Patterson

knot her catch playlist

Sweet Nothing — Taylor Swift
Rawnald Gregory Erickson the Second — STRFKR
Knock Knock — Mac Miller
Black Friday (pretty like the sun) — Lost Frequencies, Tom Odell
BOYSHIT —Madison Beer
Karma — Taylor Swift
Hush — The Marías
Wondering Why — The Red Clay Strays
Out of My League — Fitz and The Tantrums
MF Diamond — CHINCHILLA
I am not a woman, I'm a god — Halsey
this is how you fall in love — Jeremy Zucker, Chelsea Cutler
Be Gentle With Me — The Boy Least Likely To
When You Were Young — Benjamin Francis Leftwich
Like Everyone Else - Lyrah
You Are In Love (Taylor's Version) — Taylor Swift
DADDY — Cristiana Love
Sweet Heat Lightning — Gregory Alan Isakov
Gilded Lily — Cults
Need to Know — Doja Cat
Birds Of A Feather X Midnight City — Luke Muzzic
Ordinary - Wedding Version — Alex Warren
BELONG TO ME — Cristiana Love
The Spins — Mac Miller, Empire Of The Sun
She's Got You High — Mumm-ra

prologue

twelve years ago

"THERE'S NOTHING WE CAN DO."

That's not what I want to hear.

But, more importantly, it isn't what *my mother* wants to hear.

She gasps, her crystal-blue eyes filling as she covers her mouth with both hands. "Doctor, this can't be right!" she cries, flinging a nervous gesture at me. "Her perfume is *foul*."

The doctor is an alpha. And a man. Somehow, that makes his grimace even more mortifying.

"I'm aware it's not an... *easy* scent to work with—"

"I want her hormones tested again," Mom demands. "A full panel this time."

With a sigh, the doctor spares me a pitying glance and softens his expression for my mother. Alphas are always doing that—she has the kind of damsel-in-distress looks that inspire others to swing into action and rescue her. Even bonded men who know she's bonded, too.

"Mrs. Woods, I know this must be difficult for you," he continues, reminding her they've run every test under the sun. *Twice.* All to unriddle my particular brand of shame.

Or, really, the *worst* of my shame. As far as my mother—and perfect older sister—are concerned, there's plenty more where that came from.

The doctor's words echo in my head. *Mrs. Woods, I know this must be difficult for you.*

Difficult for her? I think. *What about* me?

You know? The omega who oozes *acid*?

Does nobody care about how *I* feel about spending the rest of my life alone?

I'm only fifteen. Surely there should be some sort of therapist here to break this news to me?

"Now, Bridget, we know you've always dreamed of having alphas and a pack to take you far, far away from your family, but it turns out you're medically impossible to find attractive."

When my mother sobs, I tune back in to the conversation swirling around me. "Please," she begs. "There must be *something*. She can't—she *won't* find an alpha without proper perfume."

She doesn't say the reason I don't have a prayer of attracting matches without a better scent, but she doesn't need to. It dangles over us, sucking all the air out of the room.

<u>Look</u> at her. No one will want her like <u>this</u>.

And, well, is she wrong?

Sometimes I think karma must be real, because I'm pretty sure *I'm* my mother's. A little reminder from the universe for The Great Catherine Woods: She may be the most gorgeous omega in our country club, with the wealthiest husband, most popular friends, one successful alpha daughter, and looks to kill... but no matter how well she curates the rest of her existence, she can't fix *me*.

Too pale. Splotches of freckles. Flaming-red hair. Acne. Terrible posture. Rolls of softness I can't get rid of, no matter how much she threatens me.

And now this.

Acidic perfume.

So astringent, apparently, the doctor dealing with me needs *two* face masks.

Subtle, right?

I'm not sure what Mom wants this dude to do. It's not like he can control any of this. She should know that better than anyone; she's spent *years* fighting an uphill battle against my looks, scent, and "unseemly" personality.

"Bridget can always mask her scent," the smitten doctor goes on, patting Mom's shoulder. "There are excellent de-scenters available these days. I'll prescribe a prescription-strength one."

Mom cries harder, shaking her head. "There's really *nothing* else you can try?"

The doctor frowns in befuddlement, raking tired eyes over my body. His brows leap up as the world's least original idea springs to mind.

"Has she tried losing weight?"

DOES anyone else still get those bad dreams?

You know the ones.

I'm supposed to be taking an exam—but I just woke up and I'm three hours late!

I'm in the middle of a speech—and I forgot to put on pants!

Well, this is sort of like that.

Only it's my *actual* life.

As a high school librarian and Certified Elder Nerd, I can confidently say I've always been the sort of person other humans want to stuff into lockers. So I know that, for a lot of kids, the best thing about high school is the fact that it *ends*. And the promise that, eventually, there will come a day where you never have to see those numpties again.

Unless you're me, apparently.

In which case, a guy you've spent the last nine years trying to forget is in your living room.

And he isn't alone.

What are they *doing* here?

Our parents' house is enormous—a grand assortment of lavish rooms that have gotten more ostentatious every year since they passed away. I've never been a big fan of the pomp, but at least there are plenty of places to hide.

Normally, I'm not really a "fade into the background" type of girl, but, uh... I definitely can't be seen right now.

If these are actually the alphas I think they are...

Balancing on the tips of my toes, I crane around the wall separating the first-floor hallway from the parlor.

Fuck a duck.

Yep, that's definitely them.

The one on the leather loveseat is Jesse Locke, effortless Golden Boy and my sister's friend from high school. He's as gorgeous as ever—lanky and muscled, with the sort of fluidity that hints at innate athleticism.

The years have only made him more impossibly handsome. All-American beauty—a straight nose, sharp jaw, hazel-green eyes.

Honestly? His face is just unfair.

So is the other alpha's. The one who *should* be a stranger, but —thanks to some late-night social media stalking—I admit I know his name.

And maybe his batting average.

But only because literally *every* article crows about it.

Dante Pérez.

I'm mildly annoyed that he's just as attractive as his photos. Deep-tan skin, molded onto bulging muscles. Dark-chocolate eyes, a painfully sexy smile, and a square, dimpled chin.

Like *damn*, *dude*. The bright white teeth are overkill. He's already way too hot without flashing *those*.

I really don't want to believe these alphas are here. But I would, unfortunately, recognize them anywhere. And not just because my sister used to hang out with Jesse, and Dante is Jesse's packmate.

They're famous, too. Gorgeous and single... and two of the best professional baseball players in the country. They played together in college. Now they headline the Kings, our hometown's MLB team.

Which reminds me:

What *the hell* are they *doing* in my house?

Alicia—my alpha older sister and unofficial warden—graduated with Jesse *nine years ago*. They hung out a lot back then, but I got the sense the star pitcher moved on to bigger and better things once he made a name for himself.

He found Dante, of course, and one other alpha for their pack. A catcher, I think. Though that guy's notorious for hiding from the cameras Jesse and Dante seem to love. And I don't *see* a mystery man any—

"Hiding?"

I whirl, my hands flying to cover my chest.

There's a man behind me, standing a few steps away with his fists in his pockets and a ferocious frown twisting his full lips.

Is that... a backwards Kings baseball cap on his head?

I'm gonna kill Alicia.

My throat goes rough and tight, hands shaking while I flatten myself against the wall. *Damn omega instincts.* Why couldn't they give us super strength or mind control or insane parkour skills?

Seriously? Running and hiding? That's all I get?

Stunning gray eyes glint in the shadows, even more striking beside his equally pale skin. They're... intense. Enough for me to question if my impulse to flee might be prudent.

My skin buzzes, reminding me why this whole scenario feels

like a literal nightmare—I'm only wearing a paper-thin night-gown. No one told me we'd have company.

Then again, Alicia tends to forget I live here.

I wish her new husband would also forget I live here.

It was Bradley's idea for me to move in after college. At the time, I thought he was being generous. They make the kind of money it takes to maintain this monstrosity of a house—and they're only *mostly* condescending about my job and general exis-tence. In the end, though, his reason turned out to be infinitely... ickier.

So, really, the sooner my sister has her way and gets me *out* of here, the better.

Some warning about whatever *this* is still would have been nice. Now, I'm in a blush scrap of silk, staring at one of the most beautiful alphas I've ever seen. All casual sex appeal, with his tousled, nearly-too-long hair curling from under his backwards hat. And an attractive dark-brown beard to match. *Of course.*

He keeps scowling at me, the expression impassive. *Huh.* It's not arrogant like Dante's bright grin, or gorgeously carefree like Jesse's.

Nope. This guy is... disapproving?

Of me? In my own house?

In *my sister's* own house?

The audacity.

He tilts his head slightly, gray beams gliding down my body and back up. Not *judging* me, exactly, but... looking. *Really* looking.

Which is fair.

There *is* a lot to see.

I typically pride myself on that: being a lot. A lot of thoughts and opinions. A lot of books and projects and ideas. A lot of jokes and fun. All the better to go with the hips, ass, belly, and breasts I also have a lot of.

Alicia would say that a woman "with my figure" shouldn't wear nightgowns this skimpy. In her mind, every spare moment of my life ought to be dedicated to finding ways to squeeze myself into some arbitrarily acceptable shape—all so I might have a shot in hell of finding a pack one day.

I wonder if she would still be so desperate if my weight was her only objection. True, most omegas are petite. It isn't a *rule*, though. Omegas come in all shapes and sizes, just like alphas and betas.

But *not* all omegas have the perfume I do.

Thank God I just got out of the shower. I always scrub myself with de-scenting wash. Ever since my perfume came in and the doctors started their endless crusade to "fix" it.

They each ran endless tests and wound up shrugging. *Oh well. Too bad. Guess she'll die alone.*

By the fourth or fifth doc, it was almost funny. *Almost.*

Deep down, I was devastated. My whole life felt a bit like being a puzzle piece from the wrong box, with everyone trying to jam me into slots that weren't made for people like me.

I was bigger than other girls, so that meant I *had* to be shy and socially awkward. I didn't "look like someone who worked out," so people gave me side-eye at the gym.

If I was going to be fat, I was *also* supposed to be embarrassed and humble and agreeable. And... well... I'm not.

It never made any sense to me. I was born this way. In this body, with this scent. Hating it seemed as useless as loathing myself for being a redhead. Or a Sagittarius.

Still, Alicia insisted I'd never find a pack if I had such an "entitled" attitude. Translation: *"You're burning out my nostrils and need to start settling. Stat."*

Little did she know, there *are*, in fact, alphas who like the strength of my scent. Including her creepy partner.

Does it ever piss anyone else off that absolutely terrible men without partners get to be called "bachelors," but amazing single women are labeled "tragic spinsters" by thirty?

Does it piss anyone else off that they don't *want* to be a spinster, despite how much they love giving the patriarchy the finger?

I wish I didn't care about the whole "mates" thing. I blame all the fan fiction and smut I read.

Because, really, who says finding scent-sensitive love-matches is a person's *only* chance at having the sort of companionship I've always wished for?

My stupid brain, apparently.

Not to mention my Omega.

But we don't talk to her.

Blocking out the whines squirming in my middle, I cross my arms over my chest and squint at the alpha standing across the hall, eyeing him in an exaggerated echo of the way he's glaring at me. Making a joke for myself to enjoy.

The strange alpha doesn't seem to get it. He stands taller, muscles swelling. Happy to have me ogle him, I suppose.

Game on, buddy.

Some of the sternness evaporates from his features as he skims his eyes down my body, pausing to absorb the lower curve of my belly, straining against my slip's pastel silk. That gray gaze leaps up my boobs, which are spilling around the lace cups molded over them.

Huh. Interesting.

His poker face tells me he hasn't caught my scent yet—most alphas who do scrunch their noses. The body wash and scent-canceling spray I practically swam in must be working.

Fucking Bradley.

"You, uh—" The guy pauses, roving his eyes over my chest one final time before bouncing them up to my face "—weren't expecting us?"

Us.

That word and his hat confirm that he's the third alpha. Jesse's pack member and teammate.

My mind spins with implications. Things like his name. Which—*okay, yes, fine*—I've memorized from the tabloids.

Colt Davis.

He's just as notorious as the other two, if a bit more mysterious. He avoids pictures, mostly, but in the few I've seen, he's either straight-faced or scowling.

Sort of like he is now.

I hate to admit it, but a tremor of intimidation moves through me. He's just so *big* and *menacing*, frowning like that.

His features fold into deeper creases. "Hey," he mutters, gruff. "I won't tell anyone you were eavesdropping. It's no big deal. We *are* in your house."

Fuck. The thought of him telling the others I was peeping on them didn't even occur to me. And—oh *God*—I forgot I had on these *pink pom-pom slippers.*

Anyone have a noose? Or a cloak of invisibility? I'm not picky.

"Seriously," the alpha rumbles, stepping closer. "I'm good with secrets."

Oh, I bet he is. I *see* secrets swimming in his eyes. The mysteries swirling there only multiply while he extends his hand, a tiny quirk finally lifting his lips.

"I'm Colt. Locke Pack."

His scent creeps into the air between us. Some mixture of a neutralizing cologne and his true smell. The combination is thick and refreshing. Wet, somehow, but also breezy. Its salted edge skitters down my spine and curls around my middle, squeezing. Saliva pools in my mouth, adding to my nervous nausea.

I have to shake his hand, right? I can't change my name and my face and move to Argentina? Or maybe just run and hide in the pantry? We do have Girl Scout Cookies in there.

He waves his hand at me, the gesture just grumpy and impatient enough to have me rolling my eyes in resignation. I reach out. "Bridget Woods."

His lips twitch again. "I already knew that."

Figures. Jesse probably warned them about me before they came over. I open my mouth to ask *what the actual fuck they're doing here*, but our palms brush, fingers clasping.

Everything inside me slows to a trickle. Blood pounds in my

ears, slowly filtering from my skull to my spine. Trickling through me in a hot dribble that settles between my hips. I gasp, accidentally perfuming.

Greeeeeaaaaaat.

Not only has this alpha seen the outlines of my *nipples*, but now, he's also going to *smell* me.

Colt's reaction is... average. His eyes flash with aggression. He drops my hand like a hot coal and recoils a step, staggering as if someone just splattered him with that bucket of fish guts.

See? This is the part where not caring would *really* come in handy.

But I do. So I scramble into the wall, and try to summon words. An explanation. A joke. Anything.

Before I manage a proper response, he turns, stiff as a board, and stomps right back up the hallway. Away from me.

Probably going to wash his hands, I think, guilty and oddly hollow.

He wouldn't be the first, but I wish he could be the last. That isn't likely, though. Not with Alicia trying to auction me off every chance she gets.

I've got to get out of here.

Living with Alicia, in the ruins of our fucked-up family, was meant to be *temporary.* But I've been here for two years and I still can't afford my own place. I barely manage my meager living expenses and the suppressants I have to take because Alicia would die of embarrassment if I went to any of our local heat clinics.

God forbid one of her friends sees me there. Or *scents me* there.

Little does she know, her worm of a husband acts like a slavering dog the second my pre-heat perfume comes in.

I'm uncomfortable even standing here now. If he walks by, he'll be all up in my personal space. Making the sorts of remarks that toe the line between jokes and threats.

He's smart, damn him. A lawyer. Adept at knowing exactly how much he can squeak past without giving me something solid to take to Alicia. Which is the main reason I've allowed my sister to continue her crusade to get me a pack of my own.

Footsteps approach from the opposite hallway. For a second, fear constricts my airway. Then my mind reboots, and I note the light tread—Alicia's.

The girl weighs less than my bra, I swear.

She greets the Locke Pack with a shiny hostess voice. "Jesse texted me this week and mentioned you might stop by, but I had no idea you were so serious! Are you guys really here right now?"

"In the flesh," Dante smirks. "Did Goldilocks tell you why we were coming to call? Or did he leave the bad news out as per usual?"

Jesse snorts. "It isn't *bad* news. Of course I told her. You think I'd just show up here asking for her sister's hand without warning?"

I'm sorry.

I'M SORRY.

W.H.A.T?!

A record skips in my brain, replaying his words again and again.

Her sister's hand. Her sister's hand.

Her sister's hand.

As in the hand that just sent their packmate running for the hills?

After a full minute of complete disbelief, I realize I must be missing their conversation. Shrinking down as quietly as I can, I strain to hear the rest.

And it's ridiculous.

Insulting.

Infuriating.

But Alicia actually listens. And—oh God—*calls my name.*

"Bridget? Is that you in the hallway? *Come in!*"

Her friendly bark hurtles me into motion, my desperate Omega forcing me to obey the undercurrent of command.

Crazy bitch. Now do you understand why we don't talk to her?

I stagger out from the shadows, forgetting that I don't have any real clothes on until it's too late. Which leaves me standing in front of the Locke Pack. Without underwear.

Remember that bad dream?

I'd like to wake up.

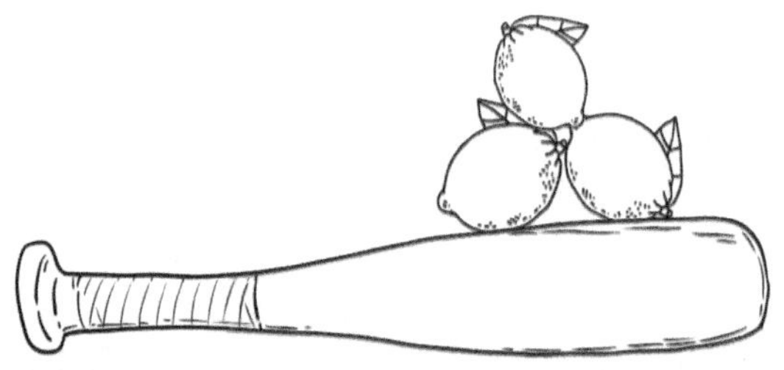

WHO THE HELL is responsible for designing women's underwear?

Seriously.

I want *names*.

I squirm on my bike seat, plucking my panties into a more comfortable position and coasting around one last corner. The groceries in my basket rattle as I steer up the first driveway on the left, the bouquet of sunflowers on top quivering.

I skid to a stop, reaching for the bell attached to my yellow beach cruiser's handlebars. It trills three times, cutting through the quiet spring Sunday.

My street is particularly sunny today. A sprinkler splashes two lawns down. A few birds tweet. And through the AirPod hooked into my right ear?

"Hold on, Em," I interrupt, tapping the earbud to mute my best friend before calling out, "Betty! It's me!"

Muttered curses and shuffling come as my answer. Smiling, I flip my kickstand down and snatch the Whole Foods bag from my white wicker basket.

The path to my neighbor's front door is overgrown and uneven, but I'm here every few days, so I know exactly which cracks to avoid if I don't want to end up on my ass. My panties ride up under my bike shorts again, and I huff a few four-letter words of my own.

"Betty! Get your old ass out here before my butt eats these shorts!"

"How about *you* eat *my* shorts?" my crotchety neighbor tosses back, appearing behind her screen door in a lime-green mu-mu. It matches the dye streaked through her short white hair. "Yelling at an old woman? What the fuck is wrong with your generation?"

I smirk to myself. Betty is a total bitch, but that happens to be my favorite thing about her. She shoots from the hip and never says thank you, no matter how many times I bring her groceries.

"Lovely to see you as always, Bets." I smile, taking the liberty of pulling her screen door open and shoving the paper bag at her. "Here. The plums you like were three for a dollar, so I got six. And I don't want to hear any lip about the green smoothies in there. Your doctor said you need vitamins, so suck it up, buttercup."

She takes the bag and looks down at the flowers on top with a snort. "We goin' steady now, red?"

My smile cracks into a full grin. "Shut up. I'll bring you your usual mid-week stuff after school on Wednesday."

Betty waves her weathered hand in a dismissive gesture. "Yeah, yeah. If you're lucky, I'll still be alive. If you're *really* lucky, I'll answer the door."

She slams it in my face a second later, leaving me to chuckle and shake my head all the way to my bike. When I click our call back on, Emma sighs, "I still don't understand why you bring that mean woman her groceries twice a week."

Her tone is so familiar, I can picture her nose scrunching as she says the words. My bestie is beautiful in that annoyingly oblivious way pretty girls in high-school sitcoms usually are. We met in college; I was getting my master's in education, she was training to become an elementary school counselor. Which, come to think of it...

"Aren't you supposed to be a kindergarten teacher? Shouldn't you tell me to 'be kind to my neighbor' and all that Mr. Rogers crap?"

Emma scoffs as I turn my bike out of Betty's drive and cross the street to my own. It's much neater, surrounded by landscaping I take pride in and the patches of hydrangeas I baby like my children. Although nowhere near as much as my cat.

"Um, *crap*?!" Emma protests. "Mr. Rogers was a *visionary*. And I'm sure he would be very proud of your altruism, but seriously? That lady has been totally rude to you since you moved there, and that was over a year ago!"

I'm well-aware. I moved into the bungalow right around the time Emma and her newly-bonded pack settled into their Florida residence last February.

Part of the reason I chose this place was its proximity to their hockey-season home. And I definitely felt their absence when they spent the summer at their mountain house.

They'll go back when her alpha finishes his season. I try not to think about how quickly those three months will fly by... and how soon I'll be alone here.

Again.

Fucking *always*.

But it's fine. I happen to be *great* company.

"Betty and I have an understanding," I reply, bending to lock my bike to my white picket fence. "We get each other."

"Whatever you say," Emma mumbles. "Hey, do you want to come over for dinner tonight? Zane's making enchiladas!"

Even if her alpha weren't a world-class chef, I'd always be down to go to her house. I love Emma's sunshiney companionship—especially when the Sunday Scaries kick in and a new week in my empty house stretches out before me.

As if protesting that thought, my tabby, Munchies, meows as I breeze through my front door. The foyer of the cozy cottage is cramped and a little cluttered, but my big man manages to saunter around a pair of ruby rainboots and into my arms.

"Sure, I can come. Around six?"

"Yep," Emma chirps. "And maaaaaybeeee..."

I brace, squeezing my eyes shut. Knowing exactly what she's about to say.

"...you could *finally* bring those alphas of yours over here with you?!"

I open my mouth to give her my usual answer, but Emma interrupts, "Let me guess: They can't come because they have practice? Or a workout? Or some sort of event? Or—"

"Em," I try. "Come on. It's not like I'm—"

"Hiding them?!" she exclaims. "Because it sort of seems like you *are*! You never bring them to parties or post pictures of them online or invite me over when they're home. I mean, seriously, we've been back here since *October* and I *still* haven't even *met* your pack."

My pack.

Ha.

Haha.

If you don't laugh, you'll go clinically insane, right?

"You know how it is, Em," I drawl, going for blasé. "Pro athletes and all."

Emma snaps, "Actually, I *do* know how it is since I'm *bonded* to a pro athlete and *related* to another. The funny thing is, Gunnar and Theo always seem to make it home *eventually*. And baseball isn't even in season yet... is it?"

Behind her, someone mutters an aside. Likely one of her alphas, confirming that baseball season won't officially start for another month.

Damn it.

Of all the things I hate about the deal I struck with the devils, lying to Emma is officially the fucking worst.

Instead of an outright untruth, I decide to go with a string of leading questions. "If there was something fishy going on, would they let me run all of their charitable trusts? And would they have bought me this house? What about all the Christmas shopping you and I did together—do you really think I'd go to the trouble of finding gifts for *three grown men* if I didn't absolutely *have to*?"

Yes, yes, and I never did receive a thank-you note for those socks.

I practically *hear* my best friend biting her lower lip. "Bridge... if something is wrong..."

Nope. I have to block out her kind offers to help. Because, lately? They've gotten a bit too tempting.

Luckily, I know Emma's one true weakness: confrontation. I cut her off, presenting a forceful ultimatum, "Look, babe, they can't make it tonight, so it's just me for dinner. Take it or leave it."

She grumbles, "Fine. But I'm making margaritas and wearing sweatpants, so don't get cute."

"Thank God."

The call clicks off. Guilt presses out from my middle while silence collapses around me like a vacuum seal.

My smile slowly fades as I look around my brightly-colored living space. The hot-pink sofa, the bubblegum bookshelves. My butter-yellow cabinets and citrus-orange barstools.

I carefully chose all of it. To be happy, upbeat. A way to keep the shadows in the corners from creeping up on me.

But, mostly, to prove that I'm *fine.*

If only to myself.

My left hand snags on my bike shorts. Or, rather, my engagement ring does.

The engagement ring, really—because it isn't *my* engagement ring. No one actually proposed. And I most definitely did not accept that pack of assholes as my *actual* fiancés.

Still.

Desperate times. Delulu measures.

I hold my hand up, scowling at the huge emerald-cut diamond in its white-gold band. The damn thing is so plain. Maybe even a little *boring*… if it weren't the size of a small planet.

Designed to be seen from outer space. Of course.

I'd bet my whole hand that was Dante's idea.

It's so like him to pee all over things that don't belong to him. Even stuff he doesn't want. I don't think it matters much, as long as it's *his* and everyone else is too scared to touch it.

Which… okay, I admit, is sort of how I wound up in this ridiculous mess. I figured, with alphas like these guys, even if our relationship was fake, Bradley would kindly fuck all the way off.

And it worked. Aside from the whole bone-deep loneliness thing.

But like I said.

I'm *all good*.

Who cares that I haven't heard from any of them in weeks? And so what if I get a pit in my stomach toward the end of every month, wondering if they're still going to hold up their end of our arrangement and pay my mortgage?

They're probably busy. Dealing with Colt's inconvenient injuries and the new wave of bad press they've caused.

I tried to mitigate it all as best I could—but there's not much a girl can do for her fake fiancés when they refuse to *talk to her*.

Jesse used to call every Sunday night. He'd check in, make sure I "had everything I needed." Sometimes, he'd share a funny story from the road or grumble a few good-natured complaints about the guys.

A couple times, he even offered to escort me to certain events. I always turned him down, knowing my sanity depended on the careful lines I drew that day in my sister's living room.

Because I might have had a nightgown on, then—but I'd be damned if I ever faced those fuckers without proper armor again.

"HE'S GONNA KNOW."

Dante kicks his cleats into his "locker." Picture air-quotes around that shit, because the thing is more of a walk-in closet than a cubby or a metal box. Part of the new team manager's many improvements to the Kings' previously decrepit facilities.

My packmates would normally love this sort of crap. Fancy new "lockers," plush carpet in the changing areas, marble showers, and cryogenic physical therapy machines. Not to mention the freshly turfed field, brand-new dugouts, and thousands upon thousands of actual stadium seats.

Apparently, bleachers are "for bullshit high school fields" and "even the good kids' teams have real seats, now."

What-the-fuck-ever.

Jesse is currently too busy spiraling to care about our new decor. He paces between his closet and Dante's, ramming both hands through his gold hair and casting wild hazel eyes between me and our other packmate.

I lean against the crutch tucked under my right arm, absorbing the scene with a pain-fogged brain. Anger roils under the nauseating burn of jealousy clenching my gut. Watching Dante carelessly toss his practice uniform into the laundry chute freezes everything over. Tempering the envy and rage into a cold blade of bitterness.

The hell am I doing here?

"This was *your* idea," I spit back, barely bothering to check over my shoulder and make sure none of our—or *their*—teammates are eavesdropping. "Now you're going postal over it like a little bitch? *You* made this stupid plan, Jesse."

He squeezes his eyelids shut and grinds out a groan. "I know. I *know*. I just didn't think we'd—"

"Fuck it all up again?" Dante supplies, dusting off his hands.

It's rare for him to make a joke these days. Which is another thing that pisses me off. He wasn't even in that godforsaken accident, so what the hell gives *him* the right to sulk about *my* injuries?

Other than the fact that the oddsmakers think the Kings' season might be in the toilet without me...

Which is one of many reasons why Jesse's next statement is all too true.

"We need this," he says, halting to turn his attention from Dante to me and back again. "You both know I'm right."

This fucking guy. He said the same thing over a year ago, the last time we were looking at two options: clean up our act... or make it *look* like we had.

Dante, of course, wasn't interested in shutting down his constant parade of pussy or the partying he claimed was our right, given how much money we make and how hard we work.

Worked, I correct internally.

Because currently? I don't play for the Kings. And may not ever play professional baseball again.

And, okay—I admit to being part of our problem last year. I slept around almost as much as Dante and probably drank the most. Definitely more than Golden Boy Jesse.

None of us wanted to slow down. Dante figured we only needed to present the *illusion* that we had. And what better way than by getting engaged?

But Jesse objected to leading some poor sap on, pretending we wanted to get married. Eventually, he made a suggestion.

We didn't *actually* have to get engaged. We just had to make it *look* like we were.

Our pack discussed it for weeks. We needed someone we could trust, obviously. An omega eager enough to agree, but noble enough to keep their word. A person the press couldn't intimidate. A woman with backbone and intelligence, but not anyone with the sort of fame that would cause a media sensation.

And, in Dante's oh-so-humble words, "hot enough to be believable."

Cue Bridget Woods.

She was Jesse's idea, too. The daughter of dead socialites—well-bred, not well-known. A good name, but nothing truly interesting.

Apart from being an absolute *bombshell* of red-haired, dangerously curved sex appeal.

I couldn't exactly hold that against her, though. On paper, she was educated, employed, and socially conscious. A veritable saint.

Volunteer work. Charitable donations. Girl Scout troop leader. A low-income librarian who single-handedly scraped together enough funds to start a citywide teen literacy program.

Jesse went to high school with the Woods girls: Bridget and her debutante, bitch-on-wheels big sister, Alicia. Word had spread through their silver-spoon circle that Alicia was trying to pair Bridget off—and it was proving quite a challenge.

I didn't understand what Alicia meant when she described Bridget as "headstrong" and "difficult to charm." Until I met the woman.

I slam a metal cage over that memory, trapping my train of thought before it sends me careening back toward blood-boiling hatred.

Maybe I should reconsider staying sober and turning down my doctors' offers for painkillers. Feeling shit sucks.

"You said you knew what you were doing *last time*," I grit. "And now we're in even deeper shit than we were before."

Jesse throws his hands up, exasperated. "Did either of you have a better idea? They were threatening to cut us!"

It's nice of him to say "us" like he was included. Jesse's never hurt a damned fly, and his position on the squad was never in question. Why would any manager cut the team's star pitcher? Especially when the extent of his debauchery amounted to sitting in VIP booths, shaking his head at us while *we* tore shit up.

Jesse was never the problem. Since we didn't have an official pack leader, most of our responsibilities fell to him. Sure, he was crap at most of them, but he did his best.

That's the real reason neither Dante nor I can tell him to shove it now.

And how we've wound up in *yet another* unholy tangle.

"Look," Dante grumbles, pulling on his pristine white sneakers and resting his elbows on his knees, glaring at Jesse from the bench. "It's simple. We can't accept his offer because we already have a deal. With Bridget."

Jesse grimaces, turning to look at me. The hopeful gleam in his green-gold eyes makes my stomach squirm.

Since when am *I* the voice of reason around here?

Christ. That's a sorry state of affairs.

"We can't take on a new packmate—a pack *leader*—and not tell him our omega is—" I check behind me again, lowering my voice to a murmur "—fake."

"She isn't *fake*!" Dante spits, way too loudly. "She's *real*, she just—"

"—isn't *really* ours," Jesse finishes, shoulders slumping. "And we can't have a new pack leader who thinks otherwise. We should tell him the truth."

"But he's also our *team manager*. We *can't* tell him without risking our positions," Dante snaps, growling.

I get it. Because, *Jesus*. We've circled this damn roundabout eighty-thousand times.

Jesse's lips pull back over a pained flash of white teeth. "We could try talking to her? Telling her about—"

"*Adrian!*"

The name of our new manager—and potential pack alpha— rings down the hall. I lean back on my crutch, swallowing a grunt when my left side protests, and crane my neck to see what's coming our way.

Dressed in his usual European sophistication, Adrian appears at the corner of the tunnel. He clocks me watching before an approaching sponsor snags his focus. They shake hands and start a conversation, but I feel our would-be leader's gaze flick to the locker room entrance—and the back of my head—every few seconds.

My voice lowers to a hiss. "You assholes are dumber than I thought if you believe we could *ever* fool *Adrian Messina*. And about *this*? He's brought Bridget up every single time we've discussed him joining the pack. He *likes* her, wants to meet her. You seriously think he won't *notice* if we keep her hidden away in a house with our names written all over it? What's gonna stop him from just showing up there?"

Dante snarls under his breath, black eyes blazing. Does he object to the idea of another alpha approaching Bridget? Or to our pack alpha finding out we're a bunch of frauds?

Either way, his dark gaze flits to Jesse. "Colt's right. The only reason Adrian hasn't gone to her yet is out of respect for our claim to her."

Delusional asshole. *What* claim? Bridget couldn't be *less* ours, as far as I'm concerned.

Jesse swallows visibly, pushing fretful fingers through his hair again. "Fine. So we tell Bridget we're ending our arrangement... Or we tell Adrian the truth and let him decide what to do."

Strained quiet swells between us, punctuated by the distant patter of the locker room showers. We all know what we need to do. It's the choice between continuing with a short-term non-solution and finally having a long-term one.

Jesse shifts his weight, toeing the carpet with his cleat. "I don't want to hurt her feelings."

For the first time all afternoon, Dante and I look at each other. And I see the truth—a quick spark behind his black irises.

Too fucking late.

WE HAVE A SITUATION?

Seriously?

That's how I started the conversation?

One Bridget hasn't engaged in yet. She read the message but didn't answer. Granted, it's Monday afternoon and she's probably at work. But, still.

We've been "engaged" for fourteen months. So I should probably be used to the fact that the woman turns me into a total *idiot*.

Actually, compared to Bee, most people are idiots. She's *smart*. Funny and sharp and intuitive. And so goddamn *pretty* while she makes it clear exactly how moronic you are.

Or maybe that's just me.

Either way, she deserves a hell of a lot more than the half-baked explanation I'm about to bumble through.

I'm not even supposed to warn her about any of this. The guys want to tell Adrian first and let him handle it. That's the whole point of having a pack alpha, for them—someone to clean up their messes the way I've been trying to for the last half-decade.

I can't do that to Bridget, though.

She should get a fair warning.

The truth is, *I* barely understand how we got here. So explaining it to someone who usually spins circles around me won't be easy.

All of this started out simply enough: I found my pack. We found this team. None of us wanted to be a pack alpha, so we let it ride and assumed we'd either find one along the way or bond an omega and let them decide.

Then the fame came. Notoriety. Paparazzi. More money than we had any idea what to do with—and I was used to having a *lot*.

Things that seemed like quirks started to become *issues*—Colt disappearing into his head and carrying around the occasional bottle of whiskey. Dante sleeping with a different woman every night. Me trying my damnedest to run our philanthropies and not having the first clue what the hell I was doing...

We had problems, sure. Who doesn't?

None of it seemed that serious. At first.

Now, I see that my particular brand of optimism probably didn't help. I never questioned any of it because I figured things had a way of working themselves out. I didn't expect the press to catch wind of all the partying, womanizing, and money misman-agement.

I definitely didn't think we would have to come up with a PR stunt to keep our positions.

A fiancée.

The whole put-a-giant-ring-on-it thing was Dante's idea. He's always leaned more toward the grandiose. Courting was one thing —and easily brushed off—he claimed. But an *engagement ring*?

I was the one who couldn't stomach pretending we cared about someone oblivious. Ironically, at the time, striking up a deal with a witting woman felt like the *kinder* option. One really big lie to paper over a whole heap of sins.

Find a willing omega who could benefit from our generosity, give her a ring and whatever else she wanted. Then we could go on with our lives and not worry about neglecting a true fiancée or attempting to court a real one without a pack leader.

I have to say, for a while, it fixed everything. Dante's womanizing ways went underground, giving the appearance of a changed man dedicated to our new relationship. Colt agreed not to miss any more practices or games and took to drinking at home. I gave Bridget our philanthropies and their funds, knowing she would whip them into shape within a week.

It only took her three days, actually.

I like to think that's why I suggested her. Talking her up to the guys, I made sure to mention how brilliant and *cool* she was. Because it's true—Bee has somehow always been one of the least-pretentious, best girls I know.

She came from a prominent family like mine, but didn't inherit any of the silver-spoon bullshit I did. Instead, she used her privilege to learn more. Grow more. Give more.

I couldn't think of anyone better for sorting out this mess.

Plus, I knew her sister was trying to pawn her off on any pack who would court her. I'm not too proud to admit I didn't love that idea. I figured—why should Bridget be shoved at a group of alphas who didn't really want her when we clearly *needed* her?

I don't know what I expected. I just know I was doomed to a strange sort of disappointment when she walked into her living room that day, sized us up, and proceeded to lay out a list of demands.

She wanted a house. An allowance. And rules.

Dante couldn't date publicly anymore. None of us could, but he was the problem there. She didn't want to attend events with us, but agreed to go by herself. She also made it clear we weren't welcome in her new home—and most especially not near her nest.

Can't blame her there.

We're basically a pack of degenerates. And nowhere near good enough for someone as incredible as Bridget Woods.

Something we proved definitively when Colt crashed his vintage Corvette into a median two months ago and nearly maimed himself for life.

The accident turned our world upside down *again*. All of Bridget's careful work and progress... down the toilet. Once the press caught wind of the fact that our packmate was on his way to a bar, we were once more labeled a group of wild partiers with no respect for our lives or anyone else's.

When the Kings' new manager showed up at the hospital, I anticipated some version of "clean out your lockers by Monday." But Adrian Messina walked in wearing one of his signature European suits and instantly took over.

It probably would have been intimidating and a little emasculating if I weren't so desperately relieved.

Since that night, things have sort of fallen into place. He's clearly the leader we've vaguely discussed for years. And he wants a pack of his own to settle down with now that he finally has his career goals sorted.

There's only one problem...

Our "fiancée."

And the fact that I think I'm going to miss her.

WE HAVE A SITUATION.

Jesse's ominous text message glows up at me from my phone. Once again, I choose to ignore it, pivoting back to my students. Just in time to catch one of the senior boys attempting to give his seatmate a wet willy.

"Dylan, we keep our fingers out of our study buddies!"

The kid in question grouses as he follows my direction and takes his finger out of his neighbor's ear.

With the retractable shades down and a cloudy afternoon brewing outside, Orange Blossom High's library is dim apart from the glow of my Smart Board. On it, a cartoon sperm swims his (or her) way to the golden egg awaiting fertilization. I note all the queasy looks on my students' faces and choke down a snort.

Teaching a supplementary sexual health course to a room of hormone-addled upperclassmen wasn't my first choice for the semester, but someone had to do it. Plus, I already had this hilarious uterus hat from the Walk For Reproductive Rights I organized last summer. When else am I going to get to wear it?

The school board threatened to cut this course unless they found a teacher who would take it on without requiring extra pay. I knew it had to be me; I have enough money from the guys. And *someone* has to help these kids before they go off to college.

I mean, really. Last week, I asked the class what labia were, and one guy thought I was talking about a designer dog bred from a Labrador and an Akita.

Your tax dollars at work, ladies and gentlemen.

Only, not really. Because they don't actually *pay* me for this.

I glance around the library while my last class of the day scribbles notes from the most recent slide. Pondering the fact that if someone made a pie chart of my life, a good slice of it has occurred in this large, airy room. With its vinyl floors and laminate bookcases. The faded inspiration posters with random nature scenes in the background.

And of course: the *books*.

Most of them are crap. Stained, dog-eared, covered in smudged plastic or penis doodles. But they're *mine*—and each one is dear to my book-loving, librarian heart.

My eye drifts to the clock hanging over the entrance. *Damn it.* The bell will ring in ninety seconds and I'm not done with this lesson. Especially since they always have questions afterward.

"So," I go on, rushing, "the sperm swims through the uterus to reach the fallopian tubes, where the egg is waiting, anddddd...."

I tap a key on my keyboard and a loud burst of gold confetti fills the screen with a BAM. The students laugh, and I smile to myself.

Some topics just call for glitter. I don't make the rules.

Our bell goes off and everyone slams their textbooks shut, shuffling their backpacks on. I call out the homework for our next session and remind them about the upcoming project info scrawled on the portable whiteboard beside my screen.

Most of the kids nod along or pull out their phones to snap pictures of the assignment, but one in particular sneers.

Ugh.

Linus.

Listen, I know every human is an individual gift with their own innate value and all that... but some kids make me wonder.

Linus doesn't show up for half of his classes. The administration lets him get away with his epic slacking because he's some sort of star athlete? I wouldn't know because I don't follow school sports, but either way, he's been in my classes for years and has some sort of beef with me being a single, plus-sized omega.

At least, that's what the insults he hurls at me every day imply. I don't pay much attention anymore. Not since I reported him to the administration and was told to "let it go."

Normally, Linus tosses in his line of the day and shuffles off to do whatever high school students do instead of attending class. Today, though, the senior takes a longer route to the exit just so he can knock his shoulder into my arm, deliberately sending the stack of quizzes in my hand all over the floor.

This gangly young alpha *loves* showing off how much bigger and stronger he is than his omega classmates. And teachers, apparently.

With a smarmy smile, he starts to back toward the library doors. "Good luck with those quizzes. It must be hard for a virgin to grade sex-ed tests."

See?

Little shit.

Rolling my eyes, I gather the papers and start to clean up the rest of my stuff. In ten minutes, the whole place needs to be clear for study hall, and I don't have time to—

"Oh, by the way," Linus adds, his grin taking on an edge of

menace. He nods at my hand. At *the* engagement ring. "I knew that had to be bullshit. Who the hell would actually want to marry *you*?"

Static fills my ears as heat floods my face. A chill of horror shoots through my veins, freezing my blood into muck so thick that my heart can barely pump. The organ flips and flails, its beats stuttering before breaking into a sprint.

"*What* did you just say?" I demand.

But Linus only chuckles, shoving the exit open with his shoulder. "The truth is all over TikTok, Miss Woods. Or should we just call you The Fake Fiancée?"

CLICK.

Familiar sounds follow the clap of the stadium lights glowing to life. Cicadas chirping. Red dirt crunching under my cleats.

And the ball, slapping my glove.

I could do this forever.

I'm almost used to the guilt pinching my lungs. After two months, it's become as much a part of practice as lacing my shoes and stretching. I swallow down the pissed-off pity and focus on Jesse's back.

All of his pitches sound different. The whistle of a fastball. A swooping whoosh for a curveball. The uneven whisper a slider makes.

This one *screams*, flying for the catcher's mitt.

He's a stand-in. The fourth one we've tried this week. And it's only Tuesday.

I cringe when the ball hits his glove and he nearly falls backward.

Damn. Jesse put some heat on that one.

"Ninety-seven."

Adrian's voice interrupts my one remaining happy place. Because of course it fucking does.

It isn't a secret that I resent the hell out of our new alpha and *all* his authority. Colt does, too.

But he isn't here.

That's the reason for the rookie catcher who can't keep his feet under him and the guilt swarming my middle.

Well. *Part* of the reason.

Cupcake.

That's what I called Bridget—the day we met, when she waltzed in and started laying out her demands. And ever since, in my own head.

When I came up with it, I had no idea the thought would stick. She just... reminded me of a cupcake. All soft and vanilla-pale, with her bright hair swirled on top of her head like a big, lickable dollop of frosting.

It even had little colorful clips in it. Like sprinkles.

Jesus. I shake my head at myself, trying to clear it. Watching Adrian approach the pitcher's mound and forcing myself to dismiss a twinge of relief.

Stupid alpha instincts.

I might not want a new pack leader, but the voice at my center seems to disagree.

It helps that our alpha is always put-together, even when he's wearing sweats and a Kings T-shirt. Any of our friends will tell you Jesse and Colt have absolutely no taste to speak of, but Adrian is like me. He somehow looks like he's wearing a Dolce tuxedo, even in joggers and a baseball cap.

I wipe my brow, sighing. Deflated.

It isn't supposed to be this way. Spring training is usually when we're at our best. Rejuvenated from the off-season, excited to dive into the next one.

Not this year.

So, alright—*fucking fine*.

We sort of *need* a pack leader.

Adrian cuts an imposing figure as he approaches Jesse and waves me over, the warm lights of King Stadium silhouetting his wide shoulders and stacked biceps.

He's not quite as tall as Jesse, but no one on the team is. That wouldn't matter if it came to blows between us—the guy may have fifteen years on the rest of our pack, but he also has about fifty extra pounds of muscle.

Muttering Spanish insults under my breath, I stomp over to the pitcher's mound, joining Jesse and Adrian on the new turf laid around it.

The older alpha's aqua eyes glint under the rim of his black hat. He runs them over Jesse's left arm—the one he uses to pitch. Genuine concern pitches a tent between his brows. "You've done too much today. We'll rest your arm tomorrow."

Seeing my sour expression, Adrian's cools into a foreboding mask. "We need to talk. All of us. Now."

Jesse's usually a glass-half-full, whistle-while-you-work type, but he turns pale. I roll my eyes. "What now, Pops? Haven't we done every goddamn thing you wanted us to do? *Jesu Cristo*, I'm so sick of your high-handed *mierda*—"

Adrian pulls his phone out of his pocket and waves it toward me. Flashing the headline.

Locke Pack Engagement A Sham?!

Oh.

Fuck.

The pack alpha cocks a thick black brow, looking from me to Jesse. "Just answer this: When did you plan to tell me that our fiancée is fake?"

IF THERE ARE sorrier sons of bitches than these three alphas, I don't want to meet them.

Pitiful is the word, really.

I still can't believe I decided to hitch my wagon to this runaway train. You'd think, after waiting twenty-some years to pick a pack, my Alpha would have been more selective. But *this* is the pack he chose.

Spent months *making me* choose.

Last summer, when I turned forty, I knew I needed to get serious about finding packmates and an omega if I ever wanted a chance at having a family.

But *this*?

This was not what I had in mind.

I watch Colt hobble around the kitchen on one crutch. He's clearly unbalanced, and I know for a fact he's supposed to be using two. Not to mention the extra strain it puts on his good leg. He's going to make his injuries worse by fighting them instead of working through them.

Try telling him that, though.

His pig-headed scowl is practically branded into his features. I don't think I've ever seen him without it. From the day the Kings hired me as their new team manager and I showed up at the hospital to assess the damage to our star player, Colt has had this look on his face like he's ready to fight off the entire world.

Or die trying.

Forget reckless—at this point, it's just plain stupid.

And I've decided these guys need a zero-tolerance policy for stubborn stupidity.

"*Colt*," I bark smoothly, setting down my tablet with a fierce frown of my own. "*Two crutches*."

He shoots me a venomous look, fighting the order. But, in the end, he snatches the second crutch from its place against the wall.

Hmm. Not even a growl. The guy may hate me, but it seems like his Alpha appreciates clear, constructive directions from mine. Yet another sign that I'm meant to be the leader of *this* pack, however hopeless they seem.

And, evidently, despite the one small detail that their omega isn't truly theirs at all.

My gaze trails over the cluttered entryway behind Colt while he limps into the equally filthy kitchen.

Fucking hell. We might have to set the place on fire.

I might have to let them burn along with it.

Anger vibrates through me, the day's headlines flashing through my mind's eye. The guys feel my undercurrent of rage snap through the kitchen. Colt collapses into a barstool, muttering about alphaholes barking orders. Dante glances over, his face carefully blank as he flips an omelet at the stove.

I catch his gaze and raise a brow. "I still cannot believe you three did this."

Dante's usually a spitfire. The fact that he simply gives a stiff shrug is telling.

"She needed a pack to take her off her sister's hands and give her a place of her own," he grumbles, petulant. "We needed an omega to fix our reputation and make everyone think we'd been domesticated. It worked."

It *did* work.

Too well.

I'd be lying if I claimed their sweet, red-headed omega wasn't the main reason I originally expressed interest in joining their pack. I've always wanted an omega to care for—and the Locke Pack's seemed like exactly the sort I'd want to worship.

Bridget is a beautiful woman. Anyone who looks her up online would know that. But she's smart, too. I've read her interviews in society papers and listened to her interviews on philanthropic podcasts. She's well-spoken and, if her constant book photos on social media are any indication, even better-read.

Over the last eight weeks, I've put consistent pressure on the guys to introduce us. I figured that would be the final step to legitimizing my place—meeting their pretty little omega and proving I deserve to be the head of her pack.

I had all sorts of plans for that.

Because, surely, they would never add a new alpha if their future omega didn't wholeheartedly approve. I should have known something was wrong when she didn't materialize right away.

Actually, I should have known when I walked into their penthouse and saw the complete shambles they live in.

Not to mention, the place smells exclusively like the three of them.

Colt's salty, oceanic sandalwood. Dante's sticky mango scent. Jesse's caramelized, toasted sugar essence.

All decent. But none of them speared me the way an omega's scent would.

I hate how much the whole thing makes sense. Why they've never been photographed with Bridget at public events. Why she never came to the dugout or any of our practices. Why she wasn't with them when Colt was laid up in the hospital.

I thought they were protective of her. Hoarding her away from me and any other alphas.

And, hell—*I respected that.*

But this explains a lot. As much as I can appreciate wanting to possess every inch of the woman, would any alpha who actually had Bridget ever leave her at home collecting dust?

Of course not.

Especially not one as arrogant as Dante.

He slides his dark eyes over to me. "You still going over there?"

I close the case of my tablet, leaving the omega's social media feeds behind. She must have seen the news when it broke yesterday, because all of her public accounts are now private.

Poor baby. I can't even imagine how hard this has been on her. And she's all alone in it.

"*We* are," I declare. "This needs to be addressed immediately."

I can always tell when Dante secretly agrees with me because he ducks his head and turns away. Without admitting he concurs. Instead, he grunts, "Whatever, Pops."

He needn't remind me that, compared to them, I am ancient. I'm already well-aware. And dreading young, beautiful Bridget's reaction when she sees the silver at my temples and the laugh lines on my face.

It doesn't matter, though.

I need to look the woman in the eye and figure out how to make this right. I may not have a plan yet, but I have a feeling I'll know exactly what she needs when I meet her.

IT'S A CUTE-ASS HOUSE.

I've always liked it. Ever since the day Bridget sent me the listing.

It was about a week after we signed our stupid agreement. Per the terms, she had a month to move out of her sister's place and into a "packhouse" furnished by us.

I remember being so surprised when I opened her email and saw what she'd chosen. Didn't she know we were millionaires? Hadn't she read the dollar figures in our contract?

This was the house she wanted?

Calling it a "house" is generous, actually. It's more like a bungalow.

A really, really cute one.

I haven't been here since the day we bought it. When I signed the papers and got the keys to the place, I came alone to check it out. Just, you know, out of curiosity.

I never imagined it would be so small and sweet. And I definitely didn't expect to spend an hour wandering from room to room, feeling the deep swell of some aching emotion that may have been *regret*…

The home is even more welcoming now. Painted chipper white with a pale yellow door, surrounded by hydrangeas every bit as blue as Bridget's eyes.

Bee.

A familiar ache yawns in my middle, stretching to fill my stomach. I'm going to miss our phone calls, however awkward they could be. Those were one of the few pack-alpha duties I didn't struggle with—that one weekly check-in, making sure "our omega" had everything she needed.

What a joke.

I never really *asked*. About her heats, her happiness, her health —mental or otherwise.

On cue, shame joins the roil inside of me. *I've been a shitty friend.* Worse than I even let myself realize before I saw the Adrian's horrified expression last night.

Most alphas would probably be put out by losing their freedom—and, trust me, I try to summon any sort of anger about it. But I just keep coming back to an almost manic sort of relief. Watching Adrian steer his BMW into Bridget's driveway feels the way I imagine a nanny would when the parents of a screaming horde finally come home.

Like, *thank God I'm not in charge anymore.* And *at least no one died.*

But it was a close call for sure.

Too close.

"This is it?" Adrian clips. He's in his usual silk dress shirt and gray slacks. Professional and put-together, with his longer black hair slicked on top of his head and the sides buzzed in a clean fade. He's bronzed, like Dante, but his eyes are a light, bright color. They narrow in speculation while he stares at Bridget's little house.

I nod, my gaze tracing the colorful wreath on the happy front door. "Yep, this is it."

"It's small," he mutters. "And... cute."

I almost smirk. He's clearly never said that word out loud. I'm not surprised.

Adrian is a ball-buster. Even at rest, with nothing to provoke him, his dominance practically chokes me.

I never could have whipped the guys into submission the way he did this morning. A few smooth barks and he had Colt actually using both crutches. And Dante *cleaning*.

Though I suspect he got less resistance than he normally would because they were both trying to put off coming over here. Seeing Bridget.

I could put this delicately, but at this point, what the hell?

They've never liked her. And she *can't stand* them.

Dante's had an issue with the omega from the moment she walked into Alicia's living room and started slinging orders at us. He fought her fire with his own; arguing with her over *every single point* in our deal. Generally being an arrogant ass. Which, granted, is sort of his default, but...

Colt surprised me. I knew his mysterious waters ran deep; although I honestly didn't think he had the whole loathing thing in him.

Until he met Bridget.

For a while, I wondered if there was something wrong with me. Was I supposed to feel that strongly, too? Alicia told me Bridget's scent was undesirable, but I've never agreed. It's a clean, fresh lemon—sharp in ways that made my mouth water.

The guys and I never talked about it, but I assumed they must have really hated her citrusy aroma. So I was the one who called her every week.

And, each time, I liked her more.

And then a little more.

The blue-eyed omega is my *friend*.

Sometimes, it felt like she was my only one.

But maybe that isn't fair. Because Adrian reaches over and gives my shoulder a firm squeeze, the same way any comrade would. "It's going to be fine."

He lifts his light eyes to the rearview mirror, pinning my packmates with reproachful, reassuring looks. "We'll make sure she's taken care of. But you each owe her an apology, and you know that."

Damn. He doesn't even have to bark. Pure, undiluted certainty oozes from every word, sinking into my center.

He's right.

I do owe Bee an apology.

Maybe even a heap of them.

chapter
nine

EMMA

Bridget please pick up the phone

pleeeeeeeeeease

with sugar on top.

and whipped cream.

and chocolate sauce.

Bridgeeeeeeeee

BRIDGET

I don't want to talk about it yet

EMMA

ok 😭

just tell me this

whose butt do I need to kick?

BRIDGET

Mine ☺

Bridget

I HAVE A MANTRA.

Cry about it today. Kick its ass tomorrow.

So tomorrow, I'll put my makeup on and do my hair and guzzle enough iced coffee to get me through work.

But for today?

I called out sick, and I plan to spend the day in my nest, crying and eating carbs.

The tabloids have every detail of my shame, splashed over gossip websites and social media.

I am officially The Fake Fiancée.

Or, according to one particularly clever outlet, *The Faux-ancée.*

Either way, the word is out. Which means, on top of being national news, I'm probably losing my little house as soon as the guys figure out how to cut their losses.

My painted patio with its rocking chairs. My back porch where I hung my hammock. My hydrangeas. My nest-in-progress—

The doorbell chimes. It's muffled in the walls of the spare room that serves as my safe space, but there's no missing the upbeat buzz.

For a second, I worry it's TMZ or something. Then I remember.

Oh, right. I ordered coffee cake.

After I give the Uber driver the requisite two minutes to get back to their car, I shuffle out of my pile of blankets and tumble into the narrow hallway.

God. It's way too bright out here. All this natural light.

What was I thinking? Didn't I know that, one day, I'd be so horribly mortified that I wouldn't want to face the sunshine? I should have thought ahead, for fuck's sake.

Still sniffling, I tuck my green floral kimono around my body and throw my front door open.

Oh.

My.

God.

The whole house seems to shiver as I immediately slam the door closed.

Oh my God. Oh my God. OH MY GOD.

This is not happening.

Not. Happening.

The Locke Pack did *not* just see me in my underwear.

Again.

Not to mention whoever that huge, handsome man behind them is. A lawyer, maybe? Here to dissolve any rights I have to my house?

Their house.

Am I hyperventilating?

Is that what this sob-breathing thing is?

"Bee?" Jesse calls through the slab. "It's, uh, me. And the guys. And, um, Adrian. He's the new team manager, and uh... he wanted to come meet you."

Come *meet me*?! I'm in a nightgown not much more modest than the one I had on last time we all had a "meeting." It's sheer luck that I happen to also have my kimono on right now. Although the silk is pretty thin...

Dear God. Did I just show Jesse Locke my nipples *again*?

And Dante?

And *Colt...*?

And their team manager, too?!

For that matter, what the hell is *he* doing here? Damage control?

Because that's me. *The damage.*

I'd be more outraged, normally, but I don't think I'm breathing. Or, at least, oxygen isn't touching my lungs. Which probably explains how my banished Omega manages to get a word in edgewise. A high, thready whine ekes out of me, the sound strangled.

"Omega."

Oh, the voice in my middle freezes, her anxiety forgotten. *Oh, hello…*

This hoe, I swear.

Even I have to admit, she has a point this time. The strange alpha's bark is pure steel, dripping with honey. I swear my blood stops pumping. Every particle in my body tunes into the commanding voice, begging me to obey.

"Deep breaths," it goes on. *"And get the door, please."*

Air hits my cramped lungs. I move, flinging the door open and stepping back, hugging my arms around myself. I realize I have no makeup on, and the irony of that—of me making my face up every day for years, only to be caught like *this, now*—nearly sends me into hysterical, snorting giggles.

Seriously, *what is my life?*

A comedy of errors, apparently, where I'm somehow always in my damn lingerie, with every effing roll and dip on display and a literal *group of professional athletes* staring at me.

Of course they all look incredible. Jesse with his blond hair curling against his collar and around his ears, hazel-green eyes glinting under the brim of his blue-and-gold Kings hat. The look on his face is a lot like relief. Probably because he knows he's about to be rid of me once and for all.

If Dante is similarly appeased, he doesn't show it. Instead of looking *at me*, he eyes my front porch with a half-sneer. Judging its size, most likely.

He might *seem* oblivious to the way his fitted white T-shirt clings to his pecs and matches the straight rows of his teeth—*and* how the pristine color sets off his rich skin, which is already extra-gorgeous thanks to the early-morning sunshine. But Dante is one hundred percent the kind of guy who kisses his own reflection before he leaves the house. Even when he has sweatpants on.

Then, there's Colt.

Glaring.

Always.

In fact, I don't think I've seen a different expression on his face since that weird moment we shared in Alicia's hallway.

He's lucky rage works for him. The dark thoughts swimming in his gray eyes go well with his thick brows and the over-long hair tucked under his baseball cap—identical to Jesse's, except Colt forever wears his backwards.

He continues glowering, even when the crutch tucked under his good arm wobbles slightly. The strange man behind him places a steadying hand on his shoulder and meets my gaze with—*wow*—the prettiest eyes I've ever seen.

It's unfair, really. No alpha should be this dominant *and* this *fucking hot*.

Tall and broad, he fills his charcoal dress shirt and silver-gray slacks like a model from a cologne ad. In fact, that's his entire aesthetic. The sort of effortless elegance that belongs on an Italian male model stepping out of a Ferrari on a cool evening in Rome. Only, this man is in his late-thirties, with a worldly air that takes him from beautiful to sexy as sin.

And his *hair*.

John Stamos, who? Plus a touch of silver at his temples?

Take me now.

As if reading every dirty, ridiculous half-thought bubbling in my brain, the strange alpha's winged brow raises slightly.

"Good morning, Bridget," he says, sending a quiver to my core. "May we come in?"

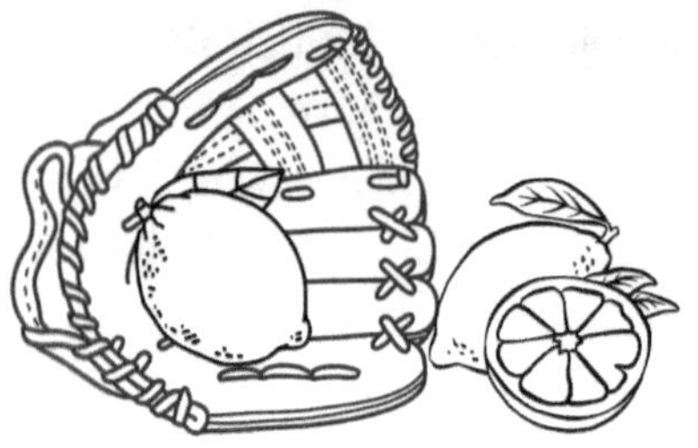

UNDERWEAR?

Check.

An actual *bra*?

Also check.

Clothing??

Check and check.

After I panicked and ran out of my foyer like my butt was on fire, Jesse awkwardly spoke through my bedroom door, telling me to take as much time as I needed to get ready. Assuring me they would wait.

Presumably, for me to calm down.

As if that's even possible.

I run my hands down my lavender skirtall, smoothing it over my tight white T-shirt. Pretending I can't hear them in my kitchen, voices low and serious. Underscoring the fact that there are *four* of them here. And that—despite each of them wearing a polite layer of de-scenter—they are still positively filling this place with *alpha*.

Jesse, in all his Golden Boy, sugar-spiced, kettle-corn glory.

Colt's general saltiness.

Dante's sticky-sweet mango.

And...

Adrian.

Simply thinking his name is enough to have me perfuming. It's taken the last thirty minutes for me to process *him*. So strong and sexy, distinguished but still young enough to pull off his trendy haircut and the three open buttons framing his bare chest. Showcasing how *all* his skin is, in fact, the same clear, bronzy color as honey...

I only got a bit of his musky scent when he walked into the foyer. He probably put on extra neutralizer before they came over here. That's considered gentlemanly when visiting the home of an unbonded omega; and despite being sex on a stick, Adrian seems like he minds his manners.

I hope not, the little voice inside of me whines.

My Omega.

Guys, she is—and I cannot stress this enough—an absolute *lunatic.*

Which is why I don't trust her with this situation one bit.

Thinking this, I reach for my scent-canceling spray, muttering to myself, "They're already in my damn house—it's not like they can't smell me all over the place."

It's still embarrassing, knowing how unappealing my aroma can be. But you know what? Better safe than sorry.

Ignoring my trembling limbs, I slip into pink Chacos and creep down the hallway. Hoping I'll be able to eavesdrop on their conversation a little. Get the lay of the land before they—

"Bridget?"

It's Adrian. I know the others' voices, but his is new to me. The rough rasp around the edges sends a melty ache to my core.

It only gets worse when warm amusement seeps into his tone. "We can smell you, little blue," he chuckles. "Do you want your coffee cake? I have it here for you."

Damn him. I *do* want my coffee cake.

And who the fuck is "little blue"?

Surely not *me*?

Blushing all over and annoyed about it, I wander around the wall separating the kitchen from the hallway.

The small, sunny room is one of my favorite spots in the house. I painted the cabinets myself, matching them to the soft, buttery yellow on my front door. I thought the color went well with the dark hardwood floors and white countertops. Plus, it adds a little brightness to all the meals I eat by myself.

Now, four huge alphas fill my upbeat kitchen and living room. Jesse leans against the wall between my pink Smeg fridge and the island. Dante is on one rosy couch, his legs and arms spread like he owns the damn thing—while Colt sits opposite him, his good knee bouncing in agitation. Adrian is perched on one of my orange barstools, waiting for me to look at him.

When I do, cool azure eyes beam fondly. He waves me toward him, an undercurrent of alpha power lacing his casual, "Here, omega."

I really wish he would stop calling me that.

I could do without the reminder of what I am—and what *he* is.

Which brings me back to: Who the fuck is this guy, and why is he in my house?

Their house.

Adrian's chiseled lips quirk up slightly. "I'll explain," he promises. "But you should eat. Come on."

Dumbfounded, I follow the pull in my middle across the

room. When I start to slide into my own stool, he hums. The sound is quiet, but disapproving. I freeze on the spot.

Then I shake that shit off because *who cares* what this *literal stranger* approves of??

Not me.

Nope.

Shut up.

Whatever manly musk I barely picked up on before is stronger directly beside him. Actually, I think it's just stronger in general. Some dark, smoky sexiness that reminds me of new cars and an old club chair next to a fireplace…

Holy shih tzus.

It's leather. Warm and supple, as if it's even possible for a scent to have a *texture*. His does, though.

What *the hell* is happening today?

Focus, Bridget.

Worldly blue-green eyes snag mine, his thick black brows drawn up. He nods at the coffee cake, served perfectly on a chipper yellow plate, with a folded napkin and everything. "Aren't you hungry, little one?"

Alright, that's it.

Whatever this is stops now.

I shoot him a dirty look before dismissing him entirely, turning to face forward and pick up my fork. "My name is Bridget," I correct as breezily as I can manage.

My focus shifts to Jesse's guilty grimace. "Are you going to explain who you brought to my house?" I ask, expression expectant. "I assume you're all here because of the news that broke yesterday."

Jesse's wince tightens. He opens his mouth, but it's Dante who answers, his dark eyes glinting across the room. "Oh, did we forget to tell you, cupcake? He's your new pack alpha."

I HATE IT HERE.

The yellow cabinets. The pink bookshelves. The fat orange cat who seems to be under the mistaken apprehension that I'm friendly.

All the evidence that Bridget has been here, happy all along, puts a deep, painful burn in my gut.

Or maybe that's her scent. Sharp lemon zest and sweet sugar-cane tingle in my lungs on every reluctant inhale. Singeing my insides until my blood feels like it will roll into a boil.

She didn't smell like this the first time we met. It was more nuanced and subtle... then, when she was embarrassed, sharper.

Remembering my reaction to all of it sets my teeth on edge. I ball my fists until my blunt fingernails nearly pierce my palms.

Look at this stupid orange cat.

Only happy people have cats like this.

Is it too much to ask that the person who destroyed my faith in humanity be at least half as miserable as I am?

I really don't think so.

Over the year, we've spent more time with our apartment building's doorman than we have with Bridget, but her expression is still all too familiar. Pursed lips, narrowed blue eyes—the same face she wore in her sister's living room the last time we were forced into a fucked-up pack meeting.

Just like that day, it's clear she wants nothing more than to get away from us as quickly as possible.

Honestly?

Relatable.

Her mind moves fast. I remember realizing that when I watched her snap our deal together last year. She didn't stand around asking dumb questions or acting affronted.

It's the same, now. She doesn't stammer denials or whine about being left out of the loop. Instead, she turns her face from Jesse to Dante and back again.

Avoiding me.

Because, like I said, the woman is *smart.*

"Then I assume he knows the truth," she sniffs, lifting her chin to a regal angle as she stares my blond packmate down. "All of it?"

Jesse's face is going to get stuck that way, I swear. His mouth pulls into a wider cringe. "Yeah. I'm sorry, Bee. I know we had a confidentiality clause in the contract."

Bridget rolls her lips together, crossing her arms under her chest and looking down at her pink shoes and purple-polished toes. "Well, someone must have broken it. We were the only people who knew, aside from Alicia, and I've already gotten a dozen calls from her, screeching about this bullshit 'sullying the family name,' so."

Her meaning is clear. Alicia is a bitch, but she had a stake in the secrecy of this arrangement, too. Now we all look like idiots.

"*I* never wanted to do this," Dante points out, drumming his fingers along the back of Bridget's couch. "I said this plan was fucking crazy, but *Jesse*—"

My anger flashes, rising high and hot, red tinting my vision. "*Jesse* isn't the one who bought the damn ring, and he definitely isn't the asshole who drives over here all the time like a stalker."

A beat of disbelief passes over my packmate's square face—because... yeah, I went there. Then Dante's eyes glint. "No, *Jesse* is the one who calls her every goddamn week like a total simp."

"I was *checking in*," Jesse interjects. "You guys *know* it was never like that!"

Dante chuffs. "Yeah, sure. Okay. Are we also supposed to believe you didn't want to get in her pants when you dragged us to her sister's house and came up with this insane plan?"

Jesse's jaw drops. A growl trips up my throat. Adrian barks a low, "*That's enough*," just as Bridget scoffs, "I'm literally sitting *right here*."

The two turn to look at each other, Adrian's gaze assessing, and Bridget's full of fire. She's really perfected that *what-are-you-looking-at* preen, but I can't let myself give her a compliment, even in my own mind.

Adrian's eyes land on hers. His mouth curves up at one corner, but his amusement only softens her for half a second before she huffs again, snapping her spine straight.

"Does it even matter whose fault this is? You guys came to me; I agreed. We all signed the damn agreement, so we're *all* to blame for our agreement," she argues. "But I held up my end of things, and you guys clearly didn't."

Being lumped in with the others chafes. In a lot of ways, I'm not truly one of them anymore. I can't play on the Kings this season. I can't do our workouts. Right now, I can't even drive.

On the other hand, I'm sick of being blamed for their bullshit. If there's one thing I can do it's keep a secret. All the partying and women and financial fuck-ups over the years... I never flaunted my flaws, but I was part of the group. So my name and career came under just as much scrutiny when the guys did.

Now we've done the same thing to Bridget.

I refuse to feel bad for her, but still.

I get it.

Adrian sighs, nodding his empathy. "You're right, Bridget. I've reviewed the deal you all made and looked over all the accounts. You've more than held up your end of the agreement. I'm sorry my pack didn't live up to theirs."

Dante mutters something that sounds like "we didn't do shit," but Adrian cuts him off with half a glance.

Fuck. The guy can really whip that dominance around.

He continues, looking into Bridget's eyes. "We'll make sure the dissolution of the contract is more-than fair if that's what you want, omega..."

But Bridget Woods—damn her—tosses her auburn hair back and snaps a laugh. "Oh *no*," she argues. "You guys aren't breaking the contract and leaving me to take the fall. You think I don't know how this will go? *You'll* all go back to being Eligible Bachelors, and *I'll* be the *Faux-ancée* for all eternity. Nope. You're going to fix this mess you made, and *then* you're going to leave me the hell alone."

Jesse's gone pale, staring at her profile as he repeats, "Fix it? How?"

I swear some of the steel melts out of her irises as she turns to Jesse. Her rounded shoulders drop at the same moment her lips turn down in a plump, pensive frown.

"I don't know," she murmurs, like she's only admitting the words to him.

Jesse's grimace cracks into an expression of pure, true pain. But Adrian stands, his bearing full of the sort of alpha power that gets shit done.

Which is why everyone's already staring at him when he nods brusquely. "I do."

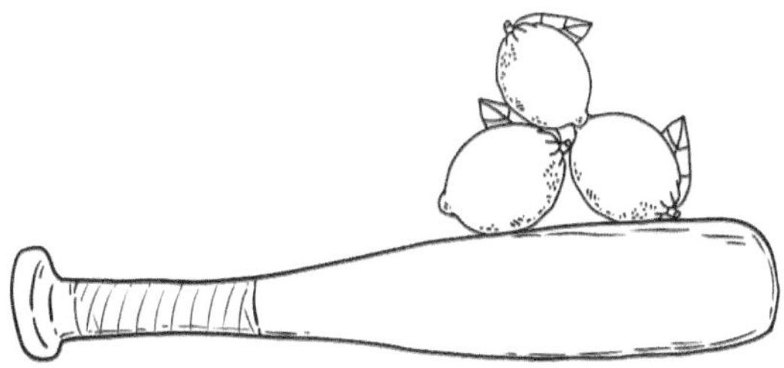

chapter **twelve**

ON THE OTHER side of Bridget's yellow front door, the world is the same orderly, indifferent place I've mastered.

On this side?

It's too chaotic to be heaven, but too sweet to be anything else.

The curvy little omega's entire house smells like lemons, but better. Far from the plain sorts of desserts I'm used to, *this* scent is rich and layered. Sumptuous and silky, like custard, but with a delicious caramelized crunch and the most tantalizing, bittersweet edge of burned sugar. All drizzled in delicious citrus tartness.

I've been dragging the drugging scent into my lungs from the second I walked in. Tasting it. Processing how it could possibly get *better* with every draw of sticky, slicing air.

As we stood in her kitchen, waiting for her to get dressed, an insistent throb started at the base of my knot, syncing with the ache in my canines.

Bite her. Claim her. Knot her. Hold her forever.

I put Bridget's breakfast together to distract myself from hunting her down.

The fact is, I'm forty and I've never met an omega *this close* to perfection. There's something about her scent that just barely keeps it from being absolutely flawless. A thread that's more unsettling than arousing.

It's maddening. Like the sensation of a word sitting on the tip of your tongue while your mind struggles to recall it.

I've experienced this before—with other, less-appealing omegas. Only a fraction of packs are actually scent-sensitive. And in all other cases? A gorgeous omega's scent is still tempting as sin, even if it doesn't click one hundred percent.

I should be stronger than this. So why is the sugared tartness swirling around Bridget's home making it hard for me to *think*?

Her reappearance hasn't helped. The de-scenter she spritzed on burns my nostrils. And she's so damn *beautiful*, I can't keep my thoughts—or my eyes—off the way her top molds to her curves. The creamy skin of her throat, her legs...

I want to drop to my knees and bury my face in those soft, thick thighs. Lap up all the sweet lemon cream between her legs. Show her the way a king treats his queen.

Fuck.

While the others bicker, I wrestle myself back, locking my muscles into stillness. Thank God control comes naturally to me, or I'd be ripping her panties right off those wide, gorgeous hips and—

No.

Focus.

She's just admitted she doesn't know how to fix this. And I suspect she's correct about the media dumping this mess on *her* doorstep if we simply sever our ties and walk away.

God. The very *thought* has my insides lurching. My fingers tingle, threatening to clench, but I only allow my eyes to move, sweeping over every bit of her pretty face.

She looks angry. Confident and in command. I admire the way she's advocating for herself, but I hate the fact that it seems to come so naturally to her.

Who's been bullying this omega, and why has she learned to defend herself so fiercely?

That should be her alphas' job.

My glare has the guys straightening. *Yeah*, I tell each of them silently. *You clowns.*

Bridget continues holding her head high, but I can tell she's more nervous than her expression lets on. Her shoulders tremble slightly, and her lovely peaches-and-cream complexion pales by the second.

I don't think she's wearing any makeup today, which is a change. In pictures, she always has eyeshadow to match her colorful clothing and appears to enjoy new beauty trends. I've seen her dolled-up face in magazines and all over the latest gossip articles.

But I came here today to see *her*.

She has freckles. Only a small splattering, but still. Adorable. Almost as cute as her little upturned nose. And her full, pouty *lips*.

Look at this beautiful baby. How did they ever let her out of their sight?

Which gives me an idea.

"I do," I intone. "I know what we need to do."

Bridget starts to react to the burst of alpha energy infused into my words. Her posture softens the smallest bit and her eyes widen before she snaps back to a sassy stance.

"And what is that?" she asks, placing a hand on her cocked hip.

I fight the urge to smile at her brattiness and settle for curving my brows at her. "We're moving in."

"WHAT?!"

Bridget and I both hurl out the word at the same time—me roaring, her in a shriek.

Huh.

There's no time to dwell on the coincidence. I have to talk our insane sort-of pack alpha out of this "solution." Now.

Shoving to my feet, I stalk from the small sitting area to the orange barstools. *Everything in this hovel looks like it was painted by an eight-year-old at Color Me Mine, I swear to—*

But the little red-haired cupcake of an omega beats me to it, spitting out a reply before I get over the way her furniture blinds me.

"Move *in*?" she shouts. "The four of you? *Here?*"

Adrian shrugs in that made-to-look-casual way that has my teeth grinding. His tone is offhand. "I assume so, unless you'd like us to move somewhere else together."

"How about Hell?" she shoots back, balking.

Colt squirms on the sofa, muttering, "*I'm* already there."

"*Colt,*" Adrian snaps while I groan a curse, and Jesse steps forward, coming to the other side of Bridget's kitchen counter.

"Bee," he pleads, "just hear Adrian out. Please?"

She rolls her eyes at him and continues pouting at Adrian, waving a dismissive hand at me and Colt.

Which...

Excuse me?

Did this woman just completely block out my *existence*?

I think the fuck not.

"If she's not going to listen," I interrupt, smirking down at her, "we should go. She's right—none of this will touch *us.*"

Jesse gapes, and Adrian glares. Bridget's eyes fly wide, but then the little brat turns her face away and *flips her hair* at me.

I feel my features fall slack and hear Colt snort at whatever dumb expression drops into place. Bridget ignores us, throwing her hand on her hip and continuing the conversation as if I never spoke at all.

"I love my house," she informs our almost pack leader. "*I'm* not moving anywhere."

He nods as if she's actually agreeing with him. "Excellent. Then we'll come live here with you, little blue."

Little blue?

That seems hella specific for a guy who just met her. But her eyes *are* really blue. Sort of like his—but warmer and darker.

Yeah, I've noticed.

Sue me.

Jesse always crows about how smart Bridget is. I saw a bit of her wit in action during our original negotiations, but now I'm actually watching her mind work. So quick, if I blinked, I would miss the understanding that zips through her gaze.

"You think that if you publicly move in with me and make it look good for the press, they'll be forced to drop the whole Faux-ancée thing?"

Ah. *Carajo.*

That *does* sort of make sense.

Denying the lie is one thing, but giving the world a glimpse of our "relationship" moving forward? It would fix the whole issue —especially if Bridget is correct and Adrian wants us to put on a whole courting charade, too.

Dates, public appearances... All the things we've avoided because this omega can't stand us, and the feeling is mutual.

But if we start taking her out and let the paps get pictures of us moving in here...

Well. There goes my sex life.

Luckily, Bridget seems hell-bent on not giving in. "There's no space here!" she huffs. "This place only has two bedrooms, and I've already converted one of them into a nest."

I can tell Adrian's thoughtful, placid expression pisses off the omega as much as it enrages me. *Goddamn this bastard for being so calm.*

"The guys and I will be fine sleeping on the floor, if neces-sary," he offers, smooth as silk. "Or we can get cots and use the sofas. Colt will need to claim one of those because of his injuries, but I don't see any reason why the rest of us aren't able-bodied enough to get creative."

I'm sure he doesn't mean to make an innuendo, but that's where my mind immediately goes. Getting *creative.* With Bridget.

All that soft, peachy skin filling my palms. Mouth-watering, lemony torched sugar slipping down her thighs—

I tune back into the conversation, only to find it's halted. And the omega is staring at me?

Mierda. My scent. It must have swelled around my neutralizer.

Bridget's features are dainty and round, underscoring those big, bright eyes and the white-hot fire licking at them. "Seriously?" she says, shooting an unimpressed glower at the semi pressed into my joggers. "*That's* what you're thinking about right now?"

That's what I've been thinking about since I saw her in her robe.

But I grit my molars. "I repeat: do you want me to leave? Because from where I'm standing, this would be a whole lot of work for *us*... to save *your* ass."

Her flame-blue eyes narrow. "Oh, I'm sorry," she hisses, "sort of like *I* saved *your* asses a year ago?"

Carajo. Why do I like it when she makes a good point?

"And, what?" she adds, peering around my bare bicep at Colt, including him in her next question. "After all this time and all the shit I've done for your pack, am I not even worth saving?"

Colt's jaw tightens, but Jesse, ever the peace-keeper interjects, "Bee, of course your ass—I mean, *you*—I mean, *yes*. We want to save your reputation, too."

Jesu Cristo. This fucking guy. He's so down bad for this girl, and look where it's gotten us.

Did we really have to pretend to ask her to marry us? He could have just taken her out for dinner. Maybe a movie?

Bridget seems just as oblivious as Jesse, blinking at him with doe-eyes so very different from the pissy gaze I usually get. "Would—could you actually do that, though, Jess? Your season is about to start, and there's barely room to do a push-up in here..."

Why do I want to argue with her over *every single thing*? Even when it means swapping sides and contradicting my own damn self from three minutes ago?

"You have a big backyard," I grumble. "And that detached garage can hold a weight bench if you move your car."

Bridget tosses shimmering red hair over her shoulder. "No need. The garage just has some renovation supplies in it, but I'm finished with most of them." Her gaze skims down to where my shirt clings to my abs as she scowls. "I *guess* I can clear it out."

"*We'll* clear it out," Adrian corrects, stepping smoothly between us, his palm settling on her arm. "You don't have to do anything, Bridget. Just say yes and it will be done."

For the first time, Bridget shrinks back, stepping away from his touch. Her arms cross under her chest again, but I barely appreciate the way they push her tits up because of the lost look on her face.

Shit. I don't want her to be *sad*.

Angry and clawing at me? Yes. But *this*?

Shrugging as casually as I can, I try to keep my tone neutral. "Whatever. I'm in."

Avoiding the way her head snaps up and—more importantly —the surprised sort of hope lighting her features, I turn and examine her tiny living room. A thought occurs to me. "Wait. You have a TV *somewhere*, right? Because otherwise I'm gonna need to buy a new flatscreen."

Jesse chuckles. The strained sound matches his swirling hazel eyes much better than the stiff smile pulling at his mouth. "I think this is a good plan," he murmurs quietly, gazing at Bridget. "What do you think, Bee?"

Our "fiancée's" lips roll together as she considers. "Maybe... if we put a time limit on it. I have my heat in two months, and I want you all gone before that."

I witness a small miracle when she turns to Adrian and *asks* his opinion. "Do you think that's enough time, alpha? Two months?"

The old bastard's face softens in a wholly unfamiliar way. "The season will be gearing up by then. Plenty of away games—it will likely take the media a while to realize we've even moved out," he muses. "I think two months is a good place to start."

Dejection melts Bridget's posture. Her shoulders slump forward and her lower lip juts out. "*Fine*. Fine! Two months. But no one touches my nest."

Or my pussy.

She doesn't say it, but that's the subtext. We can move in and save face, but we can't *have* her.

Colt starts to struggle, huffing to the edge of the sofa and then to his feet. *Ah, shit.* I forgot he was behind us. Left out of the conversation.

Jesse moves to help him, but he cuts his good arm through the air in an angry swipe. "Don't," he bleats, leveraging his crutch to stand and hobble across Bridget's hardwoods. "This whole thing is insane. I didn't do anything wrong, and I'm definitely not staying here with her."

I roll my eyes. "Yeah, you did nothing wrong—aside from crashing your car and fucking up your leg and putting us back in the middle of this tabloid bullshit."

Jesse paws at the back of his neck, wincing again. "Guys, come on."

Two months ago, this would have been a never-ending fight, and no one would have won. Adrian shuts it down in two seconds flat. Shooting Colt a stern glare and sending an electric *snap* of dominance through the small room.

"Our pack *is* moving in this weekend," he declares, arching one of his black brows. "So I guess the question is—are you part of our pack or not, Colt?"

ADRIAN HAS CHANGED THE NAME THIS CHAT TO
THE MESSINA PACK

COLT

Since when?

DANTE

Yeah, Pops, we've been the Locke Pack
forever.

JESSE

I told Adrian to change the name.

He's the pack leader.

ADRIAN

You don't have to like it.

But we need a name to present when we go
out in public.

One of the tabloids called us Pack No Name
this morning.

DANTE

Fiiiiiiiiine

COLT

Whatever.

JESSE

Has anyone heard from Bridget today?

ADRIAN

She's with her friend and she'll be clearing space in her bedroom for our clothes later tonight.

DANTE

Are we sure she has space for all of Colt's baggage?

COLT HAS LEFT THIS CHAT.

DANTE

Oops.

"I."

Whap.

"Cannot."

Whap.

"Believe you!"

Whap, whap, whap.

I snatch the pillow from Emma's hands and smack her back. "Okay, okay!" I giggle. "I'm *sorry!*"

My best friend's green eyes widen to a comical size as she screeches, "You've been *fake-engaged* for *over a year* and you didn't *tell me*?! Friendship over!"

"Shhhhh!" I hiss, shoving the blue-patterned cushion into her face. "I told you—no one can find out. Not even your pack."

I'm already regretting this, TBH. If the fretful way Emma nods and peeks at me over the top of her throw pillow is any indication, keeping a secret from her guys will not be easy. She swore she could handle it, though. And I really need *someone* who knows the truth.

That was always a very short list, but I used to have Alicia, at least. Now, after discussing the finer details with Adrian and the formerly-Locke Pack, we decided it was best to come up with a cover story for my sister, too.

She thinks things between the guys and me have progressed from fiction to reality. Jesse even volunteered to call and assure her that their plan to move in with me is one hundred percent genuine.

Ha.

Haha.

At the time, I felt relieved. Better him than me, right? But as the week has gone on... leading up to the dreaded move tomorrow...

Adrian has taken care of every detail. And I've allowed it, even though letting go is insanely out of character.

What is it about their pack alpha that makes me want to let him handle things?

I whisper the question to Em, and she shrugs, a goofy grin splitting her face. "I don't know. I've never been a badass like you, but, for me, it's like my Omega knows Knox is my alpha and wants to let him prove he can take care of me. It's so easy to give in to the impulse, I guess I've never questioned it."

I fall back onto her bed, my nose twitching when an overwhelming waft of peppermint and pine tickles my sinuses.

Sheesh, these guys smell like Christmas. That would drive me crazy in March.

Emma obviously loves it. Which brings me to my point: "Yeah, but they're your *mates*. It's different for you guys."

Em gives another carefree bounce of her shoulders. "Maybe it isn't."

You've gotta love the girl's optimism. Even when all evidence points to overcast skies and endless rain, my best friend finds a silver lining.

"Yeah," I pretend to agree, hiding my patronizing smile. "Maybe, babe."

Someone starts to knock at the palatial bedroom door, but they're cut off when another person hurtles into the room. I know without even glancing over that it's Gunnar and Zane.

Zane will be barreling toward the bed, and Gunnar will be standing in the doorway with his fist cocked.

I laugh when Emma's modelesque alpha does, in fact, leap onto the mattress beside her. Gunnar mumbles something under his breath, dragging his hand through his light brown hair and casting me an apologetic smile. "Hey, Bridget. Sorry to—"

Their dog, McKinley, bursts into the room, chasing Zane onto the bed and flopping between Emma and me.

"—bust in."

"Speak for yourself," Zane quips, snapping Emma into an embrace and rolling onto his back as he peppers her face with kisses. "*I'm* not sorry I couldn't wait another minute to get to this sexy cinnamon bun."

I hoist myself upright, finding that Gunnar and I are both rolling our eyes. He sits beside Zane's crown, which the dark-featured alpha takes as an invitation. Emma's chef scoots back to put his head in her hockey player's lap and snuggles Emma into his tight white tank top.

Gunnar chuffs but smooths one hand over Zane's hair while the other goes to Emma's blonde curls. "These two have no pause button, I swear."

"You love it," Emma teases. "Keeps you young."

"Keeps me something," he grouses, shaking his head. He snaps his gray eyes to mine... and for a second, I think of Colt.

Gunnar's gaze isn't nearly as dark or mysterious as the alpha who can't stand me, my house, or my scent. But the reminder isn't ideal.

I'm lucky I've once again bathed in neutralizer and remembered to wear my scent-blocking panties. Surely, the Beckett Pack wouldn't appreciate my acidic lemon perfume all over their bed.

"Anything new with you, Bridget?" Emma's hockey-star alpha asks.

I swallow my shame and catch my best friend's eye, noting the guilty way she bites her lip. And... yeah. I'm pretty much screwed. There's no way she'll be able to hold out for two whole months.

But that doesn't stop me from faking a smile. "Nope," I lie. "Nothing new."

chapter
fifteen

"I'VE GOTTA GIVE it to you, *cabrón*," Dante grunts, hefting three stacked boxes into his bare arms. "Of all the shit you've gotten us into, I'm pretty sure this takes the cake."

Colt growls in frustration, slinging an Ikea bag full of clothes over his good shoulder and balancing the weight on his back before reaching for his crutches. "Dante, if you don't shut the fuck up, I swear I'll break *your* leg with one of these."

He shakes his crutch at our packmate and starts the arduous path up the walkway to Bridget's front door. Adrian's there, standing just inside the foyer with his phone pressed to one ear and a sheaf of papers from the movers in his other hand.

He hired guys to get all of our stuff packed and carted over here, but he wants us to carry everything in ourselves. To keep other alphas' scents out of our *fiancée's* personal space.

It's the sort of thing that never would have occurred to me. Another way I would have accidentally hurt Bridget without even noticing.

The last few days have given me plenty of time to add up my other offenses. And, basically? The bouquet of flowers tucked under my arm and the box of donuts in my hands are nowhere near an adequate apology.

Have to start somewhere, I remind myself, following Colt inside.

The tiny house really isn't built for big alphas—let alone four of us. Adrian backs into the closet door opposite the entrance, still speaking into his phone. Colt takes a sharp right, heading for the house's one functional bedroom. Bridget promised she would find a second dresser for the four of us to share, and I see that she did—another modern piece, painted the same shade of lavender as hers.

They're crammed side-by-side against the far wall, but she's made it work. The room is pretty big—for one person. Dressed in various shades of purple and pink, the theme seems to be... bows? Of every shape and size.

They're all over her curtains and the puffy blush duvet. After a second, I realize it's all homemade; hand-tied ribbons she's sewn onto her things to give the space more color and dimension.

This whole house feels similar, actually. It's full of tight fits and awkward spaces, but she charmed each of them with cheerful paint and bright decor. Her too-small refrigerator nook? Fits a made-to-look-vintage pink Smeg perfectly. The back porch that slopes to the left? Obviously perfectly built for a hammock to hang low on that side. An awkward nook beside the front door? Perfect for the weird skinny bookcase full of... penises?

Yep. Dozens of them.

Does she collect those?

Should that turn me on?

Across the street, a flare catches my eye. The sunlight, reflecting on a camera lens. The photographers think they're hidden behind a neighbor's SUV, but I catch another flash before I sigh.

"Bridget?" I ask Adrian, mouthing the word and holding up my peace offerings.

He starts to answer, but Bee's voice bubbles in from the kitchen, along with the patter of her bare feet.

"Hey, Jess," she says, offering a smile that's only mildly forced. "Welcome to Hell."

I know she's making a joke about that shitty thing Colt said on Tuesday, but my lungs still tighten. Swallowing over the discomfort, I thrust the pastel box of donuts toward her.

"Here," I say. Like an idiot. "I, uh, got you some breakfast."

Bridget pauses for a moment, canting her head. A wild tumble of red-velvet hair falls over her shoulder, covering the strap of her navy sundress. That color looks so good on her; the rich blue setting off her lighter eyes and peachy skin. It even seems to accentuate her freckles, somehow. Highlighting the splatter across the bridge of her nose and the small constellation along the tops of her breasts...

She catches me looking. Her smile quirks higher on one side, those ocean eyes sparkling. "Thanks," she replies, then nods at my arm. "You brought your own flowers?"

Have I mentioned that I am an *idiot*?

"No, uh..." I place the bouquet on top of her donut box. "These are yours. I mean—I got them, but they're, um, for you."

Bridget's lashes flutter, her focus falling to the mix of peonies and orchids I picked out. Which suddenly seems so *dumb*. Peonies and orchids? What was I *thinking*?

For part of a second, though, it seems like I might have actually done something right. Bridget's features soften. She reaches up and rubs a petal between her thumb and forefinger—a gentle gesture that somehow scatters goosebumps down my spine.

Another camera flash glints in my peripheral vision, capturing her attention. She looks out the front door and visibly swallows before turning back.

"Oh. Smart. Good idea, Jesse."

Good idea?

Oh. Shit. She thinks I bought these as some sort of prop. For *them*.

Before I can bumble an explanation, she offers one of her warm, wide smiles and bustles past us. Adrian's head turns, his eyes roaming down the soft curve of her spine before zeroing in on her ass.

Can't blame him there. It's a gorgeous view.

Adrian notices me staring in the same direction and claps his hand on my shoulder. "She'll come around," he says. "Trust me."

I WATCH the gorgeous omega saunter into her bedroom, holding myself back.

It's one of the benefits of age—the wisdom of knowing when to chase and when to be still. Urgency certainly has its place, but there isn't any here. Bridget will realize she wants to court us for real in due time.

And these assholes will come to grips with it, too.

Jesse's already there. Longing lines the poor kid's face while he drinks in Bridget's retreating figure.

He said he's known her since high school. I wonder if his crush started back then, or if the desire sharpening his scent is a new development. Hell, I wonder if *he* knows.

Dante huffs his way inside, dramatically dropping a heap of boxes with a scowl. "There's some old bitch out there heckling us," he complains, wiping his sweaty forehead with his arm.

"That's just Betty!" Bridget chimes from her bedroom. "Tell her to bite your ass. She'll appreciate the invitation."

My eyebrows arch in surprise, but Dante's openly shocked expression is so priceless, I nearly smirk. "Do you talk to all your neighbors like that, little blue?"

Bridget emerges, holding two big trash bags labeled "donations." Before I can whisk them away, she shoves the sacks at Dante, knocking him back a step. "Be a dear and put these in your trunk for me? I'll drop them off later."

No, she won't. Because I'll take care of it before she has the chance to worry about it again. Dante scoffs, though.

"The fuck you think you're driving *my* car, cupcake," he protests. "I'll put them in yours."

She flashes a sharp smile. "Good luck with that, slugger."

Bridget heads toward her living room, leaving a tantalizing thread of lemon sweetness in her wake. The patronizing way she pats Dante's bare shoulder on her way past sends a fresh bolt of disbelief over his square features. My smile finally breaks free as I chuckle, shaking my head.

"Put the bags in my car," I direct, tossing him the keys. "I'll run them up to the Salvation Army on the way to the stadium on Monday."

He makes a sour face, but doesn't argue apart from grumbling, "What about tomorrow? We have practice at eight."

I nod. "*You* do. *I'm* going to take Bridget shopping."

Dante mutters a low string of Spanish curses, calling me a bunch of things he thinks I can't understand. Just as well—if that makes him feel better about grabbing my keys and Bridget's donations without pause, I'll take all the names he can come up with.

Colt hobbles out of Bridget's bedroom, his expression even darker than it was moments ago. "Whole place smells like lemon cheesecake," he grouses. "How am I supposed to *breathe*?"

He shuts up when he sees me watching, morphing from frustration to disdain. "She's cleared out half of her closet, but won't let me touch it," he informs. "Apparently it's for *your* shit and no one else's."

I barely resist the urge to grin.

Like I said.

She'll come around.

PACK No Name is really fucking up my aesthetic.

The three gym bags stacked next to my kitchen door are *not* the vibe.

Nor is Colt's snoring.

I hear his deep rumble from the side entrance of the house, where I do my best not to let my keys jingle too much as I let myself in.

After dodging Adrian and Jesse's offers to order dinner, I wound up going to Emma's for Gunnar's televised match. He's out of town this weekend, playing a stretch of away games. Zane went with him this time, leaving my bestie at home with her firefighter and her mountain man.

Or, as she likes to call him, Daddy.

I'm sorta glad her chef-influencer alpha was out of town. Pictures of the guys moving into my house are all over the internet, and I know Zane would have had a million questions about why I wasn't home with them for their first night as my live-in *fiancés.*

I still got some side-eye from Daddy Knox when Fireman Micah asked me how the whole day went, but thankfully, neither of them pressed too hard. It helped that Gunnar had a good game and Emma was practically frothing with excitement while we watched it.

I may have lingered a bit later than usual, hoping to come in after the guys had fallen asleep. Judging by the sounds of alpha men snoring?

Mission accomplished.

Orrrrrrr not.

Because the second I drop the deadbolt and turn to the dark kitchen, I catch a muscled silhouette ducking into my fridge.

Dante.

Adrian comes close, but of these four alphas, the all-star shortstop still *looks* the most built. His shoulders alone make my body seem narrow—which, I can assure you, it is not.

Hearing my purse land on the island, Dante jerks upright and bangs the back of his head against the frame of the refrigerator. I snort a quiet laugh as he growls, spitting a few foreign words into the appliance before slamming its door shut.

When he spins and finds me trying not to laugh, his square, handsome features drop into a glower. "Don't you know better than to sneak up on a finely-honed machine like me, cupcake? I could have karate-chopped you."

I smirk again despite myself. He's sort of funny. I never noticed before, but he has a tendency to spit whatever random nonsense pops into his mind. Which might be a trait we share.

I nod at the container of pasta salad in his left hand. "Is that for some sort of secret spy mission?"

His dark eyes flash as his mouth kicks into a crooked smile, his chin dimple deepening. "Basically. I'm not supposed to have carbs after eight when we're in training, so I have to wait for the rest of these fuckers to fall asleep."

Memories of the dozens of diets my sister—and, before that, our mom—subjected me to put a wince on my face. I step around him, going for the freezer.

"In that case." He effortlessly catches the pint of cookies and cream gelato I toss him.

Lord, his hands are quick. And big. And *strong*...

No surprise there. Given how sculpted the rest of him is.

Now that my eyes have adjusted, the dim moonlight flooding through my French doors highlights every line and dip of his exposed torso.

Jesus.

This guy doesn't just have abs. He has *obliques*—and hips so chiseled, visible shadows outline them.

By the time I manage to tear my eyes off the stacked ripples, his cocky smile has heated to boiling. "I was going to thank you for the ice cream, *querida*, but it seems like you should be the one thanking me."

He rolls his abdomen in a practiced move, punctuated with a sharp thrust toward me. My insides tweak, taut muscles thrumming between my hips.

No, I yell at my Omega. *He's mocking us, not flirting.*

I flip my hair back, rolling my eyes at him. "Easy there, slugger."

Dante sets his ice cream and noodles on the counter, still grinning. "'Easy' isn't really in my vocabulary."

A slow smile spreads over my face. "Easy—as in, you're making it too *easy* for me to make fun of you, claiming that you don't know anything about being *easy*. See? Two different ways to use it in one sentence."

To my surprise, Dante's smile takes on a wild, delighted quality. "Anyone ever told you you're kind of a bitch?"

He says it so fondly, I nearly laugh. "Anyone ever told you *you're* kind of a dick?"

Dante's answering shrug is casual. "Only like once a week."

Shit.

Of all the alphas crammed into this house—Adrian's calm insistence on shouldering my burdens, Jesse's stumbling apologies, Colt's mysterious rage—I really thought Dante would be the simplest one to keep at arm's length. He hated me; I didn't like him. Straightforward.

I never expected him to be funny and relatable. Hiding all sorts of self-awareness under the same sort of rueful quips I like to use.

I really don't want to *like* him.

So I should probably get *the hell* out of here.

CARAJO.

Of all the women on God's green Earth, I absolutely cannot afford to catch feelings for Bridget Fucking Woods.

I can't *like* my *fiancée*.

That would be so stupid. Bordering on crazy.

And, well.

Fuckin' lock me up, I guess.

Moonlight plays over Bridget's creamy throat while she works on a swallow, ducking her head. And, damn. *I* do that. Dropping my chin to hide my face whenever I need to get my shit together.

Her gaze snags on a drawer. It rattles as she opens it, revealing an assortment of mismatched silverware. The pieces are clearly thrifted, not some trendy made-to-look-eclectic set.

No. She honest-to-God went to the flea market and bought random silverware.

It makes no sense. Neither does the rest of this house. I know for a fact we wrote her a fat check last year. And a portion of my salary disappears from my account every month like clockwork. I'm no numbers guy, but the dollar figure is consistent and seems like more than enough to afford matching spoons.

Where the hell does it all go?

Does she have a Ferrari stashed somewhere? Or a yacht?

Is she some sort of degenerate gambler?

My gaze slides to the pink bookcases built into the wall behind her couch.

How much does one book cost? Fifteen bucks? Twenty? Multiplied by roughly... My eyes scan the over-stuffed shelves ...*infinity?*

My head hurts.

I take the utensil she hands me, frowning at it before diving into my snack. "We would have sprung for some cutlery, you know," I mumble around a mouthful. "Didn't anyone tell you? We're loaded."

Bridget rolls her pretty blue eyes. "Yeah, yeah. We get it, Dante. You're gorgeous and athletic and rich and have a huge dick."

I pause with a spoonful of cookies and cream halfway to my mouth. Which drops open in shock before bouncing into a grin I can't control. "Don't think I said anything about that last one. Have you been checking out the merchandise, cupcake?"

Another woman might balk or blush, but Bridget laughs, cocking an auburn brow at me. "As if you haven't been looking at my ass every time I turn around."

"It happens to be exactly my type." I shrug, talking around another bite of ice cream. "And someone mandated that I remain celibate for the next two months. I need spank bank inspo."

Even that doesn't throw her off. She chuckles some more, shaking her head. "You're a true romantic, huh?"

She has no idea.

And she never will, I remind myself. *Because, <u>again</u>, we are <u>not</u> catching feelings for our fake fiancée. We are not that guy.*

I'm talking to my Alpha. And my cock. But these bastards don't listen. Instead, my knot twitches, swelling along with the shaft pressed into my joggers.

Sons of bitches.

Don't they know this woman is *too good* for us?

Jesse may be the sort of man she deserves. Or—as much as I hate to admit it—Adrian. But me? And the fucker snoring on her couch?

I spare my crotch an exasperated glance. When I raise my head, I find Bridget smirking, looking like a cross between the world's cutest brat and some mythical red-haired siren.

"It literally hasn't even been a week," she deadpans.

Little does she know, I haven't hooked up with anyone since Colt's accident. Eight weeks is practically a record for me. Let alone the *extra* two months I'm about to pile on top of that.

My balls ache at the thought. And Bridget's scent isn't fucking helping.

I spent the better part of the evening trying to ignore the fact that it's sweeter than I remembered. Richer and more luscious and just...

Good.

So damn good.

How did I not notice before?

Is it actually getting *better* every damn minute? Or do I just *like* her more each time she opens those pouty pink lips to mock me?

Maybe it's both.

The neutralizer I wore as a courtesy must be fading fast. Either that or my scent is swelling around it. Either way, her pupils expand, thinning her blue irises.

Fuck. I just *had* to have a damn snack.

Now I can't stop wondering if she tastes as sharp and sweet as she smells. And what we would be like *together*. Mangos and lemon, sugary, tart...

A low growl snags the bottom of my lungs, roughing up my voice. "You should go to bed."

For the first time on record, Bridget looks thrown. She blinks in shock, but the motion only makes her eyes blearier. More delicious perfume leaks into the kitchen, its bitter edge darker than I want it to be.

But still so damn delicious.

Too damn delicious.

"Seriously," I rumble. "Go."

Her gaze blazes like the hottest part of a flame. "This is *my* house."

Her defiance fires my blood. I bite down on another snarl. "That's debatable. But you shouldn't push me, *querida*. You wouldn't like my Alpha if you met him."

I say the words, but they feel wrong. Untrue. Because—*fuck me*—I have a feeling Bridget might *love* my deviant side.

As if on cue, she tosses her hair back and straightens her spine.

Beautiful.

Strong.

Sexy as fuck.

"I don't speak 'boy,'" she scoffs. "So, if you have something to tell me, you're going to have to be a man about it and say what you mean."

A surge of heat rolls through my body. I move on instinct, backing her pretty ass into the kitchen cabinets and gripping the counter beside each of her hips. Boxing her in. "Listen, cupcake— you couldn't handle my kink."

It feels like an empty taunt. Because, hell, is there *anything* this woman truly couldn't handle?

But Bridget takes my provocation seriously. Outrage fills her pretty features, flaring in her gaze. "I think you're full of shit."

There are half a dozen things I could tell her. How I want to smother myself between her thighs. The way I'd watch her fiery eyes water while I stuff my dick down her throat.

But I need to shock her. Scare her off. Give her and me a chance to escape before this whole thing goes off the rails.

So I pluck up the darkest, most depraved thing I can think of. Something I've never done, but always salivated over.

"Do you know what free use means?"

Oh *shit*.

She does.

I see the spark that settles into her eyes. Her pupils get even bigger. Her perfume spikes again. Saliva wells in my mouth.

"No," she lies.

My lips quirk. She's going to make me *explain*.

Careful what you wish for, baby.

One more step and my torso presses into her softness. I love the way her body molds to mine, how the lower curve of her belly rubs the hard-on straining against it.

"It means I like to *take* what I want. Anytime, anywhere, any way—and when I tell my woman to bend over, she better show me her slick pussy and let me have it."

Fuck. I meant to scare her off, but she's so into this, the cutting edge of her tart lemon sweetness sharpens. Clawing my lungs from the inside out.

Her lips drop open as her chest heaves, those big creamy tits stuttering when she inhales me in return. Desire sparkles in her blown pupils.

"Anywhere?" she repeats.

I picture her bent over this kitchen island. Legs spread in my Escalade while I finger her in traffic. Pussy glistening under the stadium lights if I spread her along the bench in our dugout.

"Anywhere," I husk.

A red brow arches. "Any*time*?" she says next.

Prompting a whole other set of images. Interrupting her at school because I'm too horny to wait. Slamming the front door of this little house and flattening her against it *the second* we walk in. Shoving her thighs open to lick her cunt while she reads one of her bajillion books. Waking her up in the middle of the night with my cock already buried inside her.

"Anytime," I confirm.

She flicks her eyes over my face. Almost like she's looking for a joke or a prank. Waiting for me to say "gotcha!"

Something about that scrapes at the inside of my ribcage. It burns, molten heat sliding down my torso and settling at the base of my cock. My hips automatically tilt forward, grinding my erection along her belly.

She perfumes—a deep burst of sugared *freshness*. Her body trembles, but her voice is the strong, confident one I know. "Why would anyone want that?"

My answering smile feels wolfish. I glance down to where I'm sure she's wet under her dress. "You tell me, baby. You're the one pressing those delectable thighs together. Creaming your panties for it."

She tries to strangle the omega whine building in her chest, but I hear it. And my Alpha replies with a deep growl.

Fuck.

I can see the cliff we're about to drive off.

But I've never had very good brakes.

"Maybe you like the thought of not being in control," I murmur, my hands drifting to her hips. "Or maybe you're into the spontaneity."

Another thought occurs to me. And even before I say it out loud, I know I have the answer. My fingertips graze her sides before curling in her skirt. "Maybe you love the idea of me being so damn desperate for you, I can't wait one more fucking second to get inside you."

Bridget gazes up at me, her lips falling open further. And, for a second, two months here feels like a cheap joke. It's nowhere near long enough for everything I want to do to her.

But, hell. Gotta start somewhere.

She tries to swallow an accidental moan. My fingertips ghost lower and find her bare thigh. Wetness glides between my skin and hers—a layer thick enough to spill over my knuckle.

Slick.

A lot of it.

I lean back, scanning her face. Flushed cheeks, wide pupils, pussy absolutely *gushing*...

Fuck me.

Did I send our omega into a *heat-spike*?

STICKY, juicy mango bursts on my tongue.

Oh. My. God.

If I could lick the air, I would.

Because, as we've established, my Omega is a *hoe*. And, more specifically, she's practically *feral* for this dark-eyed alpha and his dangerous grin.

Anytime. Anywhere. Any way.

Why does that idea have me *pouring* slick down my legs?

Unless... *no. NO. I refuse to melt down for this man. For any man. Nope. Not gonna—*

The whine that shatters my lungs is almost enough to startle me out of the haze blurring my vision. Half panicked, I manage to blink at the living room, vaguely remembering that there might be someone in there? A snore answers me, but Dante shakes his head.

"Don't worry about Colt," he mutters. "I think we might need to worry about *you*."

An embarrassing whimper tickles my throat. And—damn it—even *that* turns me on. My nipples prick, brushing against his naked chest when I try to catch my breath.

If I could think, I might be able to determine which is hotter—Dante's usual cockiness or this new, concerned expression deepening the dimple in his chin. "Seriously," he says softly. "Colt sleeps like the dead. Don't worry about him. Are you okay?"

I try to swallow. "I—I'm f-f—"

The lie doesn't make it out before another whine escapes. A hard shudder wracks my frame, and Dante's frown deepens. "Bridget, I think you're having a spike. I'm sorry, *querida*, I didn't mean to push you over the edge."

His apology *hurts*. It carves at some tender, hollowed-out hole in my center, sending cramps up to my pounding heart.

It's not supposed to be like this, my Omega cries. *He's not supposed to be <u>sorry</u>. He's supposed to want me back.*

Normally, I'd tell this lunatic to shove a sock in it, but the room is spinning and the floor is melting... *Or is that the ceiling?*

"*Carajo*," Dante curses. The Spanish word is definitely not a nice one, but my body doesn't care. Thick perfume and slick slide down my thighs, filling the air with the slicing smell that sends alphas running for their lives.

An inhuman wail echoes through the small space. I don't realize it's coming from me until Dante's hands cup my face.

"Shhh, *corazón*," he whispers. "It's alright. You're okay."

I'm not okay, though. Because this alpha doesn't want to touch me, and he never—

Before I can hyperventilate, Dante pulls me into a hug. One of his bulging arms winds around my waist while the other wraps across my shoulder, his big hand petting my hair.

"Hey," he says, low and gentle. "Tell me what you need, huh? You want your nest? Or a toy? I could go wake up—"

My fingers dig into his naked back. Desperation and chagrin swirl into a cyclone of self-loathing that sucks at my stomach.

I try one last time to get a grip on my Omega, but the whole situation is too far gone. I can't even remember who this alpha is. Or why I feel like I'll never recover from the humiliation swamping my insides.

This dress must be made from the abrasive side of Velcro. Fabric scratches my over-sensitized skin until I shiver from the onslaught of nerve-frying discomfort. My hands fly to the straps, struggling to untie them. More pain flares there, until I find myself hiding a mortifying sob against the alpha's broad shoulder.

"*Querida*, no," he murmurs. "Don't *cry*. Is it these straps? You want your dress off?"

I feel tears streak down my cheeks and duck my head to hide my face. The built alpha pauses for half a second before his hands flatten against my body more insistently. He runs his touch up to my shoulders and plucks the bows there.

When he rubs his warm palms over my chilled skin, quivers of delight zip to my core. I perfume again, and he nudges my forehead with his.

"Is this what you need? My hands on this pretty skin?"

Another whine tumbles out of me. My body huddles closer, every muscle in my core clenching.

The alpha's black irises sparkle. My mouth wells with saliva when his juicy scent spikes. "Mmm," he hums. "You're so fucking hot like this. Needing me. Tell me what you want, baby. And maybe I'll let *you* use *me*."

My lungs expand on a gasp, thrusting my breasts into his bare chest. I feel his heat soak through the horrible fabric covering me, and I squirm.

"Shhh," he hushes. "I know. Here, let's take this off."

The itchy cloth disappears. Relief rolls over my body like a sluice of warm liquid. Wetness trickles down my thighs.

Mango succulence rolls off the alpha panting in front of me. His dark eyes trace everything he can see in the moonlight, gleaming as he pulls his lower lip between his teeth. *"Jesu Cristo, Bridget,"* he rumbles. "I'm about to come in my fucking pants."

I picture his thick cock swelling and spraying underneath his sweats. A high-pitched noise flies from my lips as I lunge for the fabric covering him.

He lets me shove the joggers down, not complaining about how dizzy and uncoordinated I am. Instead, his hands continue stroking my sides and my back, sending snaps of pleasure to my middle.

When his hard cock springs up, I feel my tongue slide over my lower lip. The alpha makes a low, predatory sound, pressing his length into my belly. The sensation of hot steel against my soft skin has me gushing more slick.

Isn't there a reason I'm supposed to be upset? Something I didn't want him to see or...?

His demanding bark scrambles my last attempt at actual thought. *"Bridget,"* he grinds out, *"Tell me to stop unless you want me to fill you up* right now."

A half-sob stutters out of me. "Alpha, *please—*"

He snaps his hands down to my hips. The soaked material covering my pussy disappears. My world swirls and shifts as warm strength grasps my wide hips and lifts me off the floor.

I barely have time to react to whatever cold surface the alpha places me on before he steps between my thighs and slams his thick cock into my pussy.

Another squeaking shriek tears up my throat. The alpha's chest vibrates on a deep rumble as he leans back, pressing his hips forward in a slow circle.

I shatter instantly. Every slick muscle in my core clamps around his girth, tugging it in rhythmic squeezes.

"Fuck, your pussy is so good, *querida.* That's it. Come all over this alpha cock. Milk it. Just. Like. That."

The succulence of his mango scent deepens. I gasp again,

struggling to breathe when he skims across the scars banded around the thickest part of my body. Everything inside me starts to recoil, some distant, foggy memory almost bitter enough to break the haze...

But then his brawny fingers find my clit and press down. My pussy instantly seizes again, rolling from one climax into the beginnings of another.

Dante groans, thrusting faster and harder. He grips my side with his free hand, holding onto my jiggling flesh. One thumb strokes at my belly just as the other swirls over my clit.

"This is so soft," he says, squeezing my side. "Feels so good to touch. And *this*," He suddenly pinches the throbbing nub at the top of my folds. "...gets so damn swollen. Makes me so fucking hard."

Having come once, I can think just long enough to wonder if he's intentionally being sweet, trying to reassure me. Or can he just not help himself?

The alpha bucks, shoving his length deeper. His knot grazes at my quivering opening each time he pumps into me, the swell hot and thick. Something deep in my body torques tight. More perfume—the good kind and its astringent counterpart—slip from my core.

Instead of pulling away, the alpha groans, dropping his face to my shoulder and opening his mouth. Slipping his lips over my collarbone. Grazing my neck with his teeth—

Ah!

His nip isn't gentle. Just like his bruising grip on my hip and the merciless way he pounds my pussy.

It's real, I realize, dazed.

He *wants* me.

Slick dribbles from my core, creaming around his cock. The alpha groans, licking over the indentations his teeth left behind. "So sweet and sharp, *querida*," he mutters. "You gonna let me in your little pussy whenever I want? Or should I enjoy this time like it's my last?"

My shriek is muffled by his broad shoulder. *"Alpha!"*

His wide shaft stretches the squelching muscles that tremble for a knot. With a snarl, he rolls his hips faster. Still rubbing the top of my clit in the softest, lightest circles.

I keen, and he growls, the sound so deep and satisfied, I suddenly can't remember how to inhale. "This little cunt is tight enough to *strangle* my dick, and you're so *wet*. You're about to come all over this big alpha cock again. And I'm going to *cover* you," he roughs out.

The alpha shifts his hips to hit the aching place inside me at the exact moment he thumbs my clit again. The room disappears in a flash of sparkling darkness. Everything inside me squeezes and bursts. Warm wetness squirts from my body, dousing Dante's knot as he buries a masculine moan in my hair.

When his body tenses, he snarls a string of Spanish curses and pulls out of me. His fist snaps to his cock as hot liquid erupts from the head. His swollen knot visibly expands while cum coats my lower belly and my mound.

Blinking, I look down at my bare body and his.

Did I mention...

Oh. My. God?!

Dante takes in the mess we made with an air of fanatical satisfaction. The expression makes no sense until our gazes meet.

And his *softens*.

For a moment, warm electricity glows between us. Not the vicious, snapping current we usually feed with banter, but something... gentle.

"Bridget," he husks, stroking my hair back. "You good? That was pretty..."

"Intense?" I laugh, but it sounds breathy and watered down. Probably because my damn eyes are welling up.

It's only natural, I tell myself. *No one's ever helped you with a heat-spike before.*

It makes perfect sense. But I'm still glad my Omega can't

weigh in. Thankfully, she's blissed out to the point of unconsciousness.

Before I can overthink, I jump down from the counter and grab my dress. It smears some of the cum cooling on my skin, and Dante curses. "Shit, here, let me—"

"No," I decide, stepping away. Pasting on an awkward smile. "I'm good! I'll just go... clean up. But, um—" *Did you feel that weird moment we just had? What the hell was that? How do we make sure it never happens again?* "—thank you?"

He mumbles some reply I don't hear. Because I'm too busy hauling my wobbly ass out of the kitchen before I drip on the floor.

Or notice just how well my sharp scent happens to pair with juicy, sweet mango.

SOMETIMES I WONDER if I look stupid.

People seem to treat me that way. As if I must be some kind of idiot. Just because I'm an athlete from the wrong side of the tracks who, yeah, okay, prefers not to bother cutting his hair.

Exhibit A: this motherfucker right here.

Trying to act like he didn't totally bone our fake fiancée on this very kitchen counter at some point in the last eight hours.

Dante inhales his usual omelet straight out of the pan, gobbling it over the kitchen sink. His eyes dart to the blank patch of countertop beside him, and he frowns.

Is he *confused*?

My packmate is normally too confident to admit confusion,

even to his own damn self. But right now, he's staring at the spot where he and Bridget boned like it's a riddle he can't unravel.

I grit my teeth, forcing down a wave of loathing. Jesse trips into the kitchen, still pulling his pants over his briefs. When he notices the way Dante considers the counter and how I glare at Dante, he pauses halfway through tucking his Kings jersey in.

Hazel eyes snap between the two of us. His blond brow lowers. "What?"

Grunting, I wave my mobile arm at Dante. "Ask him."

Our dark-haired packmate actually *winces*—dear God, *what?* —before swallowing the last bite of his breakfast and dropping the pan into the sink. "It was nothing." Then he cocks his head to the side. "I think."

"What was nothing?" Adrian's voice drifts in from the hallway a second before he appears, dressed in his usual business attire and buttoning his white shirt sleeves. His light eyes lift, drifting over all three of us. Waiting.

Dante ducks his head, avoiding the question. And as much as I would just love to spread the shitty mood I woke up in, I find myself grumbling, "Never mind."

Jesse still looks perplexed, but he wanders further into the tight space. Glancing down at the empty stretch of island in front of me, he realizes I was too damn weak to actually get into the kitchen and make myself anything. Without a word, he starts pouring me a cup of coffee from the French press in the middle of the stove.

How the hell did that get here? I know for a fact Dante can't make anything aside from eggs. He and Jesse don't usually drink coffee, anyway. I was always the only one who ignored our trainers' advice and guzzled two cups each morning.

This particular pot looks rich and dark, the way Adrian prefers it. Jesse hands each of us a mug and then sets a small carton of cream next to mine, knowing I'll want it.

And I feel like a dick.

Which pisses me off even more.

Before I can decide whether I want to thank him, happy humming interrupts us.

Bridget is awake.

And she's *chipper.*

Fucking hell.

"She came in pretty late," Jesse notes, rooting around in the fridge for one of his chalky protein shakes. "Sounds like she's in a good mood, though."

Does Dante look *nervous*? "Must be a morning person," he mumbles, motioning to Jesse for a bottle of his own.

I swear to God, all the guy does is eat. Omega pussy included, apparently.

As much as I would love to call him out, I don't actually *know* what went down after I passed out. The swirl of mango and lemon I woke up to is unmistakable, but I don't have any details —aside from how mind-bendingly sharp and sweet her perfume feels.

Was she in some sort of spike?

What would have triggered that?

And why the hell is Dante acting weird about it now? Is he— God forbid—trying to be a *gentleman*?

I have no answers, but I had to open her patio doors to get some fresh air in here before my knot exploded. Adrian's all-seeing eyes flicker to the back doors, but he decides not to comment. Instead, he pauses with his mug to his lips, humming appreciatively at the strong coffee, and gives my sling a pointed look. "You need to take that off today, Colt. The doctors said it's imperative that you start moving your arm and putting weight on that leg."

Considering my shoulder throbs just from shrugging, he and his doctors can go to hell.

I pretend to agree, nodding while I stare at my cup. It really is good coffee. And it's starting to get difficult to keep track of the good things around here that I've decided piss me off.

On cue, Bridget's fat cat meows at my feet. I sneer at him, ignoring the way my arm aches.

Jesse rolls his own shoulders, grimacing. "I might need that sling if I have to keep sleeping on the floor."

Dante grunts his agreement. Even Adrian seems a bit stiff as he nods. "Yes, I underestimated how uncomfortable cramming onto air mattresses would be. I'll speak to Bridget about it."

"Me?" Bridget herself interjects, swanning into the room.

I scowl at the perky omega and her stupid painted overalls. Covered in daisies and sunflowers to match the sunny tank top molded over her big tits and the yellow cabinets filling the walls around her.

Her red hair is piled on top of her head in two messy buns—and, unlike the first time we met, her face is made up perfectly.

Coal-rimmed blue eyes. High, shimmery cheekbones. Glossed lips.

I hate her, I remind myself, harnessing my Alpha's rage. *We hate her*.

Adrian doesn't. Clearly. He smiles as warmly as I've ever seen him, fondness and approval glowing in his ocean irises while he chuckles, "Good morning, little blue. How did you sleep?"

Amusement dances over Bridget's pert features. And—if I *didn't* hate her—I'd probably have to admit she's sort of adorable when she slants a smirk at the others. "I hate to be the one to break this to y'all, but every last one of you snores."

Dante chuffs, but doesn't deny it. It's weird for him to resist instantly defending himself. But Jesse's reaction is completely on-brand; he winces and starts apologizing.

"I had a feeling lying flat on the floor would make me snore. I'm so sorry, Bridget. Did we keep you up?"

She bounces a carefree shrug. "No biggie. I'll live."

Adrian stands, offering his barstool with a gentlemanly gesture. Bridget blinks at him, but sits down. Right next to me.

"Would you like us to move out to the living room?" he asks, settling his gaze on hers. "Or maybe you'd be more comfortable in your nest, and we can tradeoff between sharing the bed and bunking on the couches?"

Bridget's typically confident to a fault. Her uncertainty only seems to make an appearance for Adrian. The pack alpha must do things to her Omega that make her want to please him. She bites her lower lip, considering.

"We could try that," she agrees. "I sleep in my nest a lot, anyway."

Rubbing the back of his neck, Jesse replies, "I don't want to run you out of your room, Bee."

What the hell is with the *nicknames*? And how come, no matter how much she antagonizes me or Dante, she always finds a smile for our more sensitive packmate?

This one is a stunner, too—all glowy and sincere. "It's really fine with me, Jess," she bubbles. "I don't want you to mess up your arm so close to the season."

See? Such a bitch.

Adrian's stern lips flicker into a smile. "You're too good to us. But we appreciate you trying to keep our pack comfortable."

I'm sure I'm the only one who notices the way Dante glances at Bridget... and how she pointedly *doesn't* look back.

Jesus. They couldn't be more obvious.

Still, part of me wonders why they'd so brazenly fuck in here and then act like total strangers a few hours later. Usually, Dante would crow about this shit 'til kingdom come. And now he's *quiet*?

Bridget's not exactly known for being mysterious, either. She's too...

Bubbly.

The bright-haired omega blushes, her round cheeks pinking. "It's all good!" She throws her gaze across the kitchen. Hunting for some sort of distraction, I think. When she finds one, her brows arch. "Oh, good. You found your coffee."

Adrian full-on grins this time. Bridget's eyes widen at the sight. "You made that for us, omega?" our pack leader asks. "It's perfect. I'm very impressed."

The rosy tinge of her skin blazes brighter. "It's—"

No big deal. All good. Nothing.

She does that. Glossing over her attributes, acting like they're meaningless. It pinches some wounded part of me to hear her do it over and over, the same way she did the day we met. But our new pack alpha doesn't take that shit the way we did. He sets his hand on hers and squeezes it gently.

"Lovely," Adrian interrupts, his tone brokering no arguments. "Just like you, little blue."

chapter
twenty-one

BETTY

Who the hell are all those men coming out of
your house?

You running some sort of brothel now, red?

BRIDGET

Yep. $200 an hour.

BETTY

I'd pay $300 for the one in the suit

BRIDGET

You can't have him* but can I offer you the
one on crutches?

He's probably more your speed anyway

BETTY

The one with a mop on his head?

BRIDGET

That's his hair.

But yeah. Him you can keep. He's a total
grouch and he hates my guts for no reason.

Oh and he called you an old bitch.

BETTY

Never thought I'd find a true soulmate at
my age.

BRIDGET

You should have a summer wedding.

With lots of sunflowers.

BETTY

Fuck off, red.

BRIDGET

No can do, Bets. It's grocery day.

The one in the suit is taking me to run errands
in his fancy car, so your ice cream may not
even be melted this time.

BETTY

Better get two cartons then.

I COULD GET VERY USED to this view.

The interior of my X5 was custom-made. White cross-stitched leather. Black seams to match the shiny onyx exterior. Charcoal wood paneling.

I never realized how dull it felt until today.

Bridget sits in the passenger seat, filling the monochromatic cab with all her colors. Late-morning sun slants in through the window, filling her auburn hair until the lighter red highlights glow. Her buttery tank top looks brighter, too, along with the orange and pink flowers painted onto the front of her overalls.

Those are cute as hell. As a man who enjoys staying current on couture fashion, I never thought I'd be charmed by cut-offs covered in daisies. Or the kitschy blue-heart sunglasses perched on her pert little nose.

She noticed me looking at them and launched into a long explanation about her friends and their alphas. Apparently, the omegas have a little tradition where they each get a pair of heart sunglasses when they meet their packs. These, Bridget shares, were a gift from her best friend Emma when she got "engaged."

They're the perfect shade of bright Kings blue, which is adorable on her. Just like the freckles dusted over her cheeks and the teasing tilt of her smile.

"Where are you taking me, Boss?"

She's been calling me that since I showed up for our move yesterday with a clipboard. I didn't see how that was unusual, but the woman taunted me over it relentlessly; grinning and tacking my new nickname onto everything she said to me. At one point, she even saluted me.

I'm beginning to think our fiancée is a bit of a brat.

I can work with that.

"The nest store, primarily," I reply, sliding my aviators on as I steer us out of her neighborhood. Or, rather, *our* neighborhood. It's a beautiful place. She chose very well—selecting a small home in a quality location over something ostentatious and overpriced.

Each observation is a clue. To her character, her way of thinking. And, hopefully, her heart.

Because I've only been in this little omega's home for one night, but my Alpha already knows: we aren't leaving.

I can wait for her to reach the same conclusion, though. She needs to come to this realization on her own if I want it to stick. Twenty-four hours in, I already see how independent she is.

She's also whip-smart. Her light eyes narrow over the rim of her sunglasses as she picks up on my most operative word. "Primarily?"

I nod, keeping my alpha energy soothingly solid. "We have a stop to make first."

Suspicion pulls her lush lips down. "A stop?"

I smile despite myself—she's just too damn cute, even when she's glaring at me. "Yeah, sweetheart. One stop. But feel free to add to our itinerary if there's somewhere you need to go."

She wavers, trying to decide whether to stay wary or take my olive branch. In the end, she sighs. "I want to go to Whole Foods for our neighbor. I bring her groceries twice a week because she can't drive."

Knowing what I do about Bridget... Surprise lifts my brows. "You haul her food *and* yours home?"

She lifts a shoulder. "It's no big deal."

This omega barely gives herself credit for anything. I'm going to have to put a stop to that.

I mirror her shrug. "Right. It's only food. A matter of life or death." When she turns to me and blinks, I offer a kinder smile and repeat, "No big deal."

She blushes. Embarrassed to take credit for her kindness. My hand has a mind of its own, finding her thigh and squeezing. When her perfume spikes, I rub my thumb along the silky skin and leave my palm there.

She stares down at it with so much disbelief, I might be amused if her doubt didn't cleave my heart in half. Gripping her a little tighter, making sure she feels the intent behind the gesture, I lower my voice.

"You never told me why you agreed to all of this."

Behind her endearing sunglasses, Bridget flutters her lashes. "I —uhhhh... You know why. Because of the press and my sister's reputation and—"

I shake my head. "No. I don't mean *our* arrangement. I'm talking about the one you made with the guys last year when they came to you. Why did you agree to a fake engagement?"

The more I get to know her, the less I understand it. She's one of the most genuine people I've ever met. Warm and bright and honest.

How did she end up faking anything?

Bridget's creamy, unmarked throat works over a swallow. One she's probably hoping I don't notice.

But this little omega will learn soon enough—I notice *everything*.

Including the way her thick thighs have tensed under my touch, pressing together when goosebumps prickle the supple flesh. For a moment, I think her Omega may be responding as I hoped she would—feeling safer and cared for, knowing an attentive alpha is here to care for her.

Bridget's scent quickly edges from tart to acidic, though. Her chin dips slightly. "I... My sister needed me out of their house. I couldn't swing rent on my teaching salary, but I didn't want to actually *bond* with a random group of alphas for the sake of *real estate*."

Her nose scrunches adorably. I file the expression into my memory, knowing it will make me smile later. Right now, however...

She's holding something back.

But trust is earned. And I *will* earn this beautiful girl's trust. Until then, I can only ensure she knows I appreciate her willingness to share anything with me at all.

"Thank you, little blue," I reply. "For telling me that."

That same heartrending disbelief shifts over her features. Her plump mouth drops open. "I—You're welcome?"

As we roll to a stoplight, I smooth my palm up her thigh and back down, casting her a serious look. "You can always tell me things, okay? I'm here to protect you and make your life easier, omega. That's my job as your alpha. And you're going to let me do it."

Startled surprise lifts her thin red eyebrows for a moment

before she schools her expression, putting on a pout. "Good lord," she mutters, "why do I *believe* you?"

God, she's incredible. Gorgeous and funny. Practical in ways she should never have to be—but it makes me proud nonetheless.

This isn't some silly, aimless girl.

This is a fierce, intelligent *woman*. With a spine of steel and a heart that's somehow every bit as soft as her luscious body.

Perfect.

Everything I've ever searched for. Scent-sensitivity be damned.

The light changes, and I glide forward, guiding the SUV past Winter Park's most popular nest store. Bridget starts to protest, but the smirk tipping my lips stops her. That bratty pout becomes more pronounced.

I feel her debating whether to speak up, but within two minutes, I pull off the main road. Bridget sits forward, tugging her glasses off to scan the rows of vehicles around us.

"This is a car dealership."

I pop my door open, nodding. "Yes, it is."

By the time I round the front of my BMW and open her door, Bridget's mouth hangs ajar again. She moves on autopilot, unbuckling her seatbelt and sliding onto the asphalt as she gapes at the rows of vehicles like mine.

"Did you... need a tune up?" she asks.

I shake my head, rubbing my hand down her back and settling it along the lower curve of her spine. "No, little blue," I chuckle. "But you need a car."

Golden midday light fills all the hollows of her face as it contorts in utter shock. "But I—You—How—"

She's wondering how I knew she didn't *have* one. I put it together fairly fast, actually, once we moved our gym gear into her garage, and never heard a peep about where she would park going forward. That, coupled with the oversized basket on her well-loved bicycle and the worn tread on its tires, gave her away.

I move closer, slowly backing her into the closed passenger door.

"You'll learn that I'm very observant. I figured out you didn't have a car this week and went looking into our pack's bank accounts. The money Jesse allocated for you to get a vehicle is gone, but you don't have one." I arch a brow. "Which philanthropy did you give it to?"

Because combing through those same accounts gave me a clear view of her spending. She doesn't waste her "pay" from us on anything extravagant or illicit. She *gives it away.*

To people who need it more than her. Noble causes. Education efforts and environmental conservation. All of that on top of running the pack's charitable trust. After scanning the books, I'm fairly sure Bridget single-handedly doled out more than ten million dollars last year.

If I ever doubted her motives or wondered how much of her generosity was self-serving, I never will again. Her mouth wobbles as she shakes with anxiety, telling how unhappy she is to have been "caught" sacrificing her own comfort for someone else.

Her voice drops into a petulant grumble as she ducks her head, hiding her gaze. Her sandaled foot restlessly toes the asphalt. "I did buy a car," she mutters. "I just didn't buy one for myself."

Her blue eyes brighten with fervor when she turns them up to mine. She's been reluctant to counter me directly, so far, likely because her Omega wants to appease my Alpha; no matter how much Bridget hates it. But this must be very important to her, because she squares her posture.

"My best friend's brother's pack runs the Ospreys' football franchise. They have an orphanage here in town, Osprey House, and we all support it with donations. They've been able to expand and open two more houses, but one of the house mothers—the omega who runs the new location our pack's trust now funds—mentioned that she didn't have a car. She was taking the bus at four a.m. to get to the house before any of the kids woke up and the night manager got off shift."

"So you bought her a car," I guess.

Bridget sets her jaw like she's preparing to go to the mat. "Yes. I did."

I have to resist the urge to grin at her, sliding my hands to her hips and stepping close. Bridget's gaze flies wide, then slides to the group of onlookers clustered at the entrance to the dealership. She settles, thinking I'm touching her for appearance's sake.

That's fine. If thinking this is fake helps her accept my attention, I'll let her believe that.

"Very naughty, omega," I rumble. "You should have told the guys you needed more money for a car of your own." Her body trembles as I press my hips into her middle and stare down into her eyes. "I'll have to make sure you learn your lesson."

Fire sparks in her irises. "Which is what? Don't be charitable?"

I shake my head, bending closer. "Which is: you come to your alphas. If there's a problem, you come to *me*."

For one glorious moment, her expression softens. Her chin quivers. And she looks so damn *hopeful*, it might break my weathered, brittle heart.

But she's Bridget. So instead of melting, she starts to argue. The pulse of dominance I project pauses her mid-inhale.

I cup her face and press my lips to her forehead, hiding another smile when her lashes flit closed. "I don't care how we ended up here or how long it lasts," I tell her. "For now, I *am* your alpha. And you're going to let me take care of you."

MONKEY DICKS.

Can anyone tell me the exact moment my life became a never-ending series of these surreal, mortifying moments?

Because *I know* I am not actually standing in front of the fanciest boutique "nest club" in the whole damn state. Wearing space buns and painted overalls. With an alpha whose leather musk climbs over the humid afternoon breeze to warm my lungs and clench my core.

This cannot be happening.

This *is not* happening.

Except, *oh God*.

I can't stop the wet glide of slick that seeps into my panties.

They're supposed to absorb my essence—but I learned back at the car dealership that, apparently, it's time for a new pair.

Adrian immediately turns his chiseled face in my direction. And, Lord, even *that's* sexy. His neck? The muscles and tendons and bulging strength that runs all the way from his built chest to his square jaw?

Damn it. I think I have a crush on my fake Daddy-Boss-Alpha.

In my defense, how exactly does one *resist* forming a crush on a man *this* gorgeous? When he does nothing but compliment you and *buy you cars*?

Okay, well. Not car*s*.

But the cutest Mini Cooper on the planet. In an adorable shade of yellow. With custom white-and-sky-blue leather seats, nonetheless.

And now we're here. At the store of my *literal dreams*.

L'abri used to be exclusive to Europe, but that never stopped me from secretly scrolling their social media feeds late at night, drooling over the beautiful "nest-scapes" their incomparable designers curate. When we found out our tiny-but-posh Orlando suburb would be one of their test markets for launching US shops, my friends and I were thrilled.

When our location finally opened last summer, Alicia was the one to dash my dreams—informing me that *L'abri* only took customers by appointment. No window-shopping or penniless librarians allowed.

I thought it was a bullshit policy, but now? Standing here? I sort of get it. The exterior of this place is so luxurious, it practically gives me hives. Smooth black stucco, brushed brass fixtures, and their signature striped awnings—all of it is every bit as sophisticated and attractive as the alpha next to me.

The same one who senses my increasingly-acidic scent and reaches for my hand, squeezing solidly. "Don't worry about it, little blue. We have an appointment."

Seriously? I'm not even taking responsibility for the state of my panties.

This man is diabolical.

I'm starting to suspect he's planned every detail leading to the demise of my underwear's dignity. From taking me to my favorite place for iced coffee earlier, to the way he cups the nape of my neck, now, lightly drawing circles with his thumb.

I clench my core and give my Omega a very stern talking to. *We are not going to melt down here. We are in public. At the fanciest nest store in the state. With a man who looks like he could pose for cologne ads. There will be absolutely no public humiliation.*

The voice inside me whines so hard, the sound nearly trips up my throat. *But he's—*

I squash her down harder, ignoring her desperate pleas. *NO,* I bark at her. *Get back in your hole.*

She shows me a mental image of a different sort of hole and the memory of how Dante filled it last night. I snap back, *Exactly, crazycakes. That was literally <u>last night</u>. Not even twelve hours ago. You're <u>fine</u>.*

Usually, my Omega is a timid sort. She normally doesn't put up a fuss, but instead of backing down, her whines climb higher. *But—*

I cut her off with a low snarl, mentally blocking the rest of her protest. Adrian hears my strangled whimper and does the absolute worst thing imaginable: pressing his front into my side. Where I'm pretty damn sure the semi-hard *ridge of his cock* grazes my hip.

Donkey balls.

"Just a couple more minutes," he promises in the husky, reassuring timbre I can't seem to resist. "I know you're tired after sleeping so poorly. As soon as we finish up here, I'll take you home, and we can have the groceries for your neighbor delivered."

I wonder if we're early for our appointment. He paused us out here on the sidewalk, but he may be waiting for my perfume to settle.

I doubt he wants to drag me around this high-end store when my scent is so strong. Why would a man like Adrian want to be associated with the lemony napalm oozing out of my pores?

His body suddenly tenses, confirming my self-consciousness. I start to step away, giving him space to breathe, but a panted voice interrupts.

"Hey!" Jesse calls, jogging in from the parking lot. "I'm sorry I'm so late. I tried to get here by one, but my pitching coach had all these stretches and—"

He freezes at the curb, his pretty hazel eyes rounding when my stench hits him. "Uhhh..." He clears his throat. "We, um, good? To go in?"

God, this is humiliating. But I will be damned if I miss my one and only chance to go into *L'abri,* so I paper over a mortified cringe with a smile. "Yep! I didn't know you were coming, Jess."

He looks as chagrinned as I feel, grimacing. "Is that okay?"

Adrian chuckles quietly. He does that a lot, actually; like we're all so endlessly amusing. "I asked him to come, Bridget. Jesse needs an afternoon off from intensive training, and I figured he might like to help us here."

I'm still not sure what he thinks we need from this place. I've furnished my nest as best I could, turning the tiny spare bedroom into a relatively cozy space. Sure, it doesn't totally *feel* like a nest since there isn't a sunken pit in the ground. And the best I could do for the lights was blackout curtains and battery-operated Christmas bulbs from Amazon. But it gets the job done.

Well.

I *hope* it will.

I haven't done a heat there yet. Once I finally got out of Alicia's house, I used the money I used to spend on suppressants to prepay for a year-long heat clinic membership. I picked a local, low-priced place so I wouldn't run into anyone from my sister's snobby circles. And lived to regret it.

After my heat last fall left me scarred and sore for three weeks after, I vowed to take care of myself next time. Or, I guess, *this* time.

So, come to think of it, maaaaaybe there are a few things I should grab while we're here. Though I doubt they sell five-dollar twinkle lights in a beautiful place like this.

Jesse nudges my arm as we turn for the entrance, his blond brows crouched over golden-green eyes. "You sure you're okay? My Alpha is telling me you're not."

I stare, thrown. Partly because he's not wrong, but mostly because I've been upset around him nearly every time we've interacted and he's never noticed.

Or maybe he's just never spoken up.

I want to ruthlessly shush my Omega again, but she has a point. Is Jesse Locke, Golden Boy Extraordinaire—professional athlete, Prince-Charming-handsome, Honor Student—*nervous* to speak his mind?

Is he *shy*?

Maybe Colt is too, the voice in my middle suggests, remembering the way he turned his face away every time I looked at him. The stubborn set of his brows. His clenched jaw and flared nostrils...

Pretty sure he just hates us, babe, I inform her.

Which is fine because I'm not exactly his biggest fan, either. Especially since he nearly ended his own life with his selfish stupidity.

None of that is Jesse's fault, though. He's here, trying to be nice. Attempting to make amends for the last fourteen months. I should at least smile.

"This place is making my Omega a little—" *ALPHAS-SSSSSSSSS* "—extra," I tell him, ignoring the way my panties stick to my wet core. "I promise I'll be fine."

Thankfully, Adrian's unflappable control only gets smoother as he leads us into the store.

Because if I thought the *outside* of *L'abri* was intimidating... my eyes are wide as saucers as I peer around the lobby.

Its rounded alcove is dark and moody, with charcoal suede walls and flickering collections of candles. A soothing water feature fills the wall across from the door, babbling quietly, anchored behind a large glass desk and two artfully arranged fiddle-leaf trees.

Adrian doesn't appear the slightest bit bothered that I'm wearing overalls I painted myself. He whisks us up to the desk and smiles at me, barely sparing the pretty receptionist a glance as he says, "Messina Pack. One o'clock."

She types and offers a bright grin of her own. "Mr. Messina. Of course. We have the nest-scapes you requested set up for you."

My mind trips over her casual words. *Did she say he* requested *certain things? For me?!*

Seeing my stunned blink, Adrian's warm gaze flickers. "They're just a starting point, little blue," he husks. "If you don't like any of the nests I pulled, the staff will show you everything else they have in stock. We're not in any rush."

"I—I don't—"

Here I thought perpetually clicking advertisements of bedroom-to-nest conversion kits was a dirty little secret between me and my phone. How the hell did Adrian know?

Answering my unspoken question, the pack alpha squeezes my fingers. "I promise I didn't go inside your nest. But you're using the spare bedroom, and I didn't see one of these setups charged to any of our accounts. You need one, right?"

"No," I immediately deny. "It's no big deal. Seriously."

Adrian's thick black brow arches. It's the same expression he gave me when I told the car salesman I'd take any color Mini Cooper they had on the lot. The alpha's voice drops into a rougher rasp, his tone stern. "Bridget."

He sort of has a point.

I'll be going through a real heat, alone, for the first time ever. It would be good to have a proper nest structure with a sunken middle—and *L'abri* is the only place on town with custom kits to convert *any* room.

I bite my lower lip, giving in with a sigh, "Okay, okay. Yes."

Adrian flashes me his weathered, gorgeous smile, gently leading us past the front desk. "You're a fast learner. I like that."

chapter
twenty-three

I AM NOT GOING to tackle this omega into the next luxury nest we pass.

Really.

I'm like, eighty-nine percent sure.

Or maybe more like, *seventy*-nine.

From the moment I arrived, every breath I've taken has been like snorting a line of *lust*. Looking at her isn't any help, and the more I listen to her speak, the harder my knot pounds. She's so pretty and smart—and her sharp perfume might hurt, but it also makes my mouth water.

I don't even care that the scent doesn't totally "click." I'm not sure I would change it even if I could. Plus, the way it swells—

then dips, then *slices*—keeps me on my toes. I never know if it will cut me or kiss me.

This nest store is unlike any I've ever seen. There are no aisles of sex position pillows or vibrators. There are no aisles at all.

Instead, the lobby leads to a wide, circular hallway that splits into individual alcoves. Most of them are dark, but every few yards, we pass a lit one.

Those must be the nests Adrian chose for Bridget.

The fact that he could even *do* that, after knowing her for a week, puts a jealous seethe in my stomach. It also fills my chest with gratitude.

As Adrian leads her from one display to the next, appreciation edges out my envy. The look of awe on Bridget's face could make up for just about anything, I think. Not to mention how intense her perfume gets as we work our way through the "nest-scapes."

I may have a lot to learn about Bee, but even I can tell the moment she finds The One.

A gasp falls from her open lips as her footsteps snag. She darts to the left, directly into the small room.

Color greets us—rich, dark-teal velvet pads the wall, with pretty bursts of flowers woven into hidden pockets. The blooms are eclectic—purple poppies, marigolds, bright fuchsia dahlias, creamy blush peonies, small fuzzy orange buttons I have no name for. Some sit in purposeful bouquets while other arrangements drip and dangle toward the padded green-blue floor.

The cushions seamlessly blend with the walls, but the texture is entirely different—slippery silk, I think. Or maybe satin.

The room has everything: fuzzy faux-fur blankets, pillows to match every shade blooming from the wallpaper, all piled into its wide, sunken center. But it doesn't end there. With the touch of a button, hidden doors silently swoosh open, revealing exits intended for bathrooms, storage closets, or—*oh shit*—a built-in snack cabinet.

Hell, even the *sex toys* coordinate, all carefully laid out on a brass tray inside the recessed mattress. Jewel-toned silicone with gold buttons.

Bridget stands at the threshold of the display, her creamy throat bobbing on a noticeable swallow. Adrian steps up beside her. "This is exceptional. You have a good eye, little blue. Do you want to go in?"

She starts to lean forward, but stops herself. Releasing a deep breath, she shakes her head and casts her eyes to the floor. "Um, no. I—I'm good."

I don't understand. She's clearly upset, but her scent—which was warm and bright and as close to perfect as ever—doesn't turn to slicing sourness. It just... disappears?

"You okay, Bee?" I murmur.

Bridget nods absently. "Yeah. I'm just, um, hot. Is it crazy-warm in here? I mean, I know it's Florida, but *come on.*"

Adrian's gaze sharpens. He pivots on the heel of his leather shoe, scowling as he cups a hand around Bridget's cheek. Flustered, she blinks at him while he bends and presses his lips to her forehead.

Her lashes flutter faster, true shock filling her face before her eyes slowly fall shut. The look that flits over her features is as blissful as it is stunned.

Why does that tear a hole in my lung?

For that matter, why is she so surprised? A woman like Bridget should have men lining up to kiss her. Hell, I want to be one of them.

Adrian hums, his expression creasing. "You're warm, little blue. I think your Omega likes this nest."

Bridget presses one hand to her peachy cheek and the other to the curve of her belly. "I—I know. But it's probably outrageously expensive. And this is only a tiny heat-spike. Nothing crazy, just a blip from having so many alphas around so suddenly... and being here. But it's fine. I'm okay. It barely hurts."

It *hurts*? My eyes fly down her fingers, and Adrian's follow, darkening. "You're in pain and you didn't say anything?"

Bridget shakes as she shrugs, her lips pursing into a pout that doesn't match the vulnerability in her eyes. "Why would I say anything?" Her voice drops into a whisper. "It's not your problem."

Before I can draw a breath, my Alpha growls sharply. The sound vibrates in my chest, then echoes through Adrian's. I cut mine off immediately, embarrassed, but his blurs into a rumbling purr.

"Is that what you think?" he murmurs, still cupping Bridget's beautiful face. Closing the distance between their torsos.

"It's the truth," Bridget retorts, biting her lip. "*I'm* not your problem. Not really."

"Hmm," he hums, tucking a stray lock of hair behind her ear. "And what if I *want* you to be my problem?"

Yeah, I think. My insides give an eager lurch. *What if we do?*

Bridget's throat works as she stares up at Adrian for a long beat. Her scent is back, but it swoops from barely-there to a finely-honed *blade*. I suck in a painful breath, relishing how it carves into my core and sets my blood on fire.

"But my scent," Bridget whispers. "It's—"

"—making me *fucking hard*," Adrian finishes, lowering his thick brow at her. "Because it's telling me you need an alpha. Right now."

———————— ♥ ————————

THE FACT that Bridget doesn't protest betrays just how uncomfortable she must be.

I kick myself as I trail behind Adrian, watching him keep a steady hand on the nape of her neck, stroking his thumb over the exposed skin there. It's tender and reassuring—the exact type of energy an omega in a heat-spike needs.

Why couldn't I have given her that?

Why didn't *I* listen to my instincts?

"Excuse me," Adrian says, flagging down an employee. "We need a moment with our omega. Where are your easing rooms?"

The young beta nods, his face the picture of professional impassivity. "Right this way, Mr. Messina."

I'm an alpha who supposedly has an omega fiancée, but I feel like my eyes might leap out of my skull. *Easing rooms? As in places for us to—*

"Just press this button here when you're finished. The pod will self-sanitize," the beta explains, gesturing at a hidden doorbell. "This area is soundproofed."

Well, damn.

This really *is* a place for us to—

"Fuck," Adrian mutters when Bridget's scent suddenly *soars*. Sour and sweet and bright and sharp.

Haaaa-oooly shit.

It's killing me, and I can't even care. Let it cut me. If that's what she needs, I'll gladly bleed out.

I remember the way Bridget's eyes dropped to the floor when she thought I'd only bought those flowers as a prop for the paparazzi. This is different, though—there are no cameras here now. No motive other than showing her I actually care about her.

Adrian seems to feel the same. His chest rises and falls under his dark gray dress shirt, the open buttons parting as he fights for a deep inhale. Bridget quivers at the rumbling exhale that follows, her back visibly arching as fresh perfume pierces the air.

She whimpers. Adrian's face instantly softens. "Come here, baby girl," he hums, gently guiding her into a hug. "Your alpha is right here." Aqua eyes snap to mine. "Both of us are."

BRIDGET'S EYES go vacant as she watches me unbutton my shirt sleeves.

While I have her distracted, I slowly roll the cuffs up my forearms, giving Jesse a moment to decide how involved he wants to be.

The store's easing pod is functional, but no-frills. I'm sure they keep the walls bare and the floor uncarpeted to ensure easy clean-up and maintenance. There are chairs—sturdy, lacquered ones that will wipe down without any fuss.

And a lock.

Bridget is too far gone to notice Jesse dropping the deadbolt.

She fidgets with her clothes, a quiet whine vibrating in her throat as she paws at her overalls.

"Let me help you, little blue," I murmur, summoning all my self-control to avoid whisking her into my arms. "Here."

She lets me unhook one of the silver buckles over her breasts, but she trembles the entire time. I pause, reading her wide, glistening eyes.

"She doesn't feel safe here," I realize, turning to Jesse. "We need to be gentle."

Is it us? Or the store? Either way, when I finish unsnapping her overalls, she gives another barely-there squeak, scratching at the buttons over her hips with one hand while the other grips the painted denim to her torso with manic fervor.

"Shh," I hush, carefully replacing her fumbling fingers with my steady ones. Unfastening the buttons over her hips in four quick pops. "You don't have to take care of yourself this time, Bridget. I promise I won't take your clothes off if you don't want me to."

I flatten my palms to her sides, absorbing the warmth radiating beneath her tank top. "Why don't you put my hands where you want them?" I hum, standing solid at her back. Ignoring the erection that throbs when her ass brushes the front of my trousers.

Bridget doesn't take the same approach. As soon as she feels how hard she's made me, she moans, pressing her backside tight to my groin. My fingers flex automatically, eliciting a breathless whimper as she scrabbles to position my hands where she wants them.

One instantly flies up to her stuttering chest. The other slips down into her overalls.

Fucking hell. She's absolutely *soaked* with slick.

"My good girl is so ready for us," I growl, skimming the waistband of her panties. "Here?" I ask, then stretch a few inches lower, rubbing her slit through the thin, wet cotton. "Or here?"

Bridget bucks into my hand, pouring fresh slick out. Jesse

goes to his knees, inhaling deeply and shuffling closer. "Fucking *fuck*," he moans. "I want to lick her."

Our omega reacts almost violently, jerking backward. I cast him a stern look before turning my face into her hair, whispering, "Hush now, baby girl. I won't let anyone do anything you don't want. Come here."

This will be more comfortable for her if we're sitting down. Dropping into the chair at the center of the room, I keep Bridget anchored to me, pulling her into my lap. I run my touch along her mound again, hoping to distract her before she can balk over letting me support her full weight.

Her spine arches on a beautiful, lusty keen. The movement presses the soft peak of her left breast into my waiting hand. I mold my fingers around it, grasping with precision. Avoiding the tip for the first few squeezes, knowing that will just make her more sensitive when I finally—

"Alpha!" she gasps, gushing into her panties as I pinch her stiff nipple through her bra. She writhes, and I tease her more, strumming light touches over the fabric covering her core. Wetness seeps onto my fingers when her pussy sucks at the ruined panties.

Her need must be outweighing whatever caused her unease, because she starts to lower the front of the overalls. With more room, I cup her entire center, kneading my palm into her mound as I scrape my teeth over her shoulder.

Jesse's Alpha reacts to the notion of mine marking her. His chest rumbles on a growl, even as he licks his lips and stares between Bridget's thighs.

A smirk twists my mouth. "I think your other alpha needs a lesson, baby girl. Can he watch me touch you? Learn how to pet this pretty pussy?"

Bridget tosses her head in a desperate nod, leaving a swath of lemon sweetness along my jaw. My lungs heat, huffing in more. Turning my next command into a bark.

"Take her pants off, Jesse. Slowly."

He follows the order without a speck of resentment, carefully working the denim and damp panties off her hips. Her pussy comes into view, shaded by a thatch of the sweetest red curls. My chest tightens, aching.

"There you are, precious girl," I purr.

Jesse leans a little closer, his expression flashing from slack-jawed awe to raging intensity. "Dante," he growls. His pupils expand, eyes flying to Bridget's bleary gaze.

He can scent our packmate on her. *Which means they must have been busy last night after she got home...*

The rest of Jesse's meaning sinks in. *If neither of us could tell she had hooked up with Dante until we took her bottoms off...*

My purr breaks into a low snarl. I press my teeth into her neck to quell their sudden ache. "Did another alpha touch my pussy first, sweetheart?"

My scent must be strong enough to tell her just how fucking horny that makes me. Instead of quivering, our omega squirms, brazenly nodding and licking her lips again.

I land a sharp little slap to the side of her peaked breast, bending to whisper in her ear. "When I'm done making you come, you're going to suck the taste of him right off my fingers."

Bridget whines, thrusting her hips to press her soaked slit into my touch. I hum, a growly purr melding into her back while I spread her legs over mine to give Jesse a better view.

"*You,*" I bark, pinning him with another glare, "have a lot to learn. And it's not going to happen if you're distracted by your dick. No touching yourself. You'll watch her come and put your hands on her pretty thighs *if* she'll let you."

He groans, head falling forward on a pant. "Fucking *fine*. But can I—" He swallows, catching himself. "Bee," he corrects, "Can I put my hands on you?"

She hesitates just long enough for me to pause. But when she nods, a sudden rush of perfume proves how much she wants his attention.

I slap the side of her breast again, just hard enough to give her a jolt, before I clamp my thumb and forefinger over her nipple.

She cries out, dribbling slick all over my lap. Combined with the way she grinds her pussy into my touch and her ass rubs against my fly.

God Almighty.

She couldn't be any more perfect.

I tell her so, whispering praises while I work her clit with the pads of my fingers. She seems to prefer light touches... until she gets close to the edge. Then she begs for more, squirming for firm, circling swipes over the top of the pulsing bud.

Jesse watches her the entire time, running shaky palms over her thighs. Gathering her slick on his skin.

She comes when I finally snake my other hand down to join the first, stretching her fluttering muscles with two curved fingers. I bite down on her shoulder with a bone-rattling roar, closing my eyes to focus on the feel of her slippery walls begging for a knot. Knowing I'll replay the sensation every time I stroke myself off.

Jesse gasps over a growl, bending at the waist as he sinks his teeth into her thigh. The bite is almost hard enough for me to bark at him—but I see why a moment later when a dark splotch of wetness appears at the front of his jeans.

He came just from watching *her* come. So maybe he doesn't have quite as much to learn as I thought.

Smirking to myself, I lift my slick-covered fingers up to Bridget's face. Our omega's eyes are much more focused, but her lips still drop open in shock when I present her with the mess we made.

"Seriously?" she asks, breathless.

My smile widens. "Every drop," I direct. "Or we start all over."

chapter
twenty-five

JESSE

Has anyone seen my headphones?

ADRIAN

Likely in whatever box or bag is currently
hiding my tablet from me.

COLT

I swear this house is like a vortex.

DANTE

How can we lose stuff so easily in a place
that's so small?

I can't even turn around in the shower 💀

JESSE

It's only been four days.

I bet we'll get used to it.

ADRIAN

You'd all adjust much faster if you grew some
balls and started trying to connect with
Bridget.

DANTE

It isn't my fault!

She's* avoiding me*

JESSE

I keep trying to talk to her but the woman
turns me into an idiot

COLT

You say that like it's a recent development.

DANTE

Don't be silly, Colt.

Jesse's known her since high school so he's
been an idiot at least* that long

ADRIAN

If you all think there's only one idiot among
you, I have bad news.

"SO, UH..."

You know an awkward silence hates to see me coming.
Usually, I smash that shit to bits—tell a joke, start a story.

But, um...

Jesse rubs at the back of his neck, surveying the scene in the
living room. Namely, Colt, stretched across a full couch like an
absolute asshole, and Bridget, sitting primly on the sofa opposite
his. Arranging scrapbook supplies on a big foam board laid over
the coffee table.

She does shit like that all the time. Painting designs on her bookcases. Building displays for her students. And now... putting pictures of random kids on this flower-covered poster?

All while listening to the DIY Network. Naturally.

The flatscreen arrived today, along with everything else our pack alpha bought for Bridget last weekend. Including her new nest and the little Mini Cooper.

And fuck. It is *adorable*.

Of course she picked the one car and color that would make me grin like an idiot.

Doesn't she know I'm still trying to Scotch-tape my skull back together after she blew it off on Saturday night?

I'm still confused. How did we end up fucking like that out of nowhere? Why was it the most incredible sex of my life? And, given that fact, why the hell haven't I said a word about it to *anyone*?

Because it... *meant something* to me?

Colt totally knows. I see the way he sneers at me every time I stumble upon Bridget and start to freeze up. I noticed how he opened the French doors the morning after the world-class countertop sex.

He's being a dick on purpose—sprawling out with Bridget's asshole cat lying alongside him. Forcing Jesse and me to squeeze onto the other sofa with the omega doing everything she can to not notice us.

Is it bad form to kick a guy's ass while he's injured?

"We'll just..." Jesse goes on, shuffling forward. "Sit with you? If that's okay, Bee."

Bridget offers him a sideways glance and nothing more. Her seafoam fingernails flash in the low light as she sticks the last photo onto her project. Acting nonchalant, even though her voice squeaks with nerves. "Knock yourselves out."

Her attitude might be my favorite thing about her. *Aside from her sense of humor... and her hair... and her ass... and her—*

I shake myself out of my head to find Jesse hesitating like a little bitch. Shoving him, I follow behind and take the spot on the other end of the sofa. He stiffly lowers himself to the middle, his toasted sugar-and-salt scent spiking from her proximity.

While I watch, somewhere between commiseration and second-hand embarrassment, he gazes at Bridget's profile. Stringing together a lame attempt at conversation.

"Is that... a project for school?"

Cristo. He even *sounds* like a middle schooler with no game.

Bridget offers a tepid smile, carefully picking the board up and adding it to an upright stack of them wedged between the back of her sofa and her bookshelves. "Something like that."

Jesse watches as she dusts glitter off her hands and smooths her skirt down. His toasted scent gets a bit saltier. "D-did," he goes on, stammering. "Did all the stuff we picked out get here in one piece?"

Bridget's soft. I saw a little bit of it during whatever the hell happened between us. But it's even more obvious now, as she notes my packmate's anxiety and finally cracks a tiny smile. "Yeah, it did. Thanks, Jess."

"DID YOU EAT YET?"

Dios mío.

What the fuck was *that*?

I haven't said two words to her all week and *that's* my opener? Shouting a random question that has *nothing* to do with *anything*?!

Bridget's brows pinch as she tries to process my stupidity. "Nooooo. Adrian texted and told me he was bringing sushi home."

"Oh," Jesse puts in, fumbling for his phone, scanning the screen. "He didn't tell us that yet. Maybe we should, like, make a group chat?"

Colt flashes a murderous look. "I'd rather iron my own hands."

Bridget beams a deliberate, mocking smile back. "That's a *great* idea," she chirps at Jesse.

"Make sure you call it Bridget's Blue Balls," Colt mutters, going back to his book. "Or maybe The Dickless Wonders."

Jesse swells up beside me, but before he can reply, my Alpha snaps out a defensive growl. Bridget seems more disturbed by that than Colt's jeers, blinking wide eyes at me for half a moment before shooting him another saccharine smile.

"I like Option B," she chips, standing up. "Given that not *all* of you have blue balls."

Hell. She's talking about me.

Jesse freezes until she stands and saunters out of the room. Leaving a dizzying, dazzling cloud of tart sweetness in her wake. Colt's lip lifts in a sneer. My lungs stutter and cramp, turning my next dumbass question into a pant.

"Did she smell this good that day we met her?"

"Definitely not," Jesse mumbles, still fixated on the exit.

"*Good?*" Colt balks, his own sea-salt-and-sandalwood aroma smoldering. He flicks me another I'm-stabbing-you-in-my-mind look. Either because he actually *hates* her scent... or he hates *me* for pointing out how amazing it's gotten.

"Seriously," I burst, desperate for corroboration. Proof I'm not, you know, *insane*. "I'm pretty sure it was different. More acidic, I thought...?"

Jesse nods his agreement. "For sure. Maybe she was having an off day or something."

Or something.

Like three alphas showing up to ask for her hand without ever even *talking to her*.

Plus, this is her home. She's relaxed here, for the most part. It's possible this is her true perfume and has been all along. Which would explain why my Alpha's been in dumbfounded shock since Saturday.

Because this essence?

This woman?

I don't know why—but I know they're mine.

ABSOLUTE HELL, Day Five.

Also known as Wednesday.

I'm not sure exactly what happened, but ever since the weekend, things between Bridget and the guys have been weird. First, she and Dante were awkward after whatever they did Saturday night. Then, Adrian and Jesse came back from their shopping trip with obsessive gleams in their eyes.

And, apparently, a whole new nest-room thing that arrived yesterday.

Along with a new fucking *car*.

Apparently Bridget didn't have one. Which made no sense—

we gave her money. Has she seriously been riding that ridiculously bright bicycle around for... ever?

Adrian told us she spent the cash to buy a vehicle for someone else. Which really puts a damper on my "she's a gold-digging sociopath" narrative.

Although, the sociopath part would have been shot to hell by now either way, given how damn *nice* she is. Making coffee every morning, leaving leftovers out for us in the evenings. Taking groceries to her elderly neighbor. Teaching extension courses she doesn't get paid for.

She does it all with an undefeatably upbeat attitude that sets my teeth on edge. So far, I've coped by calling her Bubbles in my mind—and maybe in a few conversations with her stupid tabby cat.

I don't want to hear it, okay?

I'm here alone all day while everyone else works. Except for the two hours I spend arguing with my in-home PT every morning, I don't talk to *anyone*. And Munchies is just about the only living creature too dumb to realize what an insufferable asshole I've become.

Today's torture session—or "physical therapy," allegedly— bled into early afternoon. I'm still sweaty and pissed off when the side door rattles. Munchies meows and jumps off the pink sofa I'm marooned on.

"Traitor," I mutter, reaching for the book that's been keeping me busy this week. It's from Bridget's collection. Some anthology of political biographies featuring different powerful women in history. I hold it in front of my face so whoever walks in doesn't get any ideas about striking up a conversation.

The second I hear a cooing "Psp, psp, psp," I *know* it's Bridget.

I hate myself for lowering the book just enough to peer over the edge. Sure enough, our omega is on her knees next to the kitchen door. Wearing one of her insane outfits—a dark red dress with puffy sleeves and heart-shaped pockets stitched prominently in pink.

From the sweat darkening the roots of her pink-bowed pigtails, I'm guessing she didn't take Adrian's firm suggestion to call daily Ubers until her car gets here. I've been watching her all week, noticing that she takes her bike each morning after the guys leave. I haven't ratted her out yet, but if she keeps being so damn *annoying*…

Munchies trots off, and Bridget watches him go, blowing out a silent sigh before turning her attention to me. Pasting on a fake smile to go with her fake engagement ring.

"Oh, hi!" she chirps, perky as ever.

I nearly slip and call her Bubbles, but strangle my reply into a grunt.

"*Women Who Changed the World*," she says, reading the title of my borrowed book aloud. Her eyes narrow in faux-suspicion. "You stole that from my shelves, didn't you?"

"Borrowed it," I grunt.

Her lips twitch. "Without permission."

"I borrowed it," I repeat, ignoring her, "And when I'm done I'll put it back. You're a *librarian*. This concept shouldn't be new to you."

The obvious amusement on her face lights a fire in the pit of my stomach. She smirks, eying the book in my hands.

"That's a good one," she shrugs. "I think I liked *Not-So-Well Behaved Women* more, though. I'll *loan* it to you if you want; that way you don't have to steal it from me."

Damn it all to hell. I do want to read that. I won't *admit it*, though.

"I'm fine." My eyes glance at the clock on the wall next to her back door. It's not even four. "What are you doing here?" I ask. "Isn't school out at three-thirty?"

Bridget stands and strolls over. Her thick-soled sandals are as pink as her bows and adorned with small daisy charms. Not that

I'm *looking* at her dainty feet or the thick, shapely legs attached to them.

"School gets out early on Wednesdays. Duh." Bridget pays no mind to the crutches leaning against the couch. She moves them to my other side and takes the seat next to me.

I drop my book to my lap, scowling. "I'm sitting here."

She smirks. "Yep. Here. In *my* house. Small world, huh, Salty?"

My molars grind. "Salty?"

I watch her snort back a laugh. "Yeah. You smell salty like the beach, and you also act like a salty old man, so it sort of works on two levels."

My Alpha lurches upright, both of us outraged. But before I can even get a snarl out, Bridget's face brightens. She nudges my arm with her elbow and wags her auburn eyebrows. "Speaking of: Betty, the old bitch down the street? She said you have a shot. Want me to swipe right on that for you?"

Is this real life? Is she seriously *this* clueless?

Instead of withering under my glare, she deflates into the cushions, gazing up at the ceiling as she goes on, "You two would probably be blissfully unhappy together. You both *love* loungewear. And complaining. Betty isn't big on reading, though, so you might want to learn how to play Mahjong."

No. I am *not* going to smile *goddamn it.*

Bridget must sense she's making me somewhat less murderous because she quirks another small smile, still staring at the orange bubble chandelier.

"Of course, she's a Leo and you're a Scorpio. Great sex, but communication is gonna be a bitch. On the upside, you've definitely got the whole 'stubborn pain in the ass' thing in common."

Sunlight from the French doors fills Bridget's soft, pert features. It must momentarily fry my brain, also, because I offer her the barest lift of my brows. "Meaning?"

Bridget waves her hand, its painted fingernails glittering.

"Weren't you supposed to be off those crutches this week? And out of your sling?"

Well. Thinking I might not hate her was nice while it lasted. All forty seconds of it.

"I already had physical therapy today," I grumble, kicking out the leg trapped in a corrective boot. "I don't remember calling for a second opinion."

Bridget cackles. "*As if* I'd only be your *second* opinion."

She doesn't scold me for running off the first four trainers—she doesn't have to. Her taunt is true, and we both know it. Hell, she may even have a point about me being salty.

Back in our penthouse, it was easy to ignore how dark shit had gotten. The days started to blur together—and with our pack's constant sniping and tense silences, my general attitude fit right in. But now? Here?

Bridget makes sure I know exactly how sullen and exasperating I've become. Every single day.

She doesn't even have to *say* anything. It's *obvious*. The way she hums while she fixes her hair, the cheerful array of shoes piled beside the front door. Random, hilarious penis figurines in every color casually dotting her shelves. The dumb, purring cat who won't leave me alone.

As if it never occurred to the idiotic furball that anyone could be anything *less* than delighted to see his hairy orange ass. Because his owner is a ball of pure fucking *sunshine*.

This whole house feels tailor-made to point out just how miserable I am. Right down to the lemon-cheesecake scent currently smothering me.

And the way it makes my knot twitch.

Bridget's amused expression doesn't help. She pokes my good leg with the toe of her pink sandal. "C'moooon, you know you can do it! What if I sit here and cheer for you?"

Something painful stabs my gullet, then squirms down to my stomach. I picture myself trying to get to my feet and falling flat on my face. The image is one I've envisioned a million times at this point, and it's the reason I refuse to try whenever the PT is here.

But if that happened in front of Bridget?

My teeth grit. "No."

She narrows her blue, blue eyes. "What if I need help getting a book from the top shelf? Would you seriously say no to that?"

I make a show of sitting back and spreading my good arm across the cushions—which definitely has nothing to do with my knuckles almost grazing her shoulder. Obviously. "I'd say you've been living here alone for a year. Surely you have some way of getting your books down, Bubbles."

Damn it.

DAMN IT.

Bridget's gaze sparkles. Her elegant brows quirk. "Bubbles?"

There'll be no living with her now. I'm going to have to move out. Go on the lam. Shave my head.

The omega refuses to look away. Excitement brightens her pretty face, betraying just how long she's been waiting for me to slip up and give her a glimpse of my inner workings.

Jesus.

Bubbles?

That's the thought she gets insight into?

I have to work to keep my voice from edging into a growl. "You're... *bubbly.*"

Bridget's smirk slowly blossoms into a grin. "I am bubbly. Just like you're salty."

Does she have to be so funny? And *right?* I wave a hand as carelessly as I can. "There's another couch, you know. Get your book and sit over there. Maybe, if you're quiet, you won't be quite so annoying."

Bridget sticks her tongue out at me. "Whatever, Salty. You stink anyway."

I'm sure. Showering with crutches has been an ordeal, and I did PT for two hours today. My own salted sandalwood scent is noticeable to me, muddled by sweat and the dank must of these three-day-old clothes.

It finally occurs to me how disgusting I probably look. My hair is down to my shoulders, my beard in full effect. Both are greasy and lank, with dried perspiration at the roots. I'm sure my skin isn't any fresher. And, at the moment, I don't even have my usual baseball cap to cover any of it.

What I wouldn't give to be able to stand under hot water and actually scrub myself without balancing on a metal prop or sitting in a shower chair. I refused to even bring the one from the apartment when we moved in here.

Scowling, I pull my arm into my body, crossing it over my sling. Bridget bounces up, chatting about her school day while she scans her bookshelves. She tells me about a fire drill during second period and how she caught four girls vaping under the stairs after they asked to go to the nurse's office for tampons.

I have to admit, her stories are funny. For three days in a row, she's come home and given me a run-down of the absurdities associated with teaching high school kids. Almost like she can see under the glower on my face and somehow knows the stories really do amuse me.

I'm aware I've basically vowed not to have any positive feelings for this omega, but fuck. She doesn't make it easy.

She pulls a painted footstool from under one of the end tables and sets it in front of her shelves, giving away just how she usually gets her own books down. It's a few feet tall and clearly something she found in whatever thrift market she bought her silverware from. When she steps onto it, the legs groan, and my pulse stutters.

Because Adrian will skin me alive if anything happens to her on my watch, I decide.

Not because I *care*.

Shut up.

The stool stays put. Bridget stretches as far as she can,

reaching for a book on the very highest shelf. Her fingertips graze it. She bites her lower lip and strains a little further...

I don't notice I've moved to the edge of my seat until she balances on her tippy toes and *hops*.

My heart jumps at the same second she does. *Crutches*, I think. *I need to—*

Scrambling, I start to reach for the metal sticks, but it's too late. Bridget loses her balance. She shrieks. A book goes flying behind her head as she misses the top of the stool when she tries to land. She careens backward, arms flailing—

And then I'm *there*.

Here. On the floor. On my knees.

Only barely managing to get one arm under her head before it hits the floor.

The rest of her goes down pretty hard, though. I growl in frustration. "Fuck, are you okay?" My hand skims the side that hit first. "Let me see."

Bridget's face makes no sense. She's wincing, clearly in pain, but her plump pink lips pull into a crazy grin. "Colt—"

"No," I grunt, rolling her uninjured side onto my thighs so I can lean over her. "You might have bruising. We should get some ice."

"Colt," she tries to protest again.

I flash her a snarl. "Can you stop talking for ten seconds while I make sure your damn limbs work? What about your shoulder? Can you move your arm?"

Her smile only grows as I prop her neck in the crook of one elbow and use my left hand to bend her right arm. It seems fine, but this weird look on her face is a little concerning. Am I sure I caught her upper half before she hit her head on the floor? Is inappropriate grinning a sign of a concussion?

"*Colt*," she says again, nearly using an omega bark. I freeze automatically, my hand hovering over her chest, hunting for a heartbeat. My eyes snap to hers, finally taking in the... *smug* expression there?

What the hell?

Bridget nods at me. Specifically, at the empty sling dangling uselessly from my neck.

Oh. I stood up?

No, the self-satisfied look on her face tells me—I *lunged*. And *darted* across the room. And *caught* her.

And she planned the whole damn thing.

Her brows tweak as she takes in my gape. Her voice drops into a murmur. "Are *you* okay?"

I... am. My leg is still in the boot, and there's a dull throb blooming in my shin—probably from putting my full weight on it for the first time in months. My knees are creaky and in need of more stretching, but my shoulder barely aches. The soreness almost feels like *relief*—similar to taking off all my catcher's pads. As if I've kept my body compressed for too long.

None of it should surprise me. This is what the doctors and therapists have been saying for the last three weeks. They told me that eventually the sling would do more harm than good. And promised that I could bear weight on this leg.

I was just too stubborn and embarrassed to try. And risk failing.

Risk finding out that I would never play baseball again.

But *Bridget* figured me out. Forced my hand.

The curvy, gorgeous, evil genius sits up, then wordlessly gets to her feet. When she pauses, the smile she offers is much kinder than the one she wore a minute ago. Her dainty fingers skim the top of my head in a reassuring touch.

"Don't worry, Colt," she hums, already walking away. "I won't tell."

twenty-seven

"BEE? YOU OKAY?"

Jesse's hazel-green eyes shine at me from the rearview mirror's reflection. I duck my chin and swallow, smoothing clammy palms over the sunflower-yellow sundress Adrian selected for the occasion. It perfectly matches the gold piping on the guys' uniform shirts, a stark contrast to their sky-blue pinstripes.

His question replays in my head. *Am* I okay? Aside from making my first public appearance as their fiancée since the media uncovered our secret? Not to mention the fact that Dante's been awkwardly avoiding me all week, and my little stunt to help Colt realize his full capabilities somehow made their injured catcher hate me even *more...*?

And then there's Adrian, who's continued to be a perfect gentleman, even after our dirty, delicious moment in the nest store. Despite my spike and the way I shut down afterward, the pack leader has still offered me his seat at breakfast each morning and insisted on talking with me after dinner every night.

He always makes sure I've eaten, takes care of every household task and expense before they even register in my mind, and ends each day by scent-marking my hand before I crawl into my nest.

Which looks like something out of a GD magazine, by the way. He oversaw all of that, too. Apparently, on Tuesday, he actually *left work* to supervise the all-beta team of installers. They set up the new nest-room and didn't leave a single trace of scent behind. When he got home that evening, Adrian simply handed me a new set of keys to the room and told me to lock his pack out whenever I wanted.

It's just chivalry, I'm sure. The same as him helping me during my meltdown at *L'abri* and lifting me into Dante's enormous Escalade today.

The alpha is a gentleman. That's *it*.

Under the three layers of scent-neutralizer I dutifully sprayed on, I'm sure I smell like an atomic bomb. The longer I contemplate Jesse's question, the more Dante shifts in his seat next to me, clenching his fists and grinding his jaw as Colt leans as far back into the third row as he can.

"Yep," I finally reply. "Totally fine."

Blocking out their reactions—and the way they make my stomach scrape—I focus on the city blurring by my tinted window, running over our plan in my mind.

We're going to the Kings' first spring training game. Adrian, Dante, and Jesse will go to work while Colt and I share the pack's special box to "spectate."

Joy.

Still, Adrian's logic is sound. Spring training draws a smaller crowd and less press coverage than a regular-season game. It's

better to start here than with one of those. Or—God forbid—
their season opener.

No, this is better. We'll be photographed arriving together.
They'll each "kiss me goodbye" for the cameras. And then three-
fourths of them will disappear, and I'll just have to deal with Salty
for a couple of hours.

A *few* hours.

Why are baseball games so damn *long*, anyway?

Someone *better* get me a hot dog. And a churro.

I swear to God, Adrian is a mind reader. He casts me a soft,
amused glance as he maneuvers Dante's huge SUV into the team's
special parking lot. His deep voice has an instant steadying effect,
as if my body has started to associate the sound with relaxation.

Stupid Omega.

"I've made some improvements to the stadium since the last
time you visited, little blue. I think you'll find the box very
comfortable. You'll have an attendant checking in and bringing
you anything you want. I've made sure our best guy is on the job
today."

Alright, so maybe my Omega isn't *that* stupid. This alpha is
pretty amazing. *Whoever ends up being his mate is the luckiest
person in the world.*

The rest of these fuckers may be sorry sons of bitches, but
Adrian? There's no doubt in my mind that this man has a scent-
sensitive mate out there waiting for him. That's the way karma
works—he can't put this much good, solid energy into the world
without attracting a perfect counterpart.

And when he or she arrives? I'm going to be *long gone*.

Lest I attempt to scratch their eyes out.

The thought is startling and *unacceptable. None of your crazy
bullshit,* I tell my Omega, burying the swell of desperate longing
she pushes into my diaphragm. *Everyone is watching us today. We
have to woman up.*

She pouts at me, but I ignore her.

She'll get over it.

♥

JUST LIKE ADRIAN PROMISED, THE KINGS' stadium looks amazing. He's completely updated the worn facade—every white concrete wall is freshly painted and brand-new blue flags snap in the breeze. Hot pretzels and toasted treats leave the spring air even sweeter. Not to mention Jesse and Dante's scents.

The crowd of photographers gathered outside is smaller than I expected. Adrian leads us from our designated lot to a walkway lined with metal barriers, flanked by security. His hand lands on the small of my back as we step onto the runway.

Cameras start flashing. He keeps his face straight behind his Armani sunglasses, but bends closer, dropping a kiss onto my crown.

Just for show, I remind myself. *Not real.*

Repeating those words helps me keep my lungs working when Dante jogs up to my other side and winds his arm around my shoulders. The succulent sweetness rising from his exposed throat is enough to make me woozy. Mortifying memories flood my mind.

"You gonna let me in this little pussy whenever I want? Or should I enjoy this time like it's my last?"

Dante's forehead nuzzles the side of my face. "Long time no see, cupcake," he husks. "Did you have fun avoiding me all week?"

I scoff, leaning back to show him my outraged expression. "*Me*?! What about *you*?"

Lord, he is handsome. Especially this close up. I don't think I've ever been this near to him in the daylight. Dark eyes glitter, full of afternoon sun. A perfect balance for his bright white smile.

"You know what, *querida*?" he rumbles, roaming those coal-hot irises over my features.

I only barely manage not to gasp, covering the flustered flut-ters in my stomach by cocking an unimpressed brow. "What?"

His grin widens until it's almost *painfully* gorgeous. "I think you and I have much more in common than we think."

And—*damn it*—I want to argue... but I've had the exact same thought all week. I used him and wounded his pride by turning it into a secret. He gave me a taste of what it would be like if he actually wanted me, then took it away.

We both reacted by awkwardly—and unsuccessfully—pretending the other didn't exist.

Which sort of proves the bastard's point.

I roll my eyes, unable to keep from smirking at the cocky delight filling his face. "God help me."

Jesse practically jumps on Dante, slinging an arm around the shortstop's neck in a chokehold. They wrestle briefly before Jesse somehow knocks Dante back and takes his place, reaching for my hand.

His grin is as kind as Dante's was flirty. He also scent-marks me, but he's much shyer about it. His voice drops into a near-whisper. "Thanks for doing this, Bee. I know it's a lot."

I don't think he intends to remind me about our charade at every turn, but that's exactly what this alpha seems best at. *Except when he was on his knees—*

I try not to let my answering smile look too tense. "Of course! It's no big—"

A hand cups the side of my face from behind, covering my mouth at the last second. I recognize Colt's salty skin instantly.

Thank God he *finally* showered.

"None of that," he grumbles, already retracting his touch and wiping his palm on his shirt. "If I have to sit in a box with you for three hours, we're not starting the perky lying all the way in the *parking lot.*"

He has a point, and I'm still feeling all kinds of smug about him using his left arm, even if he only did it to shut me up.

"Fine." I shoot all four of them pointed looks and offer my best queenly nod. "*You're welcome.*"

A firm slap to my ass sends me forward a step. When I whirl

my stunned face to Adrian's, he cocks a thick brow behind his aviators. "Brat," he says without heat.

I slant my own look up at him. "If you say so, Boss."

Adrian halts us on the walkway, reaching over to grasp my chin. I inhale sharply, and he takes full advantage, pressing his chiseled lips over mine for a brief, soft kiss. When he pulls back, he flashes a glimpse of his bright blue irises over the top of his shades. His deep voice rumbles.

"While we're here, you can call me 'King.'"

I'VE NEVER BEEN in our pack's box before. It never occurred to me that I would ever spend a game up here instead of down *there*. On the field.

I'm already raging about it. Isn't that bad enough without being stuck up here with Bubbles?

She bounces around the well-appointed room, oohing and ahhing over the gold-dusted fixtures and plush blue spectator seats. The box has glass walls, giving the appearance of being in the crowd while keeping us distinctly separate.

I find myself hating that, too. If I can't play, I want to be able to at least *smell* the grass. Feel the sun on my face.

Instead, I'm here. In the air conditioning. Being slowly smothered by the thick, creamy sweetness of lemon cheesecake.

The aroma only brightens when our box attendant pops in to ask if we'd like any food. I grumble something about three hot dogs. Bridget bobs an eager nod, ordering one of her own, along with popcorn and a churro.

I try not to notice the satisfaction that seeps into my center. My Alpha can take whatever bullshit instincts give him the insane urge to feed this omega and shove them up his ass.

Bridget must notice the burning edges of my sandalwood scent because she sniffs, shifting away and smoothing her hands over her yellow skirt. The acidic notes in her half-hidden scent spike. Perverse smugness and a wash of shame collide in my middle, sending a cold spray over my organs.

I blaze darker. Bridget finally dignifies the obvious smoldering with a sideways glance. Her pretty blue eyes flicker to my boot. "Is your leg bothering you?"

No, damn it.

It's been better every day since she tricked me into trying to catch her. Almost as if following of the advice all my doctors and physical therapists have been pushing at me for weeks actually *worked*.

Go figure.

"It's fine," I grit, shifting further away from her. Clamping my teeth shut to quell the ache in my canines.

Our food arrives, offering a blessed distraction from the first inning. I twitch every time Jesse throws a fastball, watching the catcher sway, barely keeping his feet under him.

Goddamn it.

That should be *me*.

Bridget sets her half-empty bucket of popcorn on the floor beside her sandaled feet and crosses her arms at me. "Colt."

I know what I'll find if I look over at her. And I don't want her goddamn pity. Instead of replying, I rip another bite out of my final hot dog, chewing aggressively.

"Colt."

I resist the innate urge to give in. Give her what she wants. Give her every-fucking-thing.

I can't open my mouth, because I'll *snap*. The storm clouds of rage gathering in my gut have been percolating for weeks. I thought I could ignore them forever. Or move past the thunderous loathing.

But every sour breath of Bridget's disapproval and sympathy only electrifies the bitterness ballooning in my center. So I lock it down. Shut my expression off. Keep my lips sealed.

It never occurred to me that *she* wouldn't.

"*Colt!*"

The livid omega bark strikes me like a bag of bricks. I whip my head toward her automatically. Absolute fury pours from her features as she throws her hands up, exasperated.

"*What the fuck* is wrong with you?" she shrieks.

A rhetorical question, apparently. Because she doesn't let me answer before charging on.

"I know you're firmly steeped in self-righteous rage, but I cannot fucking figure out why! Or how!" She leans forward, her gaze furious. "*You* went out that night when you should have been asleep. *You* endangered your life and other drivers' by taking your car on the highway half-awake. *You* crashed and injured *yourself.*"

Each statement is a dart, striking a bullseye at the heart of me.

And she isn't done. Her gaze narrows, her scent sharper and thicker. "Do you have any idea how *lucky* you are? You could have *hurt* someone, Colt. Or killed yourself!"

Shame tightens, coiling around my intestines. Bridget tosses her hands in another fed-up gesture. "But instead of having some modicum of gratitude or—I don't know—some *remorse*, you shuffle around, snapping and scowling at everyone who cares enough about you to ask if you're doing what you need to do to *heal*. Because you *can heal*, Colt. You're just too stubborn and *proud* to try. Which also makes you *stupid.*"

Fuck me.

I think she might be... right?

She slumps backward, crossing her arms. "I've seen you play," she adds, quieter. "You're *great*, Colt. *Talented*. And you *love it*. Why would you throw all that away? And why are you mad at everyone else now that you have?"

Because.

Because if I let myself be as angry at myself as I should be, for *all* my failures...

I'm not sure I'll be able to live with myself.

The thought scrapes the back of my skull. A thick swell rises to block my throat, but I open my mouth anyway. Needing to tell her. Explain. Apologize?

Something.

But the crowd around us noticeably shifts, stealing my focus. I turn to find hundreds of phones facing us.

Filming.

MY *ABUELA* GOT me my first bat when I was three.

She got them for all my cousins, actually. A cheap Christmas gift—the hollow plastic sticks kids use to chase each other around.

But not me. According to my mother, I refused to put the thing down until I hit the ball off the tee. And then again.

And again.

It was weird, she said, because, as a kid, I mostly had the attention span of a squirrel. But I could hit that ball all day long and never get bored.

Not much has changed, I guess.

I still live for this moment, when I'm on deck and the bases are loaded.

Sanderson is up at the plate now. Whiffing. Because he's a decent first-baseman but a shit batter. Thinks too much.

Jesse's average sucks for the same reason: This isn't something you can analyze. You have to *feel* it.

The way the wind hits your face. How much tension tweaks the opposing team's pitcher. The weight of the aluminum in your hands.

My walk-out song kicks on, swelling over the stadium's speakers. I spin my bat and traipse up to the plate, absorbing every beat. Feeling it *all*.

And even before the breeze picks up and the rival pitcher, dressed in crimson, releases a slider, I know I'm gonna hit it.

Middle of the bat. Toward left field. Barely in-bounds.

The outfielder will think it's a foul ball. That's exactly what I *want* him to think. Because by the time he gets his head out of his ass, I'm at first.

He scoops it off the ground as I round second. I toss Adrian a glance to be polite, more than anything. I know he's going to motion for third, and I know I'll make it. I have to slide in, but—

My cleat kicks up a cloud of orange dust before knocking the base. Their third-baseman curses. And three points appear on our scoreboard.

I slink upright, already grinning as I turn...

To Bridget.

Not the dugout full of whooping teammates. Not the pack alpha clapping with his clipboard under his arm, or the crowd chanting my name.

I pivot toward the box situated just right of home plate, three floors up. There, the gold-trimmed open-air balcony frames what might be my favorite picture of all time—a yellow-wrapped, red-haired omega with curves to kill for, jumping up and down. Wearing the brightest smile I've ever seen. Cheering me on.

When our gazes touch, she brings her hands to her mouth and wolf-whistles loud enough for me to hear it over the rabid fans between us.

Of course Bridget can whistle like that.

And *of course* it's just about the sexiest fucking thing I've ever seen.

Our next player steps up to the plate. I find myself fidgeting, anxious to get back to the dugout so I can keep watching our omega. She says something to Colt, and he snaps out a reply, pouting. They continue arguing, but the sound of a bat connecting with a pitch snags my focus. I turn just in time to see the hit. *Fuck. A ground ball. I'm toast.*

I run for it anyway. The catcher tags me out, but at least our other shortstop gets to second. Adrian stills claps me on the back as I pass him. "That was a great hit. Three runs. Well done."

Maybe watching Bridget soak up his praise like a flower gulping down rain has had some effect on me. Normally, I'd shrug him off, but this time I try to let his approval past my bluster. And as it sinks in, I feel *good*.

"Thanks," I grunt. Jesse trudges past with a bat. Scowling. "Time for Jesse to fuck it all to hell."

Adrian smirks and smacks the back of my head. "Get in the damn dugout."

I try not to gag about the fact that his order doesn't even bother me. Ducking my head, I step down into the dugout. Orange sand crunches between my cleats and the fresh concrete beneath. Our bat boy hands me a water bottle and a towel.

I drop to my place at the end of the long bench, barely hearing my teammates. I'm already busy, scanning the crowd.

Jesse misses his first pitch as I find Bridget again. She's arguing with Colt in earnest, now, but he pauses her with a hand on her shoulder. His head turns to scan the crowd, though she assumes he's stopping their conversation so she can watch Jesse.

Her attention flies to the blond alpha at the plate. She cups her hands around her mouth and shouts something down to my packmate. I watch the words hit him, and he pauses. A strike whizzes past his shoulder.

Shit.

But he doesn't tense or screw his face up in concentration. He turns and points his bat right at Bridget, flashing the rarest, widest version of his smile.

The next pitch is a curveball. And *he hits it*. The ball goes screaming straight down centerfield. Jesse darts for first.

I barely see him, though. Because right after he points his bat at Bridget, the stands *erupt*. People crane their necks and point. Phones stick out of the crowd. Someone yells something, and another person calls back.

Except... *no*. They aren't yelling at each other. They're shouting *at Bridget*.

"It's the Fake Fiancée!" I hear.

My body feels like it's flipped inside out. There are jeers and boos as Adrian steps out of the dugout and glares up at the stadium. On the field, our next teammate at bat is so distracted by the ruckus that he strikes out and ends our inning.

The turnover only makes everyone rowdier. People start to throw cups and napkins. Hundreds of phones snap pictures. Adrian snarls a curse and stalks toward the umpire, pausing the game.

Jesse comes running toward the dugout, but he's out of earshot when Sanderson starts running his stupid mouth behind me.

"Oh shit," he chortles. "They're on to you guys, huh?"

I pin him with a murderous look, gritting, "I don't know what the fuck you're talking about."

Our second-baseman, Riggins, snorts, "Oh, c'mon. *Everyone* knows. It makes sense, by the way. We all thought it was weird that *you* were engaged to a *librarian*."

I growl before I can help myself, whirling to lunge. Knowing the entire time that I'm acting crazy.

This is how we all talk to each other—none of us mean any harm. Busting each other's balls is a time-honored dugout tradition. Like chewing sunflower seeds and spitting.

Hell, two weeks ago, I would have *laughed*.

Would have fucking *agreed.*

Me? With a woman who manages books and educates young people for a living? It sounds like a good joke, given who I am. I don't think I've voluntarily picked up a book in years... and I've always been more of a weekend-in-South-Beach guy than the Charity-Softball-Game type.

But now? I remember Bridget's sassy little hip-cock. Her quirked auburn brows. The flirty smile she flashes whenever she catches me checking out her ass.

And—*Cristo*—the way our bodies fit together. How she took me, and everything I could dish out, like a fucking *queen.* Even in a heat-spike.

How dare anyone think she isn't really mine?

She *isn't.*

But *still.*

Sanderson's eyes bug out as I grab his jersey. His blue-and-yellow Kings cap falls to the orange-dusted floor when he flails in my grip. I cock my fist, but someone snags my arm.

Jesse.

Fucker.

The pacifist alpha doesn't even try to apologize to our teammate or calm me down, though. Instead, he flicks Sanderson a loathing look of his own and nods at Adrian, who's busy shoving our second-string pitcher onto the field.

"We're going," Jesse says flatly. His hazel eyes flit to Riggins and the rest of our guys. A roiling wave of alpha aggression, unlike anything I've ever felt from him, crashes over the small space. Leaving it silent as he adds, "Our omega needs us."

chapter
thirty

IT'S NO BIG DEAL.

I've forced those words through my brain so many times, I barely hear them anymore. Hell, they're hardly even *words* at this point. More like mush.

The hallway system under King Stadium isn't as inviting as the new-and-improved floors above. Instead of frosted glass and sleek gold trim, the tunnels are simple, utilitarian concrete.

Even so, the cool surface feels good against my back as I collapse into it, remembering how to inhale on each individual breath. *In. Out.*

It's no big deal.

Out. In.

No big deal.

Colt is off his crutches and out of his sling, but it takes him a while to catch up to me. When I finally hear his boot hit the pavement at the bottom of the emergency stairwell, I've been hiding under the stadium for close to ten minutes.

He mutters to himself, hobbling around the corner at the end of the hall and staring daggers as I come into view.

"*Goddamn it*, Bridget! You can't run off like that! Do you know how many people I barked at to get down here just now? I didn't even realize you'd taken the service stairs until I was halfway to the—"

Colt's voice dies as I lift my face from my hands to look at him. His gray gaze traces the tear tracks streaked through my makeup. I sniffle, crossing my arms over my yellow eyelet sundress.

I was so stupidly proud to wear this damn dress. Knowing Adrian approved made it feel special. Now, I doubt I'll ever be able to look at sunny fabric without seeing the sneers of hundreds of hecklers.

Colt's eyes harden. His thick brows drop low. "Are you okay?"

I'm fine.

It's no big deal.

But those words don't even sound like a language to me anymore. So I swallow past a scratchy throat and shake my head.

Wordless though it may be, it's still a huge admission for me. Part of my brain braces for fallout. But Colt only sighs, moving to stand beside me, both of us leaning against the wall.

The surly alpha takes his hat off and smooths his fingers through his long hair, tipping his dark head back to close his eyes. "Why would you be?" he muses. "All of this fucking sucks. We never should have done it."

He's so correct; it's insane that his words hurt my feelings. When he feels me tense, he goes on, quieter, "I never liked the idea because I thought we got the raw side of the deal. But now I think this has been worse for you than any of us."

Am I having a panic-induced delusion? Colt Davis? Standing here with me? Speaking without grunting or grumbling?

Within a moment, I go from unsure of my sanity to convinced it's nonexistent. Because Colt *winces* and stretches his injured arm toward me. Offering his hand.

He turns his head next, peering over. The world stutters to a stop. Time melts away, jolting me back to the moment we first met, in Alicia's hallway.

For a second, that same connection crackles between us. His gray gaze glows with intensity.

"Why did you agree to make this deal, Bridget?" he asks, low and rasping. "That day we met... You knew how I felt. Why did you decide to put us through this?"

I remember his eyes flashing. How he staggered away from me with contorted features.

Yeah, I knew he hated my scent. But I made the deal anyway.

"Part of me thinks I did it to spite you," I admit sullenly, kicking the ground. "I needed to get out of there. And the way you stalked off was pretty insulting. The whole 'proposal' was, actually."

Colt doesn't drop his gaze. His brows knit, stormy confusion clouding his face. "Insulting? I was embarrassed as hell. Having to basically *run* to a guest room to *jack off*—" He cuts himself off and clears his throat. "It wasn't my finest hour, okay, Bubbles?"

Wait.

What?

A slow, stupid sort of understanding unfolds in my mind. "So you weren't turned off by my perfume?"

Colt's storm-tossed irises blaze. "Turned *off*? I was fighting for my fucking life. I thought my knot was going to explode."

I have to focus on his fingers cupping mine to keep my lungs working. Blinking at his half-cringe, I stagger back through my memories.

Did he ever *say* he hated it? Didn't he mutter an insult or *say* something to indicate that—?

No. No, we shook hands. Our palms brushed, a lot like they are in this very moment... and I perfumed... and he—

Oh. Oh *no.*

He... liked me?

"I was going to ask to court you," he rumbles, locking our gazes.

For the first time since that day, he smiles at me. It's a bleak, humorless one, though. "What a chump, right?"

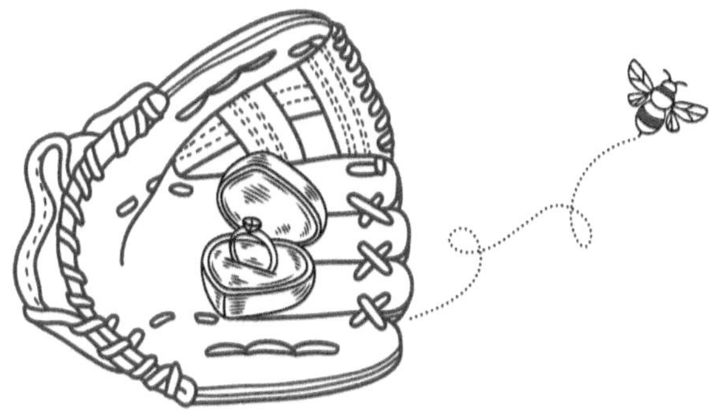

LATER, there will be plenty of time to hate myself for not trusting my instincts sooner.

This week, two months ago, last year... my Alpha's been trying to tell me all along how wrong this was.

Why didn't I listen? Why didn't I trust myself?

But, like I said, I'll have lots of time to reflect on my failure.

Right now, I'm going to *fix it*.

Dante follows me into the tunnels. That's new, too—any of the guys listening to me. Following my lead. So is the way our teammates scrambled to clear a path for me.

I'm not all that surprised, though. If I met me at this moment, I'm sure I'd get the hell out of my way, too.

When the crowd started heckling Bridget, something in my center *snapped*. And I'm not sure I want to reverse it.

The impulses roiling inside me feel *good. Right*. Even stronger than the absolute certainty I experienced when Dante, Colt, and I originally became a pack. Better than the relief when we found Adrian.

Jesus, what have I been *doing*? Letting her think every moment of kindness is part of some *scheme*? I've known Bridget was everything a guy could ever want since high school, and it's taken *this* for me to stop and realize I've never *told* her?

I stuff down my self-loathing and focus on external rage. Toward the crowd. My jackass teammates. Bridget's bitch of a big sister. Our whole stupid, messed-up society—so quick to believe she's not really ours because she works in a humble, noble profession and isn't a size two.

Dante gets more amped with every step, as well. I feel his Alpha's fury blazing hotter and higher. Leaving a trail of scorched earth behind us as we stalk down the halls.

I'm not sure how I know where to go. More instincts I've been ignoring, probably. More proof I've been an idiot.

We're both seething with outrage when we round the final corner. Our locker room comes into view, along with Colt's tall, dark-haired figure... and our omega's gloriously curvy one.

Her face is coated in dried tears and smeared makeup. The second her head snaps up, her rosebud lips drop open in shock.

I can barely process why. But then I realize—she probably had no expectation of us coming after her. Why would we miss half of our first training game for our *fake fiancée*?

Colt, at least, doesn't seem the least bit thrown. His expression is full of vehemence and lined with regret, but he doesn't so much as lift an eyebrow when he sees us. Instead, he steps to the side, away from Bridget. Making room.

Because I'm coming right for her.

She squeaks when I snap her into my arms, lifting her feet off the floor. My chest rattles, purring.

The feeling is euphoric. Bright, tingling bliss fights back the thunderclouds suffocating my lungs. I cup her head, guiding it to the base of my throat. When I realize I'm still wearing my batting glove, I rip at the Velcro with my teeth and toss it aside.

My hand flies back to Bridget's crown. Her loose red curls slip though my fingers like silk, warm and smooth.

Our omega breathes hard against my neck, her frame and face still frozen from the same disbelief I noticed before. But that only has me hugging her harder, banding an arm at the small of her back.

She starts to tremble. My purr deepens. "Shh," I soothe. "God, bumblebee. I'm so *sorry*."

She doesn't reply, but her exhales come faster and harder. Colt pivots to face us, stepping closer to our sides while Dante presses his chest to her back.

Without a speck of hesitation, our shortstop slips his hands under her skirt and grips her thighs, lifting her until she can wrap her legs around my waist. He doesn't give a shit that he has to work around my arms—he seals their bodies closer and nuzzles his face into the side of her neck.

"*Corazón*," he whispers. "Are you okay?"

Bridget's breathing stutters to a stop for a long second before she shakes her head. Just once. Just a little bit.

But Dante growls and starts up a purr of his own—uneven, rough, and deeper than mine. He scrapes his teeth along the blank, creamy skin under his lips and murmurs more Spanish. I suspect he's threatening lives, but the words don't sound nearly as ugly in his native language, and his voice relaxes the woman in my arms.

Bridget tries to apologize, but we both cut her off with dull roars.

"*Never* apologize for what just happened," Dante growls.

My Alpha snarls, putting an edge along my purr. It sends a shiver down Bridget's back. Her chest presses tighter to mine as her perfume winds into the air.

Fuck. *Yes.*

The voice in my middle loves that. Turning her on, making her feel safe enough to even *think* about sex. Especially right now.

I scent-mark Bridget before the thought registers. A small, strangled whine ekes out of her. "*Jesse...*"

God, why haven't I done this before? This should be the first thing to happen every morning and the last thing I do at night.

I'm not the only one half-crazy from Bridget's scent. Dante's dark eyes squeeze shut. He nips her again, this time hard enough to draw a whimper. He tucks his lower half against her ass, deliberately rubbing his erection there.

Bridget's perfume *explodes*, pouring out in a rush of sugared freshness so strong, even Colt grunts. My cock hardens into steel, just inches from where slick soaks through her panties and starts to creep into the pinstriped fabric of my jersey.

Shit. It's so *good.* Sharp enough to slice. So sweet that I don't care.

Let it cut me. Let it *kill* me.

As long as I get *more.*

Dante runs his palms along the outside of her thighs, audibly inhaling her scent and rasping his encouragement. "That's right. Your alphas are here now."

I feel the fight in her. The urge to protest. I can almost hear the words.

You're not actually my alphas.

This is all supposed to be fake.

It isn't fake, though.

This? Now? The fire in my body? The ache in my heart? This is the truest, deepest sort of care I've ever experienced.

In the end, Bridget sniffs quietly. "You don't have to say things like that, Dante. I'm—I know this isn't real."

We both stiffen. Dante's black eyes snap to mine, burning with angry regret. Saying all the things I'm thinking.

We fucked this up.

Colt stares at her profile like he might be able to read her mind if he tries hard enough. For a second, I feel Adrian's absence. He'd know what to say, what to do. But someone had to stay with the team and finish this damn game... and he wanted to do that for us, so *we* could fix this.

Because *we're* the ones who hurt her in the first place. It might have been the crowd today. But ultimately, this is on us.

On me.

I sigh, dropping my forehead to Bridget's crown. "Baby," I rasp, closing my eyes and drawing one last deep breath of her perfect scent. In case what I'm about to say sours it. "How can we ever make this up to you?"

LEAVE it to Jesse to be romantic as fuck when I'm too hard to remember my middle name.

Something with an H? *Hector? Hugo?*

It's not my fault, okay? There's only so much blood circulating in my body.

Jesse's question starts to snap me out of my haze, but it has the opposite effect on Bridget. Instead of quelling the desire dousing her pussy, it makes her quiver all over again. Fresh slick drips from her core as a whine pierces the air.

"I—" she stammers, then whines again. Louder. "I'm s-sorry. I can't *think*."

Neither can I. The way she smells is *breaking my brain*. And knowing exactly how perfect her curves feel molded around my body? My scent is already strong from the hours I spent playing, but it surges higher. A sticky, sweet aroma to buffer the sharp edge of her citrus acidity.

Colt growls quietly, his own salty essence answering ours. "It's the top of the sixth. The team will be back down here in an hour, and our scents are *everywhere...*"

Our scents are everywhere.

The words echo through my blank brain. Every receptor there blinks off, then blazes bright red.

Yes, my Alpha says. *Perfect.*

I'm going to claim this omega right fucking here. Let anyone call her my fake fiancée after they walk into the locker room and catch wind of how thoroughly I'm about to meld our scents together.

We'll *coat the fucking floor* if we have to.

Before anyone can move, I snatch Bridget from Jesse. Another high-pitched sound slips up her throat, but I duck my head, nuzzling her face to reassure her Omega it's still me.

That she *has* me.

The same way she did last weekend in the kitchen. One I've spent the whole week trying to understand.

I think I get it now.

She whimpers so softly, I doubt anyone else heard it. The noise hits my heart like a thunderbolt, electrifying my veins. "Come on, *querida*," I murmur, purring again. "I know what you need."

She nuzzles her cheek against the sweaty V-neck of my jersey. Clinging to me with her fingers digging into my shoulders. "W-what?" she asks.

I rub my face over her crown, turning toward the locker room. "Remember what we talked about? Wherever, whenever? Well, I need you right fucking now. You good with that?"

Her desperate whine has my mouth watering. "That's my naughty, sweet girl. Giving me this pussy whenever I want it."

I pause just long enough to look over my shoulder at the guys. "You two gonna stand out here with your dicks in your hands, or would you rather help me show our omega how 'real' this shit can get?"

I COULD TAKE Bridget in the showers. Or one of the curtained changing stalls. Or, hell, the PT room.

But I have a point to make.

I sling one leg over the padded bench angled between three walls of closet-like "lockers." Yellow leather slides against my grass-stained uniform pants, but that won't matter for long. I already have Bridget's dress unzipped.

The thought of someone accidentally walking in and *seeing* all her glorious softness edges me closer to a rut than I've been in years. Instead, I let the sunny eyelet material pool around her waist, ensuring her round, perfect ass is fully covered.

Jesse and Colt stagger in, both looking every bit as savage as I feel. My fingers rip at my jersey, tossing it aside and moving on to Bridget's bra. Her pupils expand, roaming over my exposed skin and the flaming flower tattoo branded across my chest.

I don't think she noticed the curves of black ink last time. It was dark, and she was in a spike. Now, her Omega is definitely close to the surface, but I'm pretty sure my cupcake is still in control.

I pluck her hand up and place it over my pec, encouraging her to touch me while I shimmy out of my bottoms. It's only fair since, a second later, I tug the cups covering her tits out of my way.

"*Dante!*"

God, yes. Fuck. More.

"Mm, *querida.*" I ghost my hands down her sides and catch her bright blue gaze with mine. "Is this okay? Can I take you here?"

She knows this is what I'm into, but she never actually *agreed* to let me have her any time and way I wanted. Plus, she was upset a few minutes ago. And I guess we could try—fuck, I don't know—*talking*?

People do that.

I've heard about it.

Not Bridget, apparently. She practically tackles me off the bench. I barely manage to catch her before we fall, stabilizing us with my core.

To hell with baseball. Throwing this omega around and keeping her balanced on my cock is officially my new fitspo.

Her lips are addictive. Soft, pillowy perfection. So sweet, my lungs burn, and my knot inflates.

My tongue glides along hers, sucking it into my mouth. I don't even bother looking up when Jesse's caramel-corn scent drifts closer; I just scoot us back, straddling the bench and giving him a place to sit behind Bridget.

He hesitates—and some distant, fogged piece of my brain realizes they probably haven't even *kissed* yet.

I can fix that.

Biting Bridget's lip hard enough to earn a squeak, I brush one last scent-mark on her face and flip her to face him.

There. Simple.

Like a gentleman, Jesse offers his hand to help her re-situate. When she takes it and slants a shy look up at him, his features soften.

All his concerns melt away the second he sees how self-conscious they make her. His chest rattles as he slowly moves to sit in front of her, sliding closer.

Bridget's eyes flash to our third packmate's. Colt's jaw works, grinding and clenching when he swallows hard. His hands drop to his belt. Something personal passes between them.

"I'll watch," he rasps. A compromise I don't understand, but Bridget does. Her scent brightens.

Jesse and I both groan. He slowly frames her face and bends to seal his lips over hers. They start out with a gentle brush, but soon they're eating at each other in a way that has my cock straining higher.

I hear Colt's belt tinkle. My mouth falls to Bridget's shoulder, licking and sucking the skin beside her lacy orange bra strap. I wonder if her panties match and reach under her skirt to tear them off. She shrieks indignantly when they rip.

"Stop ruining my panties!" she scolds, whirling from Jesse to me.

I bite her shoulder again. "No."

Because, *honestly*. What a ridiculous demand.

"Dante—" Her complaint shatters into a moan when my hand cups her core.

I pinch there, remembering how much she liked having her clit rubbed with her own pussy lips. Slick has soaked her whole slit, which must make it more intense because she bucks into my fingers immediately.

I slough out a growl. "Fuck, baby. All this for us?"

Bridget's moan is muffled by Jesse's mouth. When she starts to tug at his jersey, he whips it off and shoves closer, inhibitions forgotten.

"*Bridget*," he breathes, chest heaving under her hands. His eyes drop to her gorgeous breasts. His throat bobs.

This nerd, *I swear*.

I kick his shin and he jolts back into action, stroking his fingers over her arms before he moves to fill his palms with her peach-tipped tits. Bridget angles her body to encourage him.

And Jesse *snarls*.

Part of me wants to fight the fucker off. On the other hand... get it, I guess?

We've never done this before, sharing a woman. But hell, I can learn.

"Take your pants off," I suggest, nodding at Jesse's legs. His green eyes glint, understanding lighting them before they slide to Bridget's face. Reading her reaction.

She bobs her head, tugging at his uniform again. Jesse obeys, standing just long enough to shuck his bottoms and put his jersey between his bare ass and the bench.

Right. Probably should have thought of that.

Bridget's perfume floods the room in a fresh wave. I lean around her shoulder and follow her gaze to my packmate's hard dick.

I suppose it's a nice one. Our omega definitely approves, if the way she licks her lips says anything.

Fuck. I'm jealous, but it's more *compelling* than upsetting. The spark of competition just makes me want to fuck her better than anyone else ever has. Give her more than they could.

Or make sure *we* give her more than any other pack ever could.

I slip my free hand under Bridget's ass, cop a quick feel, then lift her up and forward. Her legs part to straddle Jesse. He buries his face in her neck, sucking the pristine skin.

"Fuck, Bee," he groans. "You have no idea how long I've—" He growls and purrs at the same time. Our omega turns her face into his, waiting for him to finish. Their eyes meet, and he whispers, "I've *needed* this. Thought about it a thousand times."

Bridget's pouty lower lip wobbles. The sight shreds my lungs, but the small smile that blooms on her mouth a second later heals the wound. And it isn't even directed at me.

"Next time you think about it," she murmurs to Jesse, "will you tell me?"

His eyes *burn*, shining. "Yeah," he rasps. "I promise, bumblebee."

Colt interrupts, his snarl muted but vicious. When we look over, we see him leaning against the closed door with his hand in his open jeans, peering out the window to the hallway through narrowed eyes.

"We're fine," he determines. "But we shouldn't stay here long."

Bridget nods. Her fiery hair cascades down her back when she rears up over Jesse's lap. Her red locks swing against her pale, flawless skin, the curled ends grazing the soft spot where her curves fold into each other.

And my patience *crumbles*.

Let's be real, there wasn't much of it to begin with.

Standing, I round the bench just in time to watch Bridget's face as she sinks onto Jesse's dick. She looks so *hot*—wild eyes, pink cheeks, parted lips...

Like she's reading my mind, her focus darts to my cock, bobbing inches away from her face. Jesse thrusts into her, and she cries out, reaching up to claw at my hip. She scratches my side, trying to drag me closer. When I take another step, she moans and dives for my cock.

Holy. Fuck.

My hand falls onto her head, fingers sifting through brilliant strands. I grip the strands at her nape, growling as the velvet heat of her mouth glides down my shaft.

Jesse leaves a trail of bites along her collarbone, whispering to her while he rocks his hips under hers. She's so slick, I hear every thrust.

Her tongue curls around me, licking the sensitive patch under my head. When I tug at her hair, she hums and works me in deeper.

Carajo, she's perfect. The plush cushion of her lips, the seal of her warm, wet suction. Her little moans and gasps as I start bucking my hips in time with theirs. Making sure her mouth and pussy are always full at the same time.

Lemon perfume swells while I picture putting her on all fours and spit-roasting her from both sides. *Or putting her on her back, letting her head and all this gorgeous hair hang off the side of her bed while I fuck her face and Jesse takes that sweet pussy. Watching her big tits bounce every time—*

"I'm gonna come," I realize. "Fuck, Bridget. Your mouth is too good."

She whines, plunging her lips down my shaft until they hit my aching knot. My abs harden while fire licks up my spine. Tingles echo in my balls, and the swell pumps fuller. Ready to expand and fill her up.

Bridget cries out, the sound muffled by my cock. She takes it as deep as she can, gagging on it but not caring.

My mouth falls open as I start to burst down her throat. She blinks up at me, tears streaming from her big, blue eyes. Vulnerable. Letting me use her the way I like. But also proud, with her head high.

An equal. A *queen*.

Daring me to push her further. Trusting me to know when to stop.

The look guts me. And heals me. And *ruins* me.

My heart cracks open. Tenderness bleeds behind my sternum.

And fuck—*fuck*.

Leave it to me to fall in love with a woman while she's choking on my cock.

DANTE'S dark eyes smolder as he finishes.

Warm, juicy sweetness blasts across my tongue. The taste lights every neuron in my brain. They pulse with pleasure, glowing as bright as the fervor in this alpha's gaze.

His release sliding down my throat is every bit as drugging as the caramelized scent of Jesse's skin and the low, gentle hum pressed to my breasts. His purr hitches as he watches me swallow his packmate, a growl edging his exhales.

Dante's fingers loosen at my nape, massaging the roots of my hair and recapturing my attention. I blink tears out of my eyes and pull back. He smiles, but it's not his usual cocky grin. This expression is soft. Sincere.

"You're perfect, *querida.*"

He sounds huskier than usual, but I don't have time to wonder why. Because Jesse's hands cover my hips, yanking me down his cock.

AGH!

He's *huge.*

Longer than Dante, if maybe not quite as thick. Close, though. And more than girthy enough to rub at all the nerves tingling for a knot. When he hits so deep it steals my breath, my body cinches tighter around him.

Jesse.

Jesse Locke is *inside me.* Biting my shoulder, sucking my neck, telling me how...

Telling me how *beautiful I am.*

He says it over and over, leaving the word all over my skin.

Beautiful.

Beautiful.

Beautiful.

Our position makes it hard for me to do much of the work, but that doesn't matter. He's so strong, using his bulging arms to lift and lower me into fluid rolls of his hips. The view is amazing —his broad, golden chest, his flexing abs, the flash of his teeth when he bottoms out inside me.

I whine, gushing all over his lap. Jesse hears the sound and tugs me forward, adjusting the way we're arranged until—*oh.*

Oh!

His hot, swollen knot grazes the bottom of my clit. The muscles in my core clench and flutter. "Yes," Jesse urges, bucking harder. Pressing himself into the buzzing nub begging for more attention.

A sharp sound vibrates out of me. A low, dangerous growl answers from the door.

Colt.

He's still at his post, but guard duty seems long forgotten. His closed fist flies up and down, jacking his impressive cock. I can barely see it, with how fast he's pumping his hand. But I swear I catch a glimmer studded just under the wide, ruddy head.

The wild look on his face only adds to his intensity. Veins bulge up his forearms and shaft. Pre-cum shines on his skin. He grits his teeth in a savage snarl, burning his gray gaze into mine.

"*Come on him*," he grits. "Squirt your slick all over that bench."

Oh *God*.

The tension in my core tweaks tighter. Jesse slows his pulses, letting me grind into the top of his knot with every thrust.

"Jesse! *Alpha!*"

"I'm here, beautiful," he pants. "I'm right here. Does that feel good?"

I try to moan, but it comes out as a whimper. I try to nod, but there's suddenly a lump in my throat.

They're all being so... *raw*. And wonderful. And *them*.

Will it end as soon as this does? Or will everything be different?

I'm not sure what would be *worse*.

Jesse locks eyes with me. Something gentle warms the green and gold. "I'm here," he says again, staring right into me. "I'm here with you."

I gasp to keep from sobbing. Jesse's scent spikes, his chest hitching on a growl as his cock strains. His knot expands, firm and slick against my clit.

The weight crushing my lungs pushes out another whine. All the tension inside me—physical and emotional—pops. Like a bottle of warm champagne, fizzing and bubbling bliss.

Jesse groans loudly, catching me close and burying his face in my neck as he follows me over the edge. Holding his cock deep and spraying out his release while I clamp around him on each spurt.

"*Fuck*," Colt barks. His salty scent winds into Jesse's sweetness. Both somehow complementing the overwhelming lemon perfume smothering the room.

Shit, I think, trying to clear the spots from my vision. *My scent. It's everywhere. And it's* strong, *probably not even masked at this point...*

How long until they all wrinkle their noses? Or find towels to put over their faces?

Jesse's purr melts some of the panic lining my thoughts. When I catch my breath and gather the courage to search his face, I don't find even one crease. Just his shy smile and a teasing glint in his eye.

"Still here," he murmurs, leaning his forehead into mine. "Still with you."

"FINALLY."

It's odd to have Colt say anything when I walk in the door, but that greeting is also a new one for us.

I probably shouldn't be surprised, given the very clear message they left for the *whole team* in our locker room.

Tossing my keys on the counter, I tilt a look at the three alphas huddled in Bridget's living room. "Have you three ever even heard the word 'subtle'?"

Dante keeps his bare arms spread wide—one along the back of the pink sofa and one resting on the tufted arm. His shoulders roll in a lazy half-shrug as he speaks around the apple dangling from his left hand. "Never really been my thing," he crunches.

Yeah, no shit.

Jesse's brows crouch low over his green eyes, but otherwise, he seems looser than he has in weeks. Not surprising, given the intimate way his scent and Bridget's covered the locker room bench.

Envy burns through my gut, but I stuff it down. *Patience*, I remind my Alpha. *We're letting her come to us.*

And it's *working*.

But we also had a major setback today.

I decide to start there. "The situation has been contained, but it isn't perfect. I got the footage pulled from the major networks, and security escorted any instigators out of the stadium. But it was impossible to remove everyone involved—and, of course, we have no access to their phones. It's possible someone will post on social media."

Colt exhales roughly, dropping his head back to glare at the ceiling. "This is so fucked."

I nod my agreement, scanning the room for any trace of our omega. "Is Bridget in her nest?"

Jesse nods, his whole face softening. "Yeah. She was really tired."

I haven't seen the finished room since we upgraded it, but pride still warms me. I love that her safe place is better because of me. And I'm satisfied she's finding comfort in it now.

"Poor *querida* fell asleep on me in the Uber on the way home." Dante's mouth curves up at the corners. "We must have worn her out."

I fix each of them with a serious stare. "Look, I get why it happened today—but if I *ever* find out one of you has fucked our omega *anywhere* someone else could see her, we're going to fight." I look from Colt to Jesse and end on Dante. "You will lose."

I know he believes me when he pouts instead of grumbling an insult. Colt mutters, "I didn't like it either. Made my Alpha crazy, knowing all the guys would scent her."

Mine, too. I spent the entire post-game recap with my muscles locked into utter stillness, breathing through my mouth. Seeing how many of our players had to adjust themselves after catching wind of our omega's mouth-watering lemon sharpness didn't make it any easier to hold myself together, but I was determined. Today has already been a disaster; the last thing we need is a rut.

Jesse chimes in, scratching the back of his neck while his face heats, "I liked it. Claiming her in public. I think she *needed* it."

Dante nods, as solemn as I've ever seen him. "For sure. Our girl needs more of that shit."

Our girl?

I can't help the smile pulling at my lips. "She's ours now, huh?"

"Technically, she's been ours for a year," Colt grouses, closing his eyes. "We're just saying, maybe making the deal with her was stupid. Maybe we should have just—"

"Courted her?" I supply. "Like grown men? What an insane notion."

Dante glowers at my dry quip. "Yeah, yeah, Golden Oldie. We get it. Point taken. But what do we do *now*? Just keep trying to convince her to give us a real chance?"

"If she'll forgive us," Jesse mumbles.

Dante chips back, "So we apologize first?"

Jesse looks queasy. "I think we apologize a hundred times. Then, yeah, if she'll let us, I want to court her. And take care of her during her heat. I know we agreed to leave her alone for it, but..."

I can't quite suppress the growl that builds at the thought of my little blue, alone and afraid and in *need*. I'll never allow that.

"Just because of today?"

I have to understand. This is important. I'm not going to approach Bridget—especially regarding her heat—with anything less than complete certainty. This pack has put her through enough as it is.

Jesse's face flames as chagrin burns the toasted edges of his scent. "She's always meant something more to me. I think that's why I suggested we approach her for this whole arrangement last year. I liked her; and I thought about her a lot, even though I hadn't seen her in years."

Dante chomps on his apple, staring thoughtfully into space. "I've been catching feelings for her ever since the story broke online and we came here to make it right. Before that, the only interactions we'd had were fights. I assumed we would hate each other, so I never bothered to try to get to know her. Which was *fucking dumb*, because she is incredible."

They're well-matched, actually. I didn't expect it, but something about Dante's quick fuse and Bridget's sharp mind—yes, they fight. But they also have similar inner flames. And warmth for the people they care about.

She and Jesse connect on their own separate level. Both kind souls who feel deeply. Bridget does her best to hide her emotions under humor—Jesse papers over his with politeness and people-pleasing. But in the rare moments they both strip those veneers away and really *look* at one another, they're a perfect fit, too.

Bridget and I are still building our dynamic. So far, she's everything I ever dreamed my omega would be. Brilliant, gorgeous, and sassy, with a heart big enough to love a whole pack and then some.

It's more than that, though. Some innate trust that I don't understand. She's always looked to me. Searched for my approval and praise, even when she didn't realize it.

Those moments are sacred to me. This beautiful girl, needing *me* to be proud of her. There's nothing more I could ask for.

Which just leaves—

"Colt."

We all turn to our fourth packmate. "We want to apologize to Bridget and try to court her, but the decision has to be unanimous," I say. "If her Omega thinks she's fragmenting our pack, it will devastate her. We can't do this unless you agree."

He scowls, shifting in his seat, briny scent growing saltier. He captures my gaze, intensity darkening his. "You guys weren't there with her today. You didn't see her face. An apology isn't going to fix everything."

Silence swells through the room. Colt sighs, sitting forward with a wince before adjusting his injured shoulder. His gray gaze snaps to Jesse and Dante before sliding back to mine. "She doesn't believe in any of this, Adrian. We've never given her any reason to, but I think there's more to it than that. We talked a little, after the whole thing, and..."

She's fragile.

He sees the same thing I do: under all her confidence and wit, Bridget has a big heart. And it's been wounded.

"We'll start with an apology," I determine, straightening. "You three will plan it. And dinner tonight. Bridget said she likes to grill on the weekends, so we'll start there."

If the itch under my skin wasn't climbing to a screech, I'd probably chuckle at the way they all snap upright. No one argues, though, so I push my luck and toss Bridget's new car keys at Jesse. "Might as well gas her car up and get it washed while you're out."

Colt mutters complaints about his "useless" leg, but seems completely steady as he pushes to his feet. Dante shrugs and throws his apple core into the kitchen trash can. "I know how to make grilled fish tacos."

Jesse laughs, throwing Dante a shirt. "Since fucking *when*?"

Dante pulls the tank top on. "Since forever. I just didn't want you fuckers to know I could cook and make me do it."

Colt shakes his head. "God, it's sad how much that tracks."

They all snatch their wallets and keys off the island, bickering among themselves over who has to "ride bitch" in Bridget's "clown car." Dante loses rock-paper-scissors and tries to nab the keys from Jesse, who dodges a headlock as the side door slams shut behind them.

I shake my head, but my usual glimmer of fond amusement is absent. Instead, my Alpha feels a little too satisfied knowing they're all out of the house.

Way too satisfied.

Fucking hell.

No, I tell myself. *Not today. Bridget's been through enough. She has to rest.*

The urge to rut needles at me. I grit my teeth, threatening my Alpha with a mental image of our team's new rut facility. We had them built into the latest section of the stadium—if I'm actually about to lose my shit despite all the blockers I take, I need to go there immediately.

The voice in my middle gives the equivalent to one of Colt's grumbles. Some of the pressure wrapped around my chest dissipates. I wait another moment before starting toward the hallway.

I'll just knock on Bridget's nest door, I decide. *To let her know I'm home if she needs anything.*

It's an idea my Alpha and I agree on. He wants to see the nest. I want to hold my little blue and look her in the eye after what she went through today.

But—*goddamn it*—the scent of lemons and sweet cream filling the air in Bridget's cramped hall is strong enough to knock me back a step. The moment it curls in my lungs, my vision fogs.

I grit my teeth, reaching out to steady myself. On the second inhale, my blunt nails gouge the wall's cheerful white paint.

My cock and knot are rock-solid before I have the chance to blink. When I do, a bleary film blurs over my gaze.

Shit. I'll never be able to drive back to the team's facility if I can't *see.*

And I *will not* put this burden on Bridget.

I haven't proven myself to her yet. My pack hasn't apologized properly for the harm they caused. We haven't courted her or had an opportunity to really *spoil* her—

An image of Bridget relaxing on a mountain of pillows while I worship her pussy with my mouth sends a tingling ache through my canines. They pulse along with my knot, begging.

Rut. Knot. Bite. Claim.

But I have to deny myself.

I have to...

Take her. Sink your teeth and knot into her. Never leave her side.

No. I need to—

Make her mine.

I'M NOT SAYING that having the most beautiful nest in the whole world makes what happened today okay.

But it *helps*.

I lie back on a mountain of pillows, admiring how their textures somehow complement each other. The big fuzzy magenta one, a small velvet cushion in marigold. The enormous ruby-silk blanket my Omega wants twisted around my legs for some reason...?

Psycho.

She's so extra right now. As if having an epic meltdown in public and getting railed by two alphas in a locker room wasn't enough of a day for her.

I told you: crazycakes.

All I want to do is lie here and stare at the soft pink light glowing inside the glass-bubble chandelier until I fall asleep. I'm too anxious to even scroll through my phone, knowing it's only a matter of time before I stumble over a clip of *The Incident*.

But despite the exhaustion aching in my muscles—*why did I run down twelve flights of stairs?! And who knew being bent between two alphas would be such a test of endurance?*—and the heaviness weighing down my heart, the voice in my middle will not *shut up*.

She nudges me. *The Alpha. We need to go.*

"Go *where*?" I grumble out loud. "We're already in the same house, you loon."

She isn't backing down this time, though. *To the Alpha!* she shrieks. *We have to go <u>right now</u>!*

I blow out an exasperated breath, glaring at the ceiling. "They left a minute ago. I heard them walk out."

Not <u>all</u> of them, she argues.

And, *damn it*, I know she's right. I may or may not have been paying close attention to the sounds of doors and the number of footsteps. I know there's still one alpha in the house.

Adrian.

I caught his musky, manly leather scent about five minutes ago, wafting through the closed door to the hallway. Given that I can still sense his essence even though I heard him walk away...

He must have lingered out there for a few minutes.

Was he thinking about knocking? Trying to talk to me? Or see my nest?

A small burst of perfume escapes at the thought, so I bottle it up and chuck it away. Into the dark, shifting sea full of similar notions—all the things I don't let myself think, sealed tight and bobbing on the tide. Messages in bottles.

It's no big deal.

The words are ink on the water. Oily and dark. Never quite

sinking in. Distracting me long enough for my Omega to shove closer to the surface.

We don't have time for this, she insists, bouncing frantically. *Our Alpha needs us now. Now, now, NOW.*

The last word edges close enough to a bark—I instantly pop upright and start to move. Then catch myself and huff, "Enough! This is insanity! If Adrian needed me, he'd tell me!"

The desperation in my middle yawns into a chasm of despair. *But our Alpha!* she cries. *He's hurting.*

And—curse my big, stupid heart—that does it.

I stagger to my feet and climb out of the now-recessed nest mattress, onto the perfectly dark-teal padded platform around it. Muttering chastisements at myself, I swipe at the dried mascara crusted around my eyelids and smooth my hair back.

The chemise I have on isn't exactly modest—but at least this nightgown has cups sewn into the lining. If nothing else, my nipples won't be on full display.

Unless he wants them to be.

"I cannot believe I'm listening to you," I grumble in reply, trudging to the door. "I swear, if this man isn't in the middle of a heart attack, I'm going to find some sort of Omega muzzle. Or invent one. Or, hell, I'll take suppressants again. I don't even care at this—"

Oh. Hoooooooly shit.

The smooth, warm scent of leather heats my throat, smoldering until it strikes my lungs and gives off a shower of sparks. Every tired muscle in my body braces. My nipples prick, my head swims.

Adrian's scent is thick enough to permeate every particle in the entire hall. And he isn't even here. He's...

In my bedroom.

My trembling core starts to melt, the tension between my hips gelling. I feel my face and chest flush. *He's not in* pain... I realize.

Except, the noise that echoes behind the closed bedroom door *sounds* wounded. The muffled, tortured groan skitters down my spine, landing in the wetness puddled between my thighs.

Oh God.

OH GOD.

What do I do?

I could run, I think frantically. *But would he chase me? Why do I want him to chase me? Or I could call Emma and ask for advice? Then again, her alpha rutted her into a literal tree and the HOA would have my ass if I let Adrian ruin one of their sycamores...*

"Bridget?"

His voice is unlike anything I've ever heard. Heat layered over softness. Concern with a jagged edge of command.

Light over dark. Or dark over light? It's hard to tell which part is in control—the Adrian I know or the Alpha he's clearly battling every bit as hard as I fight my Omega.

If he's so far gone, he shouldn't remember my name, though. *It must be the rut blockers*, I realize. As the only non-athlete in the pack, he's also the only one in my house who's allowed to take suppressants. They *should* keep him from tipping all the way over the cliff, but...

The strangely layered voice speaks again, this time landing closer to Adrian's usual timbre than the Alpha's growly demand. *"Bridget, you have to go. Run, omega. It's not—"* his words break off on a ragged gasp *"—it's not safe."*

Okay, well. That definitely shouldn't make me horny.

Horn*ier*.

Alright. Okay. Think, Bridget. I could run, but he might chase. I could call the guys to come back, but they may end up brawling.

Is it possible for me to slink back into my nest and lock the door? Leave him to sort himself out?

"Please, omega."

Shit, that's his Alpha. Pure desperate pain, covered in a steely layer of authority. I move toward the door automatically, coming close enough to hear him slough out a tattered snarl.

When he speaks again, he's wrestled some control. "I should have left, Bridget," he pants. "Never meant to—" he pauses, his voice dropping back into a growl "—put this on you. Go. *Now.*"

Have I mentioned I'm abysmal at doing what I'm told?

It's usually not an issue with this man. He speaks, and some innate piece of me wants to please him. It's so seamless—him caring, me obeying—I've never questioned it. Now, though...

He's hurting.

I remember the way I felt when he helped me through that heat-spike at the nest store. How my clothes scraped like nails. The painful snap of nerves, overstimulated and under-stimulated at the same time.

Motherfucker.

I'm going in there, aren't I?

❤

EVERY LIGHT in my bedroom is off. With the sun setting behind the tree line in the backyard, an orange glow bleeds through the blinds and casts everything in fire-trimmed shadows.

Including Adrian.

I've never seen him without his nice clothes, I think dumbly. Because the man I know is somehow always dressed to impress, even in joggers and the Kings cap he had on during today's game.

Was that really today?

My thoughts are laggy and bumbling. No matter how hard I try to focus, every cell vibrating within my body only wants to zero in on the hulking, hewn figure standing next to my bed. Holding onto the white frame for dear life.

Lord, there's so *much* of him. Wide, sculpted shoulders. A thick chest and abdomen, stacked with rows of ripples under tan skin. A dusting of chest hair to match the thick black locks slicked back over his crown.

I've never seen them rumpled before, but the few strands hanging over his forehead are almost as appealing as the silver glinting in his short beard. And the thin trail leading from his navel to his—

Oh.

Holy fuck.

That *knot.*

I've never seen one so big. It swells as high as it is wide—perfectly proportional to his cock and six-foot-four frame and the bulging quad muscles flexing as he roots himself in place.

He's... *magnificent.*

While we're here, you can call me King.

He looked like one in his bespoke suit, but now?

He isn't just a king. He's a god.

And I think I'm the sacrifice.

My pussy squeezes at the thought, wet muscles contracting around the empty ache burrowing between my thighs. Adrian senses my perfume before it hits, his wild eyes flying to the outline of my pantiless mound under my thin chemise. The band of aqua rimming his enormous pupils thins.

Shivers of adrenaline streak down my spine. It snaps straight, pushing my breasts out. Adrian's attention leaps to the lace and cotton straining around my boobs. His tongue slowly traces his lower lip as he stares.

Oh, dear GOD.

I'm in danger.

If he chained me up right now, I'm pretty sure I'd sob with gratitude.

A whine slips up my throat. Instead of making him wilder, the sound seems to ground him. He visibly inhales, his cut chest expanding on a deep breath.

"I told you to go."

That *voice*—the rough snarl layered over his deep velvet rasp. I tremble, pouring more perfume and slick. My head automatically falls forward, the prickle of shame I work so hard never to acknowledge scraping deep inside my belly.

I know my perfume isn't perfect. I know it's sharp and acidic. Just like I know this nightgown shows more dips and rolls than it "should."

I don't care, usually, because I can't. This is who I am. I won't hate myself because of a set of standards I didn't consent to, can't meet, and don't agree with.

But, damn.

He is a *King*.

And I wish—just for a second—that my body could fit into the box labeled "Perfect Little Omega." Delicate flower. Petite and fragile and sweet-smelling.

"*Omega*." His Alpha is winning. Adrian's next command cracks into a bark. "*Come to me*."

My feet stagger forward, closing the distance between us. Adrian holds himself still, tendons bulging in his neck from the effort. His jaw pops.

"*Naked*," he commands. "*Now*."

I can barely gasp. My lungs alternate between shriveling into crumpled balls and swelling so full of his leather richness, my head swims. A choked whimper catches halfway up my throat as my fingers curl in the hem of my chemise, peeling it up.

Oh God, oh God, oh *God*.

I wasn't nervous with Dante or Jesse—not even in front of Colt. So what is it about *this* alpha? Could it be the intent way he watches my every move? The absolute *power* rolling off him? The fact that I find his frayed self-control *insanely sexy*?

No, my Omega whispers, every bit as scared as I am. *He's our alpha*.

She keeps *saying* that. Like she doesn't understand that this is all *fake*. Just a plan we made to *survive*. Which makes Adrian a means to an end.

Except he's not.

How could he be, when he gazes at every curve of my pale,

soft flesh like it's art? A masterpiece he's waited *ages* to have in his sights. Or a feast he's been anticipating, starving himself over for weeks.

I get it. Because I can't quite keep my eyes off his cock.

It strains higher when my nightgown clears my chest. I toss the fabric aside, squaring my shoulders. Fresh lemony slick slips down my naked, dimpled thighs.

This is me. He doesn't have to like it.

A fanatical gleam fills his gaze as it roves across my breasts, then lower. He glides that scorching stare over my belly, my hips, the dents dotting my upper thighs. When it lands on my mound, he licks his lower lip again.

His body is stiff and tight as he jerks a nod toward the bed, never looking away from the moisture glistening on my skin. "*Lie down.*"

My body moves to obey automatically, but a panicked whine squeaks out of me. Adrian freezes. His black eyes snap to my face as I stumble to the right and catch myself on the edge of the mattress.

With both palms bracing on my bow-covered comforter, I know he can still see my profile when my eyes fall shut. "Please," I ask, hoping he's aware enough to hear me. "I—I'll do anything else you want, but please, don't go down on me."

He doesn't move. Not an inch. Not a breath.

His answer is a low, ominous growl.

"Please," I try again, irrational wetness pooling in my eyes. "It's... it's not good, okay? You don't want it. I promise. Just... let me present for you instead?"

There's something strange happening between us. The more I spiral, the steadier he seems. Solid dominance seeps into the air, flexing around me. His growl rolls into a deep, roaring purr.

"No."

No? Like, no, he won't let me off this hook? No, he's going to taste my sour slick anyway? Or no, he doesn't want me to present?

Every thought bumps up the panic pinching my lungs. It wars

with the instincts reveling in his purr, telling me to relax. My vision swims.

When Adrian speaks again, he almost sounds like himself. "I'll never do anything you don't want me to do," he vows.

The floorboards creak under lumbering footsteps. Hard quad muscles and warm tan skin press into the backs of my legs. "But I want to see your face." His Alpha puts a rough edge to his final plea. "*Please.*"

Swallowing, I blink the tears from my eyes and turn my head. His masculine beauty hits me all over again—the sculpted planes of his face and chest. Those chiseled shoulders and hips. His bulging arms and cock.

One of his hand lifts. I watch him pause, checking to make sure he's in control before he reaches for my hair. With a smooth flick of his wrist, all my disheveled waves are wrapped around his forearm and gathered between his flexing fingers. He tugs just hard enough for my pussy to pulse.

"*Turn over.*"

A whine tumbles out of me as fresh slick dribbles from my core. Adrian growls loudly, dropping his chin to watch. My clit throbs, swelling as if his gaze is a caress.

He waits, gently pulling my hair until I rotate. Then he wastes no time—the hand in my hair goes to my nape as his free arm bands under my ass. He maneuvers us to the middle of the mattress and drops his hips, fitting his hard length against my slit.

I shriek, my head falling back as the underside of his cock rubs against the nub at the top of my folds. There's so much *slick*—I barely feel any friction between us. Until he rolls his body and his cock slides all the way up and I get his knot.

It's big enough to cover *everything* from my clit down to my opening. The tight ring of muscle spasms against him, betraying how my inner walls clamp on air. My lower half automatically jumps, angling to press tighter to his.

His answering snarl is vicious and thrilling. My nipples ache, beading into hard points. He bends and runs his nose over each, inhaling my scent.

Rutting alphas can't torment or tease—they only *take*. A fact I'm grateful for when Adrian groans and buries his face right between the two peaked mounds. His brawny hands envelop the creamy skin jiggling around his face, his fingers plucking the tips.

I cry out, bucking against his big body. His answering growl drips approval. "*My omega,*" he husks, biting at the top of my right breast, sucking a mark into my skin. The sight leaves me gaping, my core pulling taut—almost as if I could come from watching him put a claim on me.

The emptiness scraping my insides starts to hurt. I can't contain my next whine—and the tone of it makes Adrian *feral*. He drops to his elbows, lifting and tucking his hips to *impale* me.

Shit. Fuck.

"Alpha!" I scream, clawing his bare, flexing shoulders while my eyes roll back.

Adrian roars, his body snapping into a rhythm that leaves me breathless. Deep, merciless shoves, a rotation of his hips, and a ruthlessly quick retreat. He does it over and over and—

Oh. *Oh!*

A haze settles across my mind. My brain blinks blank. Instincts take over, muscles deep inside me tugging and melting. Making way for the enormous knot sliding along my clit with every thrust.

I start to come. Adrian groans, the sound so tortured and desperate, my body reacts on impulse, wrapping my limbs around him. Pressing the top of his knot into my pussy.

I scream as he snarls. The room explodes into glitter and stardust and heat. It's *everywhere*. Buzzing inside my lungs, tingling to my toes, wrapping around my heart. Positively *filling* me.

I've never felt so stuffed. Stretched to my absolute limit, with so much cum spraying into my depths, I swear I feel it warming my belly.

My inner walls flutter and *squeeze*, a second climax tackling me before I've regained my footing from the first. Adrian growls deeply, his teeth flashing as he finds the side of my breast and bites hard enough to bruise.

Our bodies arch in unison, pleasure snapping through us in an endless loop. He spurts, and I tweak tighter. I clench, and he comes *again*. He gives me everything he has—and I *take* it.

"So good," he gasps, hoarse. "So fucking good, baby girl. Taking my big knot like you were *built* for it. Give me *more*."

I'm not sure how long I last after that. The world fades into a fog of exhausted bliss, leaving me with one final, delusional thought.

Maybe this king doesn't need a delicate flower.
Maybe he needs a queen.

"HI!"

No.

Not today.

I mean, I'm never big on random fans walking up to us and shoving their Sharpies in our faces. But especially not now. I haven't washed up since before the whole chasing-an-omega-through-King-Stadium thing, mostly because there are traces of Bridget's scent on my clothes...

And, okay, I probably need to shave eventually.

I reach out and grab a razor off the shelf of hygiene products displayed on the grocery store's aisle cap. Dante runs right into my back, huffing, "*Qué carajo?*"

Thank God for Jesse and that Cotillion class his mom stuck him in. Our golden-haired packmate manages a smile for the small blonde grinning at us from the other end of our shopping cart. "Have we met?"

The woman—an omega for sure—giggles like he's hilarious, waving a dismissive hand at his "joke." Before he can reply, a tall, super-built alpha with rich brown skin and a buzz cut steps into view. He holds up two tubes of tomato paste and shakes his head. "Zane swears there's a difference between the one that costs three dollars and the one that costs fifteen, but honestly, I'm not—"

The guy slips his arm around her waist and then pauses, realizing we're watching. "Oh. Hello." The alpha eyes his omega, tucking her closer. "Friends of yours, sweet girl?"

The omega *beams*. "This is Bridget's pack!"

The dark-eyed alpha snaps up straighter. Stony mistrust covers his face as he glances at each of us. Judging.

He offers Jesse a stiff handshake. "Micah Beckett," he says, brusque. Then looks over at the blank space next to Jesse. Like he's pointing out the absence of our girl before he introduces his own, "This is our pack's omega, Emma." The edge in his eyes grows sharper. "You know—Bridget's best friend?"

Ah, shit. We should have *known* that.

Emma claps, unbothered. "It's sooooo nice to finally meet you!" she trills, bouncing forward and snapping Dante into a hug.

I've never seen our shortstop balk from a hot woman before, but he visibly recoils, holding his hands up and scrunching his nose.

Relatable. This omega's cinnamon scent tickles my nostrils, too.

Micah seems unaffected while his girl smothers each of us. He has the settled air of a bonded alpha, which makes sense given the marks on Emma's neck and the fact that he doesn't growl while she hugs other men.

Micah's expression hardens further as he looks us over. He must share whatever he's thinking through their bond because his omega's excitement visibly dims. "I told you that's just a rumor," she hisses, smacking his chest with the back of her hand. Then, with an apologetic grimace at us, "Bridget told me what happened at your game today."

Micah's shrewd. He clearly doesn't buy our story or his omega's insistence on its validity. He meets my eye, his face nothing short of disdainful. "And we saw a video online."

"*Carajo*," Dante curses. "Already?"

He moves to whip his phone out but Jesse stops him. "We'll talk to Adrian about it when we get home."

Our little exchange must look suitably pack-like to this guy because some of the tension leaves his shoulders. His expression turns thoughtful—and for some reason, he addresses his next statement to me.

"We've been wondering when we'd meet you," he says. "It seems strange that we haven't; Bridget's over at our house a lot." Deep disapproval colors his eyes. "But I know she's home alone even more."

I'm used to burying the shame I feel by piling rage on top of it. The fury that she knew I liked her and made this stupid deal in the first place. The disgust I trained myself to harbor over the way she gluttonously spent all the money we sent her. The nauseous pang of hurt that socked my gut every time I recalled waking up after my accident and finding out she never came.

But she didn't know I liked her.

And she spent our money on everyone *but* herself.

And after what she endured today? I've gotta be honest—even the whole not-visiting-me-in-the-hospital thing feels pretty thin.

Because we've hurt her, too.

Would I have shown up for her two months ago? I want to say yes, but, at that point, I wasn't concerned with much aside from baseball and finding the bottom of as many bottles as I could.

Either way, this bonded alpha glares at me like I'm a complete fucking failure.

Like I said: this guy is *astute*.

I could have stopped our deal that day if I'd just swallowed my pride and given her the benefit of the doubt. And I'm sure I could have asked how she spent our hard-earned money anytime I wished.

I *wanted* to stay mad—because as long as I was angry, I didn't have to feel responsible for missing my chance with her. So I did everything I could to protect my anger.

Instead of protecting Bridget.

Emma chatters with Jesse for a few minutes, mentioning something about getting all of us together soon. I barely hear a word, replaying the last few months in my head. The Becketts wave and walk away, leaving me in the middle of the market with my packmates.

Thinking we'd better come up with one hell of an apology.

"YOU HAVE to let us in eventually!" Jesse points out.

"Yeah," Dante adds. I *hear* him chewing through the door. "We *sleep* in there."

God help us, but even *that* makes me growl.

I've never felt this way about anyone or anything. My Alpha might be strong when it comes to dominance, control, and sheer force of will, but his possessive impulses were never so severe.

It's hard to be too worried about it while I'm buried in my omega's body.

We've been locked together for about two hours. Long enough for me to roll us under the covers and work the tangles out of her hair. I'd moved on to massaging her back and arms when I heard the guys come in.

Bridget didn't bolt the door earlier, but the others must sense how strong my scent is. Instead of busting in, they've gathered in the hall, listening to my half-growled record of events.

My gaze traces Bridget's sleeping face. Regret burns in my gut.

"Twenty minutes," I grind out. "I just—give me twenty minutes."

They mumble among themselves and shuffle off. Sighing, I drop my forehead to our omega's crown.

The motion finally rouses her. She stretches alongside me, freezing when she feels the intimate way our bodies are tied.

My eyes fall shut as shame swirls through my stomach. "I'm sorry, little blue."

Bridget's scent—which was sweet and almost *creamy* a moment ago—sours. Almost *violently*. My arms gather her closer, purr deepening. "Do you hurt, sweetheart? Was I too rough?"

She doesn't answer, turning her face into my shoulder. My teeth grind. "Fuck, I'm so sorry, Bridget. I know how big my knot is. I had plans to ease you into taking it, if you wanted to. I never thought I'd lose my shit like that."

One big blue eye opens, scrolling up to my face. It looks like she's trying not to cry. I use the arm under her to feel around for my phone.

I'll call a doctor to come right away if she's in any pain. Maybe there's a shot they can give me to unlock us—

"It doesn't hurt," she whispers, shifting against me, blinking while her mouth trembles. "Y-you feel good."

Fucking hell. I'd rip my own heart out to wipe that look off her face. "What is it, baby?" I murmur, gathering her close and rolling onto my back so she can sprawl on top of me. My hand finds her head, petting and pressing her cheek against my purr. "Tell me and I'll fix it for you."

If anything, my promise only upsets her more. Bridget's

breath hitches—a quiet sound that lodges a dagger in my throat. "It—It's nothing. I'm f-fine."

But she isn't.

I hum and hold her tighter, dropping my face to her hair and scent-marking her with slow, thorough nuzzles. Her stuttered breaths break into quiet sobs.

Fuck. Everything I do seems to upset her more. *She may need space. Next to impossible, like this. And it will hurt like hell, but I'll give her as much room as I—*

"*No!*" she pleads, sinking her nails into my sides. "No, please. Just one m-more minute."

To hell with this.

I flip us in one quick move, putting her under me and framing her face in my hands. "Bridget. *Look at me.*"

Pained, embarrassed eyes fly to mine. Tears spill over her lashes, slicing at my heart. I drop my forehead to hers.

God, she's beautiful.

I tell her so. "Pretty blue," I purr, "tell me what's wrong."

She squirms, remolding the soft curves padding my torso. My cock kicks inside her, and she stops. Surprise flits over her features.

I try for a smile, curving the side of my mouth despite the tightness in my chest. "Nothing I can do about that if you're going to keep rubbing this sexy body all over me, little blue. We might be locked together until breakfast as it is. My knot isn't going down anytime soon."

I expected her to be distressed by that notion, but instead, Bridget relaxes a bit. She sniffles, shaking her head. "I'm sorry. I'm being so stupid."

I feel my face crease as a low rumble cuts her off. She glances down at my growling chest in confusion. "No one calls my omega stupid," I explain, "Not even *you.*"

She inhales sharply, more moisture gathering in her crystalline eyes. "B-but seriously, I know this is dumb."

I watch her mouth form the word, realizing we haven't truly

even kissed yet. *Christ.* She has nothing to apologize for, but I sure as hell do.

My lips graze hers slowly at first, testing her reaction. When her scent brightens, I hum and take her mouth. She gives in so sweetly, opening for me the way flowers unfurl for sunshine. I taste her, licking deep and swallowing her soft moans. Memorizing each one.

When we break away, my knot is harder than it was before, but I don't care. I'm not going anywhere. At the moment, I'm not sure I could stand having her on the next pillow, let alone in another room.

I tuck her face against my throat, massaging the nape of her neck. She melts into my purr, gusting a sigh.

"I didn't mean to get upset," she whispers. "I just—this is my first time being knotted by someone I know."

I feel the words crash into my mind and crumble. I stare down at the broken pieces, unable to understand.

Did she just say she's never been knotted by someone she knows?

I'm not sure what part of that statement is the most horrifying—that she's gone *without*, or that, whenever she's had what she needed, it came from a *stranger.*

My arms gather her closer. I do everything I can to keep my voice level. "Tell me why."

She shrugs, hiding her face against my chest. "I... It just felt too intimate for casual hook-ups. My boyfriends in college were both betas. And when I went to clinics for my heats last year, I didn't know the alphas or meet them beforehand. That's how it works in most places. To keep things, uh, *clinical.*"

I volunteered in those sorts of facilities for years, so I understand. Hell, at the time, that policy made perfect sense.

But now? Thinking about *my* omega being alone and in pain? Needing a knot and having to take one from a *stranger*?

Did anyone hold her or purr for her after?

Jesus. It feels like I'm having a heart attack, but cardiac arrest would probably hurt less.

"That will never happen again," I vow. To her. To myself. To the goddamned universe. *My omega will never need anything from any other alphas again.*

Bridget doesn't soften or open her eyes, but she tucks herself closer and shudders through a quiet sigh. "We'll see."

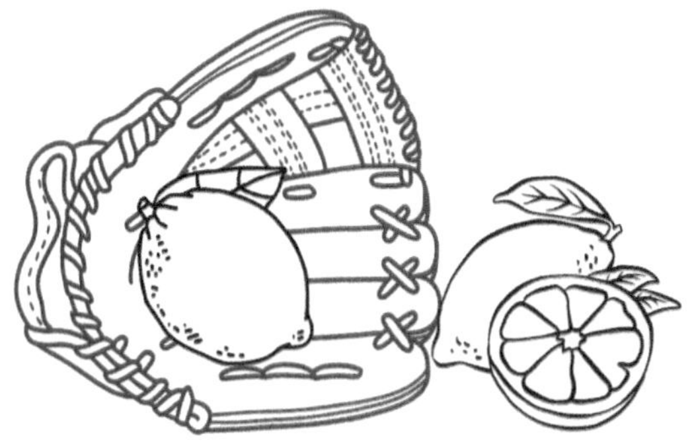

chapter
thirty-eight

BETTY

If you buy me any more kale, I will burn down your house.

BRIDGET

Please. As if you could find a lighter in those junk drawers of yours.

BETTY

Bring me margarita mix instead.

I just DoorDashed two bottles of tequila.

BRIDGET

I probably won't make it out of the house until this afternoon.

I'm a little... tied up at the moment.

Wait.

Bitch, if you know how to DoorDash WHY am I going to the store for you?

BETTY

Can it, red. You love me.

Besides, you have that fancy little car now.

"DO YOU THINK SHE *LIKES* PEONIES?"

Jesse's quiet, concerned question is the first thing that reaches my consciousness. My mind lags, wondering who he's talking about.

You! my Omega whines. *Because he's—*

I give her some *severe* side-eye. <u>*You*</u>, I correct, *could have gotten us mauled last night. <u>Hush</u>.*

Before I can react to her needling or the nauseous seethe in my middle—*are they really talking about* me?—I hear a grumpy huff.

Colt.

"She paints daisies and sunflowers all over her shit. Probably should have started there."

My stomach flips. *Oh. They <u>are</u> talking about me.*

The solid warmth under my body shifts. The motion is slight, but it's just enough to remind me where I am... and why I can't move.

Oh.

My.

God.

Adrian is knotted inside me.

And *hugging me*?

Heavy, muscled arms tighten around my back as the quietest purr I've ever heard rumbles beneath the chiseled chest pressed to my cheek. "She'll love the flowers, Jesse," Adrian says, his echoing reassurance tickling my ear. "Where did you get the food from?"

Dante mutters with his trademark petulance, "I *cooked* the food. *Cristo.* You dumbasses act like making toast is rocket science. It's literally bread, guys."

I have to smirk at that one—it sounds like a comment I would make.

You know what, querida? I think you and I have much more in common than we think.

It's true, even if it makes no sense. How can two people be alike when they don't have anything in common?

I'm not sure, but as I crack one eyelid open to the sight of Dante rolling his gaze to the heavens, my half-smile blooms into a giggle.

The annoyance falls off his face, replaced by true excitement. His onyx irises light as he bounces onto the mattress beside us. I reach my hand out, but Adrian growls.

The pack alpha clears his throat almost immediately. "Apologies," he grunts, pressing his hips to mine to remind me that he's sealed inside my body. "I may need to ease into the guys touching you, little blue. My Alpha is feeling very—" He pauses to suppress a snarl "—possessive."

As if punctuating his point, the thick cock locked inside my pussy somehow ticks fuller. I bite my lips, torn between a breathless laugh and an even-more-breathless moan.

Adrian's fingers find my nape and sink into my hair—a now familiar, deliciously dominant gesture he used repeatedly throughout the night. The alpha gently tilts my head back, gazing down at me with arresting azure eyes.

Gratitude and tenderness shine under his simmering heat. But the obvious pride floating in the Mediterranean-blue pools is what undoes me.

"Good morning," he murmurs softly. The smallest crease touches his thick brow. "How are you feeling?"

I finally manage a breath and a nod, squeaking, "I'm good. Are *you* okay?"

Adrian's always beautiful, but never more so than when he truly grins. The wide flash of his white teeth dazzles me. I blink through a dizzying swoon as he replies, "I'm perfect. Because I had the perfect omega."

Butterflies flutter in my lungs. I exhale and can't remember how to get more air in. Instead, I just stare into him, absorbing the giddiness that comes with his approval.

Adrian's smile melts into a sincere expression. He hums a quiet, "Thank you, sweetheart," and kisses my forehead.

Before I cobble my melting mind back together, a rude rumble starts in my stomach. I cringe, and the pack alpha's lips curve against my hairline.

Colt interrupts, grouchy as ever. "She has to *eat*, Adrian. Goddamn."

Hmm. Is that concern *I hear in Salty's voice?*

Surely not.

Dante smacks their leader's bare shoulder. "Yeah, dude. If you won't let me touch her, you at least have to make sure she's *fed.*"

I crane my neck to glance over at the guys. Jesse meets my eyes first, flashing his shy smile as he holds up a wooden tray full of plates. A laugh bubbles out of me. "How am I supposed to eat like *this*?"

Adrian drops his hands to the mattress, leveraging his strength to haul us both upright. He balances me on his lap, stifling a groan when the position seats him even deeper within my clenching warmth. His knot rubs at the tingling nerves buzzing around it. I shove down a whine, my fingernails biting into his shoulders.

For a moment, I tense at the rush of perfume and slick that pour out of me. But the scents of the entire pack instantly swell to meet mine. Caramelized sugar. Sea salt and ocean air. The rich musk of leather. Mango succulence.

"Easy," the alpha under me determines. "I'll feed you."

Before I can properly process how insane that image is, Dante *harrumphs*. "You got her *all night*!" he cries. "*I* want to feed her."

Jesse opens his mouth to protest, holding the tray just out of everyone else's reach, but the saltiest alpha's snarl cuts through their argument.

They all seem just as shocked as I am. We blink at his intense expression, waiting. He exhales hard, squaring his shoulders and hobbling to the edge of the bed.

He darts his wary gray eyes at Adrian, then sets his hand on top of the rumpled lavender duvet. Right over my lower back.

Shock reverberates through my body, but there isn't time to *feel* it. A storm crackles in his irises, demanding my complete focus as he roughs out, "We want to apologize to you, Bridget. As many times as you'll let us."

"OH. MY. GOD."

I nod at Emma's open-mouthed expression, pouring myself another margarita. "Yeah, I know."

She sits forward, balancing on the rickety lawn chair beneath her. Ignoring the teal metal's creak, she darts a covert glance at Betty's screen door to make sure my neighbor is still occupied inside.

"You mean, while I was at the market trying to find Zane's whole vanilla beans and McKinley's organic dog treats, you were getting *rutted*?" she hisses. Her lower lip pops out. "No fair."

I roll my eyes. "Yeah, because you *never* get rutted."

She sips from her frozen glass, shrugging. "Only like once a month. Or twice, during hockey season."

"Shut up." I laugh, kicking at her with my bare foot. "This is serious, Em. We have a *situation* here."

My best friend blinks big green eyes, tilting her head until her blonde bun flops over. "You mean the pack alpha snapping into a rut because you left your scent all over their team's locker room —*which*, BY THE WAY, we *will* be discussing, young lady—or the fact that he was barely able to let you walk across the street just now?"

I grimace. *Oof.*

The girl has a point.

Adrian *did* keep me in bed for nearly eighteen hours. Then he accompanied me to the grocery store, unloaded all of Betty's food for us, and still only *just* managed to leave me on the front porch. Where the whole pack can *see* me from their gym setup in my open garage.

Every time I glance over at my driveway, I catch at least one of them staring.

And almost always the Boss.

My King.

Oh, will you stop?! I shout internally. *You're the reason we're in this crazy mess!*

Emma follows my gaze and snorts when she catches Colt paused mid-curl, squinting at us. "Girl, I don't care what you say about fake engagements. *Look* at them!"

Jesse goes to walk from one side of the room to the other, stealing what he thinks are sneaky glimpses over at Betty's porch. Only he misses the free weight Dante just dropped to the ground and trips over it.

A giggle tickles my throat before I can help myself. They *are* sort of falling all over themselves. And Adrian hasn't looked away *at all.*

He's been on the phone from the moment I sat down, too. He keeps checking something on the screen and barking into it. If he's not glancing at his cell, his solid gaze remains fixed on me. Unapologetically.

Emma explained that it's a "pack alpha thing." Apparently, the first time Knox knotted her, his packmates had to start a snowball fight with their leader to get her out of his greedy clutches.

Of course, in her case, the four alphas were scent-sensitive to her. And fighting to become her bonded mates.

"It's all just... for show," I mutter, unsure who I'm reminding —Emma, my Omega. *Myself...*

Em leans forward, making a big show of craning her neck back and forth. "Yeah, babe, I don't see any paparazzi here. Just four men who can't keep their eyes off you. Not to mention their *scents*—holy night, I can smell them from here!"

I didn't notice that—considering their essences are all over me —but she's right once again. Their scents have swelled and drifted over to us.

"They're working out!" I argue.

Emma glugs the last of her drink and winces. "Yeah, with big boners."

Outraged, I turn to see if she's—*wow. Completely correct.*

All except for Colt, of course. But, then again, he's sitting on a bench. It's easy to see the impressive tents at the front of Dante and Jesse's shorts... and I catch the hard length under the seam of Adrian's suit easily enough, too.

My Omega snaps to the surface. *Growling.* She *hates* the idea of any other omega seeing "her alphas'" goods. Especially Emma.

She's been insanely jealous of my bestie for over a year. It was one of the main reasons I had to get so ruthless with the voice lodged in my middle.

It wasn't *Emma's* fault that she got everything I secretly dreamed of having. Back before everyone went out of their way to make sure I knew just how insane those hopes were. That it was better not to hope at all and get good at being alone.

I'm the best at that now.

When it's time for them to move on, I'll be *fine*.

Emma senses the way my insides shrivel when my scent sours. She offers a sympathetic frown, reaching for the pitcher Betty left behind when she went in search of more ice.

"Isn't it possible this could all work out?" she asks, pouring another round. "I know it didn't start out that way, but maybe it *is* real after all. Or maybe it *could* be."

"It definitely isn't," I snap back. But images of the weekend—the good, the bad, and the devastating—swamp my brain.

Colt's fingers finding mine for a few minutes. The way his gray eyes burned. *That day we met… You knew how I felt.* And this morning. *We want to apologize to you, Bridget. All of us.*

Then there was Dante, gripping my chin while I swallowed his delicious flavor. His heaving chest and husky voice. The fanatical joy in his eyes. *You're perfect, querida.*

Jesse, so thick and warm inside me. His hands cupping my face while he scent-marked my forehead. *Still here. Still with you.*

And the pack alpha. Needing *me*. Rutting *me*. Knotting *me*. *I'm perfect, because I had the perfect omega.*

No. It definitely isn't real…

But maybe it could be.

"I **KNOW** he's a huge pain in the ass, but we have to be *nice*."

Am I proud of the way I more-or-less snuck up on Bridget, just to hear her talk to her cat? Not particularly.

But when I saw her, standing on her back patio with bare feet and a yellow ribbon in her hair, I'm not sure how much actual decision-making occurred.

I saw her, so I went to her.

I suppose it was inevitable after thinking about her all day at practice. Waiting impatiently for the moment I got to come home.

Because that's what this is. What Bridget has turned this tiny house into.

Home.

I feel it in every colorful corner. Her essential oil diffusers. The over-watered plants that I suspect survive simply to bask in all the attention she gives them. Even her collection of penis figurines. And the fact that they take up shelves in the foyer, the bedroom, the living room...

She always has music playing, too. Colt claims it drives him crazy, but he must be napping in her room. Maybe that's why today's selection is more mellow than her usual songs—an acoustic playlist instead of pop music.

Bridget continues scolding her cat, who gazes up at her like she's explaining the secrets of the universe. The plump tabby meows, and a smirk curves her lips. "Yes, but he's *trying*, Munchies. No more hissing."

Since we moved in, her pet has taken to each of us with varying degrees of success. He clearly respects Adrian the most, which is typical when an alpha has as much innate dominance as ours. If our leader is present, the creature slinks around with big, hopeful eyes, waiting to be noticed.

He spends the most time with Colt during the day. So much so, the two of them now bicker like an old married couple. My packmate will grumble and grunt, and Munchies mewls in reply, arguing with the bastard.

I'm starting to suspect the creature may have figured that Colt needs emotional support, because he also insists on cuddling up next to him at all hours. The fact that Colt *allows* it makes me think he might need a hell of a lot more than emotional support.

At first, the cat approached me with simple curiosity, until I started feeding him pieces of my food. Now, the second I sit down to eat, he thinks we're best friends.

Which can only mean Dante is the tabby's Designated Asshole.

Munchies doesn't seem thrilled about being nice to my pack-mate. He lets out a deeper, bellowing meow. I smirk as I step onto the house's back porch.

"I'm with him."

Bridget startles, darting wide eyes up at me from her crouched position. Munchies speaks again, then winds through her legs. The combination sends Bridget falling backward.

I try to lurch forward, but her cut-offs hit the porch floor just as my fingertips graze her bow-tied ponytail.

"Shit," I mutter, dropping to my knees. "I didn't mean to scare you. Sorry, bumblebee."

She huffs a laugh, shaking her head. "It's no big deal. I shouldn't have my music so loud."

She has great taste, though. The song pumping through her porch speakers happens to be a cover of one of my favorites.

"I don't know," I hedge, smiling as I help her to her feet. "There are definitely worse things to come home to than good music."

Her eyes sparkle with the most genuine kind of delight. "You like this song, too?"

I nod, my fingers twitching at my sides. Aching to reach for her. For some reason, this particular tune makes me want to sweep her into the sort of slow-dance teenagers usually do around gymnasiums.

My Alpha nudges me. *Hard.*

When I listened to him at the nest store, it made everything between us more complicated, but what happened in the locker room changed things. And last weekend, when we apologized...

I promised to be better. *Do* better.

So I offer her my hand. "Dance with me?"

She blinks at my palm, her scent sweetening and dimming. Shyness creeps into the tilt of her chin. "I—Seriously?"

Ignoring the pang of chagrin that socks me in the stomach, I curl my fingers. More earnest than I've ever been. "Seriously."

Her screwed-up features are adorable—pinched somewhere between wariness and wavering. She places her hand in mine anyway, leveling me with a deadpan stare. "Slow jams only."

"Deal." I laugh, relieved. The extent of my dancing skills is exactly this—rocking back and forth.

Bridget doesn't seem to mind, though. As I pull her flush against my front, her cheeks blaze the sweetest peach to match the sudden burst of her sugared lemon perfume.

I nearly smirk at how much taller and longer-limbed I am. She has to stretch to loop her arms around my neck, while I settle my hands at the small of her back without any effort at all.

When my thumbs graze the strip of bare skin between her denim shorts and her tight white T-shirt, a shiver streaks down my spine. It lands in my groin with a hard tweak to my knot, but I ignore it, focusing on her delicate, makeup-less features. Memorizing freckles and flecks of blue.

She catches me, darting a narrow-eyed, suspicious look into mine. "What?"

My shoulders bounce under her forearms. "You're beautiful, Bee."

She snorts. "The way you say that is so funny. Like it's..."

A fact. Because it is. "It isn't *news*," I chuckle, "I've always thought you were beautiful."

A purr starts in my chest when her eyebrows leap up. She automatically huddles closer to the vibration under my navy T-shirt, pressing her cheek to my sternum. That one soft touch feels like a lightning bolt, impaling my heart. My rumbling deepens, and she hums, sounding much more relaxed.

"The last time I heard this song, I was at prom," she muses absently. Like she's simply sharing her thoughts as they drift, though I wonder if she might be changing the subject on purpose.

But that statement unlocks a memory. Likely the reason I asked her to stand here and sway with me in the first place.

She's right. They *did* play this cover at prom. And I remember the exact moment... because I was looking at *her*.

"You were beautiful that night, too," I recall. "In your light green dress."

I'm not usually one for clothes, but I can picture her exact outfit in my mind. The lightest jade silk, pooling at her waist and flowing down to a pair of strappy gold shoes. White tips on her nails. Peach warming her cheeks. A sprig of tiny pink flowers braided through her auburn hair.

Bridget slowly raises her face, gaping at me. "Y-you remember *my dress*?"

I shake my head. "I remember *you*. Standing on the side of the dance floor. With a book."

The shy version of her smile makes a brief but breathtaking appearance. "Yeah, I'm the genius who brought a book to prom and then wondered why no one wanted to dance with me."

That isn't even half-true, I realize. Because—"*I* wanted to dance with you."

The words shouldn't be a revelation. But if the last month has taught me anything, it's how little I knew my own mind back then.

Of course I wanted to dance with Bridget. Why else did I spend half of my senior prom stealing glances at her? Ignoring the burn low in my belly every time I spotted her standing alone?

Her face freezes, arrested between shock and doubt. "You... did?"

I press my palms flat to her back, hugging her closer and bending to scent-mark her forehead. Staring right into her skeptical blue eyes. "Yes." My brows crease as another memory materializes. "I actually think I ended up getting in a fight with my date because she accused me of being 'distracted.'"

My mouth flashes into a grimacing smile. "Oops."

Bridget giggles, and the quiet, warbling sound is enough to make any level of humiliation worth it.

"Oh boy. If I ever run into Brianna, I'll have to apologize."

I'm glad *she* can recall my date's name, because I wasn't one-hundred-percent certain of it. When I cock a teasing brow at her, Bridget sniffs regally, tossing her ponytail back. "What? It's not like I made a voodoo doll of her when I got home that night or anything."

The offhand way she says it makes me think that's *exactly* what she did. And the swooping ache in my stomach tells me I might have just fallen in love.

THIS IS GETTING PATHETIC.

I stare down at the neon-pink Post-It, re-reading my note.

Noticed you were taking protein bars to school for lunch, cupcake. Made you some empanadillas.

Okay, so there's also rice in there. And a salad. And *two* cookies.

I may have texted my mom and begged her to send me some old family recipes.

Sue me.

I scowl at the sticky note, wondering why two sentences doesn't feel like enough. What am I going to do? Confess my love for this woman on a Post-It?

...

I mean, I *could*...

I poise the Sharpie I pilfered from Bridget's desk over the paper, panic, and end up drawing a smiley face.

Jesu Cristo.

I'd kick my own ass if I could.

Before I lose my shit and stuff the whole meal down the garbage disposal, I snatch the glass container, slam the sticky note on top, and put it in the front portion of the fridge's top shelf. She'll see it when she wakes up and preps the coffee—now that she knows Colt takes his with milk, she leaves a little pitcher of it out for him every morning.

I'm debating whether I should pile leftover lo mein or a fresh pint of rocky road on top of the *feelings* seething in my stomach when I hear shuffling. Jolting upright, I hit my head on the inside of the refrigerator's frame. Again.

A girlish giggle bubbles behind me. "Fancy meeting you here, slugger."

Bridget waits for me to straighten and watches me rub the back of my head before she glances around the kitchen. "Have you been cooking?"

Yeah, for you, corazón.

"Nothing major," I reply, shrugging.

"It's almost one a.m.," she chuckles. "Were you that desperate for a snack?"

I flash a smile, stepping closer. *Drawn* closer. By whatever this aching, simmering *tug* under my lungs is. "Always, cupcake."

She rolls her eyes at my joke, but I notice they don't bounce back to mine. Her mouth thins, and her voice dries out. "Any particular reason for that nickname?"

I should have known she would ask eventually. She made Adrian explain his endearment for her. And Colt's slightly insulting moniker. Jesse calls her by her first initial, mostly...

I grimace, rubbing at the back of my head again. "You don't like it? It popped into my head when we first met at your sister's.

Because you looked fucking *edible* in that nightgown. And you had all those clips in your hair, like sprinkles..."

Dios mío.

Surprise flares across Bridget's face, arching her brows. But her lush lips quirk up. "You see hair barrettes and think of *sprinkles*?"

I nod, lifting her into my arms and nuzzling a thorough swath of my mango scent along her bare shoulder. "Mm. I saw *you* and thought you looked *delicious*. You know how much I like to eat, *querida*."

That line earns me her full, beautiful laugh. She winds her arms around my neck and leans her forehead into my temple. "Fine. 'Cupcake' is officially approved. Add it to the list of ridiculous things I put up with around here."

I don't think I've ever made it through one of our conversations without grinning. "You?!" I bleat indignantly, hiding my amusement against her pretty hair. "What about *me*? These nighties are *a problem, querida*."

I grasp handfuls of the silky red fabric, pushing it up her thick thighs as I bend to scrape my teeth over her other shoulder. When fresh, bright citrus warms the air, my teasing voice drops into a growl.

"Careful. We might wake the others..."

Bridget snorts, unbothered. She leans back to show me her smartass smirk. "Why? Are you going to cry loudly while you pine for me?"

Another grin flickers across my lips. "No, but when I put my head between these gorgeous thighs and turn *you* into my midnight snack, you'll be moaning loud enough to wake the neighbors. And maybe even Colt."

Bridget's legs twitch, her knees squeezing my hips. I start to smile wider, but then her scent shifts—creamy lemon, only it's... wrong?

Not *wrong*. Just... less right?

My brows fold. "I'm only teasing," I say, smoothing the nightgown back into place as I try for a flirtatious look. "Unless you're into it, then I'm totally not kidding at all."

Bridget's answering laugh trembles. Her smile looks as bright and pretty as her mussed red hair, but her eyes crease in a wince. "It's all good." Her lips slowly drop into a straight line. "We should probably stop making jokes like that, though. Since we're not, um..."

She usually isn't shy around me. With Jesse, sometimes. But those two act like they're in middle school passing notes.

And, yeah, okay, so I just put a note with a smiley face in her lunchbox, but—

"We're not what?" I ask, gripping her hips and sliding her to the edge of the counter. Fitting our bodies together, wrapping my arms around her waist.

She quivers slightly, blinking blue eyes in the dim light from the stove. "We're not... real?" she whispers.

Her scent turns again, but I don't need to sense it to see the emotion written all over her face. *Sadness*. And something way too close to *pain*.

She *wants* us to be real, I realize. But she doesn't *believe* we are.

Why would she? Because I couldn't keep my hands off her during her heat-spike? Because I fucked her mouth in a locker room? Because I spent a whole goddamn year being the worst fucking fiancé to ever live?

Mierda. I suck at this. And I'm not used to being bad at things.

Oh God. Am I bad at being bad at things?

Like I said: pathetic.

But I don't quit.

I didn't quit when my mom and I moved here all alone and I didn't know how to speak English. I didn't quit when we both had to work two jobs while I played baseball in high school just to afford my equipment and the club team's travel. I didn't quit when the previous Kings' manager told us we had to get our shit together or find new jobs.

I have a feeling Bridget isn't a quitter either. That's why she's here, right? We were her ticket to the life she wanted, and she took it.

Which means Bridget isn't just smart and funny and sexy as hell.

She's *brave*.

And she deserves alphas who have the same courage she does.

My chest vibrates, purring while I snuggle her curves into the hard planes of my torso. She feels like heaven—my scent reflects how hard my knot is, just from the press of her belly against my groin.

"What do I have to do," I murmur, "to make it real?"

I don't think I've ever been this serious about anything. Bridget must see that when I refuse to drop my gaze. She finally breaks our staring match to take in my expression, carefully searching for my angle.

She thinks I'm joking or flirting. But I wait, keeping my eyes on hers.

Her flashes flutter. "I... don't know."

It isn't the answer I wanted, but it's one I understand. And, shit, I respect her for it. She doesn't know what I can do to prove myself—and she isn't going to send me on some wild goose chase while she figures it out.

Cristo. I think I just fell even more in love with her.

"Can you let me know?" I ask, bouncing my gaze between her swirling ocean irises. "When you do?"

Her answering nod is slow. Disbelieving. "Um... y-yes?"

She's cute like this, all flustered and uncertain. I flash a smile, wrapping my arms tighter around her. "In the meantime, I'm going to do everything I can think of to show you. And you're going to let me. Deal?"

Part of me expects a snort or another eyeroll. Instead, her gaze turns glassy as she nods again. Her voice drops to a whisper. "Okay."

Victory swoops through me. My blood heats, and my chest

lights. *All because this woman agreed to let me try to convince her that I care.*

My euphoria crashes as quickly as it climbed. I might be thrilled, but she seems genuinely lost. Maybe even a little afraid.

Does she think I'll hurt her?

When she darts a shy glance into my eyes, I see the truth—she thinks I'll hurt her *feelings*.

Pain stabs into my chest, carving at my heart. I gather her into my bare skin, purring deeper. The clock on her wall hits one a.m. and an unfamiliar emotion crowds in behind my longing.

Concern.

"What got you out of bed, *corazón*?" I mumble, nuzzling her hair. "Did you want something to eat?"

Bridget shudders but plays it off as a hair toss followed by a head-shake. Her arms move slowly, hesitating as she slips them around my body. When I lean closer, pressing my erection into her soft stomach and scent-marking her crown, she practically digs her nails into my back.

"Shh," I whisper, my chest rattling deeper. "It's alright, *querida*. Tell me what you need. Let me get it for you."

Bridget swallows a whine. Some of the tension in my lungs eases. "My heat is in a few weeks," she mumbles. "And my Omega is *freaking the fuck out* when I'm alone in the nest."

God. The idea of her Omega panicking about *anything, ever,* makes that new anxiety combust into full-blown panic. My Alpha *hates* it. Which is crazy because, historically, he hasn't cared about much aside from pussy and power.

But our omega is *sad.* And he wants me to *burn the world to the ground.*

Chill, dude. We can just cuddle her. No arson necessary.

I give Bridget one final squeeze, then step back just enough to sling her into my arms. She squeaks, clinging to my neck.

Like I would ever drop her.

Psh.

Doesn't she know who I am?!

Just to prove a point, I balance her in one arm long enough to smack her ass. "Relax, cupcake. We're having a slumber party."

She starts to stammer, but exhales when I walk past her nest. I hate that the thought of letting us in there stresses her out. *I need to ask Adrian what the hell to do about that.*

In the meantime, my purr kicks higher, and I hold her closer, silently reassuring; I might be a dick, but I'll never go into her nest without an invitation.

Instead, I use my shoulder to shove into her bedroom. Adrian and Jesse are sharing the big bed tonight. It wasn't their turn, but Adrian's Alpha has had a hard time sleeping anywhere else after his rut—and Jesse's couldn't handle being away from so much of Bridget's scent.

My omega needs to be snuggled, though.

These assholes can move over.

Adrian is on the left. It doesn't escape my notice that he's sleeping with the pillow our omega used during his rut. Lying flat on his back—clutching it to his chest like it will fill the hole she left there.

Beside him, Jesse sprawls on his stomach with his head burrowed into the bed. Like he fell asleep trying to bury his face in whatever bits of Bridget are embedded into the mattress.

Carajo. Pathetic one and all, apparently.

I stomp to Jesse's side of the bed and knee him in the side. His snore stutters. "Wha—Bridget? You okay?"

He turns his head toward the woman in my arms, sensing her stress before he manages to get both eyes open. The second he sees us, he jerks upright and reaches for her.

Ha. As if.

I hold Bridget closer and nod at the bed. "Move over. We're coming in."

Jesse's mouth drops open in amazed disbelief. Like someone just woke him from a dead sleep to tell him he won the lottery.

"Really?" he asks, bleary green eyes brightening. He shakes his head at himself. "I mean—of course! Come here, Bee. Do you want to be between me and Adrian? Or me and Dante?"

Adrian rouses, grunting as he rolls onto his side. He doesn't open his eyes. "Dante? Is Bridget okay?"

"She's here," I reply, bouncing our omega. "Say hi to Daddy, cupcake."

Adrian bolts up before I finish teasing her. His arms also open automatically. "Bridget," he says, rising to his knees. "Come here, baby girl."

Fucking pack alpha bullshit. As soon as he flexes his dominance, I find myself handing our omega over. I would be more pissed off, but the total bewilderment on Bridget's face is enough to gut me.

God, she really doesn't think any of us actually give a shit, does she?

Un-fucking-acceptable.

I have to fix it.

"We should get Colt," I think out loud.

Jesse blinks at me, thrown, and Bridget starts to protest, but Adrian meets my gaze. Something solid passes between us—an understanding. An agreement.

Respect, I think.

"Good idea."

Jesse springs up. "I'll get him."

"For *what*?" Bridget asks, her whine prissy and adorably. "I'm *fine.*"

Jesse growls every bit as fiercely as Adrian and I do. Our omega's expression flicks back to astonishment as Adrian folds her against his chest and starts to pet her hair. "Little blue, your scent is practically gone. You're *not* fine." He purrs for her. "Were you lonely in your nest, sweetheart?"

Bridget stiffens. "Not *lonely*..."

She must realize how weak her protest sounds, because she doesn't bother finishing. Instead, she turns her eyes to Adrian's, and I admire the way they sparkle in the low light from the hallway.

"I-I'm sorry, alpha. I tried to sleep by myself, but with my heat coming—"

Adrian nuzzles his nose against hers, humming. "Baby girl, I can barely sleep without you either." He lies back, propping Bridget's pillow under his head and gathering her in his arms. "Luckily, there's a very simple solution."

Our omega cuddles into his side, slanting a lost look up his torso. "What is it?"

Adrian cups his hand around her cheek. "From now on, you'll sleep in here, with whichever of us you want."

She blinks, absorbing his words. Her answer is halting and unsure. "But what if..."

You leave me? You remember this isn't real? You find an omega whose scent is better?

I brace for any of the questions written on her face. But in the end, she says, "—I want all of you with me?"

Jesse reappears with Colt limping behind him. To my surprise, the long-haired bastard doesn't look nearly as grumpy as usual. His gray eyes are tired, but they seek Bridget out immediately. When he finds her, he lumbers to Adrian's side of the bed and sits next to them.

I don't know if he's ever touched Bridget before, but he stops himself with his arm extended halfway toward her. His jaw pops as he pushes through whatever halted him and rests his hand on her shoulder.

"Hey, Bubbles. You okay?"

Adrian's right; Bridget's scent is practically down to nothing. It doesn't make sense. I'm used to lung-carving, mouth-watering sharpness when she's upset. Not this subdued sort of sourness.

I bend to nose at her neck, trying to find her. Missing the way she usually cuts and then stitches me back together again. She freezes up when I scent-mark her bare shoulder. Perfume rises off her so fast, it makes me dizzy.

God, it's *perfect*. And *terrible*. I've never experienced anything like it. So sweet and delicious—so sharp it feels like inhaling glass.

We all breathe deeper, our chests throbbing on labored pants and jagged purrs. Trying to understand. Trying not to rip our own lungs out or pounce on her.

Carajo. It's *everything*. And it's *killing me*.

What is *happening*?

Bridget senses our bewilderment. The serrated edges of her scent slice deeper as she starts to squirm, trying to get away from Adrian.

"*Omega*." Our alpha's bark halts her halfway out of his arms. She sniffles, and I *die* inside, seeing the tears that cling to her lashes. Before our Adrian can continue, I tackle Bridget onto the mattress and roll her into my body.

"*Corazón*, none of us are *mad*. Or disappointed. You want us to fight to sleep next to you? I'll arm wrestle any of these fuckers. Except maybe Colt. He and I can Thumb War instead."

Jesse slides into place behind her, dropping a soft kiss to her head. "It's just me, bumblebee. Don't be embarrassed about your perfume or needing us close by. We love your body. And we want your Omega to feel safe."

Is she upset that she's perfuming? Jesse seems to think so. She's done that so many times, though. Why would it upset her now? Or at all?

Anxiety is fucking exhausting, by the way.

My restless thoughts wind down as Adrian nods, pushing solid reassurance into the air. "They're right, little blue. We'd all love to sleep with you."

Bridget glances at Colt, waiting for him to reject her. But he only nudges Adrian's shoulder with a mild eyeroll. "Move over, Boss."

The little smile on our omega's face isn't nearly as luminous as her usual grin, but when she sniffs and hides the curve of her lips against my throat, I decide it just might be my favorite anyway.

BRIDGET NAMED THIS CHAT THE ADVENTURES
OF SALTY & BUBBLES

BUBBLES

Steal any good books lately?

SALTY

No, but I borrowed* three this morning.

BUBBLES

I'm going to make you a library card

SALTY

For our bookshelves?

BUBBLES

Oh now they're OURS, huh?

Is this also OUR cat, Salty?

Because last night it looked like you'd already
fed him dinner.

SALTY

Don't be ridiculous.

I fed him two* dinners.

"GODDAMN, MOTHERFUCKING, COCK-SUCKING, PAIN-IN-THE-ASS—"

Two years ago, I was on *Sports Illustrated's* list of the World's 50 Sexiest Athletes. Number 26.

Dante was number 14, and Jesse refused to pose. Of course.

I wonder what they'd say if they could see me now. Slumped over a shower chair. Cursing at my own two feet.

"Tell 'em, Salty!"

Bridget's cheer halts my steps.

Ah hell.

It's fucking Wednesday again, isn't it?

Sure enough—it's four p.m. and Bubbles is standing in her bedroom doorway, arms crossed under those big, pretty tits.

I hate that my eyes drop to them a second after absorbing the smirk on her face. But ever since the locker room, my Alpha has been on an absolute rampage for the woman.

My obsession was already a dark, dangerous sort of thing. Now that I've seen her naked? Riding Jesse with her hair spilling loose down her back, and her face full of rapture? Swallowing Dante's cock like she would die without his cum?

Yeah.

I've ended every day since with my fist wrapped around my cock, coming all over my own damn hand. Sometimes twice. Before getting into the crowded bed with one of my packmates wedged between Bridget and me.

If any of them knew the kind of dreams her scent gives me… pretty sure Adrian would have put a rush on the new, Alaskan King-sized mattress he ordered.

This damn dress isn't helpful. It's white, for one—high-lighting the peachy blush on her cheeks and the freckles dusted over her collarbones. Everything she wears is so damn *cute*, too; all trimmed in frills, tight to her torso, with a loose skirt swishing around her dimpled knees.

I love the way her red hair curls over the straps.

I love her bright, amused eyes.

I love that we've spent two hours every afternoon this week, reading in her living room. Pretending we're not peering at each other over the tops of our books every other minute.

"Did your therapist just leave?" she finally asks, wandering closer.

I nod, hoping my voice won't sound as hoarse as it suddenly feels. "Yeah. He took my boot off and had me humping this damn walker for two hours. Then gave me a new shower chair and told me I was strong enough to get it into the bathroom by myself."

I kick the plastic chair under the front of my walker with my good leg. Showing her how the rubber gripping pads refuse to slide across her bedroom carpet. With a scowl, I ignore the mortification burning my face and sigh, "But this thing keeps getting caught on the edge of the rug."

Bridget frowns in mock-earnestness. "The cock-sucking rug?"

Funny girl. I chuckle before I can help myself. "Yeah."

"Heard he was a motherfucker," she goes on, smoothly stepping in front of me and dropping her purse onto the bed. "Here."

In one move, she plucks the chair off the floor and carries it into the bathroom. I hear the shower trickle to life a second later.

"Try to hurry up, will you?" Bridget teases, slanting me a bright-eyed smirk as she reappears. "I subbed for one of the art teachers during my free period, and there's glitter all over me."

With a grunt, I try to straighten and push the walker aside, but my right shin shrieks in protest. *Fuck.* Taking the boot off was long overdue, but doing my workouts without it was more painful than I expected.

Bridget is at my side before I can blink. Her cool fingers twine around my forearm, helping me find my footing.

I want to argue. Shove her away. This is humiliating; having to re-learn how to walk without the damn boot on. Trying to fix the body *I* broke with my own stupidity. The fact that I could have done this weeks ago, but I was too stubborn and depressed to try.

There's no hint of judgment on Bridget's face, though. Just her beautiful features, full of optimism and something that looks a lot like pride. Or at least close enough for my chest to ache.

What would it be like to be the sort of man Bridget could be proud of?

What wouldn't I give to find out?

"Well, now I get what the shower chair is for," she teases, true warmth suffusing her expression. "It's probably harder to balance on wet tile than it is on the cock-sucking rug."

Another involuntary laugh snags in my throat. "The worst part is trying to wash my hair and scrub my back. Makes my shoulder hurt like a bitch."

Bridget pulls a face, glowering at me. "Salty, I swear. What the hell are we going to do with you?"

I know what I *want* her to do with me, but now would be a supremely inconvenient time for an erection. Despite the feel of her smooth skin and frilled straps under my palms. And the way the humid room amplifies her scent.

Like everything else in her house, it's tiny. Brightly colored, in shades of green and magenta, with half-dead plants hanging over the toilet and in front of the little warped-glass window.

Bridget waits until I reach over and grip the countertop for balance. Then she steps back—

To untie her dress.

Without a care in the world, she pulls the bows at her bust loose. The whole top instantly pools at her waist, leaving her tits in a soft, strapless tube of tan fabric.

"What are you doing?"

The words come out of my mouth, but not in my voice. They sound too rough and throaty. Closer to a growl.

"Helping you," Bridget chirps back, shimmying out of her dress entirely. Standing in the foggy, colorful bathroom in nothing but her white panties and her strapless bra. With dark red hair curling over bare shoulders and grazing the outlines of her nipples.

"In your underwear?" I ask, because if she takes those *off*...

Holy God.

She snorts. "Unless you'd like me to go change into a bikini, yeah. These cover just as much, and they're bound for the hamper anyway. I'd rather not make more laundry if I can help it."

Before I have a chance to pick my jaw up off the floor, Bridget steps into the shower. She ducks under the steamy spray, letting it wet her bra, panties, and loose curls. They all stick to her pale, fleshy curves, rousing my cock from hard to rock-solid.

Fuck *me*, she's gorgeous.

Did she pick this green tile on purpose? To highlight just how lustrous her hair is? And how those pretty freckles paint constellations over her creamy, glistening skin?

Of course not.

But here we are.

I can't control the need to drift into her orbit. Count those freckles up close. See if she's truly gotten *sweeter*, or if my mind is playing tricks on me.

Plus, I really do *want* her help...

With a grunt, I shove my sweats down and toss my T-shirt aside. The edge of her shower stall isn't high enough to cause any issues, but I'm still not totally steady when I step over it. Bridget's hands find my right arm, gently clutching it until I'm inside.

It's exactly the sort of thing that shrinks my balls. I brace to find pity on her face, thankful that at least my boner will be a thing of the—

Blazing hell.

There isn't one crumb of sympathy on Bridget's pert features. Instead, I find her shooting a glare at the slippery tile under me... followed by a very interested, very *blatant*, look at my boxers.

Specifically, the bulge I'm trying to will away.

Bridget runs her tongue over her lower lip, blinking at it. "Er, um." She finally shakes her head slightly, blushing peach as she drops my arm. "Here."

She gestures at the new shower chair I hate so much. But it's difficult to summon my usual animosity when there's a gorgeous woman peeping at my dick.

Not to mention her perfume.

Fuck me hard.

It's so heady; after a deep lungful of the tart, sugared humidity, I feel nearly drunk. Which may explain why I don't notice her lathering her hands until they land on my shoulders.

Sliding down the front of my *chest*.

My knot jerks, visibly shifting the obvious erection pressed into my white boxer-briefs. Bridget doesn't notice, because she continues her work, soaping my pecs and kneading her way back toward my neck. When her thumbs find the tension pulling at the base of my skull, I groan.

Shit.

I freeze. So does Bridget.

Until... she perfumes. And *moans*.

It's a small sound—garbled by her efforts to swallow it and the hiss of the showerhead. But the second I hear it, my body *reacts*.

My cock springs out of the slit in the front of my boxers, brazenly standing upright. The tip shining with a mixture of the metal pierced there and my pre-cum. Bridget jerks behind me. Her scent swells into a cloud of bright, sweet bitterness.

I can't contain the growl that rips up my throat. But before I can put together *words*, her slippery hands start another slow glide down my front.

This time, she doesn't stop at my ribs—she goes all the way to my abs. Gently swirling her fingertips over every single ripple. Tingles of bliss trickle to my knot, my cock twitching in the steamy air. I draw a sharp breath, flooding the air with enough salty sandalwood to combat her lemon sugar.

Or actually... *complement* it?

Our two aromas mesh well, but I barely notice. I'm too busy with how Bridget traces my soaked waistband as she steps to my side, putting herself at the perfect level for me to turn my head and press my mouth to her soaked panties....

I won't, though. No matter how tempting I find the thought of denting her thick hips with my fingertips and *smothering myself* between her thighs.

I tip my head back, searching through the fog and water for her face. It's torn between lust and indecision, and I don't like the way she shifts on her feet. The flash of chagrin that moves through her eyes.

What could she possibly be embarrassed by? I roam my eyes across the beautiful landscape spread out beside me, but I only find more creamy curves.

More splatters of freckles. More pretty red hair, the striking color just visible through her wet panties.

Is it the scars on her hips? They're silver-white, just barely light enough to stand out from her pale complexion. I noticed them in the locker room and figured they were probably stretch marks, but Bridget has those, too, and she doesn't tense this way when I look at those.

I raise a brow at her, silently asking where they came from. Her scent slices deeper as her chin rises, slanting in a steely look at me.

Before I lose my nerve, I reach a wet hand over and carefully trace one. She clearly doesn't want to explain them—and I can empathize. "You don't need to worry about these on my account," I grunt. "You know I have my own."

It's true. The surgery on my shoulder left two perpendicular lines branded into it. Not to mention the incision along the front of my shin.

Bridget traces her fingertip along the tail of one healed cut, following it over my clavicle. Her gaze is considering, but soft as she clears her throat, then bites her lower lip, staring into my eyes for a long moment.

I don't understand—*is she seriously upset about being naked in front of me again? Why else would she look so embarrassed*—but a second later, she darts a quick glance down to my groin and whispers, barely audible over the pattering shower.

"Can I have it?"

Fucking hell.

I want to tell her *hell yes, take it, always.* But, also… no. Not *now*. Because I'm in a damn shower chair. Humiliated. Wearing boxers with a hole in them. And God knows I haven't *shaved* in a *minute*.

But the moment crystallizes—suddenly so clear. Her expression. Her eyes. The vulnerability there.

She's asking if she can do something for me. Asking me… not to reject her again. Or, maybe, to forgive her for assuming I did the day we met.

I know what my answer to *that* is, at least.

"Yeah," I rasp. *Yeah, I forgive you. Yeah, I want you. Yeah, I always fucking have.* "You can have it."

I never expected her to get on her knees, but I suppose I should be used to Bridget knocking me off my game. Instead of straddling my lap or asking me to touch her, she crouches between my legs and hums, slanting a small smile up at me.

"So it *is* pierced," she smirks.

And then—*shit, fuuuuuck*—it's in her mouth.

Good GOD.

A long, serrated sound scrapes out of me as plush heat surrounds the head of my cock. Bridget hums again, the vibration tweaking my knot fuller before she's even sucked the head past her lips.

Velvet suction tugs at my throbbing veins and she doesn't stop. Until I'm bumping her throat with my head, feeling the way her tongue slicks the piercing below.

It occurs to me that I should probably tell her what to do with —*ahgh!*

Proving that I've underestimated her once again, Bridget pulls back just far enough to roll the silver bar studded through the underside of my cockhead, swirling her tongue around the balls on either end until it turns. When she goes back to working my length into her throat, she makes sure the metal rolls directly over the slick warmth of her tongue on each pull.

It should probably be embarrassing how quickly I'm ready to blow my load. I can't help myself, though. This whole scene feels like a fucking dream—our gorgeous omega, glistening, with her lingerie soaked and see-through. Kneeling between my thighs, sealing her plump lips around my dick over and over. Red curls sticking to her back. Makeup and tears running down her face because she's so desperate to make me come, she's literally gagging for it.

"Bridget," I groan, winding my fingers into her damp hair and letting my head fall back. "Baby, you're going to make me—"

It's too late, though. My balls draw tight as fire barrels up my spine. Lighting my vertebrae one-by-one before flowing into my cock, bubbling up the shaft. I blast into her mouth, spurting thick and hard down her throat.

Bridget gives a small moan, her eyes dropping shut while she swallows everything I pump out. My chest aches at her expression, lungs cramping while they heave to drag in more of the thick, lemon-and-sea-salt air. The hand twisted in her hair falls to the side of her face, cupping her jaw as she slowly releases me.

Our gazes clash, locking together through the shower's steam. She doesn't look away as she swallows, the motion deliberate enough to send another twitch through my spent dick. Bridget notices; the flash of amusement that brightens her blue irises somehow puts a hoarse lump in my throat.

My scent shifts and her features lose their teasing glimmer, leaving only softness in its wake. She stands up, bending forward just far enough to brush her lips over mine.

It's quick—too fast for me to pull her in for a deeper kiss or catch how we taste together. But when she straightens, she has the same gentle smile on her face.

Ah fuck.

This little omega just tagged me out.

And I'm not sure I even mind.

chapter
forty-three

Jesse's brought me flowers every night this week.

Adrian has *three* dates planned in the next two weeks, including a "day out"???

And Colt *smiled* at me today…

EMMA

um yeaaaaaaaah.

about Adrian…

BRIDGET

What did he do now?

Em?

EMMA BECKETT GET BACK HERE

Bridget

"ALRIGHT, ladies, let's kick it up a notch!"

Our instructor calls out the pun in a chirpy cheer. Her foot slices upward before she pivots and rolls her hips. Two rows ahead of me, Dante and Jesse try to copy the move, both of them nearly taking out their neighbors in the process. Behind them, Emma's alphas—Gunnar, Zane, and Micah—barely manage not to collide with each other.

Emma snorts and I choke on a laugh, unable to fully it lock it down before the instructor calls out, "Now circle those hips!"

Jesse thrusts his forward and back, sort of like a robot doing the Hokey-Pokey. Dante sneers at him. "Like *this*, *cabrón*."

His hips move in such a fluid circle, I don't know whether I should swoon or cackle. Zane points to him. "You sure you don't want to be on any of my videos? Throw in an apron and a rolling pin and we'd be *set*."

Gunnar smacks his packmate-slash-boyfriend. "Oh, *he* can be in the videos, but I can't?"

Zane's expression is deadpan. "And risk everyone seeing your ass? I don't think so, babe." He tosses a wink back toward us. "Our omega agrees, right, gorgeous?"

Emma tries to look stern. And fails miserably. "Pay attention!"

Her alphas do seem to be treating this like a funny diversion while my guys... let's just say they're *in it to win it*.

Dante's thick brows lower over his dark eyes. He pops his hip and waves his arms while Jesse tries to keep his footing through another turn. Even Colt—who's standing off to the side, wearing a scowl that could melt glass—is shimmying.

Sure, every twirl ends with him glaring at me.

But he's *twirling*.

So I'll take it.

It's really not fair, anyway. Emma and I have taken this Zumba class dozens of times. We hop and spin through the steps effortlessly while the boys bumble around.

Until, of course, Gunnar and Dante start getting competitive. Then, suddenly, it's *Dancing With The Stars*. They throw in hip pops and jazz fingers. Micah nearly catches an elbow in the face from Jesse dodging Dante's high kick. And even Colt has to laugh when Gunnar trips Jesse *and* Dante on purpose.

They play it off quite well, in my opinion. Jesse starts to topple, but Dante turns it into a spin-and-dip.

So, basically, I can never come back to this class again.

Worth it.

My eyes slide to the hallway outside the exercise room. Knox Beckett and Adrian stand on the other side of the tinted glass, exchanging amused looks and head shakes while their packs make total fools of themselves.

I still can't believe Adrian planned this.

He even went out of his way to call the Beckett Pack's alpha for a proper introduction. It's old-fashioned—the leader of the less-established pack reaching out to the more-established group's alpha. The custom may be a little archaic, but...

What possible reason could he have for doing this, other than making me happy?

There's no PR motive to meeting my best friend's pack. Especially not here, in the neighborhood's private fitness club. There are no cameras or prying eyes. This is a Sunday afternoon Zumba class full of nanas, not the *E!* network.

You'd never know that looking at Adrian, though. With his hair slicked back and a handsome smirk, wearing a cream micro-knit collared shirt that doesn't have long sleeves but still somehow goes with his black pants? I'd swear the man just stepped out of a magazine spread on how to make European sophistication work in summer heat.

Adrian feels me watching and inclines his head, turning just long enough to raise a brow at me.

Making sure I'm okay.

When I glance at Knox, I find he's doing the same thing to my best friend. Some hybrid of checking her out and checking in. Emma blows him a kiss, and the grouchy mountain man flashes a square smile. It's handsome, but nowhere near as hot as the grin I get when I stick my tongue out at Adrian.

Emma catches my eye on our next twirl, bouncing her blonde brows. I grit my teeth at her. "Shut. Up."

She shrugs, gesturing to the way my alphas have turned Zumba into a pissing match... to *impress me*?

"I didn't say anything." Emma giggles, waving her hands to the music. "But if I *did*, I'd say you certainly look like a *real pack* to me."

And—God help me—I'd say she's right.

I WANT YOU TO KNOW, I think at the voice in my middle, hiking my school bag up higher on my shoulder. *If they made gags for Omegas, I would have slapped one in your mouth <u>months</u> ago.*

Her reply isn't really verbal. More of a pained, sobbing shriek. I sigh. My shoulders slump in exhaustion.

Turns out, fighting with yourself is a lot more exhausting than arguing with other people. With my heat a little less than three weeks away, my Omega cries to me all day long. Asking if the alphas can come into our nest and stay *forever…*

My sandals shuffle against the craggy parking lot, carrying me to the shining beacon of my little yellow car. I wish I could say driving it has been the *one* bright spot in a dismal week. It *should* be, given everything that went down at the stadium a couple weeks ago and the fact that the tabloids are *still* reporting on it.

But that isn't true. Because, the guys have been different.

Sweeter than ever.

I ruthlessly tamp down my Omega's hiccuped comment, ignoring the fact that she has a point. The guys *have* been sweeter than ever.

Since his rut, Adrian's decided that I'll eat every meal in his lap. He instantly places me there the second I walk into any room and insists on feeding me bite after bite, until he's satisfied I've eaten enough. Then he makes sure I have dessert.

Jesse carries me to our brand-new oversized bed every night, even when it isn't his turn to sleep next to me. Our pitcher is the cuddliest of the alphas. With the shortstop being a surprisingly close second...

In addition to smothering me to sleep, Dante makes me lunch every day. Midnight snacks most nights. And sends the absolute dirtiest text messages known to man. Yesterday, I got a bulge selfie —in his uniform pants—that was so obscene, I nearly passed out in the teachers' lounge.

And Colt. Where I used to find him scowling on my sofa at the end of every day, now he's there *waiting* for me. Flashing his quick grin when I bustle in the door. Offering me snacks he's assembled and a warm, wood-and-sea-salt-scented place under his arm. Not to mention how he demands to hear every mundane detail of my day.

The message from each of them is clear:

They can't undo the last year.

But they can damn sure *try*.

And maybe...

Maybe I should let them.

Sweat trickles down my back as I huff toward my car. Florida's seasonal swelter started this week, with temperatures climbing daily. It's typical for this time of year, but it also signals the end of spring.

Which means my heat is coming.

And the guys' season will start in a couple weeks.

What if they leave and never come back?

The thought is *painful*. Not just because my Omega thrashes around like a banshee every time it crosses my mind.

Fuck.

I think I might be starting to fall for this pack. *For real.*

Could I actually be their omega? They seem to truly want me, despite the fact that we're not scent-sensitive. Is that really so impossible?

What if they don't have a mate after all, like me? What if this is as close as any of us gets? Over time, maybe the world will forget about the whole—

The soles of my shoes scrape to a halt against the blacktop. My lashes flutter, disbelief and confusion spiraling into my gut. Sinking deep. Detonating into mushroom clouds of dread and dismay.

My insides heave and twist, ears whistling. The world slows to a stop.

Fresh red spray paint stands out against my car's glossy sunshine yellow. Two words.

FAKE FIANCEE.

And I'm honestly not sure which is worse—the fact that it's there. Or the fact that it's accurate.

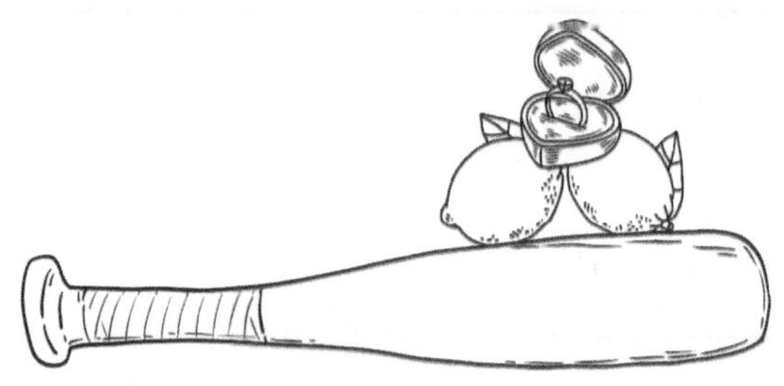

I DIDN'T WANT to call Adrian, but what choice was there?

Get in my car and drive home like that? Undo the effort we've put into convincing the world I'm really theirs?

God, maybe that would be smart at this point. Just rip out the stitches. Expose the wound. Finally accept the shame I've been trying to avoid all this time. Find out once and for all whether the way the guys treat me is genuine or just an ongoing attempt to save their reputations.

And if it is...

Alicia would be pissed, but so what? I won't get invited to Christmas or Thanksgiving? Emma's pack will probably still associate with me, assuming they aren't too angry about being bamboozled...

Hell, I'll always have Betty.

"Bridget?"

It's Jesse. I blink and see his face—the golden hair, handsome features, tanned cheeks. He's frowning, but I can't understand why he's here.

I called Adrian before I sat on this bench, right? Or did I try Colt first? He isn't working, so that would have made sense, I guess. But he can't drive, so.

Jesse gets knocked aside before I can figure it all out. Dante appears where his packmate was, leaning into my personal space without a speck of the pitcher's hesitation.

The gleaming, dark eyes I love so much look like burning coals. "*Querida?*"

I can't make my face move. It's frozen, or something. My lungs seem just as stuck. I'm unable to take a deep breath or eke out any words. My Omega is deathly still and silent, too. No whines or whimpers.

Did I finally do it? Did she finally give up?

Why does that make me want to cry?

I ignore the prickle pinching the bridge of my nose and the sting behind my eyes. A hand lands on my shoulder. I recognize Colt's fingers from recent afternoons spent with his arm curled around me. His gruff tone is also a giveaway.

"Bridget? Can you hear us?"

I think my eyelids flutter, but everything inside me is just... gone.

So is my purse, I realize distantly. And the messenger bag full of papers I needed to grade. I must have dropped them in the parking lot, because a tall, built figure cuts across the pavement, holding my stuff under one of his suit-clad arms.

Adrian.

He drops my bags to the opposite end of the bench and unleashes a wave of alpha power potent enough to knock the others aside. With deliberate movements, he comes to stand in front of me.

And goes to his knees.

Two big hands engulf my cool cheeks. *Wet*, I think, dazed. *My face is wet.*

"Bridget," Adrian husks, low and soft. "*Look at me*, baby."

My Omega must not be totally MIA, because his quiet bark still registers. I lurch my bleary eyes to his, absorbing the intensity seething in those Adriatic-blue pools.

"*Breathe*," he whispers, still dripping command. One of his hands finds mine, bringing my limp fingers to the lapel of his blazer. Pressing them over his heart.

I feel his steady heartbeat, his chest expanding under my touch, and try to match it. Oxygen spirals into my lungs.

The strange buzz dulling my senses snaps back like a rubber band. School dismissal roars to life around me. Doors slamming, kids whooping, cars peeling out of the lot.

The packs' scents hit next—caramelized kettle corn, juicy mango, a salty afternoon by the sea, warm leather and musk. My nerves spark and pulse.

Before I can worry about what *I* must smell like, Adrian nods. A steady beat of alpha approval warms my insides. "Just like that. Such a good girl for me."

I keep breathing, wishing I could hold them in my lungs.

Rumbled rattles caress my ears. My muscles loosen. I start to sway forward, but Adrian is there.

Catching me.

"Sweet baby girl," he murmurs, huddling closer. His eyes drop closed for a long moment, true relief falling across his gorgeous face. "Thank you for calling me. That was the exact right thing to do, omega."

A whine finally breaks loose, my Omega jonesing for more of his praise. Adrian responds without skipping a beat, sliding his arm around my waist and folding me into his broad strength.

"I'm going to take care of it," he vows, solid and sure, with an edge of anger lethal enough to send a shiver down my back. "Do you have any idea who would have done this?"

I'd bet all my money on Linus. He smirked at me through our entire class today, and I stupidly thought he was just being his oh-so-charming, smarmy self. I also heard some metal cans rattling in his backpack when he left study hall, but I figured he was smuggling beer or something dumb like that. I didn't want to report him and have his locker searched, so I let it go.

Idiotic.

I should have *known*.

But now that I do, I still find myself hesitating. I might loathe the kid, but playing on our school's sports teams is his whole life. His whole *future*. If I make a big deal about this, he could be booted from the athletic program. Not to mention, the last time I spoke to our principal about his behavior, *I* got scolded.

When I bite my lower lip instead of replying, Colt growls, "Fucking *Linus*."

I turn and gape at him; partially because I'm pissed he outed me, but mostly because I can't believe he's been *listening* to my stories. And closely enough to know exactly who would do this.

Adrian doesn't look away. His gaze smolders as one thick brow arches. "Linus?"

With a sigh, I mumble through some details, shame burning my cheeks. I leave out a lot of the petty things my student has done, not wanting Adrian to get overly upset, but Colt surprises me again, interjecting to stick up for me every time I purposefully omit snippets of information.

By the time we're done, even I have to admit... *Yikes.*

Adrian's jaw works for a long moment, absorbing the look on my face. He finally stands, brushing at his navy suit jacket before buttoning it. "I need a word with the principal. Jesse? Why don't you see if you can track down Linus's coach? I'd like to speak to him, too."

Jesse looks at their leader, then down at me. "I need to stay with Bridget."

Need?

Adrian takes his insistent growl in stride, nodding. "Alright. Dante? Colt? You find the coach."

They both agree. Adrian pauses just long enough to sift my hair back and place a kiss on my forehead before stalking into the school.

Dante grabs Colt's collar, practically dragging him toward the baseball diamond in the distance, behind the car lot. If the energy rolling off him is any indication...

I quiver as I turn to Jesse. "They won't h-hurt anyone, right?"

My blond alpha's face crumples in consternation. With an ease that leaves me breathless, he scoops me into his arms and shakes his head. "No, bumblebee. They wouldn't embarrass you like that."

Ignoring the looks we get while he stands beside the parking lot, holding me, Jesse presses his forehead into mine, frowning deeper. "You're shaking. What can I do?"

I don't know. This aimless emptiness inside me is unfamiliar. I'm not used to being the kind of person who can't figure out a solution.

But these *feelings?* They don't have an off switch or a resolution.

I stare into Jesse's soft green eyes. They're so full of compassion and warmth. Worry—and true, hopeful *eagerness*. He *wants* me to tell him what I need. He *wants* to give it to me.

Like the day in the locker room.

Or last week on the back porch...

Tears fill my eyes and spill over. Jesse's chest rumbles on a purr. Determination darts across his features. "Come on," he says. "I know where we need to go."

THIS WHOLE SCENE gives me *deja vu*.

I remember the days when a dinky dirt diamond like this was my entire world. The dugout, my sanctuary. Home plate, my altar. I lived and died by every practice, game, run.

There was a purity to it. No contracts, signing bonuses, or financial penalties for missed practices. Those were the days I didn't show up because someone paid me to. I showed up because this place helped me make sense of myself.

Or a place *like* this one, anyway.

It feels remarkably similar now. Stepping onto the sandy, faded-ocher dirt. Treading over scraggly grass half as thick as the turf at the stadium. Breathing the scent of damp concrete and musty gear—a high school dugout.

It's a smell as familiar as my own. One I love almost as much as Bridget's.

Clearly, I'm the only guy having a nostalgic moment here. Dante hasn't stopped muttering curses since we left our omega's earshot. I don't understand most of them, but his tone gets more ruthless as he approaches the troupe of high schoolers gathered near midfield.

I scan for an adult, but no one jumps out at me. *Great. Dealing with a bunch of snot-nosed pissants.*

For weeks, I've been wondering how the hell Bridget does her job. If I ever had to put up with a bunch of hormonal morons with under-developed frontal lobes, violence seemed like a pretty safe bet.

But as we come up to the group of losers clustered together, I mostly feel sympathetic. And maybe a little amused.

Dear God. Was I *ever* this young?

The guys finally see us coming and straighten.

One of them steps forward—a long-limbed blond kid who sort of reminds me of Jesse. He must be their captain because he has a clipboard in his hand. He tucks it under his arm and does his best to look wary instead of terrified. "Yeah?"

Dante swells beside me, ready to bite the kid's head off. I hit his chest with the back of my hand, halting him, and ask, "Where's your coach?"

A surly kid with lank black hair and acne comes to stand beside the captain. "He quit or got fired or some shit."

The captain winces. "Budget cuts," he explains with complete earnestness. Because—*yep*—this *is* the Jesse of the bunch.

Apparently, hearing these poor assholes don't even have money for a coach is enough to take the wind out of Dante's sails. He sputters and gripes, "Well no wonder you act like a bunch of assholes! You don't have a *coach*?"

Mini Jesse shakes his head. "No."

"No team manager?" Dante tries, and I do everything I can not to snort.

"No," Jesse Jr. replies, slower—like maybe he's not speaking to someone quite on his intellectual level. *Little shit.* "You guys need something? Why do you want to talk to our coach?"

Dante crosses both arms over his chest and lets his growl loose. The kids stagger back a step, and he follows, pacing forward while he grits, "Because one of you brats is fucking with *our* omega."

His dark eyes drop to one kid's shirt, then back to his face. "You *Linus*?"

He says the name like it's an insult. The kid in question seems leaner than the others—not because he's less built or taller, but because he's *thin*. For a second, I doubt he would have a cruel prank in him, but then I see what's caught Dante's eye: red spray paint, speckled over the kid's forearms.

"Yeah," Linus admits. He glares back at my packmate, all defiance. "So what?"

This time, I have to fist Dante's shirt to keep him from lunging. "So," I say, staring the kid down. "Want to explain what you were doing, vandalizing our fiancée's car?"

Linus balks, but my packmate gestures at the evidence, silently pointing out that we've literally caught the kid red-handed. Instead of quailing, the little punk narrows his eyes. "She isn't *really* your fiancée, though. Right?"

Dante mutters something in Spanish, trying to shove around me. I hold him back, ignoring the way my leg throbs when I dig my heel into the sandy grass.

"Listen," I reply, "I want to help you out here. But if you keep saying stupid shit like that, I'm going to end up letting my packmate rip your head off. That would be bad for our team *and* yours. Not to mention any chance you had at playing college ball. So, I'd maybe start showing Br—*Miss Woods*—some respect if I were you."

Linus looks paler... and even *more* determined. Scared, but no less defiant.

Hell, I really get that.

Some indistinct instinct has me narrowing my eyes. "Fine. I see how it is. Maybe we should just talk to your parents, then."

The kid sniffs, looking at his feet. His jaw grinds. "Good fucking luck, asshole."

Yeah. That's exactly what I would have said if someone had asked to talk to my mom back when I played in school. *Good fucking luck finding her sober, asshole.*

Without dropping my focus, I reach my bad arm out and grunt around the pain that shoots into my shoulder. "Give me that."

Little Jesse hands me his clipboard. One glance confirms it's an utter disaster. I hold the page up to Dante and watch his face fall.

"Here," I tell him. "Sort this shit out. Linus and I are going to have a talk."

IT'S BEEN a long time since I walked these hallways.

Not much has changed. The faded blue lockers and green-flecked linoleum are as familiar as the route to the library.

I don't care.

I'm on a mission.

Bridget has brought my Alpha to the surface once again. She does that—tugging at the deepest parts of me without realizing it.

Because it isn't the big smiles or exaggerated sassiness that pull me in. With Bridget, it's the things she doesn't want people to notice. The pink tingeing her cheeks, how her scent disappears when she's sad, how her eyes drop in shame when perfume rises off her skin.

I purr deeper, shouldering our way into the library. Emptiness echoes back at us as we step over the threshold.

Bridget sees my pleasantly surprised expression and bites down on a small smile. "It's Friday," she peeps. "No one hangs around after the last bell. But the lights will shut off and the doors will lock automatically in ten minutes."

That makes sense. The big clock on the wall above the checkout desk reads 3:50.

Fine by me. What I have in mind will take more than ten minutes anyway.

I start toward the stairs on the far side of the room. Bridget stammers and squirms, but I cradle her closer and flash a smile. "Humor me? We ran out of practice before I finished my cardio."

She gives me that wary look we've all gotten used to. I remember it from high school—how she would peek around her locker any time I stopped to talk to her. Certain I had some sort of angle, I suppose.

I guess I did, if you count wanting to talk to a pretty girl as "having an angle."

It never occurred to me before today; there was likely a reason she felt suspicious about a big alpha jock being nice to her.

Did any of my teammates bully her? How did I miss it?

Probably the same way we missed what this kid has been doing to her. She might have told Colt some anecdotes she thought would amuse him, passing her own harassment off as a *joke*. But it's clear there's a real problem here.

I hate that Bridget could possibly believe any of this wasn't a big deal. Does she really think so little of herself? Doesn't she realize how precious she is?

Has she ever?

I make it to the top of the stairs without breaking a sweat. Bridget blinks owlishly, glancing behind us like she can't quite compute what just happened. *Adorable.*

I brush my lips over her quirked brow. "Remind me, which way to the stacks?"

"Left," she replies, distracted. "Did you seriously just *carry* me up two flights of stairs? Why?"

"To get to the stacks." I shrug. "Left, you said?"

But we're already turning the last corner. Row upon row of forgotten books sit on the tallest shelves in the whole place. They make for individual dark alleys that dead-end in blank walls. I pick one in the middle.

"Jesse!" Bridget giggles. "What are we—*oh!*"

I turn and lift her, balancing her against a gap on one of the shelves. The space is just wide enough to accommodate Bee's thick hips, and the perfect height to put her level with mine.

I reach back to grab a fistful of my Henley, peeling it off in one motion. "Remember how I promised I'd tell you next time I needed you?"

The diffused light between the stacks only makes Bridget's eyes seem brighter. They glitter and glow, running over my features in a slow loop. "Yeah?"

I go for my fly, unbuttoning my jeans and rolling them down. "I need you now."

It's more that I know *she* needs *me*. My Alpha can sense it. And that edge to her scent? The bitter aftertaste that makes it just not quite "perfect"? He somehow believes *this* will fix it.

I know nothing will, because it doesn't need "fixing." That's her scent. *And I love it, because—*

Because I love her.

I love her.

Emotion echoes through my chest the same way every sound we make reverberates through this large, vaulted room. Amplifying. Touching each corner, bouncing back at me. Until it's all I hear. All I feel.

I love her.

I have for a long time.

Maybe even forever.

"You used to study up here," I whisper, helping unfasten the tiny pearls holding her blouse closed. She shrugs it off, panting as her lips fall open in awe. Her chest heaves on shallow breaths while she listens.

"You would sneak up here and hide when you were supposed to be in gym class. Coach sent me looking for you once. I knew you loved this library because—" I swallow, hoarse. "Because I watched you. All the time."

A quiet whimper catches in Bridget's throat. I wrap my fingers around her neck and smooth my thumb down the creamy column, remembering, "Your hair caught my eye whenever you came near me. The first time I ever struck out in a varsity game, it happened because I saw you in the stands. It was dusk, but your pretty hair still stood out. You were huddled next to your sister and your parents. Reading a library book."

Bridget's lower lip starts to quiver. I nuzzle my nose against hers as I go on, "So that day, when Coach sent me after you, I knew you'd be up here. I looked for your red braids. Or a ponytail with a ribbon. And when I found you hiding between these shelves, you looked so happy. Reading and doodling in your note-book. Drawing sunflowers and bumblebees. I didn't have the heart to drag you out."

How clueless was I? Even back then, something about her called to me on an elemental level. I barely knew her, had only spoken to her in passing as Alicia's little sister; but I saw her peace and wanted to *protect* it.

Bridget tries to absorb what I'm saying. Her mouth moves more deliberately, forming a word without sound. "Bumblebees?"

I nod, tracing my thumb along her rounded chin. "Where did you think I got your nickname from?"

Bridget smiles shyly—my favorite expression in the whole world. "I figured because I used to buzz around the parties Alicia would throw for the players and the cheerleaders."

My grin blooms. "You did do that. It was fucking adorable."

A faint giggle tumbles out of her. "I thought you were just too polite to call me 'gnat' like my sister did."

The throb behind my heart swells and burns. I cup my hand

around her cheek, relishing how the rounded curve perfectly fills my palm. "I should have paid more attention to the way she treated you, bumblebee. I let you down back then. I'm sorry."

Bridget shifts closer, pressing her panty-covered core to the spot between my growing knot and my navel. Wet heat kisses the trail of dark blond hair there. My lungs suck in bright lemon sweetness as she touches my face, trailing her fingertips to my jaw.

"It wasn't your fault," she murmurs. "And it wasn't your job to protect me."

A fierce, possessive urge roars to life. "I *wanted* it to be my job. I still do."

Breathless anticipation stretches taut between us. My eyes flick to the clock hanging halfway between the first floor and the second. Watching for the exact second...

Finally.

Click.

I hear the doors downstairs lock at the same second the overhead lights flicker off. Cloudy sunlight continues streaming into the first-floor windows, casting a gray glow up to the second story. The summer-blue irises staring back at me get thinner, reacting to the shadows.

Or maybe for another reason entirely.

Bridget's scent becomes so intoxicatingly *bright*, my head swims. Need pulses in my canines and my cock. Sweet slick douses the triangle of fabric between her pussy and my skin, the thick sheen glossing the top of my knot.

I groan, diving for her unmarked throat and opening my jaw to bite. Bridget squeals at the scrape of my teeth along her thin, pale flesh. Her core contracts hard enough for me to *feel* her pussy quiver and her abdominals tighten.

A feminine keen floats into the high ceiling, filling the whole library. *Fuck. I love that.*

Just like the locker room, there's something about publicly laying claim to her that appeals to the beast inside me. And this is *perfect*—public enough for my Alpha to make his point, but, at the moment, completely private and safe for Bridget.

"Need you," I gasp, reaching for her center and finding out just how soaked she is. "Right here. Please, Bee."

She nods hard enough to send loose auburn hair tumbling over her breasts. Gorgeous, with luminous strands layered over her light-yellow bra. I feel myself harden when her nipples peak, poking at the thin lace.

Fucking beautiful. Almost *decadent*. A glorious bounty.

I could wrap both hands around one of her tits and still have enough to suck into my mouth.

I thumb at her through the gossamer material, biting my lip while I glide my other forefinger through her slick slit. *Goddamn it*. Her clit is so swollen and ready for me. When I trace around the edge, she chokes on an inhale. Her opening flutters against my fingertips.

I groan as her scent hits my tongue, the sweet sharpness lighting every pleasure receptor in my brain. They pulse in time with the ache filling my balls and pumping my knot fuller.

Shit. "I want to lock us together, but I can't do it here, so I'm going to shove as deep inside you as I can get. Tease you with it."

Bridget mewls, her head falling back. Thrusting her pretty tits at me. I nip at one through the lace, then smooth my tongue over the cup. Tasting her warm skin through the textured fabric, sucking marks along the top curve where everyone will see them.

"Jesse!" she cries, rolling her hips to get my fingers back on her clit. "Please?"

I bite down on her softness, growling. "Please, what? Please fill this sweet pussy? Please plunge my cock in you so deep, you *almost* feel my knot pop into place? Rut you from behind so I can get as far inside you as possible when I come?"

Bridget cries out again. Loud enough to have my balls tingling and my Alpha snarling. He doesn't want anyone else to hear our omega.

With all the adrenaline and need coursing through me, I

barely have time to form the thought before I've flipped Bridget over and rucked up her dress. The buttery skirt pools around her waist, leaving the dimpled curves of her ass on full display.

I pull her thong aside, mouth watering, and keep the frilly strap around her hips so I can admire the way it looks while I pound into her from behind. It also makes a decent handle—I fist my left hand around the waistband and use my right to grasp the shiny red hair at her nape.

My eyes rove over her, landing on the quivering holes exposed for the taking. Need beats in my blood. My mind spins and blurs.

Fucking—

"*Ah!*" she cries out as I slide my rigid dick into her pussy. Squelching heat engulfs me, the wet walls slipping against every vein throbbing up my shaft. Slick pours from her, coating my knot and balls within seconds.

Ah, *God*.

She's so perfect, I have to grit my teeth to stop from spilling immediately. Focusing on the way her body takes mine—and how it begs for *more*.

Her back hole twitches when I angle my hips, pounding into the rough, sensitive patch along her front wall. Bridget gasps and moans, her fingers scrabbling at the bookshelf in front of us. I tug her hair a bit more, arching her back. Knowing it will make her breasts bounce on my next plunge.

"Jesse!" she pleads. "You're so—*oh!*—deep."

With my knot aching at the base of my cock, I have so much more to give her. When I start pushing the thick swell past her outer muscles, Bridget's keens turn into whimpers. Her knuckles blanch. "*Alpha!*"

Yes. Take it. <u>More</u>.

I repeat my Alpha's growled commands, thrusting faster, working my knot halfway in before ruthlessly popping it back out. It's the best kind of torture. Feeling her stretch and squeeze —a moment of blinding *pressure* when her pussy clutches me at its narrowest point—then a rush of cool nothing when I pull out.

Bridget begs wordlessly, her moans devolving into sobs. Her body squirms and flutters, both of her pretty holes winking at me each time I rip myself out of her glorious pussy. Tempting me.

I slide my grasp on her thong from the waistband to the thin strap I shoved aside, gripping it in my fingers as I skim my thumb along the cleft of her ass.

She tenses for a moment, whipping her head to the side. I keep my touch light and teasing, strumming slowly. Waiting for her to tell me to stop.

But she only opens her mouth and cuts herself off. Her eyes gloss—and I think I might have made a misstep, until her perfume *explodes*.

"P-please," she whispers, pushing back into my touch, pressing her spread pussy lips around my knot. "I—I've done it alone, but... I've always wanted to try it like this."

I picture her pleasuring herself with a toy in her ass and nearly lose my shit. A growled groan rips from my lungs. "*Jesus*, Bee. You're so *fucking hot*."

Literally *and* figuratively. Because as I work my thumb into her ass, scorching snugness greets me. Her inner muscles squeeze in tandem. Clenching and gushing, cinching and rubbing. Pulling at my knot and my thumb.

I pump into her harder. My balls swing forward, tapping her wet, swollen clit on every drive. Bridget screams—and the echo of that beautiful, needy sound finally sends me over the edge.

My cock sprays inside her, knot expanding to rub all the way from the back of her slit to the top of her throbbing nub. When she sobs a moan and pushes back into the sensation, my thumb slips deeper into ass.

"*Yes. Bee.* Fuck, your body is so damn *good*. Coming so *hard*."

I feel every wrenching pulse of the climax ravaging her. Electricity bolts up my spine, pleasure snapping through every nerve in rolling bursts. My balls keep tingling, emptying themselves in long, intense spurts that leave me hunched over her back, fighting to fill my lungs.

Bridget straightens just far enough to turn her head for a kiss. It's sloppy, both of us greedily sucking in each other's scents, trying to remember how to breathe. Sweat dots my upper lip, and bite marks emboss hers.

Our mouths brush and cling. And everything I was floats away.

Until I'm just... *hers*.

I'm starting to suspect that's all I've ever really wanted to be.

I'M STILL NOT sure what, exactly, just happened.

But somehow, while Jesse was fucking my brains out in the library, Adrian, Dante, and Colt did *the most*.

Or should I say they *also* did the most? Because, *damn*. Jesse really delivered.

I'm still a little dizzy when we use the spare ID badge I keep in my desk to let ourselves out of the library. Principal Newson and Adrian are waiting outside the administrative offices down the hall, the former trembling and sweating while our pack alpha keeps his arms crossed and taps his loafer on the linoleum.

The second he sees us, he knows what we've been doing. He

can probably scent it, given how worked up Jesse got both of us, and the fact that he made a point to come *deep* inside me.

If my beta boss has any clue, he's wise enough not to mention it. Instead, he launches into a jittery, long-winded apology, only pausing to glance at Adrian for approval every few sentences.

I try not to reveal my shock all over my face, smiling and nodding along while Jesse swipes his thumb across my knuckles in light, distracting touches. The contact feels good, though. Like the connection we shared before is so precious to him, he wants to keep hold of me for a while.

I squeeze his hand as I accept the principal's apologies and do my best not to balk when the man goes on to promise funding for the recycling program he had zero interest in last week. Or even today when I spoke with him at lunch.

All of that is crazy, but the wildest part comes just after I shake Newson's hand and he lumbers back into his office.

Without skipping a beat, Adrian glances up the hallway behind me and waves other people forward.

Not just *people*—Dante and Colt.

And *Linus.*

Colt drops the fist clutching my student's baseball jersey and nods at him, flexing alpha dominance. "Tell Miss Woods what you told me."

Linus grinds his molars, but the look in his eye isn't the malicious, gleeful one I'm used to. He seems wary. Begrudging.

"You're a good teacher, and I shouldn't mess with you like I do," Linus grits, darting a hesitant glance at my eyes. "Sorry or whatever."

I almost smirk. Biting back my amusement—because, yes, he's an ass but he's also a *kid*. And sort of *hilarious*—I scold, "You shouldn't mess with *anyone* like you do. Right?"

He kicks at the scuffed floor. "Yeah. Whatever."

My lips quirk up slightly. "So the next time you're a jerk to anyone, or to *me*, you get that I'm not going to turn a blind eye anymore, right? I'll be reporting you to the principal. And your coach."

"We don't have a coach," he mutters, sullen. Then sees the look on Dante's face and swallows audibly. "But yeah. Sure. I get it."

"Good," Colt determines. "Now what are you gonna do?"

Linus scowls at him. "Go run laps around the field until I puke?"

"Yup," Dante chirps. "And tomorrow?"

"I'll turn in all my late homework for health class," he grumbles, then snorts. "I still don't get *why* all that stupid alpha-omega bullshit is important, but—"

Adrian's alpha undercurrent cracks through the air like a shot. He steps in front of me, his body language making his protective impulses—and the threat they pose—perfectly clear. He meets Linus's widening eyes and offers his signature quirked brow. "Don't you?"

Both of Linus's hands fly up in surrender. "Okay. Yeah. Whatever you say."

Adrian's eyebrow hitches higher.

Linus gulps. "Sir."

All the alphas nod, satisfied. I roll my eyes, pushing around them. "Okay, okay. you heard him, he's sorry. Or whatever. Interrogation over."

I pat Linus on the back, eyeing him with my most intimidating teacher look. "Did you have a chance to eat lunch, or were you too busy tagging my car?"

I know he's on the state-funded meal plan. Which means he probably won't get another meal until breakfast tomorrow if he skipped today's lunch.

Before I can glance around for my purse, Colt sighs and extracts his wallet. Glowering, he hands the kid a twenty. "So help me *God* if you use this to buy anything other than dinner..."

Linus blinks at the cash. For the first time since I met him, he isn't angry or antagonistic. He seems genuinely thrown when he takes the money and pockets it.

Then a miracle occurs.

"Thanks," he mumbles, shuffling away. "Or whatever."

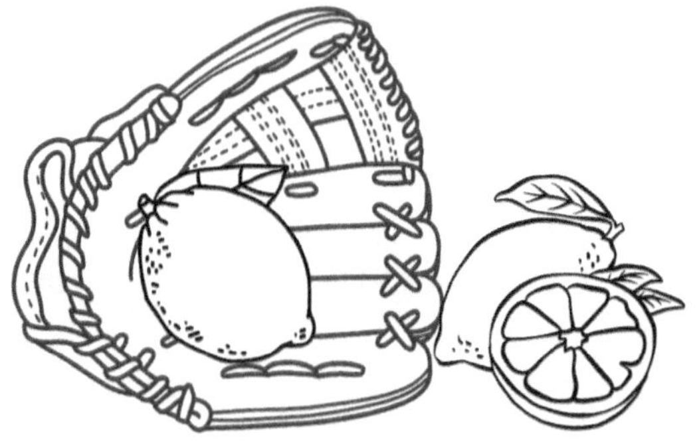

BRIDGET LOWERS her sunglasses to the end of her button nose, suspiciously peering at Winter Park's most well-appointed hotel. I hide my amusement while she roams suspicious eyes over the elegant exterior, taking in the charming European-meets-modern-traditional aesthetic.

She turns her wary gaze on mine, staring over the heart-shaped rim of her blue shades. "A hotel?" she asks flatly. "You brought me to a *hotel*?"

Her implication is clear. I chuckle to myself, passing my keys to the valet before snatching her hand, dropping a kiss on her fingers. Beyond satisfied to be able to touch her like this.

She's been more receptive to affection since our eventful afternoon at her school earlier this week. She still hasn't mentioned letting us stay for her heat, but moments like these reassure me—I feel safe to her.

And if she trusts *me*, it's only a matter of time before she trusts *this*. Us.

"No, little blue, I've brought you to their spa," I reply, wrapping my arm around her waist.

We match today—a light cornflower romper for her and a navy shirt for me. She nips her lower lip as I guide her toward the entrance, fretting, "I'm not dressed fancy enough for this place."

I nuzzle a scent-mark into her crown and leave a kiss there. "You look beautiful. But if you're feeling underdressed, don't worry—the spa will have us remove our clothing for our treatments."

Her astonishment reappears as she pushes her sunglasses into her hair. "Treatments?! Plural?"

After weeks of living with her, I've finally decided how I feel about her utter shock whenever one of us does something nice for her.

I *loathe* it.

What was originally bemusing, and maybe even a little charming, now makes me murderous. She doesn't know how to respond to gifts or pampering because no one has ever given them to her. But it's more than that.

These reactions? The shock and nervousness? The fact that they happen each and *every* time...

Someone must have told her she didn't *deserve* these things.

And she *believed* them.

That part doesn't make sense. The woman I've come to know is confident, comfortable, and at peace with herself.

Why doesn't she think she should have nice things?

The mystery continues as we walk across the wide marble lobby. Bridget darts apprehensive glances at the stately metal accents. Her scent disappears so completely, for a moment, I think the hotel is full of neutralizers. As soon as we step under an intricate iron archway and into the area designated for spa guests, the aroma of essential oils proves my theory false.

I remember her face as we signed the paperwork for her new car, how her lemon-sugar essence dissipated while she fidgeted and chewed on her lip. Much like now.

I file that information away, determined to examine it later and compare notes with my packmates. Right now, I need to pinpoint the reason for her anxiety so I can reassure her.

Despite her obvious unease, Bridget looks like she was born to be here. Her posture and bearing are every bit as elegant as our surroundings. Even dressed casually, she's always the brightest thing in *any* room.

I watch her features leap as I check us in. "Couple's massage for Messina," I tell the woman behind the desk.

She offers a bland smile to go with her nod. Bridget is much more animated, her brows rising halfway to her hairline. "A couple's massage?"

"Yes," I confirm, smoothing my hand down her side. "Have you ever had one?"

She snorts like I've asked a patently ridiculous question. "*No.*"

The receptionist overhears our conversation and beams a flirty smile in my direction, likely assuming Bridget and I must not know each other very well. I sign the iPad presented to me, fighting the urge to grit my teeth at the random woman... and the thoughtless way my omega writes herself off.

"Me neither," I return, ignoring the staffer in favor of Bridget's stunning eyes. "But we've had a stressful week."

She makes another face, silently saying she *can't* argue with me, but wishes she *could*. When her mild scent sours and she turns her narrowed gaze on the other woman, I laugh quietly into her hair.

A quiver slips down her spine as I bend to scent-mark both of her cheeks, keeping my head ducked to stare right into her. "You'll let me spoil you," I say, dropping my impassive mask to show her the need burning through my body. "Won't you?"

Bridget's whole expression softens. She sags into me, blinking as she nods. "Yes," she murmurs. "I—Okay."

The woman behind the desk senses defeat, mutters something about robes, and stomps away. I nuzzle Bridget's forehead, holding her gaze. "You can take care of your students and your neighbors and your friends—but let *me* take care of *you*. Alright?"

She doesn't answer, but tension seeps out of her limbs. She stretches onto her toes, rubbing her cheek into mine.

Scent-marking me.

Pride warms my chest. My fingers flex against her hips. "Again."

Her lashes flutter at my simple demand. Or was it more like a plea? I only know her perfume is much too faint, and I need more.

Surprise streaks across her features. "You... *want* to smell like me?"

I shake my head. "No—I *have to*. My Alpha is already pissed as hell anyone else is going to touch me. I need your scent *all over me* before we go in there."

Bridget's answering smile is a small, fragile, breathtaking thing. "Seriously?"

A hissed shriek cuts off my reply, flying at us from the hallway leading to the spa's private lounge. "*Bridget?!*"

Every ounce of color drains from my omega's face. Wide, panicked eyes fly to mine, then leap over my shoulder. Her mouth falls halfway open, squeaking, "Alicia?"

I start to turn, craning my neck just far enough to catch a glimpse of a tall strawberry-blonde alpha standing in a cluster of three women. Each of them sports similar tote bags and loungewear, topped off with the sort of understated jewelry that hints at old money.

Before I can put myself between them and Bridget, she sidesteps me and squeezes my arm. "I'll be right back."

When I start to protest, she shoots me a look as close to imploring as I've ever seen her. "Wait here?"

My brows crouch lower, but I nod. Swallowing my frustration and angling my body toward the front desk with every intention of listening as closely as I can.

Because in the last twenty seconds, Bridget went from heavenly lemon cream to a type of acidity I've never experienced before.

Is it her sister?

Or something else?

"I'll be right behind you, girls!" Alicia trills to her friends. In the mirrored wall behind the front desk, I see her wave them off and turn on her heeled sandal.

The second the other ladies disappear into the lobby, Alicia intercepts Bridget in the middle of the room. The syruped phoniness runs off her voice, leaving it dry and brittle when she snaps, "*What* are you *doing* here?"

Bridget bites her lip, leaning away with a resigned wince. As if she expected this reprimand. "I'm—I—"

She glances in my direction, catching my eye in the mirror. A darker, mottled version of her peachy blush spreads over her face as she drops her gaze to her shoes. "I didn't know you'd be here," she says simply.

Alicia throws up her manicured hands and lets them slap against her sides. "We've discussed this! Our family *knows* people here. You can't be out in polite society this close to your heat, and —oh my God—do you even have de-scenter on?"

No, she doesn't. Because I whisked her out of the house before she remembered to reapply it. I swallow the urge to charge over, watching in the reflection.

"You could have just walked past me, and no one would have noticed," Bridget mumbles. "I wouldn't have said anything."

Alicia pops her hip and props her hand at her waist. The motion is similar to something my omega might do, but also utterly different. Bridget cocks her hip to be sassy whenever she stands up for herself or others; her sister seems firmly bent on intimidation.

"We *agreed*," Alicia cuts back. "You're not supposed to come here. Or to the Waldorf for tea. The nine a.m. church service at All Saints, the Cotillion..."

She continues, rattling off a list of our town's most prestigious locales. Cold horror sinks into my stomach. Recalling her anxious face as we walked through the lobby... how her scent dipped to practically nothing.

It's more than some twisted, self-imposed belief that she doesn't *deserve* to be in places like this and have nice things.

She wasn't *allowed* to have nice things.

She was told she *couldn't* be in places like this.

I close the distance between us before the instinct even registers. Stalking to the space behind Bridget's body, winding an arm around her waist while I reach for her limp hand. She turns in my embrace, blinking. Stunned.

Alicia watches me bring her sister's wrist to my lips, brushing the delicate skin, scent-marking it, until Bridget perfumes. When she does, I ignore its acrid edge and smile, pressing a kiss to my omega's palm.

"Mmm," I murmur, "Time's up, little blue. I need you back."

Bridget's body trembles, but her muscles loosen as I start to purr, nuzzling her cheek before I spare her sister a glance. "Apologies," I drawl, making sure she sees how unapologetic I truly am. "I don't believe we've been introduced. I'm Adrian Messina, Bridget's pack alpha."

Alicia's slack mouth suddenly snaps into a twisted smirk. "No need to keep up your charade for my sake, darling," she sneers. "I'm the one who came up with the whole arrangement. Although I was surprised to hear an alpha like *you* had decided to join such a band of misfits. Especially given..."

She waves a blasé hand at her sister. I can't even think long enough to decide what she's referring to—all I see in my arms is the perfect woman.

My Alpha lunges, though, begging to take a swipe at the one undermining our pack. I fold the urge to snarl into a slight growl.

Bridget feels it in my throat and quivers, but leans closer to me. Because even when I'm the one raging, she *knows* I'm her safe place.

Good fucking girl.

"Actually," I rumble, staring into Alicia's duller blue eyes. "Bridget *is* the reason I took over the Locke Pack."

They both freeze. Bridget's gaze flies to my face, gaping every bit as much as her sister.

Fucking hell.

This bitch told *my* omega she would never have a real pack who loved her. She forced her to settle in the most degrading way, and convinced Bridget it was simply common sense.

My face conveys every ounce of hatred burning through my body as I level Alicia with a glare. "I never would have been interested in becoming their alpha if Bridget hadn't been their omega."

Rotating the woman in my arms and wrapping her closer, I look down into her bright eyes, adding, "She's incredible. Everything I've ever wanted. As soon as I saw her in the society papers and read about her work with children's charities, I knew I needed her to be mine."

Bridget's gaze roams over my face, searching. Trying to determine whether this is part of our long-abandoned rouse. When I stare back, projecting the solid weight of my certainty, her full lips tremble once, twice... then they spread into the most glorious grin I've ever seen.

My scent spikes instantly. Bridget's brightens in reply. Its slicing edge clatters to the floor as sweetness swells in its stead.

The bitterness that makes my Alpha rage in frustration is still there, but it affects me differently than before. Urging me to bite her, claim her.

Almost as if the voice inside me wants her *more* because of whatever isn't right.

Canines aching, I barely register Alicia's dainty gasp. And the deafening silence that follows.

When Bridget and I glance over, we find her wide-eyed.

Openly shocked. She flounders, her painted lips opening and closing several times before she manages, "So... you're...?"

A real pack? Bonding with one another? Getting my sister an actual engagement ring?

I wish I could say yes, to all of the above. But Bridget hasn't agreed to any of those things—and today is the time for me to *show* her how much I want to keep her.

"Staying with Bridget," I finish, giving a steady nod. "Yes. We are."

Bridget watches me. For a second, I wonder if she'll argue, but she only stands a bit straighter. Holding her head high as she bobs it once, turning to Alicia with a satisfied expression.

The woman absorbs the look on her sister's face and narrows her eyes. "Well, in that case, I suppose you wouldn't mind bringing your *whole pack* to the Ospreys' Charity Gala next weekend? It *is* your preferred philanthropy, right? And all of polite society will be there to witness your..." She pauses, raking me with suspicious eyes. "...*good fortune.*"

I start to growl, ready to chuck my manners aside and fight this other alpha for impugning my omega's honor. But Bridget's scent actually gets *sweeter*. And her smile *blossoms.*

"Really?" she bursts. "You wouldn't pitch a fit about me coming? Because I really want to go, but you said I shouldn't this close to my heat—"

Alicia's face takes on a bored quality as she examines her nails, waving dismissively. "Oh. That. Well, I assume it won't be an issue, now that you have alphas."

Bridget either accepts her blatant lie or chooses to ignore it. Either way, she shrugs, her grin growing in a way that tells me she's getting what she wants and isn't going to gripe about the details.

Practical. And too smart to dally over bullshit with a person she doesn't trust.

Which is so very *her*, it makes my heart hurt.

My patience snaps under the weight. I nuzzle my face into Bridget's hair and start to turn us away. Not sparing Alicia another glance. "If you'll excuse us, I have plans to spoil my omega."

❤

"LITTLE BLUE?"

Bridget hums, slowly peeling one eye open. I take a mental picture, knowing I'll want it later.

She's always a vision, but this may be the sexiest I've ever seen her. Stripped bare, with all her makeup washed off and her fiery hair pulled into a toppling pile. Lying on her belly, with a black satin sheet pooled at her waist and a sheen of oil glistening on her curves.

Freckles. Womanly rolls. Wide hips. The onyx fabric clinging to her round, full ass.

It's all divine; but none of it can compare to the honest softness in her brilliant blue eyes. The serenity steeped into her delicate features.

Fucking hell.

She's so beautiful.

Relaxed. With nothing to worry about except her own enjoyment.

The massages were sublime, but I spent the entire two-hour block with my head turned toward her whenever possible. Watching to make sure she was comfortable. Huffing deep inhales of her sugared brightness.

Our omega's lemony perfume has never been *this* close to perfection. It unlocks something deep inside me, but it also *enrages* my Alpha.

It's so goddamn *good*. Why does something still feel *off*?

The slightest fissure in a flawless kaleidoscope of stained glass.

So brilliant and colorful, the crack is all-but invisible. I know it's there, but I can't find it with my eyes anymore.

Is it odd that part of me misses it?

My Alpha might not love whatever keeps her from registering as our mate, but I love *everything* about her. Not being able to find the thread of bitterness I'm used to almost feels like losing a piece of her.

And every bit of Bridget is utterly precious to me.

Purring, I bend over her massage table and nuzzle the nape of her neck. "How was that, love?"

A shy, gorgeous smile curls her lips. "It was incredible, Adrian," she whispers, full of feeling I don't understand until she adds, "I've never been anywhere like this before. Thank you for bringing me."

I nip at the side of her neck, rumbling, "We'll come back. I promise. But for now, I thought we might shower this oil off and have lunch by the pool?"

Genuine delight sparkles in her gaze. I memorize it, resolving to put the same gleam there as often as humanly possible. A teasing twitch quirks her lips higher. "Okay... but you might have to carry me. I feel like I don't have any bones left."

Fuck, her perfume is so delicious. Decadent cream, lemon zest, torched sweetness. I scrape my teeth over her pulse without meaning to. When she moans, I do it again. With purpose.

"*Adrian*," she breathes, stretching under my hands. "W-what are you doing?"

I skim my fingertips down the line of her spine and span my hand against the small of her back. She arches into the touch as my purr deepens. Under the towel wrapped around my hips, my cock goes from hard to *raging*.

"I want you," I rasp. Deciding she needs to hear the raw truth instead of some playful version. "I *need* you."

God, she's perfect. Her scent climbs higher, a shiver wracking her body when she perfumes for me. Any trace of doubt or teasing vanishes, her features full of lust and genuine tenderness.

"Okay," she hums, turning onto her side. Opening her arms to me. "What can I do for you?"

Sweet baby girl.

She might be the smartest, most self-possessed woman I've ever met, but she's also the *kindest*. I pet her head, sifting my fingers through the bright strands. Our gazes lock.

"I want to taste you," I tell her. "If you'll let me."

The way her scent sharpens is enough to gut me. And tweak my knot fuller. *Fuck. Bridget.*

I love her so damn much, my heart can't contain the sensation anymore. It spills over and out, pouring through my abdomen. Pooling in my lungs. Shooting into my limbs.

I love Bridget.

And I think she might love me, too. Even if she doesn't realize it.

Because instead of denying me or curling in on herself, this time, she bites her lower lip. Earnest fear fills her face. "It—might not be... good."

Impossible.

I don't dismiss her, though. Clearly, someone put these thoughts into her mind. Made her think this way.

Massaging the crown of her head with gentle fingertips, I brush one final kiss along her unmarked throat. Shoving down the urge to *bite*.

"Do you trust me?" I whisper.

Her answering nod is quick and a little shaky. It might make me smile if she didn't seem so anxious. "What if someone comes back in?" she whispers.

I straighten, reaching over to lock the door to the cozy room. Soft gray walls glow as candlelight fills Bridget's curves with flickering warmth and sensual shadows.

"I paid for an extra block of time," I assure her. "Then tipped the masseuses enough to keep them 'busy' for a while. No one is going to disturb us."

Bridget's expressive nature has to be one of my favorite things about her. I can actually *see* the moment she decides she's ready to try. Determination brightens her blue eyes as she starts to push herself upright.

Brave, but still fretful. Casting fluttery glances around the room. "How do we do this?"

She won't be doing anything. I touch under her chin, lifting her eyes to mine. "Who takes care of you?" I demand.

Bridget swallows. "Y-you do?"

I kiss her forehead. "Good girl. Now, lie back for me."

ADRIAN SENSES every twinge of my trepidation. He smooths his purr into a dull roar, knowing the vibrations will melt what's left of my bones.

It helps that I was already so relaxed. Knowing our alpha, it's entirely possible he planned all of this to a T.

His effortless sophistication may fool others, but I know better. Any casual pretense he puts on is as calculated as everything else this brilliant man does. Including the moment he carelessly shucks his towel, tossing it onto the other massage table without breaking stride.

Holy God.

I'd say I forgot how insanely, *unbelievably* hot he is, but that would be a lie. And not a convincing one.

His masculine beauty still stuns me all over again, though. The chiseled lines and bulging quads. His enormous shoulders and muscled arms. Candlelight only accentuates every sculpted plane; not to mention, his richly tanned skin.

My mouth waters when he turns to face me, putting his cock and knot on full display. They're every bit as impressive as I remember—curving hard and high toward his navel. I lick my lips when he cups a careless hand around himself and works a pearly bead of pre-cum to the swollen head.

Oh *hell*.

My Omega whines, the sound too jagged and needy to be contained. Hearing it, the alpha pauses with his hand halfway up my thigh. His focus snaps from the place between my legs to my face.

Whatever expression I'm wearing puts a rumble along the edge of his purr. His fingers curl against my thin skin when an answering rush of slick seeps out of me.

"Tell me what you want, baby girl," he husks.

Chagrin burns my middle. My knees close automatically. Adrian allows it, but his leather musk takes on a dark, dangerous quality.

Azure eyes gleam in the dim room. "Who takes care of you?" he asks again, entirely intent on my answer. *Demanding* it.

Something inside me shifts. Or cracks. Or maybe... *soars*.

"You do," I reply.

And, God help me, I *believe* that.

Isn't this the whole reason we're here? Him, seeing how upsetting this week has been for me, and doing everything possible to relax me?

Adrian's approval is as tangible as his low, rough voice. "That's right. Smart, beautiful girl. Now, tell me what you need."

My eyes drop to his erection. I fight down my embarrassment, ignoring the impulse to silence my Omega the way I normally do. "Could I... have you? While you have me?"

Feral intensity glimmers in his gaze, a growl edging over his purr. "You're *my* omega. You can have *anything*. Everything."

A breathless moan catches in my throat. More slick gushes from my pussy, sliding onto the massage table. Adrian snaps his heated stare between my thighs. His scent swells into a dizzy cloud of warmth.

Stalking to the top of the table, he gives a sharp nod toward its edge. "Rest your neck there and let your head fall back."

Confusion creases my brows, but rightness zings through my blood when I obey his orders. The new position arches my back just enough to put my breasts on full display, the tingling nipples peaked toward the ceiling.

When Adrian steps around the table's corner, his intentions are clear. My face might be upside-down, but my mouth is at the perfect level for his hard cock. He cups my cheek, using his other hand to draw another burst of pre-cum to the tip. Brushing it over my lower lip.

"Is this what you want?"

His flavor explodes across my tongue, and I moan, opening wide to let him glide the throbbing shaft into my mouth. He snarls, snapping his hips forward. Filling my throat with a quick, deep plunge that leaves me gasping when he rips himself away.

Seeing my stunned gape, he weaves his fingers into my hair, tugging. "*Who takes care of you?*"

Oh. My. God.

"You do!" I keen, trying to take him back into my mouth.

He gives me what I want before pulling out just as ruthlessly. "That's *right*," he growls. "I'll make sure you breathe. I'll fill your belly with my cum. I'll spray it all over your pretty tits. I'll kiss your clit until you come for me. Because you're *mine*. And I take care of what's mine."

OH. MY—

"*Oh!*"

Adrian stretches his tall frame over me, reaching one arm up to balance on the table. His knee slides onto the edge of the padded surface, right beside my head. His cock hits the back of my throat the same second his lips seal around my throbbing clit.

I shriek, trying to suck in another gasp. His thick, hot hardness only slips deeper. Just as I feel the lash of his tongue over the pulsing nub at the top of my folds.

A distant part of me recognizes his game. He's making sure I'm so consumed by him that I can't think about how I might taste. Because every time I try to—

To—

OH!

"Fucking hell," Adrian snarls, licking down to my pussy. Rimming it with slippery heat. "*Bridget.*"

My throat closes over his girth. Dark, smokiness coats my tastebuds. Buzzing need and want and *rapture* light every cell in my body.

He pulls away right before I start to sputter. My hands fly up, feeling the firm swell of his knot, beating fuller every minute. When I knead it, the alpha buries his face against my slick core with renewed abandon. He groans, the sound serrated.

This is Adrian. *Adrian.* Who always looks so put together and always has a plan. Adrian... *unraveling.* Thrusting into my mouth with desperation that sets my blood on fire. Pulling my hair to guide my head. Bucking like he'll die if he doesn't get inside me.

Yet, even as he lets himself loose, he's still showing me something new. Pleasuring me in a way I've never experienced. Slipping his tongue into my quivering pussy. Licking past the opening. Molding his lips around my puffy clit and bathing it with molten *heat*, oh *God*—

He feels me quicken, pouring slick while my insides cinch and flutter. "Yes," he roars. "*Come.*"

The bark sends me over a cliff. Spinning. Flying. Dipping. Dying.

All while he blocks my throat with his thickness.

My body arches, everything coiled between my hips snapping with a rush of relief that has me collapsing onto the table. Adrian scrapes his teeth against my thigh, sucking hard enough to bruise when he groans and rips his cock out of my mouth, rising onto his bent knee and spurting across my breasts.

The sensual scent of leather probably has no business pairing with lemon, but the combination makes my heart ache. Adrian lowers himself and carefully lifts my head, banding an arm under my neck to help me see the mess we made.

His voice is a low rasp. "Look how beautiful you are."

Candlelight jumps over the stretch marks and scars banded around my middle. Slick is smeared between my inner thighs, and my whole chest is coated in a thick layer of his release. My skin shines, covered in oil and sweat.

I'm a wreck.

But I feel like...

A queen, my Omega supplies. As if it's some obvious fact.

"Come here."

Adrian gently cleans me with his towel and helps me stand. Moving slowly, he wraps me in a spa robe and dons his own before balling up the linens from both tables and stuffing everything down a concealed laundry chute.

I feel better knowing no one will see the state of the towels. But his scent is still *all over* me. And mine—

Oh shit.

Mine is all over *him*.

Mortification pricks my center. Adrian senses it immediately, stiffening as he ties his robe's sash.

He leaves the front gaping, turning to snatch me close and press his lips over mine. I start to squawk, but—

But...

The traces of me left on his lips are bright and sweet. Mellow, almost. Like a creamy dessert sprinkled with zest.

He groans when I tentatively touch my tongue to his, the masculine sound forcing a whine from my Omega. Or me.

Or *both* of us?

I'm so dizzy with relief, I barely notice him slipping his touch from my side to the hem of my robe. A moment later, he holds his palm up, showing me a glossy layer of fresh slick. Before I manage to process, Adrian paints a wide stripe of my essence down his chest. Over his flexing abs. All the way to his half-hard cock and *very* full knot.

Rubbing my scent *everywhere*.

My mouth falls open. His curves his into the most handsome grin. "On second thought," he says, offhand, "I think I'll go to lunch like this."

IT'S WEDNESDAY.

Thank God.

I don't think I could survive another hour without seeing Bridget. Especially today.

Clouds meander across the sky above me. The kind that are just thick enough to block out the sun, but not dramatic enough to signal a storm.

Fitting.

I shift on the blanket I laid out in Bridget's backyard, calling her name when I hear her cooing to Munchies. Her footsteps clack toward the back porch, and her red head pokes out of the French doors.

"Salty? Are you *outside*? In the *daylight*?"

My mouth kicks up despite the bittersweet slicking my insides. "Just get over here, Bubbles. I have snacks."

It's really more like a picnic. But we're not going to dwell on how pitifully romantic I've become.

Because then I would have to tell you just how glowy Bridget's skin looks in today's blue blouse. And how the navy eyeshadow she chose somehow turns her eyes lighter and her freckles darker. And the way both of those little details make my chest—and my sweatpants—tighter.

Hell.

I've hardly even *touched* this woman.

And she owns me.

Especially when she bounces over and plops onto the blanket without skipping a beat. She stretches out beside mine, highlighting how much taller I am. When I lift my head and find her feet level with my calves, I chortle.

Bridget sighs dramatically. "Always so damn salty. What are we going to do with you?"

Good fucking question.

I ignore the cosmic irony of her joke and reach behind me for the plate of food I assembled. Bridget chooses a strawberry and chews it thoughtfully, watching the clouds drift over us.

They don't seem to bother her, which is annoying. Here I was, wallowing in the overcast weather like it's some tailor-made omen of impending doom. But this little omega smiles, points to a particular patch of white fluff, and chirps, "Look, a duck!"

Which would be *annoying*.

Except she's so damn *cute*.

I snatch the hand gesturing at the lackluster sky and bring it to my lips, deciding the whole hands-to-ourselves thing will end now. When I brush a kiss over her knuckles, bright, sugared perfume seeps into the air.

Mm. Good fucking—

"Your heat is coming soon," I rumble, nipping at her thumb. "I can tell."

Bridget frowns at the sky. A sharper edge lines her essence. "I think it's going to be early." Her shoulder bumps mine. "Too many alphaholes hanging around."

My grin is short-lived. It fades into a solemn expression as I turn to face her. "Do you still want us to leave before your heat?" I ask quietly.

She blows out a slow exhale, gazing pensively overhead. "It's not as simple as what I *want*."

But it literally is. At this point, I can't imagine her going through that alone—mostly because the thought makes me *feral*.

Pretty sure the four of us would go out of our minds. Worrying about her. Hating whatever volunteer alphas tend to our omega with every fiber of our beings.

Dante would probably end up living in his car, parked across the street. Adrian may not even be able to walk out the front door.

And if they're traveling for road games...

Fuck.

Am *I* going to be able to stay away?

"Adrian's made it clear you're all willing to—what is called —*pinch hit*?" She wags her eyebrows at her own joke, but I sense the way her bright sweetness dulls to a subtle citrus tease. "I don't think I can do it, though."

Trying to understand other people's emotions is new for me. But for her?

I picture Bridget going to a clinic, knowing exactly what to expect. "Because it would be different?" I guess.

She snorts quietly. "No. I'm pretty sure I'd love the differences."

The urge to leave her to her secrets is strong. I've never been one to delve into anybody's innermost thoughts. But if she'd left me alone in mine, would I have gotten up the courage to call the doctors today? Would I be going in to determine the fate of my career this week?

It's odd to realize we have this habit in common—hiding our soft parts. She does it with bubbles; I do it with salt. But we're the same.

Which means she needs me the way I needed her.

I push an exhale out of my nose and hold her hand in both of mine, turning to face her again. "Bridget," I murmur, frowning when her mouth wobbles and her scent keeps dissipating. "If there's ever anything you want to tell me, I promise I won't say a word back."

She bites the corner of her lip, considering. Her eyes fall closed a second later, her expression one of total devastation. "If you stay," she starts, slow and scratchy, "I'll never want you to leave. I'll want to *bond*. And one day, you might meet someone you're all scent-sensitive to. A true *mate*."

I hear the pain layered into that one word. The longing and sorrow. I fight to keep my mouth closed, honoring my promise to let her get it all out.

Pain glows in her soft blue eyes when they flutter open and fly to mine. "I won't have mates."

Something buried in the deepest part of me squirms. Nausea and a breathless sort of denial rush into my diaphragm.

But what can I say? We'd know by now if we were her mates.

Her scent is just strong enough for me to sense its blade. Feel the way it carves canyons in my lungs. *Strong* enough, sure... but if it were right, it wouldn't *hurt*.

It's fucking infuriating. How can she be so utterly, epically *perfect*—even with this one lingering, stinging streak of *pain*?

She rewards my tense silence with an answer. "When my perfume came in, my parents knew something was... *off*. They took me to see every omega doctor and specialist they could find, but no one could figure out why my scent just got *worse*. It started off as some super-sharp version of lemon cream, but then it just got *so acidic...*"

She doesn't need to tell me. I'm tasting it right now. The electric edge of bitterness that pricks my tongue on each inhale. When Bridget sees my nostrils flare, she swallows hard. A heartbreakingly humorless smile curves her mouth.

"It's actually gotten a lot better," she mumbles. "It was *really* bad in high school. And college. But either way, it will never be *right*, like omega perfume is supposed to be. And alphas won't ever feel that scent-sensitive pull for it."

She sighs, shaking her head. Her smile grows into a genuine, achingly wistful thing. "You guys, though? There's no way you don't have a mate out there. And once you find them, I know you'll be everything they ever dreamed of."

Fuck. My *heart*. Agony cuts a jagged path through the stuttering organ. Then cleaves it into fourths.

Because this look on her face... Bridget *wanted* mates. And picturing her, younger and less confident, sitting in some damn doctor's office. Being told she would never have the security and love she needs.

Fuck.

There's more than that, though. Painted into every pained crease marring her pretty face.

She wants to be *our* mate.

She wishes we would be everything *she's* ever dreamed of.

But here she is, smiling for me. Earnestly hoping there's someone out there to make us complete. Someone she thinks would be better for us than her.

How could that be true?

Who could be better than Bridget?

I growl, unable to hold my silence when a fat tear rolls down her cheek. She lifts her free fingers to my mouth, gently pressing them to my lips before I can say anything.

The look on her face—I can't *breathe*. "Shh," she tells me gently. "You promised."

She's right.

Always right. But this time? I *hate* it.

All of this is so fucking unfair to her. And she isn't even angry about it.

She shifts to her side, finally looking back up at the sky. "Did I ever tell you why I'm friends with Betty?"

Her mind works in the funniest ways, but I've learned to go with it. She's brilliant—and I'm just lucky to be along for the ride.

When she shoots me a meaningful look, silently releasing me from my pledge not to answer her, I rasp, "No."

She bites her lower lip again, considering how much to share. I dare to scoot close enough to rest my forehead against hers, dropping my voice into a whisper. "Tell me, baby."

Her scent swells, just from that one simple endearment. The cracks in my lungs start to tear. Bridget quietly sighs at the sky.

"Because I understand her," she murmurs, scanning the clouds. "Being old and bitter and mean; that's just her armor. And I get that. Having defense mechanisms so no one ever looks too closely at why you're alone... I've lived that way for a long time. I think you have, too."

Goddamn it.

Goddamn it.

My chest shudders, a purr ripping from my very soul. She smiles at it, the expression as soft as her fingers, grazing a tender path over my temple, combing my hair back. Her brows pinch as she changes the subject again. "Your scent is different today. Deeper, like the ocean after a storm."

That's a nice way to describe the overwhelming tide of anxiety I've been treading all afternoon. I let my eyelids fall shut and focus on the places where we touch—our foreheads, our fingertips, our shoulders—hoping I can keep from panicking when I admit, "I called the doctor and made an appointment. To go see about playing. They're going to run tests."

Her perfume dulls, the sweetness and acidity fading to the subtlest of scents. "Why now?"

So smart, I realize again. *Always cutting to the chase.*

I think I might... *love* that about her.

I open my eyes to stare into hers. "Because going to your school last week made me realize how much I miss baseball. Even the piddly bullshit like high school teams. I can't explain it—but the game makes sense to me in a way nothing else does. Even that crappy field felt like coming home. And the more I thought about it... I'm not ready to be done."

Bridget absorbs every word, slowly nodding. "Then you're not done."

Our fingers entwine as she squeezes my hand. "I'm proud of you, by the way," she whispers. "For calling and making an appointment."

God.

Maybe there are a lot of things I love about her.

I smirk to clear the tightness in my throat, hoping a half-smile will hide the fear clawing at my chest. "Yeah, well. I felt pretty good about it until I came out here and saw this bullshit."

I throw my free hand toward the overcast sky. Bridget darts a quick glance upward and breaks into a true grin. "Oh, come on. They're just clouds, Salty."

I continue complaining in an effort to entertain her more than anything else. "Mm hmm. Clouds. Gray. The endless gloom of a meaningless existence. No big deal."

She laughs, a musical sound that warms my jittery insides. "I have an idea."

But she doesn't elaborate. She waits, gazing at the swirling slate sky like she has nowhere else to be.

I eventually nudge her shoulder with mine. "Well?"

"Patience," she giggles. "Just keep your eyes up above for a while, okay?"

I follow her instruction, relaxing on the blanket. My mind drifts, and the clouds do the same, swirling, spilling errant beams of gold while I consider all the secrets our omega shared.

Minutes pass by, but neither of us speaks. A warbling birdsong and the hiss of nearby sprinklers blur into the breeze. Leaves whistle, and the sun gradually starts to sink.

"Keep watching," she whispers, so I do.

And then I see it.

Nothing has changed. The sky is still overcast, with thin patches of blue between gauzy gray. Until the sun starts to set.

First, the gold glow lining the gossamer edges of the cirrus strands gets stronger. Then, a tinge of orange creeps into the mix.

More moments pass. Now there's pink layered between the frothier puffs. And all the big, gloomy masses I thought represented eminent doom?

They're *lavender*.

Before our eyes, a muddle of melancholy becomes... *beautiful*.

I see her point before she explains—if we had a clear blue day, these colors would be a thin band on a distant horizon. Instead, they reflect across the whole sky, filling big swaths with bright bursts of color, shifting and tumbling into new vistas.

Because of the clouds.

Bridget nestles closer to my side. "I've always thought it was sort of amazing," she murmurs, "how the ugliest skies make the best sunsets."

"ARE you sure you want to do this today?"

Colt grunts, shuffling into the exam room. He runs his hand though his loose, over-long hair—a new fidgeting gesture that's replaced the way he used to adjust his Kings cap all the time.

He hasn't worn it in weeks, I realize. Could that have anything to do with the reason we're here? Does wearing it remind him of everything he'll lose if he can't play again?

Oblivious to my sympathetic anxiety, Colt grimaces as he hauls himself onto the table. Sterile paper crinkles under his palms and the seat of his sweatpants. He glares at the source of the noise, then at me.

"Yes."

Alright then.

The door flies open without a knock. We both turn, expecting the doctor, but it's Dante, panting. "The fuck?" he demands. "You guys seriously came here without me?!"

Colt's bearded mouth hardens as mine drops open. We exchange another glance. *Busted.*

Dante narrows his dark gaze at us. "You fuckers! I thought you were going out with Bridget!"

Because we may have implied that we were going to tag along when she mentioned another Zumba class. Sighing, I explain, "Colt made an appointment to hear the results of his scans, but he didn't want—"

"Me?!" Dante practically shouts.

"Drama," Colt grumbles. "You know, like busting into an exam room and yelling? That sort of thing."

Dante simmers down, pouting. "Dickheads."

"How did you know we were here?" I ask. "We only told—"

Adrian steps into the room next. Moving in calm silence, of course. "I thought it was important for *all of us* to be here," he clarifies, shooting Colt and me each a raised brow. "We're a pack now."

It's all I ever wanted—and months ago, it felt like an impossible dream. Now, with Bridget at our center?

Dante's posture slumps. I can tell he agrees, but has to keep arguing because of who he is as a person. He crosses his arms mulishly. "Bridget should be here."

Colt's teeth grind audibly. "I didn't tell her on purpose. I don't want her to stress about this until they've run the damn tests."

I couldn't argue, because that was my logic the night he got in the crash. I decided not to cause our omega any anxiety until we knew what was happening.

Regret bleeds into the emotions churning through my middle. If having Bridget in our lives for real has taught me anything, it's the importance of speaking up and doing what I know is right. I clear my throat, forcing out the words I should have said a long time ago.

"I'm sorry for not calling Bridget to come see you," I tell Colt. "That was my decision. And it was a bad one."

Colt raises his somber gray eyes, staring back at me. I feel Dante gazing at my profile, too. He huffs a sigh.

"Hell, I could have done it," he admits. "Jesse was up to his knees in insurance and press and calling Adrian." My packmate nudges my arm. "You always had to do everything. I could have paid more attention."

I open my mouth to answer—or just gape—but he goes on, throwing his hands up, "And, *carajo*, while we're at it, *I* was the one who ruined our pack's reputation with the press. All the clubbing and girls and spending. *I'm* the reason we had to make this stupid deal with Bridget in the first place."

I wince, remembering. "I could have been honest about my feelings for her, and maybe we could have courted from the beginning."

Colt blows out a deep breath. "Hell, *I* could have been honest about *my* feelings. That day, when we went to her house, I'd never had a reaction like that to another omega. I should have told you guys, but I was so fucking *pissed* about fumbling her..."

Adrian looks at each of us in turn. We all glance at one another, too. A jolt of hopeless amusement hits my throat. Or maybe that's half a sob.

"We *need* her," I realize, the words crumbling.

Colt's answering nod is slow. "Yeah. We do."

Dante huffs a frustrated sound. "I know we're supposed to wait and look for our *real mate*, or whatever, but—"

But none of us *wants* a mate.

We want Bridget.

There's a certain purity to it, really. My attraction to her isn't some instantaneous, uncontrollable thing. The way we fit together wasn't inevitable. Maybe it isn't even *right*, but...

I don't care.

"I love her."

My words cut the others off mid-discussion. They each turn to me again. Adrian's eyes glint, and Colt's jaw hardens while Dante swallows.

"I love her, too," our pack leader admits.

Dante nods. "Me three."

We stare at Colt. Knowing he's usually the holdout. He manages to bob his head, though. "I didn't know I could love someone the way I love her. I won't—I *can't* imagine ever wanting anyone else."

Adrian's gaze sharpens. "Has she said that she thinks we would?"

Colt hesitates, grinding his molars. Debating whether he should share anything Bridget said to him. "She's worried about not being our mate," he finally mutters. "Thinks we'll be out the door the second we find a scent match."

Dante scrubs his hands over his face. "Are we sure she *isn't* our scent match? I mean, I know she isn't our *mate*, but her perfume keeps changing. And getting *better*."

I agree, lifting my chin. "I've noticed that, too. I thought the edge she has sometimes was just normal omega stuff—her scent getting sour or bitter when she's upset... but every time she's been really sad or scared, it's like she starts to disappear instead."

Adrian sighs, looking down at his leather loafers. "I had a similar experience with her at the spa. She was extremely muted at first, feeling unsure. Then she bloomed into this bright sweetness —until her sister showed up and threw some shit in her face. It was upsetting, obviously, and it turned her scent. But it's odd that the same emotions affect her differently each time."

A memory from high school flashes through my mind—Alicia's face, stuck in a sneer as she rolled her eyes behind Bridget's back. My lungs shudder on a growl. "What did her sister say?"

Adrian rarely looks agitated, but he tugs at his silver-blue tie, snarling, "She was horrified that Bridget would dare set foot in the spa she and all her friends frequent. Then she moved on to interrogating me and deigning to grant Bridget *permission* to go to a charity gala."

That sounds like Alicia, actually. The more I think back, the more I wonder why I ever associated with her in the first place.

I have a sneaking suspicion it was all about her red-haired sister.

"Is it the Ospreys' thing?" Dante asks, swiping his phone open. "I saw the invite for it pinned to the fridge, but I figured she wasn't going since she never mentioned it."

"She wasn't *allowed* to mention it, according to Alicia," Adrian goes on, more menacing than I've ever heard him. "She wasn't *supposed* to attend, apparently. Despite being on the damn board of the philanthropy."

Malice glints in Dante's eyes. "Oh, that bitch better *pray* I don't run into her at that gala. No one shames *my* omega."

"*Our* omega," the rest of us growl in unison.

Silence dangles between us. We all flick glances at each other, coming to grips with what we're *really* saying.

Two months ago, I might have let one of them state the obvious. Hell, one month ago, I would have looked to Adrian for a solution.

But Bridget's made me a better alpha. A better packmate and person and friend. So I take a page from her book and stand tall, squaring my shoulders. "I don't care that she's not our mate. I want to bond with her."

The room seems to exhale all at once.

"Thank *God*," Colt groans at the same moment Dante claps, whooping, "*Yes*. Fuck yes."

Adrian smirks at them before settling his gaze on mine. His steady nod drips pack leader approval and pride. "We'll take her out," he decides. "And tell her so."

"AH, FUCK."

Underneath me, Dante snickers. He holds out the hand currently not teasing the waistband of my cut-offs and wiggles his fingers. "Pay up, Pops."

Adrian glares, pulling a money clip out of his back pocket. For the fourth time in twenty minutes.

To be fair, this is only the third bet he's lost to Dante since we sat down. The first time he fished out his money-clip, he was paying for all the food spread across our picnic table.

I'm still amazed by the selection and quality. Every type of bar food or traditional ballgame fare you could think of—jumbo hot dogs, buttery bins of popcorn, churros, cheese fries, and giant turkey legs.

The guys wolfed down two of those apiece before Dante started trying to sneak bites of my funnel cake. I slap at his wrist, nearly guffawing when his eyes widen in faux innocence. "What?!" he asks. "I was getting a bite for *you*."

"Oh yeah *sure*," I toss back, snapping the crispy fried dough from his outstretched fingers with my teeth.

He watches my mouth while I chew, the sweet succulence of mango swelling around me. Its flavor teases my tongue when he plants a playful, smacking kiss on my lips.

Mm. He tastes *great* with funnel cake, actually. We might have a new midnight snack recipe on our hands.

Or breakfast... or an afternoon snack...

Basically, Dante's promise of "anytime, anywhere" has proven to be a lot more literal than I ever imagined. The man is insatiable. And the way he comes for me—so spontaneous, always *burning* with the same carnal *need*—is heady. I'm starting to think I might be addicted to feeling so insanely desired.

He isn't the only alpha in the house who's feeding my newfound compulsion. Turns out our shy, sweet pitcher has his own brand of sensual urgency—and it involves taking me in the most borderline-public place he can get away with. Our garage gym, the hammock in my backyard. And, in one particularly impressive feat, the backseat of Dante's Escalade while we sat in traffic.

Adrian doesn't love it, but his disapproval usually leads to the most delicious "lessons." Never punishments, exactly, but the sorts of mind-bending commands that truly give him the air of a king.

And when I *please* him? My rewards are certainly fit for a queen.

Colt is the only one who's continued to hold back, physically. He still steals my books, lies on the couch with me in the afternoons, and pretends he isn't halfway in love with Munchies.

Honestly? I'm pleasantly surprised by how intimate we've become. Even if my Omega has taken to hoarding his clothes for our nest, needing him *closer*.

She's sort of done that for *all* of them, actually.

But I guess what they don't know won't hurt them?

Or humiliate me...

Jesse is still pouting when he trudges back from the edge of our cage. He sets his helmet on the bench next to him and stuffs a handful of popcorn into his mouth.

"Eating your feelings, Jess?" Colt taunts dryly, turning the page of his latest book. He glances up just long enough to smirk. "You know Dante always wins."

Adrian drops into the spot beside me, shaking his head. "Every damn time."

In a tank top with ripped armholes and a matching set of gray joggers, our pack alpha seems younger and more relaxed than I've ever seen him. Striking aqua eyes glint at me from under the rim of his Kings hat. "Your turn, little blue. I put some money on you, too."

I flash him a grin. "Well, that was just stupid."

All the alphas crack up, even Adrian. Their leader's deep, velvet laugh might be my favorite sound. It warms my belly every bit as much as his heated gaze.

He reaches for Jesse's helmet, setting it on my head and tilting his chin at the makeshift "plate" we've been swinging from. "Make me proud, sweetheart."

My insides quiver and melt. And—thanks to the two ballpark beers I've shared with Jesse—I barely feel embarrassed when my perfume follows me to the edge of our cage.

This place is brilliant. Like Top Golf, but for baseball. Three floors of batting cages, built to open up onto an enormous lawn with posts demarcating different ranges. The ball machines hang from eaves, shooting balls with some sort of sensor magic that pitches them perfectly every time.

Allegedly.

I haven't hit a single ball, and Jesse hasn't done so hot either. Though he made sure to whisper in my ear and tell me it was *my* fault for draining him dry when he got home from practice earlier.

When we arrived, Adrian explained that he had public cages built into the side of King Stadium last year to generate revenue seven days a week, not just on game days. Although the idea was inspired—and proves just how business *and* baseball savvy Adrian is—their pack alpha isn't the reason we ended up here.

It was *all of them.*

The moment I walked in the door, the four alphas started rushing me right back toward it. They all seemed a bit on edge, but when they suggested changing into comfortable clothes and coming *here*, I just went with it.

I figure, if they plan on having a serious discussion of some sort, at least I'll get to hit something first.

If I can hit anything.

I might be utter crap at batting, but the view up here is gorgeous. In the distance, the cloudy sky has given way to another spectacular sunset. Big puffy collections of cumulonimbus glow tangerine, framed by pink wisps and purple cirrus.

I smile to myself, snatching the bat Jesse just dropped against the link fence surrounding our cage. As the first pitch whizzes past me, I decide it doesn't matter how terrible I am at this. The view and the snacks more than make up for it.

More importantly, the guys are *happy* here. Despite whatever tension clogged my living room before we left, Dante's been his usual ham-sandwich self—striking poses and scoring cash off the others when he kicks their asses at batting. Colt brought a book since he can't swing or drink, but he's also made more jokes and eaten more food than I've ever seen before.

Jesse may pout about losing to Dante, but his scent is sweet, and I know the shy smile on his face is real. The polite, phony version he saves for the rest of the world hasn't made one single appearance.

Of all these alphas, though, I think tonight looks the best on Adrian.

His total contentment is palpable. As long as his packmates are happy, he's completely at ease.

Well, his packmates and *me*.

The baseball's already cleared my shoulder, but he still snaps a soft bark. "*Careful*, little blue."

Oof. That definitely doesn't help the whole jiggly-melty-middle thing.

Neither does Dante's quiet, cocky chuckle. "Come here, *querida*."

He appears at my back, bending his knees to wrap his arms around my shorter frame. His rich tan skin shines under the sunset and the stadium lights overhead. Brawny hands flex over mine.

The alpha's voice finds my ear, as low and dark as his laugh. "You're thinking too much," he murmurs, nipping at my earlobe. "Relax for me."

I don't have much choice, given my spine is sort of melting into his abs. A second later, a ball comes down the chute. All the strength around me flexes as Dante strikes.

The motion is so fluid, it actually feels natural. Even to me. A metallic *zing* cracks up my wrists as the bat makes contact and sends our ball flying into the "outfield." Jesse cheers, and Adrian applauds.

Dante rubs his cheek along mine, scent-marking. "See? You're a natural."

I smile up at him. "I think *you're* a natural, slugger. I just look good holding a bat."

His hands drop to my hips, pulling me against the bulge in his loose black shorts. "Mm, you sure do."

Oh hell. These *men*.

How is a girl supposed to keep from dribbling into a puddle?

Dante reaches for his pocket and retrieves the money Adrian

handed him. I realize he got up to help me, even though it cost him a bet. My heart flutters and aches.

Why do they all have to be so wonderful?

Even Colt, who reaches his own hand out and curls his fingers. Dante pouts, ponying up more cash.

"You *both* bet on me?" I gape, swiveling from my gray-eyed alpha to my blue-eyed one.

Colt shrugs, his smirk as enigmatic as ever. "I bet on Dante being a simp."

I laugh, even though his statement pinches my lungs. It's true, though. They're all acting like the entire world revolves around me...

And it might not be forever. Or even for very long.

But it feels pretty damn real to me.

The pack alpha takes his payout, then loops a muscled forearm around my middle to guide me into his lap. Adrian removes my helmet and runs his nose along the shell of my ear. I turn my face to shoot him a look, but the intensity swirling in his eyes stops me. The small smile on his sculpted lips transforms his teasing reply into the sincerest compliment.

"I know a good investment when I see one," he murmurs.

The world could disintegrate, and I'm not sure I'd notice. The longer I stare into Adrian, the slower my breaths come. Until everything fades into a muted haze—except for this alpha's azure eyes.

For a moment—just one half of a second—I let my guard slip.

My Omega slides through that crack, snapping to the surface. *This is our alpha*, she pants, *he's really our alpha. He's really—*

Usually, her babbling optimism pisses me off. But, right now? With everything she ever wanted surrounding me? And so very much *not* mine to keep?

Unfamiliar softness throbs in my chest. *No*, I whisper to her. Aching *with* her. *No, he's not. I'm—*

I'm sorry.

I've never said that to her. Never apologized for shutting her down. Drowning her out. Verbally abusing her into silence because every word she whines breaks my big, stupid heart.

Just like I've never admitted—to myself or my Omega—that I regret taking this deal. One that's crushed my spirit and given me hope in so many unexpected ways.

Like this exact moment.

In this gorgeous, powerful man's lap.

About to cry.

A frown mars Adrian's masculine beauty. "Bridget? Are you alright?"

I open my mouth to say, *yes. I'm fine. It's no big deal.*

But the truth comes out instead. And once I whisper the words, I know I'll never be able to take them back.

"I just wish this didn't have to end. I don't know what I'll do when you leave."

fifty-three

"LEAVE YOU?"

I spit the question like a curse. Or some kind of blasphemy. Leave? *Bridget?*

Planting myself beside Adrian, I reach over to cup her cheek. My Alpha wants me to rage and shout, but I barely scrape out the words to ask, "What are you talking about, cupcake?"

She doesn't answer right away, probably because she's doing everything she can to keep the sheen in her pretty eyes from rolling down her flushed face. I glance across the table for backup, but Jesse looks just as heartsick as our omega... and Colt watches her with a calculating expression.

Carajo. Am I the only asshole who assumed this was as good as *done?*

Behind her, Adrian's worn sigh tells me, *yeah, you are.*

"Our deal," the alpha rumbles to me. "She told us we could stay until her heat, remember?"

Colt chimes in, muttering, "We agreed on eight weeks. It's been five."

"Six," Jesse whispers.

Adrian grinds his jaw. Bridget senses his upset and shrinks down a bit.

Oh, fuck no.

My omega does not *shrink.*

With a growl, I tug her into my arms. She straddles both our laps, but folds herself closer to my chest, hiding her expression against the jagged purr that rolls to life.

Her scent dwindles to a faint lemon thread—but it's still so *wrong,* I feel like I've been stabbed. A cold knife lodges itself in my gullet. Carving deep, dragging downward.

"*Querida,*" I whisper into her braided hair. "You still want us to *leave?* We were going to ask you to let us *stay.*"

My voice breaks on that last word. Bridget whines, the sound small and tight. "If you stay for my heat, my Omega won't understand. She already thinks you're actually my alphas. If you don't leave and I go into heat and you wind up helping me—"

It's not some *possibility.* If she goes into heat and I'm *fucking breathing,* I *will* be there. How could she doubt that?

Fuck. Have I ever *told* her?

I could have put that shit in writing! All those dumbass notes I leave in her lunchbox and it never occurred to me to RSVP "yes" to the woman's heat?!

I'd like to revisit the possibility of me kicking my own ass.

"—I just don't know if she'll be okay after," Bridget finishes. "Being alone."

Four growls break out, Jesse's being the loudest. "You can't *ever* be alone for your heat, bumblebee," he insists, stretching across the table to hold her hand. "It's *dangerous*. And painful."

Bridget bites her lower lip. The sour edge of her scent builds until my eyes water.

At least, that's what I'm telling myself. It could totally be a reaction to picturing my cupcake all alone during her heat haze. Hurting. *Or hurting herself.*

Jesus. I can't *breathe*. I feel sick, but there's no time for that shit. Bridget is *shaking*.

I wrap my arms around all her perfect softness, whispering as she whimpers. "Let us stay with you, *corazón*," I husk. "Please. We want to—"

I catch myself at the last second, turning to the others. They all nod, barely glancing away from Bridget's face long enough to grant their permission.

I take it, settling my eyes on hers. "We want to bond with you."

Her body goes rigid before she thrashes out of my lap. Her eyes dart around us, ensuring none of the families or couples nearby are watching when her voice drops to a hiss.

She pins me with a glare. "Don't *say* things like that, okay? Just—"

She holds up her left hand, where the Cartier diamond shimmers in the last of the evening sun. "This wasn't supposed to be *real*, okay?" she goes on, quiet but firm. "It was a *deal* we made. A *lie* we told. But then you guys moved in, and everything got so —so—"

She bursts into tears. The rest of the guys are on their feet before she can shudder through an inhale, but I stay in my seat. Staring. *Paralyzed.* Thinking about the day I bought that ring.

How I purchased the flashiest one they had. The smugness I felt about leaving without having to bother with an engraving or an ounce of romance. The way I complained about driving to her sister's to *leave it in their mailbox.*

Bridget's right. It really *does* hurt.

I stand, stepping between Adrian and Colt. Reaching for her hand and waiting for her confused gaze to find mine before I pluck the ring off her finger.

Fuck this stupid thing.

Fuck every moment we ever thought of Bridget as anything other than *everything*.

The others shuffle aside so I can cut a clean path to the edge of our cage. Avoiding the floor sensors that would prompt a pitch, I bend to pick up the nearest bat.

Silence rings behind me as I toss the diamond once. Twice. By the third time, I have its size worked out. Its weight.

I toss it a bit higher and swing.

Tink.

The sparkler flies off into the distance. Swallowed by the sunset.

I drop the bat and turn back to the others, dusting off my hands.

"Deal's off."

Bridget gapes, her mouth opening and closing three times before she finally explodes, "Dante! You just—you can't—"

"I did." I shrug, palming her nape and dragging her in for a smacking kiss. When I pull back, I nuzzle at the tears leaking from her eyes, murmuring, "Because that stupid ring and this whole dumb plan can go to hell, Bridget. I don't care about any of it. I just want *you*."

Adrian nods, drifting over to hold her jaw in his palm. "We *all* want you, little blue. *Forever*."

Jesse agrees, coming to her other side. "The four of us have discussed the future and a potential mate," he puts in. "But we unanimously decided we'd rather bond with *you*."

Colt finally joins us, releasing a long breath and staring into her depths to add, "If you'll have us."

BOND WITH ME??

Did they seriously just say that? Is this actually happening?

And where the hell is Adrian *taking us*?

I'm sure my face gave away how astonished I was—because as soon as they finished issuing their new proposal, the pack leader only watched my features for a beat before announcing he knew what I needed.

I followed them, mostly because I was too stunned to object.

I still am. While I trail behind our alpha, I channel my anxiety into unraveling my braids, a dozen questions roaring through my brain.

They want to give up the potential to find a mate? And not just stay for my heat—but forever?

What if I say yes and they change their mind?

What if I say yes and they don't *change their minds?*

Will I ever forgive myself if I let them go without trying?

Will I ever forgive myself if I let them in and they break my heart?

Adrian is unnervingly quiet. Since Dante batted my engagement ring into the sunset, their pack alpha has only spoken to give directions. We obey his low commands without hesitation; I suspect the guys are just as apprehensive about the silent intensity pouring off him as I am.

We make our way from the public batting cages to the tunnel system stretched below. Adrian uses his phone to bypass several security doors. Lights automatically flicker on and off again as we make our way from the new portion of the stadium to the refurbished part.

Adrian finally holds open one last door, waving the guys through and stepping behind me as I pass from the tunnel onto... the field?

"This is the only place in the whole stadium with cameras that turn off," he explains. "We shut them down for practices and training. No other monitor can be paused—and I've added several new angles since the incident here during our first game."

A chill streaks up my back, the memory sinking its claws into my heart.

I know my scent must be *painful* to them at this point. It's never perfectly sweet or mellow—but with the shame and doubt seething in my middle? Colt flinches when I step beside him. He's always been the most sensitive to my scent—and the wince on his otherwise unreadable face slices a little deeper than usual.

I'm *used* to this, damn it. It shouldn't affect me anymore.

Why does it still *hurt?*

And why does it hurt more *by the minute?*

Because you love them.

I want to rage at my Omega. Shove her down. Tell her to cram it. But... that voice isn't even hers.

It's *mine*.

I love them.

How did this happen? I had a plan. I had my armor on. I made smart decisions and guarded myself at every possible turn.

How did their rejection go from an inevitable inconvenience to my greatest fear?

And if I somehow get it together and let them try to be my alphas... will I ever stop waiting for them to leave me?

As if he can sense my spiraling thoughts, Jesse sloughs out a pained sound, opening his arms. Adrian leads the others toward the bases, but the golden-haired alpha pauses to hold me, mumbling into my hair. "You're so stressed, Bee. If you don't want to try this... or you don't want to do it *here*..."

His offer is implied. I know he means it—they would bundle me into the car and take me home right now if I asked them to. None of them would lay a finger on me, now or in my heat, if I said no.

I don't want to, though.

Whatever Adrian has in mind, he seems determined. His solid self-assurance has me curious.

Why did he bring us here?

What does he want them to do to me?

Wondering what the alpha is thinking is much better than being inside my own head, though. I try to focus on that, letting my mind wander over the possibilities. He doesn't keep me waiting, gesturing to the Kings' home plate with a nod.

His aqua gaze snaps to the guys. "Our omega needs us to show her how much we want to bond with her." He turns his seething, ocean irises on me. Silently asking, *Right?*

Damn him. How does he *do* this? Reading my thoughts and secret hopes and the fears I barely admit to myself?

He sees it *all*. And drags them out of me with a simple arch of his dark, winged brow.

I let my chin drop, acknowledging his wordless question with an equally muted answer. Adrian takes it, though, sending me a burst of pure pride before bending to kiss my forehead.

"Good girl," he murmurs, then, louder, "Whoever you want to ride will lay down here."

He removes his shirt and rolls his shoulders. The tanned muscles ripple. Diffused light from the cages next door pools between his cut abs as his eyes glimmer. "So, who's first, omega?"

I'm not used to listening to the voice clamoring inside me. But if this is supposed to be practice for what my heat could be like—what they could *all* be like...

For once, I tune in to my Omega's insistent nudges. Repeating the name she produces instantly. "Colt."

I expect the salty alpha to scowl at me. Or at the very least grumble. Instead, intensity snaps across his face. He pauses for a moment, then unceremoniously tosses the book in his hand to the nearest patch of turf and steps closer.

"You sure?" he asks, gesturing at his recovering leg. "I'm not exactly on my A-game, Bubbles."

Something about the dangerous gleam in his gray eyes tells me I might not be able to *handle* his A-game. Not all at once, at least.

But the wry wistfulness filling his features says something else. And I wonder... has he been holding back because of me and our situation? Or has he been worried he'd disappoint me?

I hold his gaze while I nod. Whispering one word. "Please?"

"PLEASE?"

Fuck. Me.

Bridget's blue eyes brim with earnest desire. She keeps her chin up, but her teeth worry the plump curve of her lower lip, betraying her vulnerability.

I might make an absolute idiot out of myself, but I'm not saying no to that face.

Certain things get easier every day. My shoulder still feels tight and creaky, but it doesn't hurt to maneuver out of my T-shirt and lie it on the dirt next to Adrian's. Dante moves next, adding his own Kings tank to the makeshift blanket.

We're covering home plate, which gives me an idea.

"You know," I say, stepping into Bridget's side, running my fingertips down her arm. "You and I haven't covered *a lot* of the bases yet, Bubbles."

It's true. We've barely kissed. And I'm not convinced the peck she gave me after our shower interlude should even count.

Bridget's definitely self-conscious. Instead of softening, she gives a bratty huff and rolls her eyes, puckering her lips. A bolt of warmth impales my heart, turning liquid. It spills into my center, swirling.

I ignore her mouth and press a kiss to her forehead, tucking a loose strand of shimmering auburn hair behind her ear. "Not yet," I decide.

Before the indignation fully fills her face, I drop to the ground with a grunt. One lungful of her lemon sweetness is more than enough to have my cock fighting my fly. I unbutton my jeans and shuck them in one go.

I've spent a lot of time on baseball fields, but I can't say I've ever been naked on one before. I've been *close*—

Big blue eyes roam down my bare body, lingering on my erection and the filling knot at its base. The sugary tones in her scent brighten. My mouth waters as she shifts on her feet, soaking her panties.

Adrian molds his naked front to her back, bending to rumble in her ear. "You want this, little blue? All of us at the same time?"

Gasping quietly, she whines when his teeth nip her neck. Our pack alpha nods once, deciding the matter as he fingers the waistband of her shorts.

She reads his unspoken order, lifting her face to give him one last nervous look. Adrian's bright gaze softens. He nuzzles a scentmark along her cheek. "It's safe here," he promises. "I'd never let anyone else see you come."

He means outside of our pack.

This is the first time I've thought those words. *Our pack.* Because, in this moment, they feel true.

We're a pack. This is our omega.

It should be so simple.

Bridget rubs her cheek along our alpha's jaw, leaving him with a fond smile while she shimmies out of her cut-offs. She even takes her top off, brave woman that she is.

I know we're safe here, like Adrian said, but it *feels* very exposed. *Jesse's gonna love this shit.*

Sure enough, our pitcher looks around the enormous empty stadium with a feral gleam in his green eyes. His toasty, caramelized scent deepens as he tosses his shirt to me, too.

I ball it up under my head and make an exasperated gesture at my cock, putting on an air of grumpy impatience in the hopes it might help Bridget feel more normal. "While I'm still young, Bubbles."

It works. Bridget smirks and drops to her knees. I take a second to make sure our "blanket" protects her creamy skin effectively, then—

Jesus Christ.

I've spent months—over a *year*—dreaming about getting my hands on her glorious body this way. The bare skin of her ass is silky and smooth, stretched over her supple curves. When I ghost my touch forward, to the crease where her thighs fold against her hips, I feel the scars there.

The adoration welling in my middle expands. I caress the deep silver-white lines, whispering while I look at her face, "You're gorgeous, baby."

Dante interrupts, of course. Appearing at my right side, stark naked, without a trace of shame.

He cups his hand around Bridget's jaw, turning her attention up to him. Their gazes clash. Hers flutters while his smolders. "Which base am I on, *querida*?"

Bright blue beams trace his thick dick and the balls drawn tight between his even thicker thighs. She tosses her loose hair back, preening as she nods over her shoulder.

At her ass.

Oh *fuck*.

Dante curses, low and vicious, dropping to his knees between mine. His hands are rough as he slips one under her top and uses the other to grip her neck. "Gotta at least *start* on first," he mutters, angling her for a deep, licking kiss.

She moans and meets him with equal passion, biting his lips and sliding her tongue into his mouth.

I watch, breathless with envy and lust. My fingers dimple her upper thighs, automatically pulling her forward. Notching her glistening slit against my straining cock.

I don't care what fucking base this is; her wet heat feels *incredible*. I slough out a groan, tilting my hips to press the underside of my dick further into her lush folds. Until I feel her clit throb along my tingling skin.

Her perfume spikes. Dante growls, swallowing her needy noises and rolling her nipples under her shirt. Jesse falls to his knees like he's been shot. His hands fumble for his waistband, but Adrian squeezes his shoulder to slow him down.

The pack alpha kneels on my left, rolling his joggers below his groin with much more deliberation. "Dante," he says, not quite barking. "Share."

Our shortstop swallows a grunt, breaking their lip lock and nudging Bridget's cheek with his nose. "Kiss our alpha, cupcake. I have work to do back here."

She whines, practically flinging herself at Adrian. He catches her with a satisfied rumble, purring deep in his chest while he strokes a hand down her spine and fondles her big, perfect tits with the other.

Her clit beats against my shaft, a maddening pulse I can't resist rubbing against. When I start to slowly rock into the contact, Bridget pours slick all over my lap.

I'm not the only one groaning from the scent—Dante echoes the sound, pushing at her back and dropping to his forearms. Adrian guides our omega forward, bringing her torso flush with mine. Trapping my hard cock between my burning body and her slick slit.

Jesse watches with wide eyes. He grips his own erection, working the pre-cum at the tip over his length. His mouth gapes when he glances back at Dante.

I realize why when Dante's tongue rims her back hole.

Motherfucking—

Bridget gasps, bucking forward. Perfect wet warmth glides over the entire underside of my dick. The two silver balls pierced through my frenulum tug slightly when they roll around Bridget's clit. I suck in a snarl as Adrian hums reassurances to her.

"Such a beautiful girl," he praises. "Are you going to take your alphas at the same time, little blue? Let us show you that we can cover *all* these bases?"

Bridget *keens*. The gorgeous sound reverberates into the stands, leaving her lips parted. I want to kiss her so damn badly, but I *know* I should wait. Let her focus on how good we can make her feel.

Her pussy gushes slippery lemon slick. Dante roughs out a desperate roar, burying his face as far into her cheeks as he can get. I slide my hands from her hips to her ass, spreading her open for him.

Adrian pets her hair, gripping his own cock. Holy *shit*, his knot is enormous. Thinking about her taking it during his rut has me leaking salty pre-cum. It smears along Bridget's clit. Her nails dig into my chest.

Jesse's head falls back as he moans at the combined scent. Bridget hears him and practically lunges to the right, sucking the head of his dick into her mouth.

"*Ungh*. Bee. *Fuck*." His long fingers weave into her unraveling braid, tugging at the roots when she pulls him to the back of her throat.

In one go.

Jesus.

I really am in love.

Adrian purrs his approval, his voice dropping into a low

timbre I recognize from the aftermath of his rut—it's his Alpha, speaking to her Omega.

"Come here, sweetheart."

Bridget pulls off Jesse's cock with a cry. He's hard as fuck—purple head, veins roped up the shaft, a knot that seems full to bursting.

Our omega whimpers as creamy white dribbles from the tip. She laps at it, reluctant to leave. Adrian's mouth kicks up, taking the sting out of his next command. "*Now.*"

Our girl really is a bubbly little brat. With a pout, she turns her head to the pack leader and slants a look up his torso, which roughly translates as *this better be good.*

Adrian's eyes spark. "Do you want both your alphas to come in your mouth at the same time?"

Okay. Yeah. That'll do it.

She whines loud enough to pump my knot fuller. It presses against the clenching muscles at her opening. Dante's tongue flicks down to tease her there, lapping at my swollen mass inadvertently.

It doesn't bother him, and—hell—I guess I don't care, either. Because Bridget and I both suck in sharp breaths. She bends closer to me, exposing more for him to lavish. The new position makes just enough room for my cock to kick up straight. She glances at my face, beseeching me.

Please? she said. And those pretty, endless eyes.

God, I *love* her.

That thought swirls through my center as I thrust, shoving into her pussy in one ruthless punch. Slippery heat glides around me. My piercing drags along her perfect heat. Bliss surges up my spine as my balls twitch tighter.

I'm already on edge, but fucking *Dante.* The bastard must know what he's doing, curling his tongue between her thighs. Plunging it into her ass. Making her squirm and clench around my cock.

I buck harder and faster, trying to outrun the climax barreling down my back. Bridget rides me, sucking Adrian's thick cock until he pulls her off and guides her to Jesse's. I feel one of Dante's fingers slip into her, pressing along my shaft. He keeps licking around it until he can fit two. Then three.

Shit. Fuck.

The pressure is intense, pushing at me through her thin inner walls. Bridget mewls and thrashes. Sucking Jesse down like she needs the taste of his cum to live.

"Bridget," he grits. "*Bee.* You're gonna make me—"

Adrian calmly reaches over Bridget and grabs the base of Jesse's dick, squeezing hard. "No," he orders. "You'll wait."

Oh, good fucking—

My Alpha wants to rip my packmate's throat out. And challenge Adrian. But I don't. And, instead, all that adrenaline and aggression burns into even stronger *need*.

Bridget replaces the alpha's hand, kneading Jesse's knot much more gently while she suckles at Adrian's cock. Our leader growls, low and satisfied. "That's my pretty blue. So fucking good. Are you ready for us, omega?"

She moans, nodding and taking him deeper. I snap my hips faster, thrusting into her whirling wetness while Adrian wraps his hand around her stroking fingers, helping her maintain a rhythm for Jesse while she draws his own climax to the surface.

They both snarl and jostle closer, angling their bodies to fit their heads into her open mouth. Bridget grabs at their knots while they spurt across her tongue.

Her perfume *explodes*—so fucking delicious and sharp and good *God*.

Dante chooses that moment to thrust, replacing his scissoring fingers with his cock, circling his hips to drill as deep as she'll let him. Her pussy pulses and *tugs*, cinching tight around me.

Jesse and Adrian fall back while Dante curses, squirting pure heat into her ass. Bridget's mouth drops open in rapture, her eyes rolling as she starts to come all over me.

Covering the three of us in slick. Gushing and fluttering. Grinding her clit into my knot.

The stadium blurs into a starry flash of deep blue. My body bows, straining to erupt as deep inside her as I can get. She takes it *all*, her hands scrabbling at my chest. Leaving scratch marks that will make me hard all over again, later.

I wedge one hand between us to press firm circles over her throbbing bud, and she screams my name. "*Colt!*"

Blinking, I clear my vision, wanting to memorize this moment. Knowing how she looks while she whimpers and slides into a second orgasm will stay with me forever.

Awe echoes through my mind, replaying everything we've covered. Feeling her tits, filling her pussy and her ass. Pumping into her mouth.

Second, third, home...

There's only one base missing, for me.

So, my free fingers find her nape, tangling in her gorgeous hair as I guide her lips to mine.

"Grand slam," I whisper. And I kiss her.

"ON A SCALE of one to Bianca Censori, how naked do I look?"

Emma and her sister-in-law, Meg, both cast me dubiously amused glances. "You look *hot*," Emma chimes.

Meg flashes a perfect smile, flipping her wavy blonde lob over the thin straps of her bubblegum-pink evening gown. Mischief lights her crystal irises. "A seven?"

Her bestie, Remi, floats closer and pats my bare arm. "Don't listen to her, Bridget," the sweet, honey-scented omega hums. She glances at the mirror across from us and adjusts the bust of her teal column gown, pinching the silk until it stays up.

She's stuffed the cups with boob-enhancers, but I still look like a porn star beside her. Thankfully, my girls are safely supported by this dress's butter-yellow corset.

The color may be light enough to give the impression of nudity from far away, but Adrian special-ordered the piece from a designer in Paris—and, up close, thousands of pearls line every delicate drape of lace-and-satin.

It's a piece of art, really. I still can't believe he had it *commissioned*.

Weeks ago.

Just in case, he'd explained with a heated smirk. Then proceeded to tell me he'd also gotten together with my friends' pack alphas and arranged this decadent day of primping before the gala.

Deep down, I just know *he* chose this salon—the one my sister and mother used for years. The nicest place in town for this sort of thing.

And one I was forbidden to patronize, lest I embarrass Alicia.

Remi senses the way my scent sours and rubs a soothing hand over my exposed upper back, sweeping aside the red curls styled in a half-updo. Her own black ringlets sit piled high in an artful bun, with two loosely coiled tendrils framing her clear golden-brown complexion and gorgeous hazel-blue eyes.

Before she can offer more reassurance, her sister saunters out of the dressing room, adjusting her own boobs as she glides on six-inch heels.

I swear, the girl could run a marathon in those things.

Serena flicks a curtain of glossy black hair back, turning to check herself out in another mirror. Layers of lavender tulle swish around her legs—the fabric so thin, the outlines of her legs are fully visible under the full skirt. And strategic triangles had to be sewn into the halter portion.

She pouts at her reflection, rolling her eyes. "Goddamn Tristan. I can't be a princess *and* a slut at the *same time*." She flashes the green version of her twin's hazels at me, smiling conspiratorially. "I'm happy to be either, but would it have killed him to pick a lane?"

Emma laughs, fluffing out her skirts. "Zane definitely went full-on royal for mine. I asked him if I could wear my fuzzy socks under it, but he said no."

She does look like an extra from Bridgerton, wearing a stiff A-line gown made of textured seafoam-colored fabric. With the small tiara braided into her wavy blonde hair, it's very elegant.

Serena finishes fussing with her mascara and drops a swift glance at my hands. *Oh shit.*

Of my friends, Serena Thorne is definitely the most observant. Her brows lift. "Don't you want to wear your ring, Bridge?"

Ummmmmm.... well....

I look at my bare finger, remembering how Dante plucked the ring right off it. Sent the damn thing sailing into the sunset. Like it—and our whole stupid deal—meant nothing.

Because *I* meant everything.

A small smile tilts my lips. "Guess I left it at home. Oh well."

She quirks her brow higher, but she doesn't question me. Likely because my perfume has brightened at the memory of my alphas taking me on King Stadium's home plate.

Grand Slam indeed.

Sensing the swell of my own perfume is still new for me. I'm used to being acutely aware of its existence... but not the specific smell. For one thing, it's never been quite this potent or frequent before. And, secondly, I've started wearing less de-scenter in general.

Part of it might be my heat coming next week, I suppose. And maybe a little bit the fact that all four alphas living my house groan like I'm torturing them every time the lemony aroma spikes.

Either way, it's been *different* for the last couple of days. Almost... *sweet?*

I shake the silly, hopeful thought from my mind and reach for my special de-scenting spray. Adrian bought it for me after our spa trip, explaining that it was a less powerful brand. Because, in his words, if I "insist" on "hiding my perfection," he requests I don't do it so completely.

I bite back a grin at the memory. My phone buzzes in my other palm. Our group chat—*Bridget's Ball Boys*.

DANTE

Incoming, querida.

attached image

I gasp, pressing the very nude, *very hard* picture to my chest. By the time I chance another peek, the guys have already gone off on their packmate.

COLT

Dante GODDAMN IT

JESSE

Seriously?

Right in front of my tux?

ADRIAN

Do you not have a side chat to send these pictures in like the rest of us?

DANTE

Boss is sending our omega dick pics, too??

BRIDGET

You all* send me dick pics.

More than once a day, since you've been gone.

I had to unpair my phone from my laptop 

JESSE

Maybe we should make a Dropbox.

COLT

For our dicks?

DANTE

A Dickbox

BRIDGET

Or you could just stop sending me pictures of your penises 😊

DANTE

No can do, cupcake.

I've been hard since Thursday.

48 hours is wayyyyy too long.

My lips quirk higher. They played their first "away" game this week. It was only about four hours away, in South Florida, but they've all expressed their deep displeasure about it.

Even Adrian. Within six hours of their departure on Thursday morning, he had created a whole packet for me—their full season schedule, every travel game, the specs of their team jet, which hotels they would stay in, how it all fits with the end of my semester, summer break, and the following school year.

It took me a few pages to realize what all his careful planning really was: an invitation.

A *request*.

Come with us, it said. Be *with us*.

And the schedule I sent back, showing nearly every summer away stretch blocked out on my calendar...

I suppose that was me saying *yes*.

Emma notices my expression and beams. "I'm really glad you're letting them stay with you," she murmurs, keeping her voice low for privacy. "Are you excited?"

About my heat? I nearly snort. Historically, losing my ability to take care of myself for a week has been a living nightmare. It never occurred to me that I could *get* excited about it.

But as I glance around at all the girls—all glowing, with healed bond marks and true happiness in their expressions...

My own mouth curves into a bemused smile. "Yeah, I think maybe I am."

I'M NOT sure what I expected, but it wasn't *this*.

The Ash Pack's gala is widely known to be *the* prestigious philanthropic event in Orlando. I grew up attending stuff like this —jammed into tuxedos, stuffed into ballrooms that smelled like too many things and also, somehow, nothing at all. Eating hors d'oeuvres off silver trays and pretending champagne was water... because it sure went down like it was.

Crystal and linens and chandeliers. Twelve-piece bands. Top-shelf liquor.

The Ash Pack's gala has all of that.

But it's also *fun*.

Pink bubbles shimmer inside their flutes. The chandeliers are enormous, asymmetrical art pieces befitting the huge two-story space made almost entirely of colored glass. Amber, magenta, aqua—and the largest window, encompassing the length of the entire room and the height of both stories; a perfectly clear pane to showcase the setting sun on the venue's lakefront.

I smile at the view, knowing Bridget will love it. This whole party, really. From the gold-and-white checkered dance floor to the colorful summer floral arrangements, it's exactly the sort of thing she enjoys.

Joyful.

Quirky.

Clever.

Just like her.

Which makes complete and perfect sense when I see the neon marquee hanging from the second-story's brushed brass railing.

The Osprey House Annual Gala, brought to you by the Ash and Messina Packs.

And here we are, the Messina Pack.

Utterly clueless.

Adrian steps up behind us, his voice dropping low. "I take it she didn't tell any of you, either?"

I swallow. "I knew she used our foundation funds to open another children's home under their existing philanthropy, but I had no *idea*..."

Colt—who's actually *trimmed his beard*—narrows gray eyes at our surroundings. Snapping the whole thing together before I can. "She *planned* this damn event, didn't she?"

"*Carajo,*" Dante curses, pulling at his tuxedo's lapels. "Of course she did. Look."

He nods at the photo wall across the room. Hundreds of pictures of the children our money has helped care for, all arranged on the foam boards Bridget's been working on over the last two months.

She *made* them.

Adrian's low growl doesn't make sense for a moment—how

can he be anything but *awed?*—but then he explains, "She wasn't even going to come tonight. Her sister told her she'd just embarrass herself."

After she must have spent *hours*—*weeks*—planning this with her best friend and the Ash Pack omega, Meg... Bridget wasn't going to *attend*.

She didn't even have a dress. Adrian thought ahead and had a selection of evening wear tailored for her, but...

It's no big deal.

I can hear our omega saying the words. Believing them. In her mind, all her hard work and selflessness were just... her life. Her passion. She didn't expect any credit or prestige in return.

But look what she *did*.

She took our money—the funds I never had one single damn clue what to do with—and *made* something amazing.

"Bridget did a great job with this, huh?!"

The burly blond man, suddenly shouting at us, grins as if we should know who he is. I don't, but I recognize the guy next to him—the Ospreys' quarterback, Declan Howard. He rolls his eyes and shoves his packmate.

"Jesus, Theo." Then, to us, "This is Theo. I'm Declan. We've been working with your omega to plan the event."

Our pack alpha shakes his hand, introducing all of us before adding, "We'd love to get more involved."

Theo snorts, grinning. "Are you guys kidding? You've basically single-handedly funded the new house! Thirty-six kids have been adopted so far this year because of you guys!"

Because of Bridget.

I hear my internal correction echo through all four of us. Colt and I glance at one another, then Dante. We all turn back to Adrian, who projects a steadying beat of certainty as he replies, "The recognition—for *all* of this—needs to go to Bridget, not our pack. I would consider it a personal favor if you could ensure that she receives complete credit during tonight's proceedings. By name."

The two Ash Pack alphas absorb his solemnity and look at each other, nodding. "We can do that," Declan shrugs. "Ronan, Meg, and I do the speeches. I'll tell them both, and we'll adjust our tribute."

Adrian gives a grateful sigh. "Thank you. And if we can ever help in a more hands-on way, we would appreciate the opportunity."

Theo's green eyes look a lot like Bridget's best friend's—the perky little omega, Emma. *This must be her brother.* He even bobs his head the same over-eager way. "For sure!" he crows. "You know, a lot of the kids love sports. We do football clinics for them at our facility, but adding baseball would be cool!"

Dante claps his hands, a look of sheer relief blurring into his determined expression. "Hell yeah. Sign us the fuck up."

I can't quite stifle the reflex to check in with Colt; but the alpha who used to be our resident nay-sayer already has his phone in his hand, extending it to Theo. "Put your number in, and I'll call you guys about setting something up with the kids. I know a high school team that needs volunteer hours anyway. Maybe they could help out."

A warm emotion balloons behind my ribs. Pride, I think.

I swallow mine, but Dante can't quite hide his shit-eating grin. Colt mutters, "Shut up," at both of us, and Adrian smiles the same second I do.

This is probably the first moment we've felt like a real pack without Bridget here to center us. A familiar ache swells on the left side of my chest. Longing and need—the desperate wish that I could just reach out and touch her.

Internally. Through a bond.

It's gotten steadily worse over the last two days. Being away from her has been torturous for so many reasons.

It was one thing when we got to see her and hold her at the end of every day. Test her perfume. Watch each flicker of feeling on her face. But being away? Not knowing how she is because I can't see her *or* sense her? It's been *unbearable*.

Adrian shakes the Ash Pack alphas' hands again, committing to a round of drinks with them and their pack leader later in the evening. I can barely listen, scanning the crowd for Bridget's distinctive hair. *Needing* her. Feeling my blood heat and my skin prickle.

Oh shit.

Is—am I about to—?

Dante is nearly as agitated, thrusting a hand through his pomade-styled hair. Adrian releases another deep breath, tugging at his bow tie. Colt shifts on his feet, too, grunting at his phone screen.

"She's not here yet," he mutters. "She told me she'd text me when they were pulling up."

Seriously? Then what the hell is this squirming *pulse* snapping along my nerves? Firing them up. Leaving every neuron lit. Every part of my body hard and needing and—

Oh God.

Oh *God.*

What *is* that?

Aside from soul-crushing, life-ending *perfection*?

Shit. Fuck.

No.

It *is* a rut.

Because this? The air I'm breathing?

The scent *ruining* me?

It's *our mate.*

fifty-eight

I WAS NEVER the type of moony asshole who imagined finding my mate.

I didn't think about it much at all, really. What good would it do? I figured it would happen the way it happened—*if* it ever did.

I didn't even want it to, once we found Bridget.

All her fretting? Colt's brooding? Adrian and Jesse and their murmured reassurances?

I thought they were all a smidge *dramatic*, to be honest.

Cristo.

How fucking stupid am I?

This feeling isn't human. It isn't even *earthly*.

My body is my job. Honing the muscles, training the reflexes.

But my entire being suddenly feels alien. Like someone plucked out my mind and put me into a foreign form. One that twists and smokes and sparks.

All because I dared to *breathe*.

Fucking *fuck*. It is *so good*.

My lungs flip inside out. Throbbing on shallow scrapes of the sweetest air I've ever tasted. Mind-bending. Life-ending. Pure electricity, thundering through my veins.

But—*no*.

No, goddammit.

I feel my soul snap forward, reaching, reaching. But my heart slaps it down. *No*, I say again.

Because I promised Bridget I would.

Because I looked into her blue, blue eyes and I swore *she* was the one I wanted.

My Alpha can go to hell and take my stupid knot with him. I don't care that my mouth is watering. I don't care that my teeth ache. I don't care how pumped up my sticky mango scent is.

I *have* an omega.

And I love her.

I love *her*.

The colorful room—*Bridget's* colors—blur around me as I lock my muscles down. Fighting the beat rearing up in my center. Automatically wheeling around to find my packmates. Hoping I'm the only one. Praying I'm *wrong*.

They all feel it, though. The absolute focus etched into Adrian's features. The desolation in Colt's burning gray gaze.

And—ah *fuck*—Jesse. Snapping into a *rut*.

Everyone stares. Whispers and shocked sounds filter out of the crowd shifting around us. Backing up and off, leaving our pack in a pocket of open space as the voices rise higher.

"That alpha is in a *rut*."

"One of them said '*mate*.' Their match must be here."

"Oh dear, isn't that *Bridget Woods'* pack? Her *fiancés*? And their mate is *someone else*?"

Holy shit.

This is her nightmare.

And it's *actually happening*.

Fisting my packmate's jacket, I hold my breath, doing everything I can to avoid the scent attempting to wrap itself around my soul. "*Jesse, no,*" I bark, trying to keep quiet. "No. What about—"

"*Bridget.*" Colt croaks the word, pure pain breaking over his face as he scans the hundreds of people watching us. "We need to get out of here."

Adrian shakes off his self-imposed lockdown, nodding. Opening his mouth to speak. But Jesse suddenly rips himself out of my hands, turning to the source of the heavenly, silken scent.

And lunging with a roar.

I GIGGLE as I fluff Serena's skirt out, tossing a handful of tulle out of our limo.

She casts me a dark look that reminds me of her MMA fighter mate. "Thanks," she adds flatly. "It's gonna be a long night."

I feel exactly the opposite, actually. After receiving a collection of scorching hot pictures and downing half a bottle of champagne at the salon, I doubt much could put a damper on my mood.

I'm here. At a society event. In this beautiful dress that one of… one of my alphas had made…

…with my pack.

The venue is every bit as modern and gorgeous as the day Meg and I toured it last summer. With the enormous windows and the timing of the gala, I knew we'd be perfectly poised to capitalize on this glorious sunset—and I was right.

Golden blush and tangerine-tinted lavender pour across the sky as we step onto the pavement. I tilt my head back, smiling to myself. Giddy. Genuinely overjoyed.

And... proud.

Of myself.

I look around at the beautiful building, my amazing friends dressed to the nines. The row of ultra-luxury vehicles queuing to valet behind us.

This is a really big deal.

My happiness only sails higher when we hit the "pink carpet" leading to the entrance. Paparazzi and our own event photographers clamor for group shots of us. Remi fusses with Meg's strap while her twin adjusts the butterfly clipped into Remi's bun. Emma grins at me, holding out her hand. When I take it, she surprises me with a twirl and a dip that leaves us both laughing for the camera flashes.

We accommodate every photographer's requests. Even, surprisingly, a couple who want pictures of me alone. And not one of them calls me the Fake Fiancée.

Once they're finished, we hurry into the building's grand, glass-and-gold lobby. Anticipation sparkles through my body as we step toward the row of doors across from the entrance. I know they lead to the event space, and I *can't wait* to see the guys.

My pack, I think again.

Our alphas, my Omega adds, shoving me hard.

Urgently. Almost as if something is—

All the girls pause at the same moment. Meg throws her arm in front of me, freezing as she tilts her head. Listening, I realize. Hearing something I can't through her bonds.

Behind me, Serena spits a vicious curse, and Remi gasps. But still, I don't understand that there's a situation. Not until Emma's hand scrambles to find mine, squeezing hard.

I turn to her crest-fallen face. "Bridget," she whispers, bone-pale.

"What?" I ask, wide-eyed. Looking at each of them in turn. "Did something happen? I don't have an internal observation deck, so one of you better tell me what you're—"

The rattle of one set of double doors shoving open cuts me off. Four alphas—one from each of their packs—come rushing out. Meg's quarterback, Declan. Emma's fireman, Micah. Serena's huge former-linebacker, Jonah. And Remi's broody goalie, Cassian.

They all look distinctly on edge. And relieved to get their hands on their omegas.

Cassian strides right over to Remi, cupping her face in his palms. Their eyes lock, and he barely has time to snap her into his arms before she starts to cry.

Jonah gazes at Serena with a similarly pained expression. "*Manamea*," he whispers. Just one word, but her lips wobble before blazing anger snaps over her features. "No," she asserts, stomping her heel on the marble floor. "*No.*"

Her alpha sighs at the pleading note in her denial, pulling her close. Declan silently steps into Meg's back, clenching his jaw as he wraps a solid arm around her. Holding her up, I realize. Because she's so upset, she's *swaying*.

Micah tries to embrace Emma, too, but she throws him off with a small, pained sound. Wrapping her arms around *me* instead.

Clinging to me like—

Like she's *holding me together*.

Which is the moment reality finally sinks in.

Oh.

This is about *me*.

But no one explains what's happening. Or why. They all just stare at me. Grimacing or frowning or—in Remi's case—sobbing.

I feel tears drip from Emma's cheeks into my hair. And a strange sort of certainty sinks into my center.

Oh, I think again. *Right. Of course.*

"Say it," I whisper to my best friend. "Tell me."

She tries. I feel her inhale and fight for the words. But, in the end, it's Micah. Stepping forward and placing his hand on Emma's back. Leveling me with his dark, sympathetic eyes. Admitting, "Bridget, your—*the* Messina Pack..."

And, with that one small correction, I already know. I *know*.

"They were here, waiting for you, and Jesse snapped into a rut," Micah finishes. "Because their mate is in there."

ALL HELL BREAKS loose in the lobby outside the ballroom.

Meg charges out to the valet, waving her hands and directing attendees to the lakeside deck instead of the main event space. Declan snaps to, corralling the photographers that way as well.

Remi and Cassian set off to find the security liaison and make sure they have the correct measures in place. Absently, I have the rueful thought that *yes, they do*. Because I coordinated with them a couple of weeks ago.

After Adrian's rut.

Memories of him locked inside me, warm and sure all around me... My scent must do something unholy because Emma squeaks, squeezing me tighter against her side.

"We'll get your ride back any minute, Bridget," Micah assures, holding his phone to his ear. "The driver left, but he's turning around. Hopefully, the valets will have the backed-up cars cleared by the time he—"

My ears don't quite work, I think. Or maybe they're just reacting to the washes of fire-and-ice cascading over my face. Mortified, reddening heat; cool, gut-twisting dread. A buzz echoing against my eardrums, then silence, the beat of my own heart, more hushed voices.

"Avery isn't answering me," Serena mumbles to Jonah. "Is he—"

"*Helping*," Jonah nods, "yeah."

His subtle inflection somehow registers where nothing else does. But, of course, if Jesse is in a raging rut in the middle of a public ballroom and won't leave because his mate is in there... naturally, the professional fighter would help hold him back.

My numb features twitch into a wince. "T-tell him to be careful with Jesse's arms. P-please," I murmur, thinking of the golden alpha's fluid grace, striking out opponents. His genuine smiles, humble and small, shaded by the brim of his cap—but still, always *striking*. Even up in the stands or on TV.

My heart spasms with pure pain at the thought of losing those. I've already lost them, though, right? The shy, sideways grins. His long fingers weaving into mine. The glow in his hazel eyes.

Still here, he'd said. *Still with you.*

He won't be, now. He'll be with *them*—his mate.

And he isn't the only one.

Adrian, with his solid devotion and unyielding certainty. Commissioning dresses, custom ordering cars. Slaying my dragons and holding me like I'm a priceless, precious *prize*.

Who takes care of you?

Dante—all his stupid Post-It notes and dumb jokes and always *chewing* something, damn him, but still so fucking gorgeous and fun and impassioned. Carving into me with those coal-hot irises. Burning bright and *true*.

What do I have to do? he'd whispered. *To make it real?*

But it never could be. For this exact reason. And out of all of them... I think Colt feared that.

Deep down—in his terrible, wonderful, breathtaking *depths*. Too honest, maybe. Too damaged and lonely. *Lost*.

But *strong*. Stubborn in a way I understand. Working, fighting himself with literally every step. To be better and *do* better and *give more*, God—

Can I breathe?

Yes, I must be. Because here, darting out from the farthest gap in the row of burnished glass doors to the gala, is an all-too-familiar figure, shrouded in delicate lemon verbena.

Alicia.

She clacks over the wide, white floor, an imposing column of elegance dressed in solemn black. As if she anticipated the death of my hopes and dreams at this fucking party when she chose her ensemble.

My sister essentially says much, pointing a slender finger and harrumphing, "I *knew* it! I *knew* you shouldn't be here. Out at *events*. With your '*pack*.'" She throws up air quotes. "Now everyone—*everyone*—will know they dumped you! Here! In front of the *entire world*!"

I flinch away from every harsh, accurate word. Her herbaceous smell starts to edge closer to sour citrus.

Not as "bad" as mine, of course. *Never as bad as mine*.

That may be the worst part about sisters—even when you hate them, they can still read your mind. Alicia's nostrils flare the same second I have the shame-filled thought. Her eyes bug out. "*Oh my God, Bridget! Are you even* wearing—"

I don't get to hear the rest of her demand, though.

Because a deep, pained *roar* echoes from the ballroom. My Omega tries to fling my body toward it, pleading with cries so desperate, I can't even understand her.

Jonah barely manages to offer a hand to keep me on my feet. I think about how my acidic essence must be all over his hand now and cringe back.

Alicia's entire body jolts. The other alphas have the decency to try to hide it, but they all balk, too. When Emma accidentally whines, Micah braves the air around us to stand between my sister and me. "Who are you?" he demands. "And what gives you the right to speak to Bridget this way?"

Alicia stares for a long second, her pretty features ravaged by disgust. Instead of answering the other alpha, she addresses me again. "Obviously, this is all too much for you, Bridget. You shouldn't be here. Your scent is *awful.* And so *strong.* How could you fathom that any alpha would want to endure *this*?"

It's embarrassing how unprepared I am, how soft I've gotten. She shared these thoughts daily when I lived with her. Eventually, they just rolled off my back. Hearing them now, though, after the way the Messina Pack has treated me...

Shame tightens around my guts like a noose. Cinching tighter, yanking bile up my throat. Dizziness swirls my thoughts into a dust storm of self-doubt.

Should I not be here?

Was this irresponsible or stupid?

Am I going to ruin this philanthropy?

A fierce omega snarl cracks through the lobby, bringing me back to reality. I turn to my friends, wondering which one of them took a snap at my sister. Stunned faces blink back at me— even the alphas.

Oh. Was that... me?

No, my Omega said. *It was us.*

Before I can figure out what the hell propelled my Omega out of her timid nature, my sister falls back a step. She stammers—and maybe I should care about her ashen face or her trembling shoulders, but all I see is her sneering expression, seared into my brain.

I want to tell her that her own sniveling husband used to leer at me, but I know she won't believe me. I mean, for fuck's sake, she saw me with Adrian. And she's still standing here, telling me no one will *ever* want me. I don't know why she needs me to believe that—and I'm not sure why I let her convince me for so long.

Was it the doctors? Our parents?

Does it even matter? Enough is *enough*.

"You always said no alpha could ever want me," I bark. *"But that was a lie. They did. They love me. They knew we weren't mates and they wanted to bond with me anyway. So I guess that makes you wrong, Alicia."*

I'm crying by the end. Shouting through tears. Yelling to hear myself over the voice in my center, who's once again sobbing and screaming.

They're our alphas! They really are!

My heart breaks. Not with a loud bang or a sharp snap. More of a quiet sort of crumbling. My world disintegrating into ash.

And this voice, the one I've spent *years* silencing? She stood up for me. She's *here,* with me. *Part of me.* Feeling my pain as her own, pumping her hurt into my soul. So many wishes and dreams, shattered to bits.

Because all this time? While I denied my feelings and told myself I had gotten over my silly romantic fantasies?

She held onto them for me.

How did I ever hate her for that?

Regret swamps my stomach, the unfamiliar urge to be gentle bolting onto my throat. Have I ever spoken to her with any sort of empathy? Or *myself?*

No, I start to whisper, deep down, weeping with her. *No, they aren't ours, Omega. I'm sorry. I'm really so sorry—*

"Bridget."

The alpha bark pierces my buzzing eardrums. Low and urgent, but not altogether loud. I'd know it anywhere, though.

Underwater. In a cyclone. Buried six feet under.

Adrian.

He's there, in one of the doorways to the gala. Behind him, the entire event has fallen silent. I can only hear my own breaths...

And Jesse.

Barred by two rows of alpha bodies blocking his exit. Fighting with everything he has. Growling and roaring into the ballroom's stilted silence, while Colt barks quietly, and Dante grunts with the effort of holding him back.

I recognize Serena's fighter, Avery, pinning Jesse's right arm as carefully as he can while the blond alpha twists and bucks. The other men sandwiched between Adrian and the rest of his pack are familiar, too. The rest of my friends' mates, all trying to keep the rutting alpha from getting into the lobby.

Beside me, Alicia shakes her head back and forth, an expression of outraged dismay expanding across her visage before mortification sinks in. Realizing this is about to become a public altercation, she ducks her head and scurries away. Embarrassed to be associated with me, as per usual.

Did that bother me a minute ago? It's crazy how much I don't care.

Can't care.

Because my Omega is finally talking. Or, rather, I'm finally *listening*.

Our alpha, she says, panting. As if she's been drowned, thrashing against my hold, fighting to break the surface to tell me, *Our mate. HE'S OUR MATE.*

But *no*. She's *confused*. I can't have mates. My scent is—

Wrong?

Alicia was wrong, though. She's the one who told me a pack would never like my natural scent. The doctors did, too, but... they were all incorrect. Weren't they?

The gears in my mind spin out, trying to process.

But were they mistaken? My scent did just strangle all my friends' alphas. Despite all the de-scenter I—

Wait.

WAIT.

I try to remember actually *spraying* the neutralizer on. I know I picked it up, didn't really want to wear it, decided to use it anyway, got a dick pic from Dante, and—

Oh.

Oh, *holy shit.*

Adrian is already moving, striding right for me. Rushing me off my feet and into his arms. Folding me into his warm, masculine musk. So strong and pure and rich. So *perfect*, it shoots burning sparks of bliss through my lungs. Sends dizzy swirls of desire and need and adoration through my whole being. Dribbling pure, raging want into my core.

And he feels... like mine.

But how? Is this even possible? Why now?

I've been de-scented around them before, and no one ever—

"Shhh," Adrian soothes the endless churn in my mind. Pulling me into his broad strength like he'll never let me go. "Shhh. I'm here now. Your alpha's here. Who takes care of my baby girl?"

I'm still *sobbing*, damn it. My chest stutters and aches. A sloughed whine scrapes up my throat.

Adrian hums, bending to skim his lips over my pulse. "I'm here now, little blue," he says again, a deep purr rattling against my corset. Peaking my nipples and sending fresh slick down my thighs. "I'll always take care of you. I promised, remember?"

The moment feels surreal. Like a dream.

But—what about their mate?

What about—

"I *knew* it." Adrian repeats the words Alicia stabbed me with, erasing my sister's venom with a slow, sweet scent-mark on my forehead. "I knew you were meant to be mine. *Our mate.*"

IF I CAUGHT A FALLEN star in my arms, it wouldn't be this precious.

If I learned every secret of the universe in one blink, I couldn't feel as complete.

If someone saved my very life, I'm not sure I would be more grateful than I am right this moment.

Holding Bridget is elation and vindication. The clang of victory. All-consuming *joy*. Wrapped around the deepest roots of *truth*.

This woman is *mine*.

The love of my life.

The center of our pack.

Our *mate*.

Part of me always knew. When I saw her picture in the press, scrolled through her Instagram. Learned her face and body. Saw her mind and heart, stitched prominently onto her sleeve.

She was the reason I chose this pack.

The best damn decision I've ever made.

Her round blue eyes blink up at me, filling with tears. "Alpha —*Adrian*," she murmurs, letting me hold her. "W-what's happening?"

If the glassy sheen hazing her gaze is any indication, I'd say her heat is setting in early. Probably due to all this excitement—or perhaps her Omega knowing we've finally *seen* her.

I'm not sure if our away game has anything to do with this chain of events. Did we have to get some space to realize how perfect her scent is? Were we desensitized to it before?

I think it's more than that. We've all noticed the gradual change over the last couple of months. Brightening, sweetening. Always, ever closer to the exact sensation I just experienced.

Absolute *rightness*. Perfection.

I can tell she forgot to put de-scenter on. That, coupled with her pre-heat perfume... I must have caught her scent the second she got out of her limo.

An irrational burst of pride warms my chest at the thought. Being able to sense a mate in a crowded room is one thing—but feeling one when they aren't even in the building yet? Our match must be strong.

Which all makes perfect sense, given the way I've felt about this woman since the day we met. *Of course* she's my mate. *Of course* there could never be anyone else as right for me as Bridget.

But the confusion on my little one's pert, pretty features also makes sense. Because, no matter how any of us *felt*, the final piece didn't completely snap into place until right now. Today.

Why?

Her perfume has already shifted, nudging closer to the version I'm accustomed to. It doesn't matter, though. The one faint trail of her absolute perfection was enough. My Alpha is convinced.

In fact, knowing his mate has been in there all along, hurting for him... he's *obsessed with her*.

Hell, we both are.

We *need* to make sure our omega never hurts again. Which, given my rutting packmate trying to fight his way to her, might not be simple.

I have to grit my teeth to ignore Jesse's pained roars, focusing on Bridget's dismayed face. "We were in the ballroom, waiting for you," I explain, cupping my palms around her arms and chasing her chills. Noting how warm her skin feels.

"Your scent hit me like a freight train," I go on, growling low for privacy. "I've never—It was different than your perfume has been, but still so clearly *you*, little blue. By the second or third breath, my Alpha finally knew what I've always known."

Bridget blinks, hope rising in her azure irises. "B-but what about...?"

An involuntary grin spreads over my face. "Your other alphas? Yeah, sweetheart, them too. We all panicked for a moment, trying to process. But they know it's you. Even Jesse. Look."

I direct her attention to the rest of our pack. Showing her the raging intensity in Colt's eyes and the way Dante's body strains toward her, even as he does everything he can to hold Jesse back.

"B-but," Bridget whispers. "Someone said Jesse scented his mate and got upset. Then snapped into a—"

I shake my head before she's even done, not wanting that thought to germinate in her mind. "No, Bridget. He scented *you* and *immediately* went into rut. There wasn't enough time for him to think about it. None of us could confer until we had Jesse reined in. But the second we got to focus on the scent, we knew."

I lean closer, kissing her forehead. Allowing my lips to curve up in a rueful smile as I share one detail I know she'll love. "Colt figured it out first."

Her little gasp and the accompanying burst of creamy lemon

decadence pump my knot fuller. All too aware of our audience, I pet her hair softly and add in a murmur, "Jesse might not be able to understand what's happening yet, but I think he was heartbroken that it might *not* be you."

The poor kid. He's out of his mind now, but I know his last conscious thought was the same panicked, painful one we all experienced before the full strength of her silky, lemon meringue scent sank in.

Bridget's posture straightens. I watch her mind spin behind her clear blue eyes, weaving itself around my words. Her manicured fingers curl into my sleeves.

"Let him come to me," she begs breathlessly, crumpling her face into a pleading look.

My protective instincts lurch upright, lodging a swift *no* in my gullet. But I hold the word back, moving my focus over each tiny tremble in her expression. Debating as my thumb gently strokes her cheekbone.

Everyone will watch them.

But, then again, <u>*everyone will watch them*</u>.

Meaning nobody will *ever* question our undeniable connection to this woman again.

Bridget's heat must be closer than I thought, because a whine rips up her throat, and she doesn't even attempt to block it. "Please, alpha? I need to *help him*."

Being with Bridget has truly made me into a better man. A better leader. Because two months ago, I might have refused. Taken the safest course. Tried to manage everyone's feelings instead of *hearing* them.

Instead, I let her instincts speak to mine. Absorbing her absolute entreaty. The intent focus sharpening her blue gaze despite her clear pre-heat haze.

I'm here to protect her—and she's *our omega*. If she needs to care for one of us, I want to support her.

Besides, if anyone can handle whatever is thrown at them, it's my *mate*.

I project my full confidence, along with a burst of alpha approval. "Of course you can, sweetheart. You were so perfect during my rut. But he's fighting the guys pretty hard, and you feel very warm—"

She's shaking all over, too. Of course, that doesn't stop our perfect little mate from tossing her fiery hair and insisting, "I can do it."

Her scent is already returning to the absolute glory we experienced in the ballroom, but when I nod and step behind her, the brilliant lemon sweetness practically *glows*. I pull her into my chest, letting her feel the rumbling purr layered under my clothes. Bending to skim my lips along her shoulder, imagining how it will feel to sink my teeth into the thin, unmarked skin.

I angle a look at the other alphas. *"Let him go."*

There are gasps and titters from the onlookers. Several people in the audience jostle farther back. But I know it's safe—the only person Jesse's Alpha has eyes for is wrapped in my arms.

The tattooed Thorne Pack alpha drops his hold, swooping over to practically tackle his own omega. As I expected, Jesse doesn't even turn his head. The second Dante and Colt let go, he's a blur.

Aimed right at Bridget.

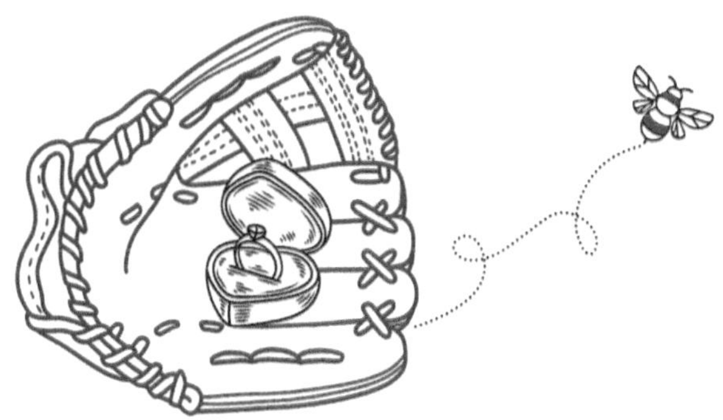

THE WORD SURREAL may lose all meaning to me after today.

I thought I understood what I was forfeiting when the doctors said I would never have mates. I thought I *knew*.

But nothing could have prepared me for *this*.

Because it feels...

The same.

I loved them an hour ago, and I love them now. Their scents have spoken to me for as long as I've known each of them... and they still do.

The only difference is *me*. Listening to the piece of myself I've denied for so long.

I was afraid of her, I think. Scared to feel this soul-consuming want. Terrified that wishing and hoping would only lead to more of the pain I'd pushed down my entire life.

Never quite right. Too big and bright. Too strong and sharp.

Not just my scent, either.

I told myself I was better than all of that. Above it. But really, this whole time, I was hurting myself. Punishing my Omega for wanting things the rest of the world told me I couldn't have.

It was never her fault.

Or mine.

But I let fear control my whole relationship with an essential part of myself. I wrote her off as some flighty, stupid, insane voice. I hated her for needing things because, deep down, I was scared *I* needed those things, too.

These things.

The security of Adrian at my back. Solid and steady. So warm. Literally vibrating with approval and strength.

Dante, grinning like a lunatic and gazing at me with the craziest gleam in his dark eyes. Like the rest of the world has gone up in a plume of smoke—and he's *glad*. Elated only to see me. Sense me. Want *me*.

Colt, too. His intense stare is so much more intent than I've ever seen it. Pouring pure, undiluted devotion into my body. Even from across the room.

And Jesse. Lunging in a blur of black fabric and golden hair. Arrowing toward me like he'll punch a hole in the fabric of time before he slows down.

A sane person would be afraid, but whatever scraps of sanity I have left are history the moment I gasp, inhaling...

Them.

All four of them. Together. A combination I've surely breathed a hundred times, but this time... I'm *listening*, tuned in to the way my Omega scrabbles. Begging me to let them *come*, let them *bite* us, *bond* us.

Please, our mates!

Every muscle below my waist gels and squelches. Perfume pours off me in a wave of—oh.

Oh.

It isn't bitter or acidic. It isn't even sharp. No. I smell... tart and sweet and *smooth?*

Adrian's body stiffens behind me, the iron ridge of his cock pressing into my backside as Colt *snarls.* He and Dante both snap straight, then follow Jesse, approaching with glimmering eyes and clenched jaws.

But their rutting packmate finally reaches me.

And *crumples* to the ground.

"Omega," he pants, pained and dazed.

His hands find my hips, fisting the fabric. I remember Adrian's rut, bracing. Waiting for this out-of-his-mind alpha to tear my dress off. Instead, he sloughs out a growly groan and buries his face against my belly.

I feel his lips through the silky fabric. Skimming and nipping at me. His fingers blanch as he holds my sides, jostling us both with his quivers.

"O-omega?"

Hearing the way his voice stutters, I realize he's confused. If his last coherent thought was truly that he was about to lose me... or *hurt* me...

I weave my fingers into his hair and let myself purr for him. The sound is dainty and pitiful, but he reacts as if I've just sucked his raging cock into my mouth, moaning plaintively, loud and low, into my soft stomach rolls.

People are watching and whispering, but it's impossible to care. Especially when Dante and Colt slot into place at my sides.

My injured alpha seems wary of his rutting packmate, casting Jesse a sideways look before cupping my face. Jesse is too far gone to notice, even when Dante slides his arms under my bust and squeezes me.

"*Querida,*" he whispers, dropping a reverent kiss to my bare shoulder. "I missed you so damn much."

My mind feels fuzzy, lagging as I process his words. *He's missed me for the last few days. And* that's *what he wanted to tell me first.*

Colt sees everything, those gray eyes flickering with his uncanny ability to read my thoughts. "You were already ours," he murmurs, scent-marking my temple. "This just makes us yours."

He's... *right.* They wanted me when they thought I wasn't their mate. And now? They're looking at me exactly the same way they did before.

Oh God, is this *all my fault*?

Jesse's Alpha senses the bittersweet turn of my thoughts and moans again. I whine at the needy grimace on his face, guilt swarming my stomach. Adrian's arm tightens at my waist, his purr deepening. "Shh, it's alright, sweetheart. No one is mad at you."

"B-but I could've—I didn't—"

Colt hums, his own chest expanding on a rusty rattle. "You didn't know, baby. None of us did. Something must have changed for you today, right? Something new or different?"

I turn to him, gazing into blazing gray and attempting to muddle through the blurry fog encroaching from the corners of my mind. "I—Adrian set up a spa day with the girls at a really nice salon Alicia made me avoid... And this dress actually *fits* me and looks decent—"

Dante's quiet, biting snarl cuts me off. My lips twitch shakily as I correct, "Looks *good* on me. I forgot my de-scenter, and my heat is coming, but..."

I didn't have de-scenter on every minute of every day for the last couple of months. And my pre-heat perfume started well before they left for their away game this week.

Colt waits patiently, staring steadily into my eyes while I ponder. Jesse bites the fleshy part of my hip through my dress, and my pussy squeezes. Memories fly by faster, running together as my haze thickens.

Stumbling out of the salon in my heels. Laughing and taking selfies with the girls in the limo. Pulling up the venue and—

That new, *beautiful* perfume winds into the air again. Just a little—a single thread, maybe. But it's enough.

I freeze. So do all my alphas. Until Adrian uses his free hand to cup my jaw, angling my face toward his.

"Tell me," he intones. So smooth and approving, I wonder if he hasn't already guessed what I'm about to say.

A whimper catches in my throat, turning my voice into a rasp. "W-when I got out of the car, I looked around at everything and felt... really proud. Of myself."

I sense Adrian, Dante, and Colt absorbing my words. They all move at the same moment, each of them getting their hands on me however they can, with Jesse nosing at my core.

"You should be *so damn proud*!" Dante crows, pressing more kisses to my shoulder. "This event is *incredible*!"

"*You* are incredible," Adrian agrees. "We are so fucking proud of you, little blue."

Colt's gaze snags mine again, glowing so fiercely he doesn't have to speak at all. I see that he *gets* it.

He knows it's never been about compliments or praise—because they've all given me those. It was me, not letting myself hear them or believe any of it. Me, telling myself that everything I accomplished was no big deal. My sacrifices didn't matter all that much. I was fine. *Fine.*

Then they came along. And started to catch how I spoke about myself. *To* myself.

None of them pushed or shamed me or tried to make me feel worse. But in their own ways, they all showed me how I should be treated, even within my own body.

They changed me.

Or maybe... *I* changed me.

Which reminds me of the one other change I decided on today. Gazing to Adrian over my shoulder, I admit, "There was one other thing. Back at the salon, and again when I arrived here...

I was thinking of you guys. As *my pack*. Calling you that, in my mind."

Dante's arms hug me tighter as Adrian flashes his sexy smile. "Because that's exactly what we are," he confirms, kissing my forehead. "*Your pack*."

A cloud of tart sweetness warms the air surrounding us, my perfume unleashed in another tidal wave of lemon cream. Jesse growls another groan, huddling close and wrapping his arms around my thighs in a vise. Adrian's purr stutters on a deep hum.

Dante practically sobs, dropping his forehead to my shoulder. "*Goddamn it*, cupcake. Warn a man so he doesn't come in his pants."

Colt just smiles. His rare, smoldering grin. So heart-stoppingly sincere and teasing and intensely beautiful, I perfume *again*.

The whole world tilts. A thick mist settles over my thoughts, burying whatever logical pieces I had left. Leaving me untethered, with four sets of arms anchoring me to the earth.

The stormy-eyed alpha's lips twitch higher. "I think it's time we get out of here," he says, glancing at the others. "I want my mate."

sixty-three

BEFORE BRIDGET, I never would have thought watching my girl ride my best friend could be so *fucking hot*.

She practically tackled Jesse the second we got in the limo. Dante and I didn't even have to guide the poor bastard out of the venue—Bridget cupped his face in her hands, whispered something, and he followed. Eyes glowing like a zealot who'd been touched by his goddess.

Fuck. Can I blame him?

She looks like a powerful, ethereal creature as she rucks her silk skirt up to her waist, baring the patch of fiery curls between her thick, deliciously dimpled thighs. With vacant eyes fixed on her core, Jesse literally tears his pants down, rending the tuxedo's fly as Adrian finishes issuing terse instructions to our driver.

The partition glides into place. A few of the windows crack open.

Dante balks, outraged. Echoing my own dismay. "You're going to let her perfume out!"

Adrian nods brusquely, unfastening his cufflinks. "We're her alphas, and she's vulnerable. We need to keep a clear head until we get her safely into her nest. Especially once Jesse knots her."

Bridget's breathy whine at the mention of her nest has my cock fully erect. I grit my teeth, adjusting myself. Knowing Adrian is *right*, damn it.

Watching him navigate apps on his phone, launching into prep mode for what's to come, I'm once again struck with begrudging gratitude for the older alpha. Back in the ballroom, when Jesse snapped into a rut and Dante spun out, he was the one who looked at me and saw what I was thinking.

Part of me hopes he can't read my mind now, though. Given the sickening swoop that sails through me when Dante groans, "Fuck, *corazón, I can't wait* to bite you."

I ignore the seething sensation, forcing my focus to where Dante's gathered her skirt in his fist, exposing her glorious ass. Just in time for her to sink her soaked pussy onto Jesse's raging purple cock.

Holy—

Her thighs are shiny with slick. A wet sound squelches from her body as she keens, crying loudly enough to pull a purr to the surface of my chest.

Everything about Bridget is so delicious, I swear I could come from watching her hips and ass jiggle as she pounds herself onto Jesse's cock. I let my mouth fall ajar, staring from my prime position across from their bench seat.

His knot and balls are already impossibly full and tight. I don't have a single clue how the hell she'll fit the swell into her body when it's already so thick, but our girl is *determined*.

She's so single-minded when she's turned on. That makes me hotter. *I'm going to let her use me and my knot for the rest of my life.* And I'll love every fucking minute of it.

Jesse snarls and grunts. His hands are bloodless from the way he grips her hips, but he buries his face in the cleavage bouncing out of her corset with distinct tenderness. Adoring her, even when he can't think long enough to remember who either of them is.

The purity of his need touches Bridget. She whimpers, hugging her arms around his head and scent-marking his crown while she rides him faster. Pumping her spread, pink lips halfway over the thick, swollen skin at the base of his shaft.

"*Jesus*, you're so hot," I grit, gripping my hard length through my suit pants. When Bridget's blue beams flash across the limo to me, I smirk. "You gonna work that fat knot into your sweet little pussy, baby? Let me watch you take it."

Bridget's moan hits my balls and my heart at the same damn time. Drawing them up. Drawing me closer.

I find myself on my knees by her side, forfeiting my view so I can stroke her spine. "So beautiful," I whisper, nuzzling her shoulder.

Adrian appears behind Dante, sliding his phone into his pocket. He reaches around our packmate, gently ruffling our omega's hair. "Everything is ready for us, little blue. So whenever you feel your heat haze coming on, just let go and give in to it. We've got you."

Bridget's body stutters, her hips losing their fluid rhythm. Fear crosses her face, dulling her scent enough to rip a roar from Jesse's heaving chest. She blinks, eyes shimmering with tears.

"Y-you won't leave?" she sniffles.

We all snarl, but Dante is the loudest. His hand snaps up to her jaw, whipping her face in his direction. A fanatical twinkle lights his gaze as he grinds out, "We are *never* leaving you."

Adrian purrs his agreement as Jesse scrapes his teeth over the creamy tits spilling out of Bridget's gown. But even with all of them reassuring her, I'm the one she turns to.

Because she expects me to say no.

It's her Omega, I realize. I pushed her away so many times, in the beginning. Now, the fragile voice inside her doesn't know if I want them.

I huddle closer to her side. "*Never,*" I vow, then tack on a rueful smile that reflects the pang in my chest. "You're stuck with me, Bubbles."

And I hate that for her.

How can I keep her when I have no idea what kind of future I can give her? I might not have a career come Monday. And without baseball, I don't know who the hell I am or what I'll be able to provide.

The deluge of sweet lemon silkiness that pours off her can't be denied, though.

She *wants* me. *This.* All of us.

Adrian pushes limp red curls off her sweat-misted forehead, gazing at her with undeniable adoration. "Do you still want our bonds, baby girl? Because we want *yours.*"

My gut tweaks again. But Bridget whines loud enough to shatter my thoughts, trying to shimmy her hips and fit Jesse all the way in. Imagining how full she must be distracts me just long enough for an idea to spring up.

"Need some help?" I murmur, darting a glance to our pack leader. I don't really mean to look to Adrian for *permission...* but I'm pretty sure I *am.* His solid nod loosens my airway; a louder purr rumbles up my throat.

Most alphas would try to decapitate another person who touched them during a rut. But, as I suspected, if Jesse is so far gone, he hasn't noticed Dante and me putting our hands on Bridget, he won't care about this either.

I only get a slight snarl when my hand closes around the widest part of his knot. Bridget soothes him with a filthy, licking kiss, swallowing his growl. Below my wrist, I feel his balls tweak tighter while I knead the hard swell of his knot between my fingers. Narrowing it just enough to pop into Bridget.

Her pussy lips and the quivering cunt stretch over his heated bulk. The wet sound of her tugging his knot *all the way* inside is enough to have me biting her upper arm, needing pressure to quell the ache in my canines when her bright, sugary cream gushes over my hand.

Fucking hell. I'm going to come.

Bridget screams, bucking her hips even though they're locked against Jesse's. His eyes roll back, body jerking as he sprays out inside her. I feel his balls emptying and slip my fingers around to Bridget's clit. Two brushes of the throbbing bud send her into a screeching orgasm to match his.

My teeth dig further into her flesh. And I want to do it. *Bite her. Mark her. Make her mine.* Drag a thread from her bright, brilliant soul into my tattered, overcast *mess*.

My purr stammers as my salty scent deepens into something briny and unpleasant. Bridget's hazy gaze searches for mine, but she's barely able to focus once she finds me.

"A-alpha?" she mumbles, the words mushy, "What's wrong?"

I expect judgment from the others. Heavy glares, disapproving scowls. After all, here I am, putting doubt back in her mind.

But I can't ignore my conscience, telling me she deserves the whole truth. And when I chance a glance at my packmates, I only find concern and confusion on their faces.

"Bubbles," I whisper, sighing quietly as I cup a hand around her nape and press my forehead to hers. "I might not ever play again. If you don't want to bond me because—*mmpfh*."

Bridget's plump lips slant over my mine, sucking my fears off my tongue. Her slick heat invades, sliding over mine with an insistence that has my knot pounding as hard as my pulse.

The tart taste of lemon juice invades my senses, and I can't hold back—my hands clasp her tighter as I delve into her mouth, kissing her with all the pain and need and love blistering a hole in my abdomen. "I fucking *love you*," I snap when she draws in a gasp. "And I need you to be happy and safe and—"

She releases an impressive omega growl, silencing me before she plunders my mouth again. When she's done, she pulls back with a fierce expression. "Then you better *bite me*, alpha."

She turns to glare at rest of the guys. "You *all* better bite me."

Dante grins so wide, I swear his face will crack. "Try and stop me, cupcake."

Adrian's smile is warm and fond. "Anything you want, sweetheart. Forever."

Which, considering Jesse is currently floating in outer space, just leaves me, I guess. Bridget tosses her hair over her shoulder as she regards my expression, waiting impatiently.

Goddamn this woman.

I couldn't love anyone more.

"Alright," I agree, then throw in a wicked smile. "I'll bite you, Bubbles. *Hard*."

Jesse starts to come to. His growls roll into a steady purr. The way he rubs his face between her tits turns undeniably gentle.

"Bee?" he murmurs. "Is it—is it really you?"

Bridget whines again. The sound upsets my Alpha, but I'm grateful she's finally letting those noises out. Allowing her Omega room to communicate when she's distressed.

She nods wordlessly, hugging him closer. Jesse sloughs out a labored, broken breath, kissing his way up to her neck. "Bumblebee, thank *God*. I scented our mate, and I was so scared—*Fuck*. I love you. I love you so damn much, and I'm an idiot for every second I didn't tell you."

Bridget's creamy, citrus-covered essence brightens into something almost *painfully* perfect. Dante jostles closer. "Me too, *querida*. I've been in love with you from the moment you told me to man up because you don't speak 'boy.'"

We all chuckle at that, snorting at our packmate. He doesn't give a shit, though. He's too busy kissing Bridget, weaving his fingers through her hair.

When they break apart, Adrian strokes his knuckle down her cheek, his eyes burning. "We all love you, omega. And we're going to get into your nest and make you ours."

Bridget keens, launching herself off Jesse's lap and into Adrian's arms. He catches her, but we all blink in shock.

They should have been tied together for at least another hour. Why did Jesse's knot go down so fast?

The urgency on Adrian's face when he kisses her forehead says it all. "Hot," he rasps. "Too hot."

Oh fuck.

Our girl is officially in heat.

OUR LIMO IDLES at the curb for ten minutes, and I let them pass.

The time for counting seconds has passed. What Bridget needs now is all the affection and attention we can give her, with no agenda or hurry.

So I sit on the leather bench seat, holding her across my lap, purring. Kissing her in slow, deep plunges. Focusing on her taste, the warmth and weight of her body.

Being our pack leader means my energy sets the tone. And I'll be damned if we make this anything less than magical for our mate.

Colt sits beside me, rattling us both with his own purr. His hands cup the back of Bridget's head, carefully removing her hair-pins and massaging the roots.

She whimpers, quivering through another climax when Jesse's fingers draw gentle circles over clit. Dante kneels at her side, between my legs, stroking her tits. Pinching her nipples as her body arches.

We have to move her now. Our easing has helped calm her enough to build her nest, but the muscles visibly contracting low in her belly will only get more insistent. I want her settled long before they cause her any pain.

Bone-deep satisfaction pours into my body as I watch her lips fall open on a cry. Purpose—solid and soul-altering—settles into the deepest part of me. An anchor and an inspiration.

I will give her everything.

She deserves to be pampered and protected, simply because of who she is. Her beautiful heart and soaring spirit. Her kindness and quirkiness and undefeatable humor.

I'd want to provide for her for those reasons alone. The fact that she's been so hurt only ignites my determination.

All this time, the slicing edge to her scent wasn't some malady or proof she would never find mates.

It was *despair*.

Shame.

Guilt and humiliation that her mother and sister conditioned her to feel. Convinced her was appropriate, given how unap-pealing *they* deemed her aroma. Despite it being a sweeter, more potent version of their own.

What would have happened if one single person had simply *complimented* her? Or if her family had kept their toxic opinions to themselves and let her finish developing before writing her off? Would her perfume have developed into this rich, creamy deca-dence years ago?

To think she's been walking around, hating this piece of herself so vehemently that it's colored every moment of her life. Damaged her Omega to the point where the poor baby *never* let that aching weight go, not even when she was here, in her home.

Knowing what I do now, I truly don't understand how Bridget managed to put on a brave face and project such confidence. Most omegas would have curled up and let misery destroy them, but ours showed up for her life and her loved ones in a hundred profound ways.

Volunteering, befriending her impossible neighbor, rescuing Munchies. Hell, even her little house with its yellow door.

She didn't wait for us to save her or make her happy. She did that *on her own*.

And I don't think I've ever respected anyone more.

Bridget's peachy cheeks blaze with heat as she rubs her face against my shirt. She whimpers, wanting my skin instead of fabric. A soft pang echoes in my chest, rising to fill my throat. "I know, precious girl. We're going to get cozy right now."

The others follow my lead, moving with care while we step into the dusk. It only takes a moment to get everyone inside, where the whole pack pauses, ignoring Munchies' greeting while we stare at the closed door to Bridget's nest.

Tightening my arms around her, I nuzzle a scent-mark over her burning cheek. "Can we go into your nest now, little blue? Is that okay?"

She squirms, another whine piercing my heart. "Nest," she gasps, garbled and breathless. "Please, Alpha, it *hurts*."

My packmates' scents spike the same moment mine does, all of us blazing with the need to chase her pain away. The combination somehow makes perfect sense, now that her true essence is finally threading us together.

Tart acidity to balance Jesse's caramelized sugar. Something creamy and refreshing to match Colt's beachy, oceanic sandalwood. Dante's succulence, complemented by the pucker of lemon juice. And my own smokiness as a dark, musky counterpoint for the rest of my pack.

My pack.

Pride swells behind my sternum. "Yes, omega," I purr, "we can go into your nest right now."

Dante shoves the door open, already whipping his clothes off. Jesse follows suit, gathering the pieces into his hands so our girl can use them to make her sacred space even more inviting.

Which seems impossible, honestly. I vividly recall every detail of the design she chose at the nest store, but the memory didn't prepare me for how utterly perfect she's made it.

The deep teal walls and colorful bursts of flowers are definitely the same ones we selected, but they've been rearranged. Instead of interspersing the built-in pocket vases, Bridget put them all on the far wall, turning it into a floral display worthy of a queen.

Her cushion pile looks suitable for royalty, too. A sloping mountain of satin and velvet, with silk duvets and fuzzy blankets woven throughout.

A dozen or so unfamiliar pieces catch my eye. A bundle of gray. Something black. A stark white shape.

And a scrap of the Kings' signature sky blue.

Colt inhales, coming to the same realization I have on scent alone. "Our clothes," he rasps, his sea-salt smell swelling into a potent wave. "She's been putting them in here."

The way Bridget trembles, huddling closer to my chest, tells me she's embarrassed. Even before the sharp edge of shame creeps back into her perfume.

Now that I understand the difference, I see why my Alpha hated it so much. Why it always felt so *wrong*.

I open my mouth to reassure her, but Dante beats me to it, groaning loudly as he presses his bare chest against her other side. "*Corazón*," he breathes, "You stole our *clothes*? And you've been *using* them in your nest? That's the *hottest fucking thing* I've ever heard."

Bridget keens when his lips land on hers, moving her mouth in desperate, chasing licks. Dante gives another deep moan, cupping her head and eating at her in return.

Colt appears at my side, his gray eyes bright. "I'll undress her. While she's distracted."

He begins working on the ribbons of her corset while I set her down. She whines as her feet touch the floor, but Dante steps directly into her, sealing their torsos together with an arm around her waist, sucking and biting at her lips.

Our omega rubs her hard nipples over his tattooed chest. She cries out as her spine arches. Perfume explodes into the room, drowning it in sweet brightness. Her pained squeak tweaks my knot fuller.

Jesse finishes setting their clothes aside, taking my place at her back so I can strip my tux off, too. My cock is so hard, it smacks my abs as it springs free. I hiss, earning our omega's dazed attention.

She whines—a full, uninhibited omega noise. Music to my ears, after hearing her strangle the sound so many times.

"A-alpha? Can we—" Pain pierces her gaze, another whine eking out.

I can't bear it. And it will only get worse when she loses these last few moments of lucidity.

With a firm tug, I lift her into my arms and step into the cushioned hollow. My skin must feel as incredible for her as hers does to me, because she starts to bounce in my grasp, rubbing her curves along my torso while I maneuver us into the mountain of pillows fit for my queen.

Grasping her hips in my hands, I slide her under me before sinking onto my forearms, stretching out on top of her.

"Come here, baby girl," I murmur. "Who takes care of you?"

She can't answer, and I don't make her. The tears on her lashes have me cupping her slick, molten core, teasing just long enough to ensure she's fully coated in the slippery lemon cream before I line my cock up. In one roll of my hips, she's stuffed as full as she can get without a knot.

Bridget wails, her pretty tits spilling backward when her body arches. I bend and skim my teeth along one of the peach-tipped globes. She gasps, pressing up into the contact.

"P-please," she begs again. "Can we—c-can—"

Whatever she has to say is keeping her on the edge of her haze instead of releasing her. Nuzzling her neck, leaving my scent across her skin, I purr, "What, baby? Can we what?"

Her nails gouge tingling stripes into my back when I tilt the upper half of my knot into her trembling heat. The pressure—squelching around my swollen, tingling skin—snaps pleasure up through my core. I grind my teeth to keep from lunging for her blank throat.

She whimpers at the stretch, suddenly dropping her hands and reaching out. Needing *all* of us.

The others come without hesitation. Colt slides into her side, while Dante takes her other hand, and Jesse crawls to the other side of the nest, lifting her head into his lap.

The second we all have our hands on her, I pull myself halfway out of her pussy. Giving her time to absorb their caresses and purrs. Feeling how much we all want to give her whatever she needs.

She makes another tiny sound, pumping her hips for more friction. I set a slow pace, rocking into her clenching wetness. Her eyes roll back for a moment, a delicious moan filling our nest.

"We want you to let go, sweetheart. Tell us what you need," I husk, nipping the swell of her breast.

Her eyes are bleary, but she fights to flutter them open, briefly looking at the four of us. "Can w-we bond?" Bridget whispers. "N-now? I don't want to be alone this time. I—I'm scared."

My heart cracks in half, then breaks again. All the pieces expand. Swelling to fill my chest until it's heaving, sawing out serrated purrs as emotion thickens my throat.

Of course she's scared. All her heats have been traumatic, with strangers who didn't take proper care of her, or medications that knocked her out. As far as I'm concerned, this is the first time she's even had a proper heat, in a proper nest.

Her Omega needs to feel the absolute devotion rooted deep in my soul. The adoration pouring from the ripped, reborn organ pounding in my chest. And this *desire*. Scalding my blood, razing my veins to ash.

I glance at the rest of my pack, seeing their blazing certainty and eagerness. The last piece inside me snaps into place.

So I press my knot into Bridget's glorious pussy and sink my teeth into the side of her neck.

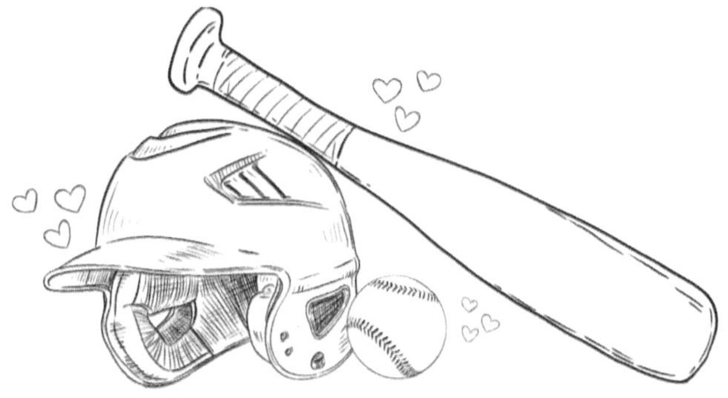

I'M FALLING in slow motion.

For a moment, the only thing I feel... is all the things I *don't* feel.

No panic blaring behind my lungs. No coiled barbs of heartbreak curled around my gullet. No stomach-seething mortification.

Four sharp, snarling gasps rend the air a second before it hits me—*perfume*. A beautifully balanced smell. Creamy citrus. Tart and silken and *sweet*.

It's... *good*.

Everything my scent never could be.

Except... *I'm* the only omega here.

So, it's good. But it must also be... *me.*

A symphony of alpha essences explodes around me. Each delicious on their own, but when I inhale them all, the nest dips and disappears, burned away by the fire licking at my limbs.

The scents and silky textures surrounding me *make sense.* They're perfect, actually. Balanced so precisely, the distant voice in my brain wonders what kind of genius assembled them.

Then I remember—it was *me.*

This is *my pack.*

And our alpha, lying on top of me. Gazing at me with an unfathomable look on his square face.

Did I ask him to bond with me? Did he answer?

The murky thoughts loop faster and faster. My chest throbs, fighting to pull more of this blissful combination—*my mates, my mates, my mates*—into my lungs. The air strokes a warm path down my throat, but hits the inside of my chest in a cool burst. Soothing the tingly burn behind my ribs.

Instead of flaming out, the sensation slips lower. Liquid fire, dribbling down to my core. Heating with every panted breath. Getting *worse*, somehow—*oh no, oh God.*

Coiling tight, it snaps around the thickness buried in my pussy, trying to suck it deeper with wrenching *tugs*. My alpha's eyes sparkle, the pretty color darkening.

Please, the voice inside of me whines. Or maybe that's just me. *Please, alpha.*

It's like he hears me. Staring so intently, I swear he reads the desperation spilling from my soul.

And answers it.

With a graceful lunge, the pack leader sinks his knot into my fluttering wetness. Stretching every sizzling nerve, rubbing each secret, needy spot.

Filling, filling, *filling* me. Until I can't imagine how I ever needed *anything* else.

Aside from—
From—
Oh!

His teeth break the skin on my throat in a smooth, painless *snap*. A tidal wave of ecstasy rears high and floods my body. Washing away the nest, the need. Until my blood is burning, shimmering bliss.

His cock pulses, jetting hot lashes into my depths. Dousing the flames between my hips with spurts of pure euphoria.

A silken tether unfurls, winding a soothing, sinuous path to my center. Smooth as satin. Strong as steel. Beautiful, but *unbreakable*.

The diamond band anchors itself in the deepest parts of me. Piercing the place that always hurt too much for me to look at it.

But I have to now.

Because *he's* there.

Solid and *powerful*. Squashing the squirm in my stomach. Filling the aching hollow between my legs. Flexing thick, and *oh —oh!*

I whine, my body rolling from the first climax into another. This one vicious enough to wring tears from my eyes.

My mate grunts, spilling into me again, licking at his bite. I feel his purr against my chest *and* inside it, somehow. *Here I am,* it seems to hum, right under my heart. *Where I belong.*

I start to sink into the sensation, drinking it up, wishing I could hold on to it. But a twinge at my core tweaks so hard, I can't float deeper into my haze. My canines throb, saliva welling until all I can think about is the manly musk rising off his throat.

I nuzzle into the perfect warmth, fitting my teeth around the front of his collarbone. A big hand lands on the back of my head, pressing me closer. "Yes," the alpha growls. And inside, that hum agrees, somehow. Vibrating deeper. "So perfect, baby girl. *Right there.*"

The soft bark sails to the center of my mind. Sinking into it like an arrow. Graceful and sharp.

I bite. And it's—it's—

Adrian.

The rumble in my soul becomes a *voice. His* voice. His name slips through my mind like a veil in a breeze, but I know *him.*

Steady support. An iron will. Elegant and dominant and cool and warm. Aqua eyes, always watching. Observing so he can lead. So he can *give.*

Daddy Alpha.

The burst of amusement that shimmers over my insides brings a certain smile to mind. His beloved face appears in my memories; ocean irises shining, lips quirked up. And when I open my eyes? A heartrendingly tender version looms over me.

"That's right, sweetheart," he purrs, scent-marking my forehead and dropping a lingering kiss there. "Who takes care of you?"

I know the answer. He hears it the second it springs up, even though the words tangle with a whimper in my throat.

Daddy takes care of me.

A brilliant version of that adoring grin blazes to life before my very eyes. "Damn right, baby." And in my heart, *Daddy will <u>always</u> take care of you.*

Emotion bubbles into my throat. Gratitude and disbelief.

I love him.

His own deep-rooted devotion smolders in my center. *I love you, too, Bridget,* he says, speaking through our tether of impenetrable, sparkling stone. Where only *I* can hear him.

The brush of his forehead matches the nudge under my ribs. Images fly through my haze—and I barely have the ability to realize, *they're his.* My face, in social media pictures. A rumpled, makeup-less, somehow-better version in person. Smiling at my blond alpha with empathy. Smirking at the gray-eyed one. Cocking my hip when the dark-featured devil tossed me his scoundrel's grin.

I knew you were perfect, the pack leader husks, *But I never imagined anyone could possibly be <u>this</u> perfect. For <u>all</u> of us.*

Somewhere under all the good, there's a nagging thread of unease, pulling at me. The alpha senses it and huddles closer, letting me feel his weight, his knot, the invisible link connecting our bodies in a totally different way.

I want you to see, he says and then, out loud, so the others hear him, "Are you ready to claim the rest of your pack, omega?"

I'VE NEVER BEEN in an omega's nest or part of a heat, so I'm not sure what I expected.

A frenzy, maybe. Or at least anxious urgency.

This is different, though.

This is *everything*.

Adrian has kept the energy soothing and sacred. Even when he spontaneously bit her, I watched him soak in her every move. Reading all her needs and providing for them like a true pack alpha.

I used to feel inadequate at times like these. Now, I'm *inspired*.

I can do that. *Be* that.

For her, I think I could be just about *anything*.

Adrian's body senses her heat the same way mine did. His knot deflates within a minute, setting off a fresh round of whines from our omega.

Our *mate*.

I don't know how or why she chooses me next, but I trust her instincts with every fiber of my being. When she turns her foggy blue eyes in my direction, my face splits into a soft grin.

My bumblebee.

She's still in there, fighting with everything she has to stay present for this bonding. Our gazes meet, and Bridget tries to lurch upright.

Adrian helps her to her knees. A brazen gush of slick and cum dribbles down her thighs, the heady combination soaking into the nest's special cushions. Musk and sugar, tart and warm.

The scent of her would draw me anywhere, but the look on Bridget's face is what has me rushing to gather her into my arms. Scent-marking her everywhere I can—her breasts, her shoulders, her face and neck and hair.

"Hi, beautiful girl," I whisper, snuggling her close. "Me next?"

She whimpers, her eyes desperate behind laggy blinks. "She can't remember your name," Adrian explains, coming up behind her and kissing her nape. "She feels very guilty about it."

Something inside me flips. A seethe strikes my stomach and sparks scatter, lighting my lungs. A deep purr rattles them.

"That's okay, Bee," I murmur. "You don't have to remember anything right now. Just let me take care of you."

Balancing on my bent legs, I spread my knees for stability and lift her into my lap. The position reminds me of our limo ride home, and how frantic I was to have her. The crushing fear I felt before the rut took over.

"I was so scared," I confess into her hair, guiding her hips in a fluid roll. Letting her use my pulsing shaft to rub her clit until she gasps. Groaning at the slippery burst of slick dribbling down my knot and balls, I force myself to focus.

I've spent so many years trying to be decisive and commanding. All the things I thought an alpha needed to be... Now, I wonder if maybe *this* is my role, for her.

Honest. Vulnerable.

She needs to hear this.

"When your true perfume hit at the gala, I was fucking *terrified*," I go on, panting. "I needed it to be you, Bee. Back then. Now. That's why I brought the guys to you. That's why I called you every week. I've loved you the whole time. It always had to be you."

Bridget's haze is so thick, she's past the point of speaking. That's alright, though. I see her emotions, glowing in her eyes. Even under her fog, with her pupils expanding every second... *she loves me.*

I feel it in the way she clings to me. Tears stream over her cheeks, and she turns to the hand cupped around her shoulder, nosing at my fingers. The gesture is so sweet, the bridge of my nose stings.

"Yeah? You want to bite me there?" It's so *Bridget*, I can't help my small smile. "Right where everyone will see it when I throw a pitch, huh?"

She whines shyly, slanting a sideways look at me. *God.* Our mate might be one of the strongest, smartest women in the world, but her Omega is a sweet, tender-hearted creature. I bury my face into her hair and hug her closer.

"That's a perfect spot," I rasp, plucking up her left hand and bringing it to my lips. "Here. We'll match, okay?"

She loves that idea as much as I do. Her grin is lopsided and goofy, but I don't think she's ever looked more gorgeous.

I memorize the expression, catching the exact moment pain starts to pull her expression into a grimace. My purr snags in my chest. "Come here, bumblebee. I'll give you my knot and sink my teeth into you right now."

She nods desperately, red hair cascading over her pale perfection. I lift her again, sinking myself all the way inside her on one plunge.

Goddamn it, she feels incredible. Slippery and hot, her muscles cinched and *squeezing*. I buck into her, circling my knot into the quivering heat. It expands instantly, pressing into all her walls.

Bridget's eyes slide closed, a small cry tripping up her throat. I brush my lips over hers slowly, reaching between us to stroke my thumb over the top of her swollen nub. Rubbing it until she sobs against my mouth and starts to come.

My bite breaks her skin the same second her orgasm crests. Bridget wails, bouncing on my pounding knot, kneading it. I choke on a snarl, lapping at her skin and spurting deep. Glazing her insides while I suck her fingers.

Our mate takes my hand much more gently, placing her teeth wide across the back. Branding me with one steady press through the thin flesh.

My lungs stammer, oxygen spiraling into an abyss but never touching me. Because the only thing I feel—all that I *am*—is the loop locking into place between us.

It's so *soft*. The papery whisper of pages. A silent sigh while you sink into a steamy bath. Safe and quiet, but also *bright*.

Sunrise, maybe, or serendipity.

Whatever it is, it's mine. *She's mine.*

And she's so damn *beautiful*—deep down inside, here in my arms—I don't even try to stem the tears that flow from my eyes.

She loves all of us so much. I feel her trying to tell me, but her haze is already overpowering, and getting thicker by the minute.

Funneling reassurance into her, I hum and rub at my claim mark, tending it while she rides me to another trembling finish. "That's it, beautiful. You use me however you want. I love you so damn much. You can feel it, right?"

Adrian makes himself known with a thump of approval, followed by a sweeping tide of pride. *Isn't she perfect?*

A growl of agreement deepens my purr. Bridget whimpers when the rumble vibrates my knot and her pussy. Her little cry draws Dante closer. He's been watching, dark flames licking higher and hotter in his gaze every minute.

I'm surprised that her soft sound of distress is what finally snaps him into action, but as he approaches, his usual recklessness is nowhere to be found. Instead, he roams his solemn, heated eyes down her back, noting the way she squirms when my knot unlocks us.

Chest heaving, he slowly extends his arms. Meeting my gaze with a solid sort of respect in his, he simply says, "Please."

Adrian's surprise echoes my own, bouncing from his side of our bond into mine and back again. His approval climbs, easing some of Bridget's restlessness—enough to allow me to carefully turn her toward our packmate.

Colt crawls closer, too. Watching with his singular intensity. Dante barely notices, though. He's too busy beaming at our girl, taking her from my hands like the priceless treasure she is.

Instead of staying on his knees, Dante lowers them both into the pillows, curving a protective arm over her head and using the other to anchor their bodies together. Our omega clasps her thigh over his, fighting to get him into her right away.

The curve of Dante's lips is warm and adoring. "It's like that, huh, *querida*? Okay, baby. You can have it. You can have as much as you want."

He bends to whisper to her, but I hear him, because her haze is too thick for her to filter anything out of our tether.

"Love you more than life," he roughs into her ear. "Take this big alpha cock and use me, *corazón*."

They collide. Bridget reaches for his cock and pushes it inside her. Dante hooks his arm under her knee and lifts her leg to show us her slick and our cum, creamed together, seeping from her slit as his dick splits it.

Nerves tingle in my center when they start eating at each other, kissing deeper and faster to match the stroke of his cock. I didn't think about this before. Witnessing my packmates bonding from the inside.

Adrian senses my anticipation and nudges my arm. "It's amazing."

He's right, of course. When Dante finally chooses his mark, at the top of Bridget's left breast—somewhere between Adrian's spot and mine—our mate's pleasure crests into an electric wave.

Adrian braces, but I'm too late. When Dante sinks his teeth into Bridget's skin, their shared bliss floods my body too quickly to control. I come again, groaning and spraying over the nest cushions. My balls draw up again as Bridget claims Dante, her answering bite savage compared to the ones she gave me and our pack leader.

It takes up the whole front of his neck, spreading like a collar across his Adam's apple. Dante groans, his knot tying them together while he blasts into our bond like a cannonball.

Color and bright, blinding light explode into our tether. A zing of pure energy. Bouncing and boundless.

Adrian and I start to shuffle back on instinct, but Bridget?

Bridget rushes *into* it. Opens her arms and wraps them around Dante. All of his excess. The heat, the hurt, the hedonism. She doesn't let any of it scare her. She *wants* it *all*. Every last bit of *him*.

"It was the same way with you," Adrian confirms out loud.

I find myself struggling to believe anyone could love me this much, this hard. But I *feel* it. I can *see* it, here at the heart of me.

It's *her*, actually. *Her* heart.

And it's big enough for all of us.

chapter
sixty-seven

IF THE BONE-SEARING, jaw-grinding perfection spilling from between our omega's thighs is any indication, she's fully in her heat haze now.

So it hits my chest like a flaming arrow when she slides off Dante's spent dick and clambers straight to *me*. I catch her with a breathless laugh, ignoring the twinge of discomfort that zips down my arm as we fall backward onto the nest cushions.

Bridget may be gone, but her Omega obviously knows me just as well. Her blown-out gaze only lags for a moment before shifting to the tail of my scar, branded over the curve of my shoulder. She whines and nuzzles it. A bittersweet slurry slicks my soul.

"Hi, baby," I murmur, kissing her face. "How's my girl, huh? You need me?"

As I speak, my hands skim down her sides. Over all the glorious, creamy softness. To *her* scars.

Our mate quivers on top of me, but her scent doesn't sour with chagrin this time. It *dwindles*; sadness blotting out the creamy, sugared lemon.

I can't sense what she's thinking, but the guys can. Adrian's purr rolls into a dangerous growl to match the gleam in Dante's feral eyes. Jesse swallows hard enough for me to hear it.

Goddamn it. My blood is *roaring*. I need to claim my omega *now*.

But I won't do it while tears stream down her peachy cheeks.

"What is it?" I rasp, a horrible realization dawning. "Is it me?"

Fuck, that would make sense. If she's changed her mind and doesn't want to be my omega—with my entire future up in the air —then that's fair. And I suppose I can wait for her, if that's the case.

I'd wait *forever* for this woman.

I grit my teeth to quell their ache. Preparing for her rejection. Resolved to handle it so fucking differently this time. *I'll earn her, and fight for her, and never let my stupid, stubborn pride—*

Adrian's sudden, ear-splitting snarl yanks me from my thoughts and puts me on the defensive. I roll automatically, tucking my mate underneath me. Ready to protect her from—

What?

My packmates look like they've seen a ghost, but nothing has changed. *Right?*

"Tell me what the hell is happening," I grind out.

"It's—" Jesse tries to explain, but he shakes his head.

"Her scars," Adrian rasps, clearing his throat. "They're from the heat clinic she went to last time."

Dante growls low. "They put her in one of those stupid omega cages. For knotting."

"But it wasn't designed for her body," Jesse whispers. "And no one noticed... or cared so—"

It tore her up.

Being rutted from behind while the metal scraped her skin. Hurt her. For *days.*

Alpha energy snaps through the nest, each of the guys barely reining themselves in. Adrian holds the others back with his hands raised in front of them, though.

He meets my gaze, impressing the importance of his next statement before he even opens his mouth. "In the bond, she's asking us if she ever has to go back there," he says, then raises a brow. "You want to answer her?"

The words melt through the clouds shrouding my mind and plunge *deep.* The last shred of control pulled taut at my middle *snaps.*

I grasp Bridget's gorgeous face between my palms, growling a final vow. "*Never,* omega. You will never have another heat without us."

It's not enough. Her eyes are too unfocused, her skin too hot to the touch.

And I want to make damn sure she understands.

So I slide down her body and find the scars etched into her left hip. Kissing each one before I open my mouth and claim her.

My teeth sink through her supple skin, pressing deep and sure. Indelible. Just like her scars and mine.

We're part of each other, now. And neither of us ever have to be alone again.

Our omega writhes, wailing for a knot to clamp down on as she comes. I rear up, barely able to slide home before she bolts forward and *bites.*

Bridget.

Fluttering heat swirling around my cock. Brilliant sunshine beaming into my soul. Outside, all around. Inside, luminous and all-consuming.

Bubbling into my blood. Wrapping my cock in perfect slick-soaked softness. I fly straight over the edge without attempting to slow either of us down, filling her with my release while her own clutches me tighter.

My knot expands the same second our tether glows to life, locking us together. *Hi*, I whisper, pouring the hoarse words directly into her heart. *Hi, baby. God, look how pretty you are, inside and outside. My bubbly girl. I love you.*

She feels it—and, more importantly she *believes* me.

HAVE you ever seen the Grand Canyon?

It's one of the Seven Wonders of the World. My mom took me once, when I was eight—I remember the view so clearly. Endless golden color. Carved so deep, it turns your brain inside out.

But that shit?

It's *nothing* compared to Bridget.

Standing at the edge of our bond, gazing into her soul, feels a lot like standing at the edge of that canyon. Only *better*. Fucking *more*.

I don't know how. Or why she chose *me*.

But I *know* I will be worthy.

Because it's my life's mission now. And we all know how I get when I want something.

Like this omega, eating her damn coffee cake.

"One more bite, *querida*," I promise, sending a rush of reassurance into our bond. "I can feel how hungry you are."

And it's driving me *insane*.

Our mate may be a sassy vixen, but her Omega is a total sweetheart. She huddles closer to my chest, curling in on herself when she senses my frustration. I set her breakfast down instantly, purring as I plant kisses all over her face.

Seeing this vulnerable side of her should probably freak me out, but I only love her more for every quiver of her full lips and each droplet in her crystal eyes. I tell her so, humming the words in both of my languages, scent-marking her face.

"I'm not mad, *corazón*. Just worried about you. I want you to eat some more for me."

Food has been my responsibility for this heat. Cooking it, making sure she eats it. Eating *her* as a bribe when she refuses...

Colt's taken on her showers, insisting he be the one to wash her every day. No matter how much she fusses, he finds a way to coax her onto his handy shower chair. Then takes his time massaging her sore limbs and washing her hair.

Jesse is the one she counts on to help rebuild her nest whenever the mood strikes. She also tends to go to him if she needs someone to purr her to sleep.

Adrian has surprised me the most. Sure, he runs this shit, pumping out his particular brand of dominance to keep everyone in line—but Bridget isn't the only one he's caring for.

No, he observes *all* of us. Issuing reminders that we keep up our water intake. Ensuring we get at least a few hours of uninterrupted sleep every day. Pitching in to do his fair share of the chores and keeping up with team business, too.

It took a few days, but eventually—sometime around three a.m. last night, while we sandwiched our omega between us—I begrudgingly had to admit: I appreciate the bastard.

Bridget feels my remembered gratitude and perks up a little. It's so fucking sweet how her Omega just wants all of us to be happy—and is willing to do just about anything for our approval.

I won't rest until she knows she doesn't have to *do* anything. She has my whole fucking heart, forever. No matter what.

I can't even decide which version of her I love more, at this point. Her angelic Omega, or my fiery red-velvet cupcake.

Jesus.

Colt is right: I *am* a simp.

Our catcher isn't much better off, though. The awe smoldering low in his lungs reflects the adoration vibrating in my own. He glances up from the scrap of Kings' blue in his hands, casting our omega a tender glance.

I can't believe she stole this, he thinks, holding up the cap.

Jesse abandons his musings on what sort of lotion our omega might tolerate for a massage later, tuning in to our conversation. He looks at our sleeping pack leader. Determination sparks in his center when he decides not to wake Adrian.

"You stopped wearing it," Jesse points out, whispering. "Was that just because she took it for her nest?"

Denial lurches into Colt's throat, but he deliberately swallows it. Hoarse, he answers, "No. I—It didn't feel right anymore."

I was embarrassed, he admits, deep down where only we can hear. *I used to wear this damn thing everywhere. Every day. And then it became a symbol of all my fuck-ups...*

He doesn't have the words to complete his thought, but I understand anyway. So does Jesse.

Bridget wanted it, our blond packmate finishes. *She liked it enough to hide it in her nest. Because she loves you.*

Every piece, Colt agrees, examining the cap again. Wonder swells under his diaphragm. *Even this one.*

Because she's perfect, I reply. *Our mate.*

Bridget burrows closer to my purr when it stutters. Her scent-mark puts a soft smile on my face as I roll her into her queen-worthy pile of pillows. Silky lemon cream fills the air.

It definitely isn't causing as much urgency today, which probably means her heat is winding down. After four days, a part of me is sad to lose this bubble we've been in, but another piece is relieved. Even with all our extra care, this has been hard on our girl's body. She deserves some quality rest.

None of us are willing to rush her, though. This Omega can have as many knots and as much pampering as she can handle.

Carajo, but she looks like a jewel. Her rich auburn hair and peachy blush. The way her blown pupils have turned her sky-blue eyes to sapphires.

She gives a tiny whine, begging for another knot. Which is fair. I *did* promise her a treat if she ate her breakfast.

Colt hears my mind racing through the possibilities and latches onto the distraction, setting his hat aside as he tosses out a mental image. One filthy enough to turn Jesse's low purr into a stammer and transform our girl's whimper into a *keen*.

Oh, fuck yeah. She likes that idea.

Wicked delight swoops through my stomach. "Wake Adrian up."

Our pack leader has definitely gotten the least sleep, but he won't want to miss this. Especially since it will be a new experience for our omega.

Sure enough, his bleary blue eyes clear within seconds, sharpening while he runs over the details swirling in Colt's mind.

Goddamn.

The guy's a *freak*.

I'm a little proud.

Jesse snorts at my thoughts. Reminding me, once again, that I should probably *turn that shit off* occasionally.

We all should, for this, Adrian agrees. *Things will be messy enough without one of us going off early.*

As embarrassing as it is to admit, that has been a bit of a problem since we bonded. Feeling five people's lust at one time, not to mention how motherfucking *glorious* Bridget's scent is...

It's a good thing we have forever to practice not coming all over her pretty pillows.

And maybe an even better thing that our girl doesn't seem to mind.

Colt might be ruthless with the rest of us when it comes to this shit, but he's always exceedingly sweet to our omega. He thoroughly scent-marks her forehead and his claim mark before helping her onto her knees, clutching her close and kissing her with plunging licks.

Squirming for more, Bridget whines and gouges her nails into his skin. When she hits his bond mark, Colt hisses, dropping onto his back and spreading his legs. The look he casts me is impatient.

As if he isn't asking me to perform a highly skilled maneuver on the fly.

"If you're not up to it..." Jesse taunts.

Bridget squeaks her desperation, earning each of us stern looks from Daddy.

I mean *Adrian*.

"Don't make my mate wait," he bites out, making his way to her face. Pressing gentle kisses on her cheeks before murmuring praises to her.

I take advantage of Jesse's distraction and move into position, lining my cock up with Colt's pierced dick. It twitches, bumping our heads together.

Carajo. This might be hard.

Pun *completely* intended.

Bridget's already gushing slick, so I scoop up a palmful of her gorgeous lemon cream and glide my hand over myself, then Colt. He grits his teeth when I slip over his knot, a low growl vibrating against Bridget's chest.

She needs to be like this, I think, sending Adrian a mental picture before I close my internal curtain.

He weaves his fingers into the hair at her nape and tugs. "*Present*, omega."

The gentle bark works instantly. Bridget lets her upper half sink fully onto Colt's chest and lifts her ass higher. Jesse watches her assume her new position, slowly stroking himself as he bites his lip.

God, she's so beautiful. He shuts his part of the bond down after that final thought, turning his attention to where I'm hard at work.

Trying to fit two alpha cocks into one gorgeous cunt.

Colt and I grunt when I stretch my fingers around both shafts. His silver piercing grazes the underside of my head, sending a tingly *snap* to my balls. Combined with the sensation of sweet citrus slick sliding over my swollen skin... my knot is already half full by the time I line us both up at her entrance.

Bridget's next whine launches me into motion. My hips buck forward, punching myself into her wet, silky heat. Colt snarls, lifting his body to replace mine when I start to pull back. Beginning a rhythm where we take turns filling her.

Fuck *me*. It's been five days, and she just gets more perfect *every time*.

Her inner muscles massage the top of my throbbing cock while Colt's piercing rubs along the other side, keeping me balanced on the edge of a blade. I ignore the way my knot screams, shifting and moving my knees to straddle Colt's right leg... so Jesse can get to Bridget's ass.

Our omega thrashes, a wail of pleasure tearing from her chest as he slowly works himself into her. We've taken her this way dozens of times since her heat started, but never with *two* dicks in her pussy.

The stretch is *intense*. I feel the hard ridge of Jesse's massive erection pressing through the thin, scorching skin separating us. Everything inside Bridget seizes up, trying to tug us all deeper.

"Shh," Adrian soothes, thumbing her cheek. He hooks her lower lip. "Open up for Daddy, sweetheart."

Dios mío, the way she lunges for his dick is *so hot*. Colt groans from underneath her, his view even better than mine.

Jesse must like it, too, because he's already panting. Drilling her ass in smooth, deep plunges. Creating constant friction on both sides of my raging cock.

Bridget starts to clench around us, the pressure pressing my knot into Colt's, rubbing those damn silver metal balls over my frenulum until I'm gasping. "Fuck, *fuck*. Gonna come, *querida*."

Adrian's low growl reminds me of our original plan. I shove as deep into her cunt s I can while Colt snarls and slides out. I go off the second his piercing rubs the base of my knot, popping myself all the way into Bridget just in time.

Unghhhhhh fuuuuuuck. I'll never get used to feeling her lush wetness locked around my stretched, pulsing skin. How she massages every nerve with her trembling muscles.

My omega screams around our pack leader's dick, still coming as Colt empties his balls all over her pussy, paying no mind the fact that he sprays Jesse and me in the process.

Our blond packmate hisses a second later, tugging himself out of her ass so he can add his cum to the *waterfall* of slick and seed covering her. "*Jesus*," he moans, watching himself spray out. "Bee, you're so goddamn *sexy*."

Colt groans his agreement while I pant, flicking a look to Adrian. He's borderline feral, hard enough to drive nails as he gently pulls himself out of Bridget's mouth and nods at me.

My knot has barely deflated enough to slip free, but he's beyond caring. Our alpha flips her over, jacking his thick cock with fast snaps of his wrist. Holding our girl's face in one palm while the other milks a thick stream of white down her belly, across her mound, and *all over* her cunt.

"*Alpha!*" Bridget pleads. And, inside our bond, she begs with a single image.

Appreciative snarls ring through the nest as Adrian's chest swells with smug pride. *Daddy knew you would want to taste all of us at once*, he murmurs to her. He bends to rub a sweet scent-mark along our omega's cheekbone, reaching down for the hot fucking mess between her thick thighs.

He scoops up the mixture, bringing it to her lips. Watching

her lap it up with a fanatical gleam in his eye. We all groan again, but he wraps his free hand around her throat before reaching for another taste of us.

I collapse into her side, snuggling close. She feels a bit cooler now, which was Adrian's aim. I'm not sure how I feel about it.

On one hand, I get my mate back. On the other, I'll miss the Omega I've fallen *madly* in love with.

I don't think she's going to lock her Omega down again, Colt replies, stretching his limbs before he comes to sit between her legs.

Jesse crawls to Bridget's crown, sifting her mussed hair back to plant a kiss on her forehead. *That's the beauty of this*, he thinks, adoration filling his chest. *We get to keep them both.*

I gaze into her bleary eyes, love rising to fill my throat as I nod. Glancing at my packmates. Absorbing the moment and agreeing. Promising.

Forever.

ORLANDO ORTHOPEDIC SPECIALISTS

This is a message for Colt Davis. Please contact us for the results of your recent exam immediately.

I WAKE with a whine still vibrating in my throat. The vocal chords involved feel distinctly worn, which likely means I've been whining *a lot*.

Embarrassing.

But not nearly as mortifying as calling one of my alphas Daddy for the last four days?

Yet, somehow, I can't shake the urge to grin as I tell my Omega, *We are so not friends anymore.*

She snuffs a mildly indignant sound, waving me off in a *yeah, yeah* gesture. *Were we ever friends?*

Her question hits me harder than it should. My Omega feels my stomach coil, but stays silent, waiting.

I think I want to be, I finally reply. *If that's okay?*

I don't deserve the instant burst of excitement she bubbles back at me. Her joy is wordless, but the sentiment is clear—the two of us working together? Being *friends*? That's all she's ever wanted.

My Omega's happiness quickly fades into a pleasantly exhausted stupor. She starts to fade into unconsciousness, curling back into her usual place at my middle. Forgiving me effortlessly.

Guilty tears clog my throat, welling behind my closed eyelids. The urge to stuff them down is strong and familiar. I seriously consider it, especially since I really don't want the guys' first impression of me as their bonded mate to be incoherent sobs.

But I forgot—*they're here.*

Part of me.

The haze fully recedes, snapping back like a rubber band. Four deep purrs invade my senses, followed by the feel of my alphas' muscled bodies cuddling closer. I don't even have to open my eyes to know who is who.

Adrian's thigh is under my head, his fingers massaging my scalp. Jesse spoons at my back, unbothered by using our pack alpha's leg as a pillow.

The over-long hair tickling my belly is Colt, of course, which means his arm must be the one banded around my hips... and Dante has my feet in his brawny hands. He's completely still while they all listen. Actively holding their reactions in, I suspect, so they don't overwhelm me.

Jesse speaks first, his whisper broken enough to confirm they've heard everything. *Bumblebee,* he rasps. *Babe...*

Images flood our bond—a picture from high school; me,

ducking behind my locker door when a group of his asshole friends passed by. One of him sitting in the Kings' weight room, staring at his phone; wanting to call me and ignoring his instincts. The night he watched Colt walk out of their apartment, knowing his packmate was too tired to drive, but actively held in his objections.

It's impossible to explain how, but he also shows me the emotions each picture invokes—and how those feelings have transformed since he started trying to move forward. *Learning from your mistakes takes time*, he adds, *but it's worth it. You taught me that.*

Colt's arm squeezes me softly. *And there isn't any rush*, he adds, gruff. *We'll all be here while you figure this out.*

He reminds me of our day in the shower, the afternoon under the clouds. How I tricked him into catching me, just to prove he *could*.

You were always there for me, he murmurs, quieter. Shades of longing and fear shadow the words. *I hope you always will be.*

That finally snaps my eyes open.

Adrian's face is the first one I see, gazing down at me with a blend of tenderness and concern. I lurch upright as much as I can while wrapped up in four alphas, casting Colt a scolding glare.

"Of course I will be!" I burst. "How can you even think otherwise?!"

My fierce protectiveness lights Dante's chest up. He groans, reaching out to tug me away from the others and into his lap. "Fuck, *querida*, I *missed* you. Let's fight about something."

He truly wants to, which is both hilarious and adorable—but I need to kick Colt's ass first. *How can he possibly think, after all of this, that I wouldn't—*

Oh.

All four of them share their versions of the same memory. I tune into Colt's, instinct guiding my focus.

A phone call—from the only number Adrian programmed to allow calls from during my heat.

Their team doctor.

The message came just after our last round, once I'd passed out. Colt recalls the man's careful words, how he skillfully delivered the killing blow to my alpha's career with a few sympathetic sentences.

I barely hear the words, too caught up in the tidal wave of devastation swamping Colt's stomach. The way his hope had soared, caught fire, and crashed into a burning heap. His dreams, his passion—*gone.*

"No."

Their purrs stutter as Colt snaps, plucking me from Dante and framing my face with both of his shaking hands. Gray beams bore into my gaze. *"No,"* he repeats, softer but no less intense. "My dreams are *not* gone. My passion isn't either."

He rests his forehead on mine, letting his eyes fall shut. *Because you're here.*

It's insane to think there was ever a time when I would have doubted him. Now that I can feel the true depth of his love, how much he means this—his thoughts, swirling with words like *saved me, found me, gave me a purpose, made us a family.*

And it's not just him.

My other alphas reflect his sentiments, flooding my soul with their own adoration. I soak it all in, pouring right back out. Into Colt.

His chest shudders when I wrap my arms around his neck and hold him close. *I'm so proud to be your mate.*

The deep vulnerability he used to reserve just for me is on full display. But he doesn't recoil, speaking his fear for everyone to hear. "Even now?"

I sidle closer. *"Especially* now."

My words sink into his wounds, filling them with light. He nuzzles his face into my throat, huffing a thick, rueful laugh. "Ah, fuck," he sniffs. "This means Dante was *right.*"

We all laugh, except for my dark-eyed alpha. He crows, *"I told you.* Our girl is *perfect.*"

Jesse's hand finds the back of my head, stroking my hair. His golden gaze shines. "She really is."

Adrian's warm hum draws my gaze to his handsome grin. "Best decision I've ever made."

Colt lies back in our mountain of perfectly scented pillows, bundling me into his side. He presses a kiss to my crown. *Hi, Bubbles.*

The thought is accompanied by the strangest, fizzy sensation. I nearly giggle when I realize—they're *bubbles*. Inside him.

Me, inside him.

Flowing like champagne. Sweet, golden effervescence that tickles his veins and swells behind his heart.

Dante and Jesse drift closer, drawn by the happiness rising off me when I feel just how much they all still want to be near me. Even after six days in here.

I really was *touch-starved, huh?*

Adrian fits himself against my back, petting my hair. Projecting the calm certainty that there's no reason for any of us to leave this nest until we're *all* good and ready. Pouring a layer of pride and adoration over his soothing purr. "What does it feel like for you, sweetheart? All of us together?"

I close my eyes, exploring the new alcove carved into my center for the first time. It's beautiful and unique. Like a sunset. Changing from moment to moment, but always exquisite. Bright and serene—colorful and comforting.

It's *them*.

Adrian is the sun, of course. The anchor of my universe; the one I've turned to without hesitation from the day we met.

He's also steady. Predictable in the best way; no matter how dark it gets, the sun will rise. And Adrian will be there for me. For all of us.

The bright, gorgeous colors? Those are Dante, blooming in the most unexpected ways. Gentle, then *brilliant*. But always *warm*. Spreading joy and humor and heart.

Jesse would be the sky itself. Clear, brilliant blue. Endlessly holding everyone up, holding *space* for each of us to shine. Taking on our pains and triumphs. Reflecting our moods and various shades. Giving everyone room to roam.

That makes me the clouds, huh? Colt asks, his dry tone a direct contrast to the wonder lighting up his heart. The others watch as he replays our afternoon in the backyard, revealing just how touched he was by everything I said.

Everyone huddles closer, settling in together.

And it occurs to me that this moment? Is a lot like that sunset.

The end of something beautiful—bittersweet and luminous. But promising a thousand new beginnings.

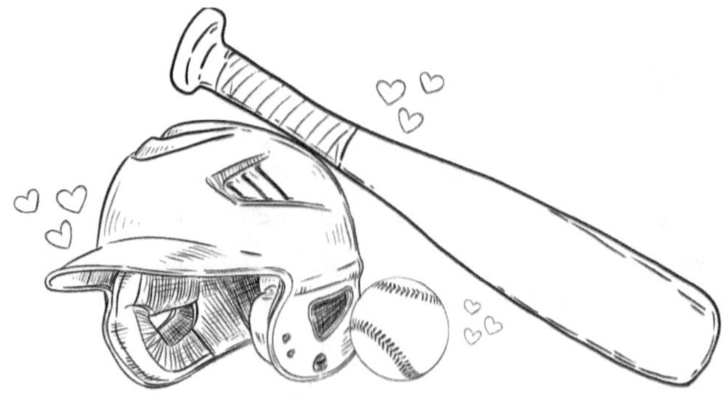

DANTE'S HAND clamps around my neck, his palm firmly pressed over Adrian's claim mark. When I squeak, my shortstop chuckles darkly, pumping his hips faster.

"*Shhh, querida,*" he purrs, all teasing sternness. "This is a *library.*"

This *asshole.* In retaliation for all his taunts, I work myself onto his hardness fast, drawing out a surprised hiss and another squeeze to my throat.

Mine, he thinks, pumping with renewed abandon. *My fucking <u>queen</u>*.

Colt's gray irises spark as he watches his packmate use me. Beside him, Jesse glances swiftly around the stacks, even though he knows damn well the doors locked ten minutes ago.

Who would have guessed that my shy alpha would turn out to be *such* an exhibitionist?

And Colt such a voyeur?

He may not be a fan of sharing my scent, but he certainly enjoys seeing his packmates use me. And Jesse really loves flaunting me. Marking his territory anywhere less-than "appropriate."

I love that part, too. Probably because both of us grew up with so many social obligations and expectations—there's nothing I adore more than moments like these, when he's wild-eyed and drained dry. Panting from all the release my body just wrung out of him...

...Except for maybe how Dante casually asserted that he was up next. Right before he bent me over and hooked his forearm through both my elbows, arching me to give himself access to my throat.

He nuzzles a succulent scent-mark there, humming his approval. "Such a good little mate. Letting me fuck her whenever I want." His hips punch harder, the swollen head of his cock hitting deep. "Wherever I want." He circles, teasing my quivering opening with the knot I know he won't give me. "However I want."

I make another high-pitched noise, and he snarls a laugh, rearranging his hand to shove two fingers into my mouth. "Quiet, cupcake. Or everyone will hear you coming on my cock."

Guys, I swear, this was *so* not the plan today.

My alphas work me over, nonetheless, giving me two more orgasms before Colt guides my mouth onto his dick. He takes turns thrusting back and forth with Dante, until I'm boneless, dripping with their release.

Well, we wanted him distracted, I think, watching Colt's irises burn as he smirks down at me, memorizing the sight of me licking his cum off my lips. *Mission accomplished.*

The second Jesse finishes kissing a leisurely path up my left thigh, sliding my panties back into place, a slow clap starts behind us.

Fuck a duck.

We all whirl, sagging with relief when we find our pack leader leaning against the second-floor guardrail, his bright gaze piercingly blue.

Blushing hard enough to heat the room, I bite my lip. "Oh. H-hi, alpha."

"Hi, little blue." The fond curve of his lips is enough to set my heart racing all over again. He holds out his hand in a wordless command, curling his fingers twice. "Come see me."

The happy hum in my heart has become my constant companion. Every morning, when I wake up wedged between whichever two of my mates won their nightly arm-wrestling competition. Every afternoon, when I come home to find Colt and Munchies arguing over what we should have for dinner. And every night in my nest, whether we're watching movies or trying out new configurations for our pack's version of a Grand Slam.

My joy only multiplies when Adrian twirls me into his chest. Today's white sundress flares around my knees before he catches me, kissing me soundly, pulling back to arch an eyebrow.

"Letting them have you without me here? Sounds like someone needs to learn a lesson," he murmurs, all silken promises.

Anticipation zings through my veins. Sometimes, his protective dominance makes me desperate for his approval and pride. Other days...

I stick my tongue out, earning myself a hard slap on the ass. When Adrian laughs at my put-on outrage, I huff, "How did you even get into the library? It's *locked*!"

He squeezes me tighter, pressing the bulge at the front of his slacks to my belly. "I have my ways." He shrugs enigmatically, leaning closer to add a quiet growl. "Did you really think Daddy would let you be locked in here if he didn't have a key?"

Before you ask, *no,* "Daddy" is not a thing.

Shut up.

It's totally a thing, my Omega says, bubbling.

With an internal sigh, I let her show me all the images from our heat... and the numerous other times I've accidentally called Adrian that since.

Okay, okay, so it's a thing.

Don't tell Emma, I end up replying. My Omega gives the mental equivalent of a salute, then nudges me back to Adrian, urging me to find the patch of musky skin along his neck. While I nuzzle my scent-mark, our pack leader sends me an image from last night. When he massaged my entire body and spent nearly half an hour between my thighs...

These men! Why do I even bother wearing panties?

Oh. Right.

The reason is currently seeping into them *as we speak.*

Adrian chuckles at my resigned expression, then glances at the big clock over the stairs. "We'd better get out of here. It's almost four-thirty."

Colt finishes buckling his belt and approaches, scowling. "Yeah, what did you need a ride for, Bubbles? Didn't you take your car?" As he reaches me, he skims his hand over my hip and adds, *Not that I mind a break from being bored at home. Especially this one.*

He's so funny, acting sweet in the bond and externally pouting like a grump. I smirk at him. "Maybe I just wanted all my alphas to come running to my rescue again."

Jesse slots into place behind me, setting his chin on my shoulder. His tone is teasing, but the earnestness blooming behind his ribs pricks my eyes. "Anytime, bumblebee."

Dante keeps us entertained on our way down the stairs, talking about all the restaurants and clubs he wants to take me to when we go on their next road game near Miami. His plan is outrageous, given how early they have to wake up for conditioning the next morning, but his enthusiasm is as contagious as ever. By the time we hit the school quad, Adrian has his phone in his hand, booking reservations.

It's a gorgeous afternoon. Sunny with a few gauzy clouds. Plants all bursting in full Florida bloom. I listen to Jesse and Dante exchange barbs about their upcoming game, sinking into Colt's side.

He lets me into his part of our bond, showing me the wistfulness swelling in his throat every time he thinks about watching the guys play without him. Admitting, just to me, that it hurts.

He's amazing, though. No matter how many times these feelings spring up, he consistently turns them around and finds a way to support his packmates. Sometimes it's messy, but he always fights to find a path to gratitude. Reflecting on his appreciation for everything the game gave him—

Namely, me.

Our pack.

I listen to his bittersweet thoughts, actively stuffing my reactions down. Not wanting to give anything away.

"You know," I say, offhand, "Meg told me that Colt was working with the kids at the Osprey House's field day last weekend."

My grump rolls his eyes, but I feel how the memories of bright-eyed young players hanging from his every word spark joy for him. "It was easy," he grouses. "Whatever."

That one word nearly splits my face into a grin. "Yeah." I shrug, reaching into my messenger bag. "Whatever."

I pull out the hat tucked under my planner, reaching over to show Colt the orange baseball cap emblazoned with my school's logo.

Well, *our* school's logo.

He blinks at it, brow furrowing as my other alphas fall silent. I finally let all my secret memories tumble forward—the meeting I had with our principal, calling their college for a copy of Colt's degree, lobbying the PTA to give my ex-pro-baseball star a shot, me standing over their crummy little field, wondering if I'd miscalculated.

You said you weren't ready to leave the game behind, I whisper where only Colt can hear me. *Maybe, this way, you don't have to.*

Bottomless gray beams gaze back at me. Blazing and beloved. *You did this for me?* he asks inside. *You seriously—it's actually—?*

His awed disbelief finally sets my grin loose. *The job is yours if you want it*, I assure him, wincing as I recall the moment I insinuated to Linus and his friends that they might be getting a real professional player as a coach.

There was *a lot* of shouting.

Mostly in a good way.

Colt watches the memory, his slow, gorgeous smile stretching across his face. We both feel the rest of our pack watching, bursting with half-baked excitement, waiting for my final explanation.

Instead, I stretch up onto my toes, brushing a kiss to Colt's cheek. "Practice starts in ten minutes," I chirp, passing him his cap. "You better get going, Coach."

epilogue

one year later

"THE CLOSET NEEDED to be twice this big."

Bridget angles a sassy look over her shoulder, flashing pretty eyes full of mischief. "Maybe *your wardrobe* needs to be cut in half."

We both know *my* wardrobe isn't the problem anymore. Between Dante and me, Bridget's collection of designer clothes, accessories, and jewelry has reached critical mass.

It doesn't help that she's incredibly fun to shop for, between her eclectic taste and love of color. Not to mention how damn *beautiful* she is in *everything* we commission...

I've made it my mission to ensure she has all of the beautiful things and special experiences her sister kept from her. I was already determined to provide them for her, but that desire morphed into a full-blown *need* once we found out Bradley was the one who originally broke the story about our fake engagement to the press.

It took a few months to prove, but after Alicia's behavior at the ball, I had a sinking suspicion it had been one of them all along. With a hefty bribe, the investigator I hired was able to get one of the tabloids to reveal their source.

Apparently, he missed having Bridget around to sniff after and harass. He thought outing us would cause a "break-up" and force our omega to move back under his roof.

Bridget didn't know how to feel about the whole situation for a while. It was hard for her, knowing her own flesh-and-blood could find out something so vile about her spouse and still choose him over Bridget. Eventually, though, our girl decided to give Alicia an ultimatum: she should either sponsor an annual summer sports clinic for Osprey House, or our pack would do a tell-all interview detailing our *entire* story.

Including her husband's betrayal, the way she constantly belittled Bridget *for years*, and—of course—how she basically *sold* her own sister.

Needless to say, the kids' sports camp is now incredibly well-funded.

Though maybe not quite as luxe as my mate's closet.

"The size of this house is already obscene," Bridget goes on, pouting as she adjusts her denim skirt and shrugs into Jesse's yellow letterman jacket—the one from high school, which he dug out of storage as a gift for her. "We did *not* need a two-story closet."

I loop my arm around our omega's waist, running my palm over the ribbed orange tank top molded to her curves. Nipping her ear, I argue in a purr, "The bedroom is already two floors, with your nest-room upstairs. What's the harm in adding a second level to the closet, too?"

Bridget softens automatically, giddy bliss sparkling through her veins as my rumble soaks into her spine. When she feels my answering burst of amusement, though, she snaps upright again, tossing me another dirty look. "How do you make something so unreasonable sound like common sense?"

I can't help but smile at her. *Because I'm always paying attention, little blue. Learning <u>all</u> your secrets.*

Through our tether, I show her memories of the month after we bonded. How her features fell ever so slightly each time our pack discussed moving into a larger place and leaving her little house behind.

As far as I'm concerned, buying the decrepit property behind hers and building our new home around her bungalow *was* common sense. We got to retain pieces of the place she'd worked so hard on, stay close to Betty and Emma, and have a house large enough for everyone, without sacrificing any nostalgia.

Hiring the best architects in town, coming up with a floor plan as unique and cozy as her little house, finding a way to incorporate the structure's original facade...

Bridget feels the sincere emotion layered into every memory, recalling them along with me.

Our pack fell in love here, I think, repeating the words I'd told her the day I presented her with my plan. *Why would we ever leave?*

Sighing in defeat, she lets go of her irritation and embraces the desire to snuggle into my arms. I kiss her temple, flashing mental pictures of my imagined two-story closet. Showing her all the pretty things I've already ordered for her to put in it.

"Adriannnn," she whines. "You *have* to stop spoiling me like this."

Never, I think immediately, giving an easy shrug. *Daddy will always spoil you.*

Her heart flutters. I feel it in our bond and physically, through the thin fabric of my white shirt. I rub one hand down her back, cupping the other around her nape. Holding her against my purr.

It's been a year since Bridget first let her Omega come to the surface—and once her heat ended, it was obvious how touch-starved she'd been. We've banished that issue, of course, but I still like to put my hands all over her every chance I get.

As if you need an excuse, Dante cuts in. *Now, come on. You're hogging our omega, Daddy.*

Jesse chuckles in the bond. *Plus, we're going to be late.*

Yeah, that too, Dante agrees.

Bridget misreads their excitement as anticipation for tonight's main event. Little does she know, we have a *whole* separate plan.

Still, their eagerness puts a grin on my face. When I glance down at Bridget, I catch a similar expression on her pert features.

"I suppose they have a point," I muse, playing off my sudden wave of exhilaration. Weaving our fingers together as I nod at the door. "Let's go, sweetheart. We can't be late for a playoff game."

THERE COULDN'T BE A MORE perfect evening to play ball.

Except, maybe, if Betty would stop cat-calling us.

And the other team's coach.

And—*oh God*—did she bring a *flask*?!

Bridget hears my mental balk, giggling. "She always settles down by the second inning. Besides, it's not like they have the same policies here that Adrian has at King Stadium."

It's true. The Orange Blossom baseball field is much less

formal, even after all the renovations our pack donated last summer. Bridget arranged the upgrades as a surprise birthday gift for Colt—something for him to come home to after our summer of constant road games.

The dinky diamond now boasts brand-new bleachers, a beautiful concession stand, fresh turf, and a proper fence. All of it trimmed in the high school's signature orange-and-yellow, of course.

Beside me in the stands, Bridget matches our surroundings perfectly. Right down to one of Colt's Orange Blossom baseball caps perched on her head.

Just outside the dugout, our packmate calls out his team's batting lineup. Without pausing, he shoots a thought at our mate through the bond.

Hat thief.

A breathtaking grin spreads over her face. She sends back an image of all the books piled beside his reading chair in their new home library. *Book thief.*

That finally cracks Colt's stern Coach Face. His lips twitch slightly as he finishes reading out names and turns to the horizon.

The sun has begun sinking below the tree-line. He shoots Bridget an image of his view, along with a fierce burst of affection, before his tether blinks off.

It's our custom whenever one of our teams plays. We decided we would shut the interior curtains to focus. A rule Dante frequently breaks to send our omega filthy ideas whenever the mood strikes him.

"Can you *blame me*?" my packmate guffaws, winding his arm around Bridget's waist. "*Look* at her."

She's as exquisite as ever, of course. But as I gaze down at her, taking in our surroundings, my mind flings me back in time. To the night I struck out because I couldn't keep my focus off her brilliant hair, falling in front of her face while she bent over a book.

Bridget feels the tide of devotion swamping my stomach and

scoots closer, nuzzling her face into my neck. Dante's mouth drops open in outrage.

"I compliment you and he gets cuddles?" His dark eyes snap to the green-haired elderly woman beside him. "Betty, back me up on this."

Our neighbor scoffs, "As long as she's shagging one of you enough to keep these nachos coming, I don't give a shit which one she picks." She crunches on a tortilla chip, unbothered when my packmate steals one. "Besides, Blondie is much quieter than you when he goes off."

Oh, good God.

My face flames as Bridget bursts into musical peals of laughter and Dante chokes on his nacho.

Betty's stooped shoulders shrug under her orange mu-mu. "Not my fault you're about as subtle as a fireworks show," she tells us. "Close your curtains every once in a while. Goddamn."

She's not wrong, Bridget points out, unbothered. She slides her blue heart-rimmed sunglasses off, balancing them on top of her head as she turns to look around.

Where is everyone? Adrian was supposed to meet Emma's pack out front and bring them over.

Anxiety lurches behind my sternum. Dante flings a death-glare over our omega's head, hissing where only I can hear, *Be cool, cabrón. Damn.*

Our pack leader flexes a solid beat of reassurance through the bond. *We're on our way, little blue.*

My heart aches when Bridget immediately takes him at his word, snuggling back into my side. Her trust means *everything* to us. Which is one reason why planning our surprise has been insanely difficult.

Not to mention how brilliant our mate is.

Bridget snaps her crystalline eyes to my face, her brow tweaking. *Everything okay, Jess?*

I stare down at her, absorbing the way it feels for our souls to brush. The others have always described Bridget as light, bright, bubbly, and full of fire. But for me? She's peace and quiet. Truth and destiny. All the things I ever wanted and never knew I needed.

I hold her closer, letting my memories of this field and what it means to us flood the tether between our hearts. *Perfect, bumblebee*, I think, because it's the truth. She's perfect now; and she always has been. *Because of you.*

"HE'S GONNA KNOW."

The familiar words invade my senses, throwing me back to that day in the Kings' locker room. A spark of fond amusement lights the base of my lungs, but I smother it, snapping a glower at the players huddled over a phone.

They know those are forbidden in my dugout. I suppose they figured I'd be too distracted by our loaded bases to notice.

Keeping my focus on the field, I hold my palm out, curling my fingers. Linus grumbles a curse, dropping his cell into my hand.

"What's the rule?" I ask, narrowing my gaze at the opposing team's pitcher. *Damn, he's good.*

"Save the stupidity for after the game," my players intone.

I nod, pocketing the phone. "Something more important than winning this playoff game, Linus?"

To my surprise, he doesn't grunt a comeback. Instead, our second baseman elbows him in the ribs, cackling, "Linus found an omega."

Oh.

Damn.

I remember the day he told Adrian he didn't understand the point of Bridget's sex-ed class; and learning all the "stupid alpha-omega bullshit." Amusement tickles my throat.

Of all the things that have stunned me about this job—mostly, how much I love it—I think I've been most surprised by how fucking funny teenagers are. Watching them fight and fail and figure things out is touching, but it also gives my omega and me plenty to chuckle about at the end of the day.

It's the same when my pitcher—affectionately known in our house as "mini-Jesse"—strikes out. He's pissed as he jogs back to the dugout and receives my requisite slap on the back. But I'm old enough to know that one day? All of this will be a fond memory for the guy.

That same perspective has me smirking at the stormy look on Linus' face. It's clear he fully appreciates the irony of his situation, which only makes it funnier.

Bridget is going to love *this,* I think. *I can't wait to tell her tonight. After—*

One of our outfielders gets a decent hit, sending one run in and leaving the bases loaded once again. I shift my gaze to Linus, nodding at the field. He's on deck.

"Your omega is here?" I ask, handing him a helmet.

Linus is smart enough to know that none of us are going to leave him alone. Especially given the merciless way he's mocked some of his teammates for their relationships.

He blows air out of his nose, admitting, "He's here."

An involuntary grin splits my face. "Better not embarrass yourself, then."

He won't. Linus is, ironically, my best player. I can tell before his walk-out song even ends that he's about to smash this shit.

Sure enough, his bat makes contact on the first pitch. The crowd goes berserk as the ball goes screaming over the outfield and clears our new fence.

Bridget breaks our standing rule about keeping our curtains closed during games just long enough to send me a rush of pride and excitement. *Grand Slam!*

My grin only grows.

Not my favorite kind, I tell her. *But I'll take it.*

BY THE TOP of the ninth inning, I've discovered that I, in fact, am the one who needs to be *cool*.

Jesse and Adrian immerse their thoughts in the game easily enough. But I cannot keep my mind off the surprise burning a hole in my pocket.

We unanimously decided that I should be the one to hold it. I'm also supposed to give it to her. Just as soon as this inning ends...

Jesse's team is down one run. If they can close this down and score just two runs during their final turn at-bat, they can still win it.

Luckily, our mate is fully immersed in the action—and her conversation with Emma, who's sitting beside her with a matching mint-green version of Bridget's sunglasses perched in her blonde curls.

The two omegas bounce and cheer when our pitcher strikes out his third player, sending the opposition out to the field. Adrian tenses next to me, doing everything he can to hold back the urge to interrupt Colt.

I swear, you'd think Daddy was the assistant coach for all the work he does with this team. Our whole pack spends a bunch of time here, actually. And not just because we like defiling our librarian in her natural habitat.

Although...

Bridget senses the bent of my thoughts and casts me a sharp look. *Don't you <u>dare</u>, slugger. I am <u>not</u> missing the end of this game.*

Normally, such a challenge would only make me hotter. But I doubt I can get her to the car, undress her, make her come three times, *and* put her skirt back on before this inning is over...

Maybe *twice*...

Focus, Adrian growls internally, leaning over with his forearms braced against his knees. Peering at the field like this is the World Series. Out loud, he adds, "Colt already has a player on base."

Oh shit.

The next five minutes are enough to put me in a chokehold. We're all on the edges of our seats when Linus comes up to bat again.

The bases are loaded, and we have two outs.

This is it.

Everyone in the stands holds their breath as Linus swings and misses. My heart fucking stops when he gets a second strike six seconds after the first.

Colt is outside the dugout now. I watch him give the player a solid nod. Reassuring the kid.

Another fastball flies forth. Linus swings and gets a chunk of it.

It's not as perfect as his last hit, but it's *enough*. The players on base sprint. One hits home before the other team retrieves the ball. They move to get it to first, trying to tag Linus out before we can get a second run...

FUCK.

The first second baseman catches the ball and turns to tag Linus as he slides in, mirroring his teammate's desperate attempt to hit home before the inning ends.

A plume of orange dust explodes over the plate, engulfing our runner, the other team's catcher, and the umpire.

The cloud settles, revealing the umpire's stance—arms spread straight across, palms down.

"SAFE!"

WE WON!

The words swirl through our bond from all sides, surrounded by delirious joy and dizzying exhilaration.

Maybe *that's* why I don't notice how my pack somehow gets us to the field within seconds.

The team is still whooping and shouting, celebrating their victory in front of the dugout, when Adrian guides me onto the turf. I blink, trying to clear my mind enough to understand how we got here so quickly.

Unless, of course, our pack alpha planned it this way.

Of course he did, I realize, noting the steely determination on his handsome features.

I assume he simply had this plan in place because he suspected we would win and knew I'd want to get to Colt as quickly as possible. He's not wrong, either.

I break into a run as soon as I can, darting for my salty alpha. Colt grins as he scoops me off my feet, spinning in a circle.

"I'm so proud of you!" I gush, pressing kisses all over his face. "Best coach ever!" *Just like I knew you would be.*

Colt hears both sentiments, grinning. "Of course you find a way to take credit, Bubbles."

I laugh, trying to feel my way into our tether. Wanting to show him how immensely happy I am for him.

But, uh...

Why do they all *have their curtains up at a time like this?*

My alphas have formed a circle around me. I cast each of them a questioning look, trying to figure out what they're doing.

The stands have gotten inordinately quiet, with our players shushing the spectators until the hum of cicadas is the only sound interrupting the pearly purple dusk.

Narrowing my eyes, I cock my hip at Colt. "What in the—?"

Before I can finish, our pack alpha drops to his knees.

In his suit.

In the dirt.

Jesse follows, reaching out to squeeze my hand in a reassuring gesture. By the time I turn back to Colt, he's kneeling too. Along with—

Dante reaches into the pocket of his shorts, extracting a small, sparkling item. He pinches it between his thumb and forefinger.

A *ring.*

But not just *any* ring.

It's the one he batted into oblivion. I can tell, because the platinum band has a noticeable scuff on the side.

If it weren't for that one small detail, I wouldn't recognize the piece at all. Because instead of the one flawless diamond I always disliked, *four* colorful gems glitter in the field's overhead lights.

They're each different colors.

Yellow for Jesse, like his letterman jacket and bumblebees and the sunflowers he brings me every week.

Blue for Adrian, of course. His special nickname for me, his gorgeous ocean gaze.

Amethyst purple to represent Colt. And all our evenings under these ombre sunsets, watching the way the clouds glow lavender.

Which leaves the pink for Dante. *Post-Its in my lunchbox, the back of his head, always framed by my pink refrigerator. All our nights in the kitchen.*

I note the solemn intensity in his dark eyes, my middle melting. *Of course* he's the one giving this to me, now. Wanting to make up for the last time he gave me a ring.

Emotion rises to block my throat, my heart aching. Even before Adrian clears his throat, his Adriatic irises burning hot on mine. "It's engraved, little blue."

I turn the band, tears welling as I read the words carved there.

There are two lines. One small and stricken out; and another, carved in deep, beautiful cursive.

~~*Fake fiancée*~~, it reads, with a clean, permanent line through it. Followed by a two-word correction.

Forever fiancée.

A watery smile spreads across my face. "Forever fiancée?"

"Or wife!" Dante blurts. "Or both!"

Adrian chuckles, scent-marking my left hand. "Whatever you want, Bridget. But we're yours. We always have been."

Jesse meets my gaze, his brimming with affection. "We wanted to give you the proposal you deserve. Here, in front of everyone."

"With a ring we made," Colt puts in, his mouth quirking up. "One to match all your colors."

Please, baby? he adds in our bond. *Say yes.*

I honestly didn't know how I'd feel about wearing another ring from them. I should have guessed they would make it an irresistible offer. A spectacle worthy of a queen.

I stare into Colt's stormy eyes for a long second before giving each of the others the same consideration. *My soulmates, my sparring partners, my caretakers, and lovers.*

YES! the voice inside me begs. Bouncing with joy, lighting me up. *Yes, yes, y—*

"Yes," I whisper, my heart igniting like a Roman candle. "I'll wear your ring."

Adrian grins, sliding the band onto my left hand.

Now the circuit is complete, Jesse thinks, mentally tracing each of their bites. Colt's on my hip. Adrian's at my throat. Dante's half-moons over my left breast, and Jesse's—branded over the hand still in our pack alpha's.

Somehow, their glimmering ring feels like one final piece, snapping into place. Tying all of us together, bonding us to our past and all our promises for tomorrow.

And the next day.

And the next.

Until the end of forever.

Thank you for reading Knot Her Catch!

Ratings and reviews help indie authors do what they love and write more amazing books for everyone to enjoy! If you loved watching the Messina Pack get their HEA, **please consider leaving a rating** or a review.

Want more Messina Pack?

For access to any extended epilogues, ARCs, and other fun goodies, sign up for Ari's mailing list! There's even talk of a book of extended epilogues for all the packs that will go out to email subscribers as a special treat... just saying 👀

a note from ari

Hello lovely readers!

I'm overjoyed to share Bridget's story with you!

As a plus-sized woman, this book is very special to me. A lot of thought and care went into every part of Bridget's pack.

I refused to write a story wherein my heroine's relationship to gravity was a "problem" for her to overcome, but I wanted to highlight the very real psychological effects of being told your body isn't "right" at every turn (by society, medicine, family, etc.). Moreover, how that constant toxicity can slowly erode our most important relationship: the one we have with ourselves.

So for all the readers out there who tell themselves to suck it up, it's no big deal, I'm *fine*—I see you. I feel you. I *am* you. And I hope Bridget's journey to self-kindness brought you as much joy as writing it gave me.

xx,

acknowledgments

Kelly gets all the thanks, because none of us would be in this crazy Ari Wright Omegaverse without her! Kel, I love you for being my sounding board, task-master, second therapist, and all-around best friend. You are the best assistant, mom, wife, and BFF out there and I'm so insanely blessed to have you.

To my dearest Katie: I know this one was emotional for both of us, but I seriously could not have made Bridget all she is without you. She took little pieces of both of us and I honestly couldn't be more proud of that fact. Thank you for helping me create this magical story and give it to our readers. I love you even when you don't love you; and I know you'll always do the same for me 🖤

And, also, THANK YOU RICK (this is me, shouting across an ocean). We appreciate you sharing your wonderful Katie with us and helping shove certain banners into certain boxes. We won't talk about it.

Another huge thank you yo my unhinged enabler, Amanda—knowing I can always come running to you with ideas, tears, or insane stories is such a comfort and a privilege. I am so grateful the universe sent you to us.

A big thanks to Mekhala and Katelin for stepping in and helping me get this one over the finish line at the eleventh hour! I appreciate you!

Lastly, to my husband: these stories bloom from the heart you water. Thank you for being here to remind me what true love feels like.

about the author

Ari Wright was once entirely sane, but then she realized sanity is overrated and decided to write sporty Omegaverse smut.

Because life is short, you know?

When she isn't writing unhinged romances, she enjoys drinking coffee to the point of excess, kitchen experiments, raising her littles, and trying to keep her plants alive (just kidding, her husband does that).

She loves really embarrassing music, moody weather, and any story where the bad guy gets the girl.

Because what's Happily Ever After without a little (or a lot of) spice?

You can follow her works in progress, favorite reads, and very pink aesthetic on Instagram—or check out her exclusive reader Facebook group!